Nightmare Therapy

Nightmare Therapy

Kevin McCaffrey

To order additional copies of this book, contact:
Xlibris Corporation
1-888-7-XLIBRIS
www.Xlibris.com
Orders@Xlibris.com

Contents

FOR ELIZABETH, AIDAN, MARY AND GEORGE

Prologue

Bland Dystopia

Clear Liquids was a cramped, filthy bar on the third floor of an old office building. No signs on the street—or anywhere else—advertised its existence. People either knew it was there or they did not. It was called Clear Liquids because only clear liquids were served there. The drink menu consisted of such beverages as gin, vodka, white rum, white wine, schnapps, water, and other liquids which were perfectly clear or, at most, colorlessly cloudy. There was no food menu. Why the owner of the bar had settled on this particular scheme he never made clear. In addition to the sale of clear beverages, an ample drug trade took place on the premises.

Drugs could be bought either from the bartender or in the bathroom from a seller who worked for the owner. Other drug dealers were actively discouraged from working at the establishment.

It was a dark place with an old linoleum floor, no decoration, no plants, a wooden bar, some bar stools, some tables and chairs. Large, dirt-spattered windows looked onto a shabby street, a tired city. At Clear Liquids there was no music.

Karla and Bruno were two people who knew where Clear Liquids was.

They sat together at a table in the waning hours of the May

afternoon. Though the afternoon was warm, the windows of the bar were closed. There was no air conditioning and it was hot in the bar and the air was thick with smells of sweat, cigarettes, liquor, and a hint of the vomit which had not been thoroughly washed away from a corner of the room.

Karla said, "Well, what's your mindset, Bruno? I mean really?"

Bruno said, "I can't complain."

Karla looked out the window, then back at Bruno. He could see that she was formulating a thought, a thought which was causing her some anxiety.

"I'm not here to ask you for anything, Bruno, but I just want to know—is it easier . . . is it better for you being with her than it was being with me?"

Bruno put down his glass of vodka. With his finger he traced a design through wetness on the table. He said softly, "Karla, we've been through this before. I'm happy now. Or less unhappy. Not that I care a lot about my emotions. Things just work better with Ashley. It's more . . . uh . . . efficient. More mechanical."

"Mechanical," she replied, raising an eyebrow in a way he remembered well. "What's funny to me, Bruno, is you always told me that you thought Ashley and I were so similar, that we were cut from the same boring cloth."

"I know," Bruno replied. "I still do."

"And you told me before that you thought I was more . . ."

"Karla," Bruno interrupted, "We don't need to get into this."

He looked at her. He knew her body well. Almost as well as her mind. She was beautiful—a pallid, five foot eleven inch, emaciated, languid goddess with long legs, thin expressive hands, high cheekbones, blue eyes, short-cropped blonde hair. She looked back at him intently with an expression which, despite the complexity of her personality, was almost one of innocent befuddlement. The perpetual gee-whiz look of a faun, Bruno thought to himself, or a lamb. Or a child. Ashley, on the other hand—his Ashley—was shorter and not so very thin as Karla.

Her image formed in his mind and he conducted, as he had many times before, a mental comparison. Ashley's lips were fuller than Karla's, her nose broader, her hips wider, her cheekbones lower, her breasts smaller, and her legs not as impressively long. She was less angular. Her lines were softer. Her hair—brown and shoulder length—was less distinctive. But Ashley's personality held for him an as yet unresolved mystery. She balanced a prematurely world-weary cynicism with a mild, yet constant, enthusiasm for life. Easily bored by topics that most people found interesting, she often displayed great enthusiasm for topics generally considered mind-numbingly dull. Her disposition, her spirit, seemed poised equally between the twin concepts of "why" and "why not?" At any rate, Karla and Ashley were nearly the same in one respect: each thought the world revolved around herself. This might have been too much for him, but their beauty compensated for their self-centeredness.

Karla cleared her throat. Bruno brought his attention back to her. The weakening light of the afternoon was playing tepidly now on her, daubing half her face and half her upper body with yellowish light.

He picked up his glass, took another sip, said, "This vodka gets to you."

She did not reply, turned instead to look out the window. She saw workers in skyblue uniforms sweeping the street. Freedomworkers. They swept around the prostrate body of a man who had been shot recently. Blood formed a pool around his head. The sweepers were careful to avoid the blood with their brooms. Then she noticed the sound of a police siren, still far away. Funny, she thought, she could not even remember a gunshot. Her eyes climbed the office building across the street, rising like the dead man's soul might have risen, though she doubted it. Death was death. Final. A billboard was on the roof. It depicted small, diaphanously clad children on a beach. Their eyes were closed. They were pallid. Their bodies looked stiff, contorted. They were dead too. Dead children on the beach. The billboard advertised a unisex cologne called No Future.

She said, "Well, tell me what it's like. I want to know what it's like living with Ashley." She turned her gaze towards Bruno.

Bruno looked away. Then he looked back at Karla and, using one of the expressions common to the young people of the city, he said, "It's bland. We get along pretty well."

"You mean," Karla said, "you don't have the arguments that we used to have?"

"Oh, we have some arguments, but look, why do you want to talk about this? She's your best friend."

"Yes," Karla said, "she is my best friend and I've tried—we've both tried—not to let you come between us."

"Has that been hard?"

"Yes. At times. Very hard," Karla replied. She thought for a moment; her expression became wistful. "Jesus" she exclaimed with a trace of enthusiasm. "Do you remember this is the same sweating place where we first met each other?"

"Yes, " Bruno said. "When was that? Five or six years ago?"

"Yes," she said, looking at him, looking at the same time into the distance of the past. "This place had a different name then."

"It did. What was it called? Something like The Palace or The Chalice. Something that made no sense."

"No," Karla smiled, "I'm sure the name referred to some kind of emotional state. It might have been Malice."

"No, " Bruno said. "I would remember if it had something to do with feelings."

"Like you have them, ugly."

"I do, when it's appropriate."

"Who cares about that? It was named Malice."

"It wasn't."

"Well," Karla replied, her voice girlish and insincere, "we rarely agree."

"What's the point?" Bruno said. "Sometimes I just prefer to

be disagreeable." Then, leaning forward, he changed the subject. "What do you think of the dream therapy sessions?"

"Oh, them," Karla said. "Bland. Mildly bland. Bland squared."

"And what do you think of Dr Bentley?"

"She fits her role perfectly, I think. If someone is going to lead me through my nightmares, I want it to be someone like her."

"Yes," Bruno said, "You're right about that."

"So how are your dreams, Bruno? How is your dreamlife?" Karla smiled.

"The same. Nonexistent."

"Nightmares?"

"Never," Bruno answered. "How about you?"

"Oh, my dreams are boring, I mean really. But I'd love to know what you're actually dreaming these days."

"Believe me, Karla, my mind is blank."

"You say that, but I'd like to think," Karla said, "that you're dreaming about me at least once in a while."

Bruno said, "Well, I do daydream about you occasionally."

Karla smiled, "I know you do."

Bruno raised his eyebrows.

"Perhaps," she responded cryptically, "I know more than you think."

Bruno looked at her more closely and let it pass. He had seen this manufactured mysteriousness before. He took another sip of vodka, then he said, "I'm glad you've been able to maintain your friendship with Ashley. That's important to me."

"Oh. Why?"

"Because something tells me," Bruno said, "that when I'm gone from both your lives, you'll still have each other."

"Maybe you should write the inscriptions for sympathy cards," Karla said. "That's such a deeply touching thought."

Bruno pursed his lips, then he looked out the window. "No, I'm being sincere," he said.

"Sincere? Bruno, the day that you or I or Ashley actually say what we really mean, or even know if we . . . uh . . . if we mean what we're saying—that will be a banner day in . . . in . . . well, it will be a banner day, whatever that is."

Bruno did not respond.

Then Karla said, "You know, I thought up a story, maybe yesterday or the day before. Would you like to hear it?"

"Yes."

"Napping. The story goes like this: there were two twins, two women. Identical twins. And they were almost exactly alike in every respect. Of course they weren't the same person, but they were almost like two . . . uh . . . manifestations of the same person. Absolutely identical, like I said. And there was one guy . . . one of the twins was in love with this guy. Needless to say—just to make the story more interesting—he wasn't really worthy of her love. But what is love if not a sacrifice of ourselves to something that is not worthy of such a sacrifice, huh?"

Bruno grunted, "That's today's definition of love, anyway."

"Anyway," Karla smiled, "one of the twins was deeply in love with this guy, this specimen, this unworthy fellow, and he's in love with her. In so far as that's possible, I mean. Yet, the other twin—it would be too trite to call her the evil twin—decides that she wants to sleep with this guy. Who knows why? She's bored maybe. And so she finds an opportunity to pretend that she is her sister, and she sleeps with him—and guess what?—he doesn't know the difference. Imagine! So, this goes on for months, maybe years, with the one twin, the surrogate, pretending she is her sister, and neither her sister nor her sister's boyfriend ever know that there's a . . . third element in their relationship."

Bruno nodded, "That's napping. What happens in the end?"

"Who says there's an end, you pessimist? Maybe the end is that the sister and her boyfriend die and they are buried side by side and so the twin decides to kill herself and she buries herself, or she has herself buried, between the two of them. Or better yet—she has her sister's coffin exhumed and hers buried in its place. Just to keep up the pattern. That would be a pretty good ending, huh?"

"Yes, that would be an excellent ending. Would you like another drink?"

"I would." Karla got up and walked to the bar, ordered herself a vodka, ordered the same for Bruno, came back. She carried two old jelly jars filled nearly full with the clear liquid. They drank, they smoked cigarettes. They did not say much for a few minutes. Then Bruno had an impulse, an impulse he instantly knew he should discount, stifle. But for some reason the impulse moved from impulse to verbalization so quickly and smoothly he could not stop it.

He said, "So how would you like to go back to your apartment and make love?" He felt his face redden, but he held Karla's eyes. "In a way, we would be acting out the story you just told. Obviously."

She looked at him, then looked down at her drink, took another sip, puffed on her cigarette, exhaled.

She said, "Give me a moment to think about it, you ugly fucker."

Comme un tout jeune oiseau qui tremble et qui palpite,
J'arracherai ce coeur tout rouge de son sein,
Et, pour rassasier ma bête favorite,
Je le lui jetterai par terre avec dédain!

Charles Baudelaire

Chapter 1

Nightmare Therapy

Ashley extended her arm and looked away.

She gasped when she felt the needle prick.

For a moment she thought she would not, but then she began to fall asleep.

She lay on a futon mattress in a shadowy, expansive room. Around her, a group—all younger people except for the older woman next to her—sat cross-legged, their eyes intent on the almost sleeping woman.

"Think bad thoughts," Dr Bentley said, putting the spent syringe on a table.

In her early forties, Dr Bentley was both older than the rest of those at her session and more conservatively attired. Everything about her—her gestures, demeanor and dress, a stern charcoal business suit with austere touches of silver—said "successful professional."

She sat down next to Ashley on a round, blood red cushion, folding her long legs under her and looking slowly at each of the participants and then at the silent, reclining form of Ashley.

"Chant," she said, and the group began to chant quietly an eerie, repetitive melody.

At the fringes of her dissolving wakefulness, Ashley heard the chanting; the sound led her into a dream.

*　　*　　*

The cemetery is empty and calm. The heat of early spring warms the fecund soil which surrounds the graves. Little flowers sprout in the grass.

She stands on the top of a hill. For miles on every side of her rows of graves extend.

She hears grunting and tussling off to one side. Two black dogs of moderate size are mating on top of a new grave. Their paws sink into the soil. She tries to see the name on the headstone but she cannot.

Her attention is drawn back to the dogs. The female dog now has a human head. It is Ashley's head from when she was a child.

Her younger self looks up at her with pleading eyes.

"Please," her long-forgotten voice says. "Please."

Ashley runs down the hill.

Each of the gravestones has her name on it.

Ashley Quick.

As she runs, she feels herself changing from an adult to a little girl. When she finishes running, she finds herself struggling to catch her breath in the ominously quiet corridors of a home.

She steps softly. She does not want to be heard. No one must know she is here. No one but the boy who is walking with her.

She turns to look at him. Anguish wells up within her, anguish and something else, something ineffable and base. But she cannot see his face. He turns his face away when she turns to look at him.

"In here," the boy whispers.

Black drapes make the large room dark. Only one beam of sunlight cuts through, illuminating a casket surrounded by flowers which fill the room with decaying sweetness.

She feels herself moving ahead to look in the open casket.

The skin of the corpse, of the face and of the hands drawn

together on the dead man's stomach, is like thin, translucent leather. The man wears a military uniform covered with ribbons and medals.

She senses the boy joining her at the casket.

"That's my father," he sobs, reaching out to brush his father's mouse gray hair with his pale hand.

She watches him brush his father's hair and she shuts her eyes.

She knows what she will see if she opens them. Perhaps this time the dream will not repeat itself, but it does. She hears the boy gasp, "Daddy, daddy," then scream in soul-wrenching horror.

There is no need for her to look. Turning, running blindly, she opens her eyes only when she is far away from the death room, walking through a cathedral of trees.

She knows these woods. They are part of the Arboretum near her home. Her childhood sneakers crackle through orange and yellow leaves which carpet the ground. It is autumn. Abruptly, the day ends. Much too quickly the daylight recedes; the color bleeds out of the leaves. Above her now, night sky. The moon is there, the stars, and vague, twisted clouds, each looking like an animal running in fright from something beyond the edge of the sky, the scope of the night.

She carries a bow and some arrows.

She wonders why and yet somehow she knows she is only going to do what she has done before.

"Here, Ashley. Over here," the boy's voice beckons.

He stands by a twisted tree, holding a length of rope in his hand. She cannot see his face.

"Tie me to the tree," he says, weeping gently. He has taken off his clothes.

"You look like an angel," she says. His pale flesh is blue-white in the moonlit darkness, shivering with the cold, the fear.

"Tie me!"

She binds him to the tree so tightly that he cries out. She feels his blood's warmth where the ropes have cut into his skin.

"What do I do now?" she asks him.

"You know."

"Yes, I know."

She takes up the bow and arrows and places herself about ten child's paces from him. The wind rises up and kicks a swirl of fallen leaves around her. She raises the bow, pulls back an arrow and lets it fly.

It transfixes the boy's knee.

He does not cry out.

"Try again," he urges.

It has become brighter. The moon and stars shine with new intensity. She sees blood rushing from his knee, staining the porcelain of his shin, forming a steaming pool on the ground.

"I can't do it."

"You must."

She pulls a second arrow back and holds it, feeling the intensity of her heart beat, the tension of the bowstring. She cannot do it.

"Ashley!"

She lets the arrow loose and it transfixes his eye. The boy screams as the arrow quivers. A thin stream of blood flows from his torn eye socket across his cheek. He asks, he implores her to shoot again.

She shakes her head. She drops the bow and arrow and turns to run a few steps into the surrounding night but he, his voice, calls her back. She must finish it.

She readies herself.

She lets the arrow loose. She has hit her mark, straight through the boy's chest and into the heart of the tree. She watches the arrow quiver before blood spurts, a fountain, from the boy's chest. As the hot blood falls in a shower on her hands and her face and her legs and on the leaves around her, the trees in this dream glade let loose, all at once, their dying leaves so that they swirl and whirl about her, filling the air with dry rustling.

Descending, whispering vortices.

Dying leaves for a dying boy.
She screams and wakes screaming.

*   *   *

Dr Bentley, clinically calm, looked down at her.

"What a nightmare!" Ashley gasped, body slick with sweat, heart pounding.

"Good, Ashley. Very good," said Dr Bentley. "That's what we're here for."

Someone brought Ashley a cool drink, and, sitting up on the futon, her legs folded beneath her, Ashley related her dream, prodded here and there by Dr Bentley.

While she spoke, her feeling of terror left her to be replaced by a sense of vague unease. Face by face, she looked at her fellow participants in the nightmare therapy session. Ten of the total of eleven participants in the weekly therapy sessions were present that evening.

They were young men and women who, like Ashley, were in their twenties or early thirties. The eleven could be divided, Ashley thought, into two distinct groups, two basic character types distinguishable most obviously by dress and attitude. The first group, into which Ashley put herself, mostly wore ripped, tattered clothing and leather or denim jackets adorned with decorative elements such as skulls, spikes, chains, the images of demons or cartoon characters, or the logos of failed corporations, although at times some might favor bright polyester, platform shoes, or other outlandish stylings of the 1960s and 70s. But whatever their fashion sense, all were remote in their postures, distant in their attitudes.

Others in the class, whose dress was more conservative yet still informally laid back, were earnest, more or less troubled introspectives who had been influenced by various New Age and Post-New Age disciplines and trends ranging from past life regression and aroma-therapy to macrobiotics and astral communication with alien or disembodied beings. They had come to Dr Bentley's sessions driven by the same impulses, the same core beliefs, that motivate most disciples of "holistic" belief systems—that an unveiling of the innermost essence of oneself will make the pieces of one's life fall into place and set in motion a radical improvement in its quality. By exploring their nightmares, they hoped to gain deep insights into themselves. Ashley did not share their hope of self improvement through bad dreams. She attended Dr Bentley's sessions purely for kicks.

Ashley's eyes met those of her best friend Karla, tall and blonde, who despite her outwardly carefree disposition would recount a hideous dream of a world in which the sun was dying after she emerged from her experiences with the nightmare inducing drug. Ashley looked next at Irma, an almost gnome-like artist who dreamed of death beneath the city in rancid sewers amidst foul, fecal manifestations. A horn—thick and stubby like a rhinoceros's horn, though much smaller, more modest—rose from the center of her forehead. It was a detachable model; not an implant. She looked at Jessica, fleshy and fish white, whose dreams were of Gothic battles between angels and demons, between Christ and Satan; at Jerry, who dreamed that his body was covered with huge, hideous, pus-filled sores. As if a physical signal or marker of his terrible dream, Jerry's face was flecked with acne. Ashley looked next at Brandon, a wide-shouldered, handsome, practical joker who worked in a natural foods store and whose nightmare was of being held confined in a small dark space; at Dominic, a khaki-and-Oxford-shirt-wearing preppy who dreamed in a past life he had been a guard at a death camp sending thousands to their deaths; at Jane, mousy, nondescript in appearance, who dreamed that worms were infesting her body; and at Alvin, the retro-Hippie who dreamed of car crashes and graveyards.

Finally, forcing herself, she looked at Eric. He returned her gaze with a look Ashley could not define but which made her uneasy. Of all the participants in the sessions he held himself most aloof and detached. He rarely shared much of his dreams when he spoke, although he obviously writhed in terror in the drug-induced nightmares which Dr Bentley brought about.

The eleventh member of the group, Ashley's boyfriend Bruno, was not present. He alone of the group did not experience nightmares or, in fact, dreams of any sort. When he went under Dr Bentley's drug he did not dream at all. Boring, Ashley thought. So lovably boring. Awake or asleep, his mind clung to its emptiness.

Her gaze returned to Dr Bentley and Ashley wondered what the psychologist who seemed so much in control of her life dreamed, or if she ever subjected herself to the same sorts of terrors her clients faced. If Bentley did have dark visions, she never shared them.

When Ashley finished relating her dream, she heard some of her fellow "dreamworkers" exhale. Jane sobbed quietly as she usually did. Dr Bentley smiled.

"Good work, Ashley."

"But, Doctor," said Brandon, the cut-up of the group, "what does it all mean?"

Everyone laughed except Eric.

"What indeed?" replied the doctor, brushing back a strand of white-blonde hair which had slipped across her face. "We pursue these dreams for a more basic reason than to discern meaning. That is a relatively easy thing to do. The source of Ashley's dream for example can be traced, I imagine, to some deeply-situated guilt about something so horrible that she has forced herself to forget it.

"So what?" she continued. "We dream these dreams because they are powerful things in and of themselves. Nightmares are the lightning bolts of human consciousness—a natural shock therapy with curative, not negative, effects. You'll see."

"I think that just about answers my question," Brandon said, his voice low with false earnestness.

"Natural shock therapy? That's a little hyperkinetic, don't you think?" Jerry sneered to Jessica. She looked away.

*   *   *

The dog knew something was wrong.

Very wrong.

Up until this moment it had been a standard evening for the dog. He had eaten. He had napped. One of his masters, the woman, had talked to him, petted him. Then he had left the home where they kept him, exiting the room where the man and woman fed him his food through his own dog door into the chill of night.

The air was slightly cold and was scented with the salt of the ocean. The wind tossed leaves from the trees.

He was a good dog. Not a bad dog. The man and woman told him so.

And, it had been good to follow his own familiar trail from the house through the places near where other people—not the man and the woman—lived until he had come to his own private passage under the fence into the place with all the trees.

Sometimes the man called him White Fang or Cujo or Lassie though he did not think that these were his names, really. He was only a terrier.

A frightened terrier.

He turned and turned. Looked in all directions.

Nothing.

Trees. Stones. Wind. Shadows. Bushes. Brambles.

He used his nose.

Something.

Something bad was near.

He ran from the bad thing, scampering as fast as he could through the passages between bushes, stones, trees that he had traveled night after night since he could remember.

It was right behind him, the bad thing, pursuing.

The dog heard footfalls on the leaves. Something whistled at his ear. It hurt him. He felt sick.

He made a sharp turn under some low thorn bushes, tore his way beneath them.

The branches pulled at his sides but he remembered this route. He would come out of these sweet smelling bushes and be in a clear space where he could run.

His head felt hollow.

It was quiet here in the thorns.

He stopped and listened, cocking his ear.

A sound.

It was a man whistling like the man at his house whistled, but more quietly.

Different, quieter. But the same. Whistling.

Perhaps it was the man. His man who lived with his woman. His masters.

Maybe he had done something wrong. And so the whistling man had thrown something at his head, a punishment.

It was very dark here in the thorn bushes, very dark and peaceful.

The terrier felt his eyes closing.

He felt himself moving towards sleep.

The chase had been just a bad dream. Like a rabbit would have.

It was all right.

It did not matter now.

His name was Charlie.

*   *   *

Later, after the conclusion of the therapy session, Ashley and Karla walked to a small club in the city's industrial district which, gradually abandoned by business, dying, had given rise to a scattering of clubs, galleries, and artists' studios which thrived and died almost as quickly, brightly, as wild flowers on abandoned lots. Block after inactive block, the district of former factories, warehouses, machine shops, office buildings, and supply houses covered much of the south side of the city. People in the city called it the warehouse district, if they spoke of it at all.

The club was called I HATE SPROUTS. But besides the inclination of the clientele to leather or polyester apparel and general unhealth, there was nothing overtly anti-health food about the place, though that the name of the club was represented in capital letters seemed to be important somehow. Here and there on the club's concrete walls hung large photographs of vegetables and fruits.

Ashley and Karla sat at a table at the back of the club, looking out over a claustrophobic rectangle of warehouse space that contained a small stage, a smaller dance floor, some tables, and two bars which ran lengthwise along either side of the club. I HATE SPROUTS was illuminated only by candlelight. Shadows played against the walls, creating a flat, flittingly distorted double-world.

The music was slow and very soft. In slow motion on the dance floor some men and women danced by softly knocking into each other, now groping and entwining at random, now falling away in a dance called the slow slam.

"Who's that?" Karla asked, pointing to a couple who walked through the frail light at the other side of the club.

Ashley looked. A tiny woman led a huge, flabby man with a shaved head by a short choke leash. On his upper body he wore a leather harness; a studded collar ringed his neck. He also wore tight leather shorts, green-gray *lederhosen*, and his legs were fat.

Ashley yawned, sneered, said, "Hush now, ugly. We must not pry. Besides I want to hear this song."

On the stage one of the members of a band made some noise on a guitar. The club grew quieter. The music that had been playing over the loudspeakers stopped. The dancers stopped, looked toward the stage.

The lead singer stepped to the microphone, strummed his acoustic guitar, and sang.

> *I could'a been a flower but I stayed a weed*
> *Even that was too much*
> *I should'a stayed a seed.*

This stanza was followed by a shout from the rest of the band:

I tried to fail.

The singer went on, joined between verses by his shouting bandmates:

If I was Jonah
I would'a stayed in the whale
doing nothing all day
in the fish's entrails
and I wonder why Jack
even picked up the pail.

I tried to fail.

Bland! I am a steam engine all covered in fur
I don't "think I can" cause I haven't got gears.

I tried to fail.

The song stopped abruptly with only the drummer playing on. Then, his beats trailed into silence.

No one clapped.

The lead guitar player dropped his guitar and walked off towards one of the bars. The singer brushed his hand through the weedlike lavender curls which rose from the top of his head but not from the close-shaved back or sides. He put his guitar on the floor. Then he walked towards Ashley.

They kissed with listless passion.

"A short set," Ashley observed as she took her mouth away.

"What do you expect? An opera?" he asked. "How'd you like that . . . song?"

"Trite," Karla responded archly. "Trite and . . . sweaty."

"A failure," Ashley replied.

The singer, now a speaker, tried to mask his pleasure. He almost blushed.

"That's too bad," he coughed. "We tried to make it worse."

"Yes. You tried to . . . uh . . . fail," Karla said. "I heard."

The singer looked at her questioningly, looked away.

His name was Bruno, Bruno Passive—a name his parents had nothing to do with. His band was called the Pacifists.

The Pacifists at the moment were emerging as one of the more "important" of the dozens of bands in the city, at least to those who felt empowered, or inclined, to judge such things. At a time when most bands—yet again!—were vying to be the loudest, the fastest, the brashest, the most feral, Bruno Passive and the Pacifists tacked against the prevailing wind. Their music was soft, listless, dull. "We try not to be noticed," Bruno said sometimes, "so we are noticeable." It was not that they were Post-Techno or anti-Electronica or *Punk Nouveau*. All the bands were to some degree. It was that they chose to play their three repetitive chords more quietly, that they chose to shout rather than scream.

Now as he lit a cigarette in the flicker of a candle, his face shone as if within a pale cloud. Bruno surveyed the club.

"Bland," he exclaimed, seeing that in a far corner the woman who had led the man in on a leash had placed a box of dog biscuits on the table next to her glass of amaretto and that her man-pet squatted now on all fours on the floor beside her, drinking from a silver dog bowl. Bruno was too far away to see that the bowl had the word HUMAN engraved on its side in large, capital letters.

"Bland," Ashley agreed, following her lover's stare.

"Bland squared," Karla observed, craning her neck to look, her voice charged with wonder.

"What do you think?" Ashley asked.

"I have just begun to think," Bruno replied.

"What does he think about what?" Karla asked.

"What does he think about what we see here before us—a man apparently reduced to being a pet," Ashley said.

"I don't know what to think . . . or how, actually," Bruno said, rising, "but we'll see. I hope his bark is worse than his bite."

"And hers too," Karla smiled.

"No one is barking now," Ashley observed.

He walked over to the woman and her prone companion.

The woman, strangely distant in her blood-red leather motorcycle jacket, blood-red micro-mini, and blood-red fishnet stockings did not look up.

Bruno drank in the woman's attire.

On her tiny feet she wore blood red-hush puppies so that she could walk, he presumed, in comfort.

"Madam," Bruno said, "you stun me."

The man pet growled subtly.

The woman rolled her eyes, commanded, "Silence." Something was strange about her accent.

The man at her feet cowered; Bruno did too. He stepped back.

"Were you speaking to me?" Bruno asked. "Because if you were, you don't know how to take a compliment."

The woman replied with soft malice, quoting in French some lines from Charles Baudelaire.

The meaning was not lost on Bruno. Nor the source. He had glanced himself at *Les Fleurs du Mal* before he had given up reading.

He inclined his head deferentially and observed to himself that this woman, despite her fluent French and her apparent knowledge of poetry, did not appear particularly refined. The first impression she made—her voice, bearing, gestures—seemed plain, standard. Maybe she was a working class Francophile, he thought, but his mind jumped elsewhere. He noted the engraving on the side of the silver dish. He smiled, showed all his teeth. He had big teeth; his was nearly the goofy smile of a simpleton.

He said, "I just want to talk to you."

"What would you like to know?"

"So many things," he replied, taking a seat, unbidden.

The man at his feet was subdued. For the moment anyway.

She picked up her glass of liqueur, toyed with it.

"Ask."

Bruno glanced at the man at her feet, then at the mistress. Her face was superbly impassive as if it had been constructed of some alloy of skin and steel.

"What's your name?" Bruno asked.

"Next question."

He paused.

"What's the story with the man at your feet?"

"Next question."

"What brings you here tonight, to this dump?" Bruno asked.

She fixed him with her stare. She had bloodshot eyes.

"The atmosphere," she responded, sipping. "And you."

"Me?"

"Your songs."

"Songs?"

"He likes them," she said, nodding to the man at her feet. "*Mon petit chien.*"

The crouching man smiled. His incisors were long, doglike.

He sat up on his haunches. She gave him a biscuit which he chewed with delight, making crunching sounds.

Bruno addressed him.

"What do you like about my . . . uh . . . songs?"

The man, glistening droplets of sweat beading amidst stubbled hairs on his shaved head, regarded Bruno. First his expression was without emotion, next he tilted his head to one side quizzically, then the man leapt at Bruno, emitting a yowl of rage and pain. His teeth were bare and flecked with moist biscuit crumbs. Heads turned throughout the club. Voices stopped.

The woman yanked him back with the choke leash and slapped him soundly on the skull.

"Bad!" she rebuked her unusual companion, who cowered

once more. She looked at the man pet a moment. He could not hold her eye. Then she turned towards Bruno. "I think it is time for you to go," she said, smiling.

"Yes," said Bruno rising, "I've never been good with . . . uh . . . pets."

The prone man looked at him from the floor and smiled. Bruno returned through bodies and shadows to Ashley and Karla. They sat for a moment in silence.

He looked at Karla.

She held her arms up in a gesture of bafflement and said, "Let's hear it for leash laws, huh?"

He rolled his eyes.

Ashley said, "Now that is one person I would like to meet."

"Who?"

"The woman you were just talking to."

"I don't think she likes people much," Bruno said.

"Oh, Ashley shrugged, "who does?"

Bruno asked, "How was the therapy session."

"Nightmarish," Ashley replied.

"Ashley was the guinea pig tonight," said Karla.

"Yeah?"

"I don't want to talk about it," Ashley said. Then her attention moved to someone across the club. She saw Eric looking at her expressionlessly. She averted her eyes.

Bruno got up, said, "Use you later." Karla and Ashley nodded. Bruno returned to the stage. It was time to sing again.

* * *

Eventually Bruno and Ashley left the club. It was three o'clock in the morning. The moon dusted the neighborhood with a tepid light which covered and shone from everything like glowing flour. Then it went away. It was June.

"Which way home, my ugly little lover?" Bruno asked, taking Ashley's arm. It had rained briefly but voluminously just after midnight. Now, the air was vaguely, mercifully cool after the warmth of the nightspot. A clammy mist rose three or four feet off the ground.

"Alleys."

They turned into the darkness between two tattered structures. Ashley removed her arm from Bruno's and took his hand. They walked on through shadows, rat sounds, the weak stink of dumpsters long forgotten by removal companies, and spent buildings ghostly with traces of former use.

They walked in silence and with care, wary, excited.

"What's that?" she asked.

By the foot of a loading dock lighted by a single, wire mesh-encased bulb lay a mass of fur and blood. A small, dead animal. Its head had been cut off, set a few inches from the larger mass of its body. Smoke rose from near the remains of the slaughtered animal, intertwining with the mist. By the dead animal's side there was a candle, blood red, which flickered in the moribund breeze that came from the harbor.

For a long moment Bruno looked down in silence.

"A terrier," he said finally, scrutinizing the severed head.

"Ugh, how nerve-wracking. How fucking sweaty. This is one sick society," Ashley said, then started to walk on.

Bruno remained, drinking in the details.

Although the dog looked freshly killed, flies already swarmed on the entrails which spilled from the slit gut.

Bruno knelt and put his ear close to hear their sound. Perhaps it would be the inspiration for a song.

Ashley returned to his side.

"What are you doing?"

"Listening to the flies. . . . Look!"

He took the dog's collar from where its neck had been, careful to hold it where it was not slicked with the dog's blood, and found the tag. The dog tag.

"Charlie," he read. "What the fuck?"

"Charlie? Oh my god!"

"Jesus!" He turned to see her face crack.

She shoved him aside and knelt by the dog, taking both its head and torso in her arms so that the dog's head and body were rejoined—a slightly Cubist figure of a dog.

"Charlie. Oh, Charlie. Who did this to you?" she cried, her voice becoming that of a shattered child. It was her mother's dog, the family pet.

When she was done weeping, she took off her leather jacket and placed the dog's head and body in it. She carried it close to her through the alleys, her body convulsed by spasms of sadness and disbelief, her studied posture of aloof nihilism for the moment dissolved.

$$*\quad*\quad*$$

Mrs Quick lit her thirteenth cigarette of the very early morning and flicked it before an ash even had a chance of forming. On the refrigerator she kept a daily chart of how many cigarettes she smoked. She was already nearing her daily quota. This was part of her ongoing efforts to limit, to control, her smoking. But, she was too worried now to concern herself with the triviality of counting cigarettes. She wanted to know where her pet was, but she did not know. This not knowing was causing her a great deal of anxiety which she was trying unsuccessfully to hide from her husband and from herself.

Mr Quick looked up at her from the newspaper he was reading at the kitchen table, shifted gears in the mechanism of his attention, said, "What's the matter, dear? Really?"

"Oh nothing. Nothing is the matter," his usually perky, fiftyish wife replied too quickly, an edge to her voice.

"Darling," her husband countered, "I can tell when something is wrong, and something *is* wrong. You are not your usual self, brimming with optimism, alternatingly praising then chiding that little dog"—at this Rex Quick paused—"that's it. The little dog. Where is Prince Charles? Where is Charlie?"

"I . . . I don't know. I can't seem to find him anywhere."

"Honey, he's probably taking a nap somewhere," Mr Quick said. "He does seem to be a nocturnal creature. In fact, he didn't seem to be around at all when I got in last night."

"Oh, what time was that?"

"Late, my dear. Too late. Work at the lab is absolutely out of control. The whole week looks like it is going to be unbearable."

"I'm sorry." Her voice lacked sympathy.

Cassie Quick walked to the kitchen door, opened it, cupped her hands around her mouth, yelled, "Charlie. Charlie." Then she stepped into the backyard, wrung her hands, crossed her chest with her arms, patted a hand nervously across her hair. Her mind, her senses raced. It was chilly. There was a faint smell of sea in the morning air. Predawn light. Haze over the Arboretum. Thousands of trees of all varieties. The dog loved romping there.

Indoors, Rex could hear his wife calling the dog. He shook his head, hated to see her so distraught. He turned the page of the newspaper, *The Traveler*, and a small item caught his attention.

Pet Slayings Baffle Police

A series of bizarre pet slayings, apparently ritualistic in nature, has occurred in and around the city over the past three months, the Police Commissioner said yesterday.

Police report that seven household pets have been found dead since mid-March, all apparently killed by the same slayer or slayers.

"Pet owners should keep a close watch on their pets and keep them indoors especially after dark," Commissioner Raymond Trump said.

Police have no leads in the case, but are working to identify possible suspects.

He turned the page, folded the paper, laid it on the kitchen table. He removed his thick glasses, and, momentarily lost in thought, wiped them with a paper napkin.

Mrs Quick returned.

"What am I going to do?" she asked, lighting another cigarette. "I can't find him anywhere."

Mr Quick rose and hugged his wife. He patted her on the back.

He said, "I'm sure he'll turn up. I wish I could help but I have got to get to work. There's a very important meeting I have to put together about the company's chair policy. I've got to draft a whole new policy concerning which staff members are entitled to have which kind of chairs. You know what I mean: swivel chairs; stationary chairs with arms; or swivel, high-backed chairs with arms, and so forth and so on. There are more kinds of chairs than you'd imagine, dearest, I'm sorry to say. Amazing, really. It's all got to be based on position in the company obviously, but we've also got to factor in other things such as seniority and age, not to mention special needs. It's complex, very complex. And very touchy."

"Why don't you just assign chairs based on the smell of people's assholes," Mrs Quick snapped. Then she started to weep.

Rex Quick was taken aback. That sort of comment was unlike Cassie. Very unlike. This Charlie thing must be putting her nerves on edge. He tried to think of something soothing to say, but she ran from the room. After waiting quietly for a few moments, listening to his wife weeping in a distant part of the house, he departed. She was not like this often, but when she was it was best to leave her be.

Soon Mrs Quick returned to the kitchen, looked anxiously out the window. Her thin, straight hair—mouse brown streaked with gray—was pulled back in a ponytail. Her face was faintly girlish, lightly freckled with a slightly upturned nose, but it was creased with lines of age and worry.

She puffed at another cigarette. Number fifteen.

The telephone rang. She took it from its cradle on the wall, held it to her ear, said hello.

"Ashley," she responded woodenly. Then her tone changed. "What is it?"

She listened for a moment more, asked that the information be repeated. Her face became a gray mask of dread. Her eyes rolled up into her head and she fell back against a wall. Crumpling slowly to the green and yellow tiled floor, she muttered, "Charlie."

Over the unconscious woman the phone swung, importuning, "Mom! Mom!"

Chapter 2

Hunters and Gatherers

She is chasing, chasing her dog Charlie through the Arboretum. How fast he runs and how excitedly. He is always just ahead, just out of sight. Now she is running through trees. Across a meadow now. She can hear Charlie, but she can't see him. Who is there with her? Not with her, but above her. Sitting in the trees. Eric? Dr Bentley? The dog's bark seems closer. She runs faster. Tears are streaming down her face. When I catch that damn dog, she says to herself, I'm going to kill him. Someone is laughing. She can't see who. How can you kill him, the unseen voice laughs, when he's already dead?

* * *

Ashley woke up with a start. She had been crying in her dream. A dog was barking in the apartment above. Not at all like Charlie's bark, his yip.

"Shut-up," Ashley moaned, then she sighed, tossing the bed clothes aside. Her room was half-dark, strewn with clothes, jewelry, magazines, things picked up off the street, pieces of junk, an automobile muffler she had found. In one corner a television set, not working, tuned to no channel, bathed part of the room in graygreen light. As the nightmare faded from her consciousness, she turned on a lamp, pulled on a T-shirt and a pair of jeans. Her radio was on. It was some kind of call-in show.

"It's like I can think what people are going to say before they say it," a woman said.

"It's happening more and more," a man responded. "We're in the midst of a telepathic revolution."

Ashley closed her eyes and tried to think what Bruno was thinking now. Nothing. She could not pick up any telepathic messages.

She left her room.

In the living room, Bruno lay face down on the couch, asleep or too listless to move even when Ashley turned on the record player on a table at the front end of the room.

Herb Alpert and the Tijuana Brass.

The living room was dark. The walls in the room were off-white and bare except for a huge photo of Ashley's parents in a gilded frame. The frame shone where it was touched by the light which slid through a gap in the heavy blankets that hung across a picture window in the front wall. In the photograph, Ashley's mother and father both held bows and quivers of arrows in front of a huge target. Her family enjoyed archery. On the floor beneath the picture was a vase filled with dead flowers. Dry, red-black roses. Ashley had stolen them from a graveyard. Between her parents was Charlie, his tongue lolling from his mouth, his eyes smiling. In the past.

Bruno covered his ears, said, "Double-o-nine, Ashley! I hate music. Even good music like this."

He rolled over on his back, wiped sleep from his eyes.

"Come here, ugly," he beckoned.

She came to him and lay down next to him on the mildewed couch. He put his hand under her shirt and she slid hers, sighing, onto his thigh and then into his boxer shorts. She knew what he was thinking now. She pulled his shorts down and he helped her take them off. He sighed and she bent her head down to his thigh and kissed it. Then she paused.

"Oh, forget it," Ashley said, getting up and walking to the record player. She turned it off, bathing the room abruptly in absence of sound.

Bruno smiled.

"That's my girl," he said.

"I'm not a girl," she said, "I'm eusocial." As she turned back towards him, her smirk was caught perfectly in a shaft of sunlight, a glistening smirk; the rest of her face remained in shadow. Moving quietly, quickly, she gathered some things, getting ready to leave.

"Use you later," she said, waving, as she closed the apartment door.

"Use you later," Bruno replied as much to himself as to her.

She was gone.

She walked out of the apartment and down five flights to the street below and her neighborhood of apartment houses which stood on the southwest border of the warehouse district. All the previous night it had rained and, though the sun was now taking full possession of the morning sky, the sidewalk and the street were patterned with puddles from which mist rose knee-high. A mini-fog. She walked along the front of her building and turned into an alley. In the alleyways behind the apartment buildings the mist was thicker, rising two, three feet above the ground. The ground was covered in mist, yet, when Ashley looked up she could see a sliver of the sky, grayblue and spattered with fat clouds. Here and there along the alley walls people had painted words, messages, slogans.

POST-GOD

HIP GNOSIS

WHAT FREEDOM?

She whistled. She felt alone. She walked on. We must confront our fears, she said to herself. We must find what we fear most and confront it. That's what Dr Bentley says.

She walked deeper into a tangle of alleyways and abandoned streets, vacant warehouses, garages, and factories. It was only natural, she told herself, that she should feel that someone was following her. It was only natural that she should think, from time to time, that she heard footsteps. These fears were only natural. They could be easily explained.

She heard something. She turned.

Nothing. Only fog and tangles of sound.

No one.

She hurried on, stepping carefully. Overturned garbage cans and bright clothes were strewn across the alley floor as if limbs, torsos had occupied them and had disappeared, leaving only blouses, pants, socks, a pair of stained women's underwear, shoes. The clothes gave way to newspapers, a gas can with a gaping hole in its side, a pile of bricks, a discarded microwave oven, never used. She tripped over a shopping cart which lay, a trap, across her path. She broke her fall with her forearms and palms. "Shit," she yelled. The sound moved along the alley, faded. Around her she saw discarded compact discs, a headless figurine of the Virgin Mary, a television set without a screen. She pushed herself up. The heels of her hands were scraped. Beads of blood rose on the damaged skin. This was no time to look at her hands.

She hurried on.

She hurried around a corner and stopped short.

In an unnatural pose a woman stood. She was surrounded in mist—a feathery halo, a moist aura. Something evil? Was it? No. Only a mannequin wearing a plain black robe—ankle-length, patterned with silver buttons and studs—last year's fashionable attire. Post-Goth Revival IV. A hood covered the mannequin's head, obscuring her face, and a hand-lettered sign hung around her neck. "Who are you today?" it asked in flowing cursive letters.

It was then that Ashley knew—knew in her gut—she was being followed.

She turned.

The figure of a man about twenty yards away.

No time to gather details.

A voice in her head cried run and she ran—her footsteps reverberating —towards any outlet from this warren of alleys and silent walls. She heard the sound of other, heavier footsteps joining hers in a slightly different rhythm. Slightly faster. She increased her pace. She emerged onto a major street. There was no fog there. Only clarity. She saw cars, pedestrians, a knot of vagrants sitting, lying on the sidewalk, talking, smoking. She looked back into the alley.

Nothing.

Her fear fell from her. Soon forgotten.

*   *   *

Karla, too chipper for such an early hour, was waiting for her at a diner called Rockwell's, a greasy spoon where surfaces shone with oily brightness, the fruit in the pies with artificial sheen. Plate glass windows displayed the street through a coating of grime. There were plastic *bonsai* trees on pedestals throughout the cafe.

Karla wore a tattered leather jacket adorned with silver skulls and the heads of small dolls, a leather skirt and penny loafers. She had streaked her short blond hair with black and the black make-up on her lips and eyelids made her face seem more pallid than usual.

She said, "What's your mindset?"

"User friendly," Ashley replied, sitting down.

"Napping," Karla replied.

"Multi-bland," said Ashley.

She sat down alongside Karla at a table. Both of them had their backs against the wall, positioned so that they could see the rest of Rockwell's. Ashley had an unlit cigarette in her mouth. Ashley was eager to speak. She said, "Let's take as our premise that humankind is not really on the right track." She took a lighter from her pocket, lit the cigarette.

"Huh?" her friend said, looking around the diner. The place was half-filled.

Ashley closed her eyes for an instant and let the babble of voices fill her mind. It was funny how the sum of so many people speaking English all at once sounded like some language from the Middle East. Then she resumed: "I was saying that we should take as the first premise of our conversation—if we are going to have one, Karla—that humankind is not on the right track."

"Who could argue?" Karla shrugged.

"But have you ever thought about why?"

Karla had not.

"It is because we are all doing things that we were not intended to do," Ashley said, exhaling a plume of smoke which joined the cloud that hung over the tables at Rockwell's.

"Well, Ashley, what are we here for, I mean in the big sense?" Karla asked. "I have the impression that you're going to tell me and, frankly, I'm dying to know."

"Sincerely?" Ashley asked.

"Sincerely," Karla confirmed.

"Napping," Ashley nodded.

"Napping squared," Karla returned, completing the exchange of slang approval.

A waitress brought Ashley a cup of coffee, refilled Karla's.

Ashley resumed, "If we go back to the dawn of time, to the very beginning, way before even history began, what did we humans do? We hunted. We gathered food. We fucked. We sought shelter. In fact, that was it. These sweating things were the entire menu, you might say, or the whole can of . . . uh . . . worms. There was no art, no artifice, no artificial preservatives, no artificial emotions. Everything was completely lifelike."

"Cave paintings," Karla exclaimed, relishing the words. She considered as she said it what it might be like to do contemporary cave paintings on her apartment walls. Probably too much trouble. Oh well. She focused again on what Ashley was saying.

"Not art *per se*, ugly" Ashley was countering, looking serious, "but bland roadmaps to where the mastodons were, according to the most contemporary anthropological thinking."

"You're making that up," Karla said, pouting.

"Karla! You question my . . . veracity when I am just trying to understand the basic questions of life. Anyway, that was what we humans were really designed to do, hunt and rest. That is our optimum design function."

"I've never gone hunting," Karla said.

"Who has?" Ashley replied. "But let's look at what we do instead. Take the standard office worker, I mean if her office still exists. She spends the day manipulating reams of information, working through stacks of paper, applying endless rules and procedures and systems that are all far from the natural world. It's so fucking hyper-k. Or take the bureaucrat. Ms Government. She does the same thing—manipulates information about a national system that is more and more divorced from reality."

"That's a form of hunting—searching for all those viral facts and figures, all those solutions," Karla sighed, looking at the wall. There was a print there of a boy in a doctor's office many years ago, his pants down, about to get a shot.

"No, it's not. It's fundamentally absurd, fundamentally unsatisfying. People are spending their lives in arbitrary activities that have rewards and penalties based on what?"

"I don't know. Interest rates? Soybean futures? The imperfect nature of the marketplace?" Karla said, pulling phrases out of thin air, feeling pleased with herself.

Ashley nodded, "That's just it! Abstractions. We are having heart attacks for abstractions."

Karla was lost.

"But it's not all abstract," she said slowly. "What about the guy in Pakistan making the no-tech radios?"

"How do you think that little radio-maker feels as he stands on the line making his five thousandth radio of the day?"

"I don't know. Tuned in?" Karla smiled. "On the right wavelength?"

"Don't you think he might get the idea that there might be enough radios to go around already? In fact, there are. The world could easily churn out enough radios and cars and record players and electric toothbrushes to give everyone in the world a lifetime supply, assuming, that is, that the fucking things worked. In fact, ugly, there should really be no reason for anyone to work at all! We should be able to just sit back and atrophy, waiting for our latest supply of groceries to come in from the Farm Belt or wherever food is grown," Ashley said.

"Ashley! I didn't know you had such ambition," Karla said. "Maybe you haven't noticed though that there's a permanent recession—or something—going on. The economy is completely double-o-nined. Lots of people aren't working. Food and other things don't seem to be in such abundant supply."

"Yes," Ashley acknowledged, "we are in a . . . uh . . . severe downturn, but that's just here. Our multinational corporations are doing a hyperkinetic business just about everywhere else. Soon, after they've bulked up on sucking the Third World dry, they'll have to come back to the U.S. and get the whole sweaty process started again. After all, we are the belly of the beast."

"Now, that's my trite optimist," Karla smiled admiringly. "But, of course, all this economic stuff doesn't affect me in the least. Recession, depression, who cares? I don't need to do anything personally. My trust fund takes care of everything. So my question is, oh wise one, if I've got everything, why do I always want something new?"

"If you can't kill a mountain lion . . . you might as well buy a mountain bike," Ashley said, stretching.

"Huh?"

"Karla, the point is that we don't do what we are hard-wired to do. Our lives were supposed to be a bland, beautiful adventure. It was supposed to be us against the mastodons, the prehistoric boars, with a feast and a screw afterwards. Now, we have to channel our desires into things, useless things. We have to manufacture our adventures."

"I certainly wouldn't want a putrid mountain bike," Karla yawned. "But I would like two of almost everything else.

Ashley rolled her eyes, then brought them back, wide.

"God," she whispered. "He's coming in here."

Karla looked towards the entrance to Rockwell's.

In walked Eric with his unique walk. Sloping forward, his gait mixed arrogance and lack of balance, deformity almost. His body was squat and powerful, but the angles were too harsh. The same with his head; it was as if the angles had been molded too harshly and never smoothed to softer curves. His route through the tables took him right by Ashley and Karla. He smiled at them as he passed. His teeth were very small and white.

He sat off at a table in a far corner of the diner, positioning himself in such a way that he could watch them from the corner of his eyes.

He sat under a picture of a young girl trying on her mother's make-up before a mirror on a dresser.

"A reptile," Karla observed.

Ashley nodded.

"Now, back to our topic."

"Oh, please," Karla said, "let's just be quiet for a moment."

"You've hurt me, you ugly thing," Ashley said mockingly. No one wanted to listen to her ideas.

They sat quietly for a while, drinking their coffees, letting the various other conversations of the cafe enter and leave their minds one at a time until they found something worth listening to. They called this mental process, this turning the dials of their attentions, "being radios." Here was Walter the actor-waiter gossiping in a stage whisper with the dreary busboy. Over there someone was complaining about the trouble she had had with a shop clerk. Now a heartbroken young man in a tweed jacket was telling a companion how sad he was but how he could rise above his sorrow if only. . . .

Karla motioned with her head. She had found a promising transmission.

The first thing Ashley noticed about the voices was the contrast between them. The feminine voice mixed precision with earnestness. The masculine was tired, self-mocking.

The voices went with the speakers, Ashley noted, glancing at them, the interlocutors, two tables away. She was in her early twenties, olive skinned with vaguely oriental features, her hair pulled back severely into a bun. Wearing a wrinkled greenish business suit, he flopped in his chair and puffed a cigarette.

"Describe the colors of the inner organs," he said curtly. It was almost a command.

"Yellow and pale, for the most part."

"Even the heart?"

"You've got to remember there is no blood. The blood has been drained from the entire body. It's pale."

"The lungs?"

"Pale yellow unless the person was a smoker. Then they are black."

"Describe the most repulsive thing."

"The smell. Without question."

"What is it like? Rotting meat?"

"As you would expect. Rotting meat and formaldehyde. Especially in the summer. There is no air conditioning in the room."

"What measures are taken against the smells?"

"Some cover their mouths and noses with handkerchiefs or surgical masks. Most students always wear the same clothes in the room and change before they go. It's impossible to get the smell out."

"The smell of death. How about air freshener?"

"Not allowed."

"Describe the room."

"It is a huge room, voluminous, with row upon row of tables. The walls are dull gray. Along the walls are shelves filled with bottles of preserved organs that the instructors use in demonstrations."

"Do you ever work there alone. Late at night for example?"

"Yes."

"It must be . . . unsettling?"

"It is unsettling. Yes."

"I can imagine that some students must have terrible nightmares about the cadavers. Has anything frightening ever happened to you?"

"Not to me, no. But to a friend."

He was quiet and she went on.

"At the end of the tables are waste buckets where parts are discarded. One night my friend was in the room alone. She heard a rustling. She did not know where it was coming from. It sounded like there was a stirring in the waste bucket."

"What was it? Did an organ . . . reanimate? Did a finger begin to wag?"

"It was a mouse. There was a mouse in the waste bucket."

"God, how . . . unsettling," Ashley said, turning her attention to Karla, but Karla's eyes were closed and she was breathing deeply. She had fallen asleep.

* * *

When Bruno left the apartment that morning nourishment was the only thought on his mind.

His stomach was empty. Gastric acids had started eating at the stomach lining, yet he passed by his usual breakfast spot, a drug store with a lunch counter. He felt the heat of the day begin to beat down on the city. Another hot July day was gathering force. The sides of his head, shaved and fishwhite, felt the heat especially. He needed a hat or a bandana. It was about 11:30.

My skin is warm, my stomach is warmer, he thought to himself. Maybe that could be the lyric of a song.

He passed a restaurant where a neon pitcher poured electric coffee into a crackling cup. Tempting, but he would walk on for a while. He began to feel sweat in the small of his back, in his armpits. He came to a park where children baited a limping dog.

Their eyes were gleeful and their chortling rose above the sounds of the street.

Bruno stopped, watched through the iron bars of the fence surrounding the park.

The children has sticks with which they poked at the dog. Not especially hard, the poking, but repeatedly, so that the dog, a cocker spaniel, whimpered and cowered.

One of the children wore a Donald Duck baseball hat, the hat brim a thick, yellow plastic bill.

A crowd formed to watch the dog being baited. Some watched silently. Others began to cheer the children, spurring them on to greater cruelty.

For a moment the dog broke free, scampered to the side of a vagrant who lay on the grassless dirt, drinking from a bottle. The man pushed the dog away.

Now the children, dressed in tattered jeans and sweaters and filthy, laceless sneakers, surrounded the dog, whacking at it furiously as it lay on the ground.

The eldest, a boy about eleven, began to kick the dog in the head. The violence was giving the other children such excitement they stopped beating the dog and began jumping up and down—dancing almost—their cheeks, their faces ruddy with exertion.

"Kill it," an aristocratic man with horn-rimmed glasses yelled. Others in the crowd joined in: "Kill the dog. Kill the dog."

Bruno could see that, at last, the sticks were opening gashes on the dog. He began to push through the crowd toward the gateway into the park. He pushed through the surging mass of transfixed onlookers, each of them pushing to get to the fence to have a better look, standing on tiptoes, craning necks. Bruno's nostrils flared. The crowd had the smell of primal, bestial excitement—a smell, Bruno thought, like sweat and concrete.

"Excuse me," he yelled, pushing ahead, almost attaining the gate. "Excuse me!"

A woman glared at him.

A man turned, shoved him.

Bruno looked at him. "Excuse me."

But the man would not let him pass. His face was red, beaded with sweat. He was a thick man with a gut which ballooned out beneath the hairy chest which his half-opened shirt revealed. He moved left, then right so that Bruno could not get around him.

"Excuse me!"

"Fuck you," the man yelled, putting his face up to Bruno's.

Suddenly, the virulence of the crowd sputtered and the yelling which had in fact become a unified chant died. The man took his face from Bruno's and turned. Bruno stood up on his toes, looked over the man's shoulder.

"Stop that! Stop it now," a women shouted. She had stopped her car in the middle of the street. The driver's door was open. Traffic had stopped. Drivers and passengers watched from their cars. No one honked or yelled. Something out of the ordinary was happening.

Onlookers stepped aside as she moved through the gate and strode toward the children and their canine victim.

"Stop!"

The eldest let loose one last half-hearted kick against the dog's side. The thud was dull but audible in the new silence.

The children dropped their sticks. Their heads hung in shame. A little girl in a plaid skirt and knee socks fidgeted with her hands behind her back while the woman knelt by the dog, patted it reassuringly.

She picked the dog up. She turned and walked toward her car saying nothing, looking straight ahead until, for some reason, she turned and looked directly at Bruno. She stopped.

A long thread of blood-flecked drool hung from the dog's mouth.

"Bruno," she said, "you should be ashamed of yourself."

He felt his face coloring with shame and he looked at the sidewalk. It was severely cracked. Weeds grew through the cracks.

Everyone in the crowd turned and looked at Bruno, then away from him again to watch the woman take the dog to the car, open a rear door, place it gently on the back seat. When the dog was settled, she closed the door, got in the car, drove off.

The woman was Cassie Quick.

Muttering under its collective breath, the crowd cleared. Traffic resumed, swallowing up the rare interlude of silence. Still lying on the ground, his arm propping up his head, the homeless man bellowed, "Best show I've seen in days. Best show I've, hell, ever seen. Ever seen."

Bruno stood by a crumbling stone gate post and watched the children.

On the stone was painted the word ABJURE. The letters had dripped a little.

The children stood, doing nothing, sticks still in hands. The little plaid skirted girl kicked at the dirt and clods of earth sprayed a companion. The eldest said nothing, turned around, and began to walk. He was a tall, thin, open-faced boy with brown, disheveled hair and brown eyes. The children followed, walking or skipping toward the other end of the park.

"Best goddamn show ever, kids."

Bruno followed.

He passed a man—horrible acne, flecks of dandruff in his moussed hair and on his gold Century 21 jacket—who whispered, "Pain for sale. I've got Pain."

The dog beaters walked on, dropping their sticks. They became more childlike, more sweet, jabbering, laughing, each vying to make his voice heard. The girl began to sing "Old MacDonald," her voice sweet and tart as a small green apple.

Leaving the park, they crossed a street and turned down an alley between apartment buildings. The heat had long since burned away the early morning mist. The apartment buildings looked mostly unlived-in. An old man sat on a chair by the alley's mouth, picking methodically through a garbage bag.

"Hello, old timer," the eldest boy laughed.

The man nodded. Avuncular.

The brick walls of the alley were painted with slogans.

ABJURE

PICKLES FOR NARNIA

2009!

HAIL MAGAZINES

ABJURE PAIN

TERRY R.I.P. NOW YOU HAVE A HOME ON THE OTHER SIDE

EAT MEXICAN, NOT MEXICANS

INFORMATION=DEATH

He was thirty paces behind the children. They paid him no heed. He fought his reluctance and kept going. He did not fancy being hit with sticks. He was past that stage in his lifework.

REGRET

When the children turned into a shadowy passageway that led into a forgotten courtyard, Bruno stopped short. From the edge of the passageway he could see the old tenements surrounding the courtyard rising upwards, their windows bricked or boarded or broken. Across the courtyard sagged rotted clotheslines. The light in the courtyard was dim. The children had become silent.

Some of the children looked back at Bruno. Only for a moment. Then they turned back to their play. A spontaneous and simple game of tag, played simply, unhurriedly, without rancor. They played in silence.

Bruno's palms and underarms sweated but the sweat dried quickly in the sluggish, shadowy coolness from which he watched.

The balance of his indecision shifted, as it so often did, for no good reason.

He approached.

ABJURE

The children stopped their activity, looked up with expressions of expectancy.

"Hi kids," Bruno said.

The children remained quiet, shy. Some looked at their feet, their sneakers. Not the eldest, the leader. He looked at Bruno.

"What you want?" the eleven year old said, taking a step toward the adult. He wore jeans and a striped, short sleeved shirt. Though he spoke with the brittle accent of this northeastern, coastal city, he had a farmboy look, healthy. His face and his arms were tanned. His eyes were hard.

"I just want to talk to you . . . about the dog," Bruno replied.

A child giggled nervously. Rosy cheeks besmirched with grime.

"Why you want to know, mister?" asked the boy, his hands balling up by his sides.

Bruno looked around at the children. Their eyes seemed bright. Bright lights in the dimness.

"Just interested."

"You want to turn us in. To the 'thorities."

"No way. I have nothing to do with the authorities."

"But you're not a kid," the boy said, then pondered. "You like dogs or hate 'em."

Bruno weighed his answer.

"I don't care either way, really."

He looked at the walls around the courtyard. There was one window that was not filled with bricks. Someone was looking down at him. The realization filled him with dread. He could make out only that it was a human form, sexless in the gloom and distance, shapeless with a shape that signified only someone watching.

The boy followed Bruno's glance.

"City of eyes," the boy said softly, then spat on the ground. "By which I mean—somebody always watching."

The form retreated. Bruno looked back down at the chief child, met his eyes.

"We don't like watchers do we, kids?" the boy said.

The children shook their heads.

"Uhn-uh."

"You a watcher, mister?"

"No. A follower."

"You followed us here, didn'cha?"

"Yes."

The boy thought for a moment, then he smiled. Hatching a scheme maybe, or just having an amusing thought.

"Maybe we should sing him the song. Wha'cha say kids? Should we?"

Silence.

The little girl with the plaid skirt looked at him with wide-pupiled eyes. All the children were in tattered clothes except her. She looked as if she should have been on her way to parochial school, Bruno thought, not here. She was a perfect little doll, not even four feet in height, except that she had, on one side of her face, a discoloration of her skin, a stain, that reached from her forehead across one eye down across her cheek and half of her chin. In color it was between red clay and lavender.

She said, "Do you really want to hear the song?"

"Yes," Bruno answered.

"Fetch the singing box, then," the eldest said.

Two boys went to a corner of the courtyard and brought back a crate. They set it down three feet in front of the adult.

"You sing the song, Beatrice," the eldest said.

Shy, the little girl in the plaid skirt stepped up onto the box. Even elevated, she rose only to Bruno's chest.

She sang:

Whatcha going to do when you're feeling low?
Going to a pet show.

Whatcha going to do when you're feeling down?
Chase a pet all over town.

Whatcha going to do when you can't get it up?
Run over a pet in a pickup truck.

Talking about Pet Hunter. Pet Hunter.

When she finished, she smiled.

The others stood there silently but Bruno felt the menace growing.

"Now you sing," the eldest said.

Bruno stammered, "Me . . . I can't . . . uh . . . well, what do you want me to sing?"

"Now you sing."

The children took a step towards Bruno.

His voice cracked when he began to sing. He stopped. Embarrassed.

"Mister, you have to get up on the box to sing," Beatrice said, her voice sweet but her eyes cold.

"Yes," the eldest said. "On the singing box."

Bruno towered above the children.

He sang the first song that came to mind. He saw the children's leader make a subtle movement with his head and the children circled Bruno while he sang. His impulses said run. He kept singing. He finished, surrounded by children who looked up at him with cold, feral faces.

The leader considered.

"That was nice," he said.

"Thanks," Bruno said. "I think I'd like to go now."

"Okay. Bye-bye."

He stepped down from the box and turned. The children stepped aside and let Bruno pass.

Chapter 3

The Interpenetration of Dreams

Everything in the station was broken, rusted, encased in grime, damp, beaded with moisture. Steam escaped from broken pipes. Water flowed from doorless public lavatories so that a glazed wet covered the platforms and dripped down to the pit that cradled the tracks. Filth and mold patterned the yellowish walls, nearly obscuring printed instructions to commuters. Instructions like this:

> If for some reason your train does not arrive on time, please wait with patience. We apologize for the inconvenience.
>
> City Transit Authority

Here to this broken station, broken people hobbled, shuffled every evening to make an exodus from the center of the city on barely moving trains. Tonight they began to gather at about half past six. The passengers were nervous, wondering if police or National Guardsmen would swoop down on them this evening with dogs and clubs to herd them off to one of the Freedomworker camps outside the city. They were quiet in their wariness and so the station was quiet but for the incomprehensible announcements which at random moments overrode the continuous static of the public address system.

Tonight an unfamiliar figure joined the outbound throng. The others eyed him.

He was marked by cleanliness, health, gait, demeanor, bearing, attitude, by brightness of eyes, by lack of abrasions, deformities, odors. Earlier today some would have approached him, asked him for things, or hoped just to stand near him, feeding on his health, thinking his thoughts.

Now, at the hour of leave-taking they, these outbounders, held back from him. From Alvin. He was not one of them.

He carried a backpack and a sleeping bag and he wore sandals with thick, hiking socks. Alvin was ready. He was determined, too.

When the train finally arrived, Alvin sat alone. Others stood rather than take a seat near him. The train began its movement through the tunnels.

Alvin listened to one man speaking to himself, "Is there anyone who really enjoys riding the subway these days? No. Perhaps not. But I do. I find it so restful. Now we are going to a place of final rest."

They were, but not entirely by train.

The train, after it had ascended from the tunnels into the less dark of night, inched some blocks through neighborhoods of three-deckers and high fences before it broke down.

Cursing or silent, the riders detrained into the almost cold October evening.

They formed a slow, disorderly parade moving over a series of gently rolling hills towards an endless expanse of open space. From behind high fences, dogs yowled at them as they passed.

At last they reached their destination. Here, in Final Rapture Cemetery, the homeless made their nightly encampment. They slept on the graves. Many had set up cardboard houses and hovels. The strongest, the canniest, lived in mausoleums where their fires singed the marble floors and walls with soot, with burn marks.

Alvin walked down an avenue of these mausoleums, these opulent homes intended only for the dead.

Well, there goes the neighborhood, he smiled to himself. His inner voice sounded odd to him. It made him afraid. He felt the others looking at him, thinking about him, as he walked by their marble hovels. It was funny in a way how this neighborhood—suburb really—of the dead was being ruined by the influx of the living in much the same way a mausoleum placed on a residential street would engender decline. Alvin shook this thought from his mind. Even thinking made him uneasy. He wanted a blank mind.

As he walked further into the graveyard Alvin grew more nervous. A little beyond the lane of mausoleums he stopped. Turn back! Turn back! He fought the impulse. He visualized his fear and his will struggling within him. He exhaled. He saw his breath in the chilly air. His breath shone in the moonlight, then disappeared. A fleeting apparition. He walked off the cemetery lane, taking a footpath which climbed towards a tiny hill. The moonlight guided him. The sounds of the homeless encampment diminished to leave a graveyard silent but for the sound of his footsteps, his breathing, and the wind. His fear grew as he walked on but he was determined now. He must look his fear straight in the eye and overcome it.

Leaving the path, he pushed through bushes and brambles until he came to a clear space on the top of a the hill. Here there was a single grave marked by an old stone. The grave was overgrown. Forgotten. Bushes ringed the hilltop. Alvin could not see over them. He could only look up.

He stood for a moment, panicked, fighting against the panic.

This was his nightmare. To be alone with a grave in a graveyard in the dead of night.

Each night he dreamed this. The dream always began with a scene like this one—walking, pulled by unseen forces to a secluded spot, and then . . . he slammed the steel door of his will shut on what came next in his recurring dream. Or tried to. His heart pounded and his arms and legs began to shake uncontrollably.

"Unbland!" he yelled. He heard his voice die in the expanse of night.

Fumbling, he took a bottle of vodka from his backpack, removed the cap, gulped it down.

He took another gulp. That settled him.

Hot quietness radiated from his stomach up into his lungs, down into his loins. He drank again.

Then, feeling calmed, he sat on the headstone and looked up at the moon. A half disk in a cloudless sky. Wind was blowing up from the sea, increasing in intensity.

Alvin laughed with the pure pleasure of feeling his fear subside. Look! He was here alone and nothing was happening. No strange voices, no apparitions, no movements underfoot, no . . . well . . . he did not even want to think about the things which were not happening when the fact was nothing was.

Nothing.

Just nothing.

But it was chilly. He zipped up his jacket, took another drink. He looked at the pint bottle and saw he had already emptied half. Half empty or half full, he smiled to himself. Standing up, he felt off balance. He steadied himself, undid his zipper, and pissed on the ground, steam rising from his urine.

Piss drops glistened on cold, wind-blown grass in the wan lunar light.

Lovely, really.

Perhaps he should go.

He had come, seen, conquered his fear.

"No! It is not enough," he said aloud. His voice sounded strange.

He had come to spend the night, to see dawn come and nothing happen. It would only be then that he would have beaten back the nightmare that had poisoned his mind. But, he told himself, what a hyperactive hassle it would be sitting here in the chilly grass, especially when it was turning out to be so easy, so much easier than he had expected.

Using a flashlight he had brought with him, he examined the name on the gravestone.

> *William W. Roberts*
> *1900-1977*
> *A loving brother*

He sat with his back against the gravestone and looked up again at the night sky.

Just killing time.

Bland.

*   *   *

In her handsome home in an exclusive enclave of the city overlooking one side of the spacious Arboretum, that splendid park, Dr Allison Bentley, dressed in sheer, loose-fitting white garments, lit a pungent stick of incense.

Her third floor study—capacious and ornate—was filled with the statuettes, masks, and ritualistic implements of ancient and primitive cultures. Goats' heads and gods' heads stared down on the thick Persian carpet, antique furnishings, and a huge mahogany desk which dominated one part of the room. A glass-topped specimen case along one wall was filled with ceremonial daggers. Rubies, sapphires, emeralds and other jewels glistened on polished silver or gold handles inlaid with occult images or words and signs from arcane or long-dead languages. Another case alongside it was filled with crystals which seemed to glow with thick, almost greasily palpable auras in the light from the half dozen candelabras which lit the room.

There were a few pictures on the walls amidst the many masks, including —directly below Dr Bentley's diplomas from Mount Holyoke, Berkeley, and the Katja Institute for the Study of Sleep Disorders—a triptych referencing the Passion of Christ. However, in these three small, blasphemous paintings it was Satan who was subjected to humiliation and crucifixion. That the pictures were drawn in a clear and sentimental manner only enhanced their sinister effect.

The center of the room was free of furniture except for a meditation cushion and a Japanese sidetable from which, sitting cross-legged atop a hard, circular pillow, Bentley took a syringe and vial. She drew the contents of the vial, the drug, up into the syringe, prepared her arm, and injected herself.

Primitive, ritualistic music played quietly over the Doctor's exquisite sound system: an undertone, an undertow of sound. The speakers were subtly hidden in the paneled walls of the room. Drums and voices whispered, begged, screamed—the chanting gliding always towards climactic resolution, never attaining it.

She put the spent syringe back on the side table, her movements serene and precise. Then she settled down into a meditative posture. Her eyes closed and her expression became placid.

This was her meditation:

She began by letting her mind grow absolutely clear so that she was conscious of nothing, not even of herself or her lack of self-awareness. This had taken years of practice, this letting her mind become a far-reaching vacancy into which nothing would come, no hint of thought, sensation, emotion, desire. Then, when the appropriate time came, her consciousness, now self-willed by her deepest self, was freed to wander wherever it sought to go, to past or future, or into others' consciousnesses, their dreams, or their nightmares.

*　　*　　*

Despite the setting and the cold, Alvin found himself fighting to keep his eyes open. He looked at his watch with a flashlight he had brought with him. One o'clock. He stood up, stretched, felt a pleasant crackling in his spine. Getting the energy channels aligned.

Putting his back to the old stone once more, he sat down again, his mind bubbling slowly with thoughts. He unrolled his sleeping bag but he did not bother to slip inside it; instead he just pulled it loosely over his body. He thought about his job, about the quietness of the cemetery, about how he would like a girlfriend, about how he used to go with his family to the lake in the summer when he was little and his mother would make pancakes on an old iron stove in a cottage up on the hill by the lake, the blue lake, cold as a fish when you pulled it out of the water as his father did standing up in the green boat yelling "I've got you, I've got you, Mr. Fish" . . . and Alvin slept.

He dreamt.

*　　*　　*

The Priest prays over the grave but Alvin cannot make out the words.

Is he speaking Latin?

It seems he is saying the "one potato, two potato" nursery rhyme.

That can't be.

He looks at the faces at the graveside. Mrs Beamis dabs at her eyes with a handkerchief. She cries red tears. Blood tears. Mr Beamis glares at Alvin with a hard, cold look. Alvin looks down at the grass.

The groundskeepers are doing a terrible job. The grass is long and yellowing. Shoots of ivy trundle through the grass; they seem to grow as he watches. Someone should mow it, cut it back.

But he knows no one will. It makes him uneasy. He hears children crying. He cries too. Everyone is wailing.

He feels something strange, as if there is someone or something watching his dream, an unseen, but palpable, presence.

He sobs uncontrollably, hot tears streaming over his cheeks. Rosalie is dead.

The only woman—girl really—that he has ever loved is dead. And he . . . no! . . . he killed her.

Abruptly he is driving in a car on a rain dashed road. The tape player is playing loudly and he is laughing. Rosalie is next to him, laughing. Loudly laughing. They laugh with the pure joy of living, of being young and in love. He looks over at her in the darkness of the car. Her hair hangs, a tangled mass of black, down onto her soft white shoulders. She radiates serenity, warmth, caring. She is the kind of girl who is wholesome, good, and solid. She is Alvin's anchor. He knows that she will always stand by him.

Her lips are full and she smiles at him with kind eyes. A look that says "forever."

"Kiss me," Alvin says.

"Not while you're driving, you goof."

"Kiss me," he says with mock insistence, but he really does need her reassurance all the time and he looks over at her intently. "Please."

She leans toward him, lips parted, and he leans towards her.

She leans towards him and . . . something terrible is about to . . . no! . . . her body flies forward against the dashboard, her head—face-first—smashes into, through the windshield glass and his body lurches forward and there is the awful sound of a collision. Metal twists and screams. Glass sprays.

He lies in the mangled car.

He hears the tape playing and his horn blaring.

He is wedged in metal. He cannot feel his arms.

He cannot reach out to Rosalie. He watches her slumped body heave with the effort of trying to take another breath; the sound reminds him—horribly—of a plugged vacuum cleaner. The front of her head, her face, is . . . has been torn off, sliced away at a sharp angle that runs from where her nose had been to the center of the crown of her head.

Slowly, she turns to him and . . . she is gone. He is back at the funeral; an electric winch lowers her coffin into the grave. Then workmen slowly shovel soil down onto the box that holds her, his Rosalie.

Eventually the others leave. Mrs Beamis tries to get Alvin to come along, but he shakes his head, stays.

It is early evening. A half moon appears in the night sky of wind blown clouds. The moon is halved just as his life is cut in half, his heart. He stands at the foot of the grave alone, wracked by uncontrollable sobbing. He kneels on the soft soil, his hands covering his eyes. His knees sink into the warm, easy dirt.

"Alvin."

It must be the wind, some wind trick.

Again. Softly.

"Alvin."

He drops his hands, looks up. She stands in front of him, looks just like she always looked.

"I knew that you couldn't live without me," she smiles, "so I came back. It isn't so hard if you love someone. Love is stronger that death."

She is wearing jeans and an India print blouse, just what she always wore, and her hair is pulled back in a pony tail. Just like . . . before.

She beckons to him.

"Get up, you silly goose. It's me."

It is her voice. He rises, steps back. His dream heart swoons with chilled warmth—awe mixed with longing.

She stands on her grave, not an insubstantial wraith but warm, animate. Not clothed in some windy, transparent ghost wrap, but just as she had been that last night.

"Alvin, aren't you glad to see me? I know I'm glad to see you."

Moonlit lips glisten, shape words which are not ghost words. He tries to speak, cannot.

"I have missed you so much." She steps forward; her foot sinks to her ankle in the soil of her fresh-laid grave. "And I have a wonderful secret. I am not dead. I live."

He gasps. He whispers her name.

"Rosalie."

They embrace. Their kiss is the primordial kiss—simultaneously a kindling and a consummation of desire.

He feels her living in his arms, their hearts beating together. He pulls back just to make sure.

She smiles and the upper half of her face slides off her head, leaving a savaged wreckage of brains, skull, cartilage, blood. Her nose, eyes, forehead, and the front half of her skull—still topped with a part of her scalp and her thick black hair—form an unnatural wedge which slides between them until it is trapped, hot and wet, between their embracing chests.

He recoils, steps back, and the half face falls to the ground and slithers then towards him like a horseshoe crab of torn human flesh from the top of which human eyes, her eyes, glare up at him with hatred and, at the same time, her faceless body simply sits like a tired little girl sits on the grave, the still intact mouth singing:

> *"I lost my face, it's true,*
> *and it's all because of you, Alvin.*
>
> *We took a drive, a pleasant drive,*
> *now I'm not alive, Alvin.*
>
> *And it's something I can't face*
> *because I haven't got a face, Alvin."*

A voice in his dreaming mind asks what is happening. His dream has changed, become so much worse than ever before. Rosalie's face slithers after Alvin as he runs. But thick brambles and hedges have grown up in a tight circle around the grave.

He runs within the circle around the sitting body of his lover, pursued. He is screaming, howling inexpressible sounds of fear and in her study Dr Bentley's tranquil face became perplexed.

Beads of sweat formed on her brow. Her thin, dry lips formed a word.

"No," she said soundlessly.

Now, the face is leaping at Alvin.

*　　*　　*

He woke writhing on the grave and heard, faintly, what sounded like a woman laughing. Not a happy laugh.

"Jesus," Alvin gasped.

He fumbled for his flashlight and switched on the reassuring beam, throwing the light wildly around.

Nothing. It must have been the sound of wind through the trees.

He stood up, throwing his sleeping bag aside. His body was clammy with sweat.

With a sense of dread he realized that he had fouled himself. A warm stickiness weighed in his pants.

Somehow he managed to catch his breath.

The cemetery was quiet but for the wind.

"I must not run," he said aloud to himself, miraculously retaining a vestige of courage. "It was only a dream."

The flashlight shone on the grave stone.

No.

Her name was engraved there.

Rosalie Beamis

The name remained there for an instant, then withered, faded into *William W. Roberts.*

He heard her voice—Rosalie's voice—whisper his name. "Alvin."

* * *

Detective Thomas Costello, faintly handsome despite a thin scar running from the top of one eye across his forehead and into his balding scalp, sat with his feet up on his desk at Police Headquarters. This was one of those rare moments when he had nothing to do. His case file was cleared, or almost cleared. Only a few cases lingered on, unsolvable, their thick manila folders full of many leads maybe pointing at, but not leading to, perpetrators or motives. Physically Costello looked spent. Every aspect of his appearance insinuated that he was in the midst of a slow, but ceaseless journey towards dissolution. There were holes in one of his slumping socks and in the sole of one of his shoes. The thighs of his slacks were shiny with wear. His shirt was stained, unpressed. In a limp loop hung his tie, a slack noose. He needed a shave. His red hair, thick at the sides of his head though not on top, was unbrushed, curly, unruly. His face, though still keeping some of the thin singularity of Costello's relative youth, was becoming simultaneously pudgy and strained.

Though it was nearly 8 p.m., he still felt the effects of the previous evening's drinking. During the course of the day he had tried to eat, beginning with lunch, but food made his stomach flip.

Closing his eyes, he put his head back. At least the feeling that today held some exquisitely terrible assignment was subsiding. Just four more hours and—mercifully—his shift would end. Then he could have a drink, or two, to put his shattered mind back together. Soothing alcohol soaking the arid material of his brain, turning it again into pleasant mush—that was the ticket. Thinking now of drinking, he visualized water turning parched dirt to cool, coherent mud. Well, he might feel like a man made

of dirt now, but soon the deluge! Perhaps he would allow himself
a catnap to help his waiting.

The phone's ringing quashed his reverie.

One eye opened. Then two.

"Shit."

He knew who it was; he sensed it. He removed his feet from
the desk top.

"Costello," he answered.

"Thomas," exuded Lieutenant Francis Finnerty in tones of
silken sarcasm, "have I disturbed you?"

Costello pondered, replied, "Do you want the truth?"

"I hope I did not wake you," Finnerty continued, not missing a beat, "but perhaps you could come to my office. After all,
Thomas, it is our sacred duty to protect the public and perhaps
we could discuss how we could use the last few hours of your
shift to best do our duty. Perhaps you could come now. Now would
be a good time."

The way Finnerty chortled at the conclusion of his request
was not a good sign.

Costello put the receiver down, then picked up a cup from
his desk. It was a thick, porcelain cup. He considered it for a
moment, felt its weight. Then he threw it hard against the wall of
his office. The impact made a small explosion not unlike the
report of a revolver. He pondered the impression the cup had
made in the wallboard. The door of his office was thrown open.
Another detective looked in. Samuelson.

Samuelson took in the scene.

"You okay?"

"Yes, I'm fine," Costello said. He lit a cigarette. He sounded
calm. "Someone threw a coffee cup against my wall, that's all."

Samuelson stepped into the office. He looked bored and concerned at the same time, Costello noted. Not an atypical
combination here at Police Headquarters. Samuelson looked
around the office again.

"Someone?" he asked.

"Someone with an anger problem," Costello replied.

"Oh," Samuelson said. "I thought you offed yourself."

"Sorry to disappoint," Costello said.

"It's been that kind of day," Samuelson replied wearily, then left, not closing the door behind him.

Costello got up, walked down to the lieutenant's office. People eyed him from their desks. Why not? He was armed.

"I take it," he said, placing himself in an uncomfortable chair in front of Finnerty's file-strewn desk, "that you have an assignment of particular shittiness for me."

Finnerty eyed him with chilled bemusement.

"Costello, I love the way you talk," the lieutenant said, leaning back in his swivel chair and focusing on the wall calendar. "'An assignment of particular shittiness.' In fact, you might notice I try to address you on your own terms and to give you an assignment worthy of someone of your education and . . . position within the Department."

"You're just jealous," Costello smiled, "because unlike yourself I can think."

"That's it," Finnerty said, smiling at the detective, taking pleasure in the interaction. "I am jealous of you—your education, your sense of culture and . . ."

"And?"

"And I am particularly jealous of your next assignment."

The lieutenant paused, pouted when Costello did not take the bait.

"Detective," he continued, "did you know that throughout our fair city some mad fiend is slaughtering pets?"

"Pets?"

"Do you not know what a pet is?"

"Shit," Costello said.

"Ahhh, no," Finnerty said, savoring the words, "a pet is not shit, my young friend. Pets produce shit. Dog shit. Cat shit. Bird shit. Snake shit. Other kinds of shit."

Costello put his face in his hands.

"Your assignment, should you decide to accept it . . . or not, is to find this aforementioned fiend, apprehend him, and bring him to justice."

"Come on, Lieutenant! Isn't this a job for somebody else. Animal Control for instance?"

Finnerty rolled his eyes.

"Costello," he said, "do you think our duty stops with human beings, that the rights of pets are beneath the notice of the police? You've got to get with it. Times are changing. We are . . . ah . . . Postmodern now."

"Huh? Jesus," Costello sighed, "Postmodern." He needed a drink.

Abruptly the lieutenant's tone changed.

Leaning forward, he said, "Look, Costello, let's put bullshit aside. This assignment sucks. Neither you or I give a fuck about pets living or dead, especially when the homicide rate is growing exponentially. But this shit comes from the top. The mayor is beginning to get an earful about these goddamn pet murders. He wants it stopped but obviously he is not going to mount the investigation himself. You are, I hate to admit, one of my few competent guys. No argument, you're an asshole. But you're a cop. Here's the file. Find the fruitcake. Make him stop."

Finnerty tossed the file to Costello. He opened it, glanced at a photo, grimaced. Blood and fur.

"Leads?"

"No. None."

"Well, any insight as to how I might proceed? Based, naturally, on your own vast experience."

"Yes," Finnerty said, the mirth returning to his eyes. "Go out, drive around. Interview some dogs and cats."

Costello nodded.

"Thanks."

He rose, turned. Finnerty's voice caught him at the door.

"You know what they call what you're about to do?"

"No. What?"

"Pooch patrol."

Costello smiled.

"Perhaps I should request a canine unit?"

"It's a dog-eat-dog world," Finnerty replied sagely, carrying—as was his habit—the conceit a step too far.

* * *

Dark and blustery.

Costello drove in an unmarked car. Something was wrong with the engine. It clanked. The car shook noticeably when it idled and Costello could smell exhaust inside the car. Anyway, it drove.

It amazed him—impressed rather—how many bars and clubs lay in the southwest sector of the city. Neon lights flashed in buildings that were a step above rubble. Here and there, groups of homeless people huddled around trashcan fires; all of them appeared to be living, at least for the moment. Now and then a dog or cat scampered along ill-lit streets. Animals seemed to be moving more quickly these days.

As he passed the bars he felt pulled toward them, but something, duty maybe, kept him driving. He swung deeper into the warehouse district. It was a strange place—sparsely inhabited either by vagrants or by members of yet another wave of young people in all the standard, tattered panoply of youth. They were still into music that sounded much the same as music had sounded for decades, still into sex and rebellion and drugs, though now the drugs at least were new. With names like Chaos, Sadness, Belief, Trust and Henry James, these new drugs induced—or biochemically replicated—certain human emotions and mindsets. Biotechnology and neuroscience had certainly taken an ugly turn, Costello smirked. That was progress for you. He passed a neon sign.

I HATE SPROUTS

The Detective did not know what to think anymore.

His had been the most traditional of working class Catholic upbringings— working class neighborhood, parochial schools— until his break came, a scholarship to a private school which had led in time to an exclusive college. Great education.

It had changed his diction though not much else.

He had become a cop just like his father, his grandfather, his uncle, his sister. At St. Aidan's he had married a pretty neighborhood girl. They had had three kids in rapid succession—all wonderful—and then they had split up, or, more accurately, he had split, not being able to deal with the sobering fact that this was all there was to his life. Now he devoted his off-duty hours to drink. He was a wreck, but at least he was a wreck who sent regular checks to his wife, his former wife, and who stopped in on the family on most Sundays.

Shit, he hated to think about this. He heard what sounded like a pistol being fired somewhere behind him. He let it go. He swung the car onto an on-ramp for the elevated expressway and headed away from the squalor of the city. After less than fifteen minutes he left the expressway. The exit led to a road through a large shoreline land preserve. Soon he was driving along a clifftop road, looking down onto the blackness of the ocean. He rolled down his window, feeling the bite of the cold night air. It felt good. There was something purifying in this coldness and in this being alone. When he had been young this road had often been full of cars at this time of the evening. Lovers had come here to this space of natural serenity and beauty so close to the city; they had come here to be in love.

No one did that now, of course—not so much because love had declined so much as because hate, or indifference, had so significantly increased.

At the overlook which marked the end of the road he stopped the car, ignoring the warning sign which a lone streetlamp illuminated.

UNSAFE TO STOP AFTER DARK

He stepped out of the car, leaving it running in the small

parking lot. The wind whipped against him. Leaning into the wind, he walked to the edge of the cliff and looked down at the sea. After a moment he could see the crashing of the waves on the rocks below. He listened. He could hear the sound of the waves under the drone of the wind and the car's spluttering engine. He sat on a rock, his legs dangling down toward the ocean. His ankles were cold.

When he had been a boy, he had often come to this place with his mother and thrown rocks at the seagulls as they hovered in the air, floating on updrafts. She had never minded his throwing stones. He had never hit the damn birds anyway. Flying rodents, they had seemed to know enough to hover just out of range. But she had told him again and again to stay away from the edge.

Once he had jumped off to crouch on a ledge four feet below. He saw it below him now. His mother had screamed like he had never heard before. He could not forget the expression she had as she looked over the edge. A look of terror and loss melting into a mixture of relief and anger. He had hugged her while she wept.

He sensed someone was behind him now.

Someone was. Not his mother.

Military boots, slim legs, camouflaged fatigues, an Uzi. Pointed at him. Strands of red hair falling from a black beret. Pale skin. A bandanna obscuring the lower half of her face. Pretty, from what he could see. Lively eyes.

"That your car?" she asked.

"You need a ride or something?" he asked.

He looked beyond her.

Six other gun-toting women.

"I think you should get up and put your arms over your head," she suggested.

He did, standing with this back to the precarious cliff, the abyss.

"Hey!" another woman said, poking her head into his car. "A radio. Wow. Are you a cop or something?"

The first woman repeated the question.

He nodded.

"Then you should take your gun out very slowly and throw it into the ocean."

"All right," he said. "I've always wanted to do that."

He started to reach inside his jacket for his gun.

The woman before him was a little above average in height, thin, well-proportioned.

"Please don't do anything that would make me shoot you," she said politely.

"Don't worry," he shrugged. "I'm a policeman. We try to avoid violence."

"Napping," she said.

He tossed his gun over the cliff. Throwing brought back memories. He wondered if he would hit a gull. They both heard the sound of the gun hitting the rocks a hundred feet below. The gun discharged. The other female commandos ducked, looked around, pointing guns every whichway. Not the woman holding the Uzi on Costello. She smiled.

They had him sit on a broken bench while they took the license plate from his car.

Some of them wore berets. Some wore leather jackets like motorcycle cops wear. They all wore fatigues and bandannas across their faces and carried Uzi sub-machine guns, one of which the first woman still trained on him with intriguing nonchalance.

"Who are you?" he asked, looking up at her, making conversation, awaiting his fate.

"We are Women Against Cars," she declared.

"Again?"

"We are a group of women who believe that cars must go—that they have already damaged the earth's fragile eco-system far too much—and so we're getting rid of them one at a time."

"Oh," Costello said.

He started to say something else, to ask another question, but he was interrupted.

"Esmeralda," one of the other women called to his captor. "We're ready."

"Then do it."

The women shifted the car into neutral, rolled it towards a place where the boulders spaced along the cliffside edge of the pavement had given way and tumbled into the sea. They pushed the car off the cliff. It caught for a moment on the edge, teetering in slow motion, nose down, before dropping into the rocks below.

The women shouted like children.

"Another big mother for the Great Mother!" one yelled.

Costello eyed the woman before him. She had never taken her eyes off him.

"Me next?" he asked.

"What?"

"Cliff? Me?"

She laughed.

"Of course not, ugly. We're not Women Against Cops. You can go in a moment."

"Then . . . uh . . . why don't I give you my card. You should call me sometime."

"Why? So you can arrest me?"

"No, so I can ask you out for a drink. Quite frankly, I was getting sick of cars myself. They're so un . . . un . . ."

"Unwhat?"

"Unsomething."

She let Costello reach into his pocket, produce a card, hand it to her. She looked at in, put it in her pocket.

"You're lucky, Detective Thomas Costello," she said.

"Lucky?"

"Your new anti-car beliefs come just at the right time. You're going to have to walk home from here."

"Walk?"

"Or atrophy."

He got up slowly.

She nodded at him, walked backwards a step or two, turned

and strode away. She and her companions mounted bicycles that had been hidden in the shadows—mountain bikes and old three speeds—and raced off into the night.

Costello watched them recede into the darkness, women bicyclists with machine guns strapped across their backs.

"This will be very hard to explain," he said. Then he laughed. A genuine laugh bubbling up from the belly. It was the first time he had laughed like that in months.

He began to walk.

* * *

After Costello had walked for a little more than an hour he came to Final Rapture Cemetery. It was quicker to cut through than walk around, so he slipped through two bent rods in the fence and entered the extensive burial ground. When he had squeezed into the cemetery, he stopped to look up at the moon. It was a bright incomplete circle amidst stars and high clouds. He looked at it for a moment. He was not much of a moon watcher. Perhaps he should be. People said nature was beautiful, calming, consoling. He headed in the direction of the dwindling fires of the homeless encampment on the other side of the graveyard.

Fifteen minutes later, he walked through groups of sleepers huddled in cardboard boxes and sleeping bags, groaning and snoring, crying out. Some were awake; they stared at him, eyes bright with the light of campfires.

Then he heard screams.

* * *

A conversation late that evening in a bar in the city.

"Hey, do you mind if I join you?"

"No," she replied.

"What?" he said.

"Sit down if you want to."

"So, how are you," he said, sitting down at the table at which she had been sitting alone. "What's your mindset?"

"Bland."

"You looked lonely sitting here alone."

She said, "Cut the bullshit. You know and I know you just want to get into my pants."

He paused. "Under your skirt, actually."

"Good point."

"So tell me what I have to do to get to know you better?" he said.

"First, buy me a drink."

"Easy enough."

She told him what she was drinking. He went to the bar. As he waited for the bartender, he looked over his shoulder to make sure she was still there. He was not worried about another guy trying to sit down with her. That would not happen here. Not to him. He brought two drinks, two vodkas, back to the table. She sipped hers quietly.

He said, "So what else do I have to do?"

"Give me some drugs."

"Sure. What else?"

"Tell me your dreams, ugly."

"I don't remember my fucking dreams."

"That's a lie," she said. "Tell me a dream you've had recently . . . a trite one."

He did.

She yawned.

"Napping," she said. "But, why don't you tell me what you really dream about. Your real nightmare."

He looked at her, laughed derisively, spread his hands, nodded, said, "Whatever you want, ugly. Whatever you want."

Chapter 4

Airborne Messages

The blimps were ready and so was the message, the big message. The local television and radio stations were broadcasting the important announcement live.

Mayor Edgar Paninni spoke forcefully to the crowd, the respectably substantial crowd, that stood in a semi-circle around the raised stage on one side of City Hall. From his wide, high cheekboned face and the jet black hair receding from his glistening forehead to his short, pear-shaped body, Paninni looked uncannily like an Italian-American Mao Tse Tung. Though not conscious of his resemblance to the historical figure, Paninni was now hoping to ignite a Cultural Revolution of his own.

Keeping his feet planted on the dais, not moving his lower body at all, Paninni swiveled his chest and head from side to side, sweeping the crowd with his gaze, gesticulating with stubby hands to enhance his points. It was he who controlled this moment. Watching from amidst the shadowy cement columns of City Hall, Paninni's aides were happy. The attendance was unexpectedly good. Of course, there were the usual "community activists" and "neighborhood leaders"—people who were called on again and again to add legitimacy and "turn-out" to mayoral events, but this crisp mid-fall afternoon there were also dozens of people the aides had never seen before. If they had looked more closely, the aides might have been puzzled by the signs and placards these strangers held by their sides or on the ground, their messages hidden from view for the moment. But these went unnoticed.

"Perhaps the mayor has caught on to an issue here," one aide whispered to another.

"He's brilliant. He's really captured the imagination of the public on this one," the other aide agreed.

Mid-way through his prepared remarks, Paninni was saying, "If we are to continue to prosper as a great city, a world-class city, we have to return to the old virtues. Too many of our citizens have given up. They no longer adhere to the straight and narrow. They no longer believe in the time-honored virtues of honesty, hard-work, and personal initiative. Punctuality, politeness, and even personal hygiene are now in sad decline."

Awkwardly he waved an arm at this last point and paused as his prepared remarks prompted him to do. On cue, one of the mayor's aides, standing in the crowd, started to clap. Others joined in. From the rear of the crowd someone yelled, "Personal hygiene! All right!"

The mayor nodded and refocused on his speech. He was doing well, he could feel it, even though he knew he was mispronouncing some of the words in his text. This was going to be a great issue. Behind Paninni on the raised wooden stage stood leaders: men and women from an assortment of important fields of endeavor. Bertrand Dumas, the president and CEO of Crowe Poussin Enterprises, the largest business in the metropolitan area, was directly behind the mayor. To either side of Dumas stood other business leaders, educators, and members of the clergy, as well as representatives of the city's public relations and advertising sectors. These communicators were an essential part of the mayor's new program. They were crafting the mayor's messages and helping him bring them to the city.

"That is why today," Mayor Paninni continued, "I am joining with people from across the city to initiate a campaign to restore common virtues. From this day forward, the BACK TO BASICS campaign will carry its message to every family and to every citizen through billboards, through advertisements on buses, subway trains, and trolleys, through public service messages in newspapers and on the radio and television, and . . . and on the sides of a fleet of blimps which local businesses, led by Crowe Poussin Enterprises, have so kindly, so generously, donated to our city."

At this moment, a number of blimps ascended from behind City Hall to hover gracefully and at substantial height above the city. It took them a few minutes to rise to the ends of long tethers. People applauded while they rose. Messages, old and new homilies, were displayed on the sides of the blimps, one piece of sage advice on each flying Leviathan:

POLITENESS COUNTS

THE EARLY BIRD CATCHES THE WORM

HARD WORK IS ITS OWN REWARD

LISTEN TO YOUR MOTHER

ALWAYS WASH BEHIND YOUR EARS

This last one, this exhortation to basic cleanliness, was the mayor's favorite.

Mayor Paninni looked back over his shoulder at the blimps, then turned, beaming, to his audience. He was not prepared for what he saw.

Many of the attendees at his press conference had put on masks, masks representing dogs, cats, other creatures. They had raised their signs. The signs and placards contained messages that had nothing to do with the BACK TO BASICS campaign. SAVE OUR PETS! one sign demanded. Another read, MAYOR PANINNI FIDDLES WHILE DOGS AND CATS ARE MURDERED. This sign was decorated with what looked like bloody paw prints. Another sign asked, HOW ABOUT SOME COURTESY FOR PET VICTIMS, MR. MAYOR?

Paninni was startled. He looked off to the side of the stage at his press secretary. The press secretary stood rigid, unmoving, uncomprehending. After mumbling a few incoherent words, Paninni managed to put a short sentence together.

He said, "Uh, are there any questions?"

That was a mistake.

"Yeah," a dog-headed man yelled from the back row. "How come City Hall isn't doing anything about the slaughter of innocent pets?"

Paninni was given no opportunity to reply. A chant rose up from the crowd. "Save our pets. Save our pets." Shaking signs, fists, the protesters growled, barked, meowed, cock-a-doodle-dooed. Paninni scanned the faces of those behind him on stage and in the throng before him. Many of the civic and business leaders looked like it was all they could do not to turn tail and run. Some allies! What fairies! Bafflement and anger waged a battle for control of the mayor's ordinarily impassive features. Summoning his wits, he smiled, waved at the television cameras positioned in front of the stage, and moved resolutely towards the nearest entrance to City Hall. The television cameramen and reporters ran after him, shouting questions. He picked up speed as he moved. He held his arms up. Not out of concern for the cameras. The protesters were pelting him with dog biscuits and kitty litter. Animal droppings too.

"Nice event" he growled at his press secretary as he stormed past him. "You're fired."

*   *   *

In the quiet of the night, outwardly quiet himself in the midst of dark stands of trees and gently rolling meadows, Detective Thomas Costello thought about the distasteful events of the day just passed. He had been sitting at his desk in Police Headquarters just after lunch, poring over the few files the department had on known animal offenders, when his phone had rung—Finnerty giving him an earful about losing his car. For some reason, the lieutenant had doubted the veracity of Costello's report. Then, an hour later, the commissioner himself had summoned Costello and Finnerty to his office where, in a very convincing way, he had screamed about pet activists attacking the mayor. His face, through the brief meeting, had become increasingly red. Flecks of spittle had formed at the corners of his mouth. "I want results. I want results now," Commissioner Raymond Trump had hissed through clenched teeth. "What have you got for me, Costello?" The commissioner had not been impressed by Costello's explanation that he had been on the case less than twenty-four hours.

"Goddamn it, you lazy, incompetent fuck" the commissioner had yelled, while Finnerty had looked intently at the floor. "If you can't get the job done then I'll assign this to someone else who can."

"That might be a very good idea, sir," Costello had replied. That had been a mistake which had prompted a look of malice to appear brilliantly, instantaneously in the commissioner's eyes. "Costello," Trump had said, "you've got one week—seven fucking days—to make an arrest in this case. Otherwise, you'll be buried so low in this organization that people will wonder whether you're a dead fucking pet yourself."

"You'll be missed," Finnerty had whispered to Costello as they had left the commissioner's office. That had been consoling. Now, eight hours later, Costello was staking out the Talcott Arboretum. According to the information that he had been able to put together in his initial research, the rash of pet slayings had begun seven months ago, in March. In that time, fourteen killings, apparently attributable to the same perpetrator or perpetrators, had been reported, although there had probably been more which had either gone unreported or fallen through cracks in a system which was not efficient in recording crimes against humans, much less animals. His research also indicated that a fair number of the crimes had probably been carried out here in the placid expanses of the Arboretum, though there was evidence the slain bodies had been removed on a number of occasions to be left elsewhere.

The Arboretum, acre after acre of well-maintained woodland, wetland, walking paths, and meadows, totally surrounded by high walls and fences, was supposed to be devoid of users after the fall of evening, and for the most part it was empty tonight. Around ten p.m., a pair of sweethearts had walked through, arm-in-arm, to some secluded spot. Occasionally the night watchman drove along the few park roads, his noisy jeep preceded by headlights. But, the detective noted, the place was frequented by pets—dogs and cats stealing out from the surrounding neighborhoods to experience the closest thing to a natural environment they would ever see.

Sitting quietly, unmovingly, on the top of the park's highest hill, a place from which he had a fair view of much of the land-scaped preserve, Costello's mind turned to the woman who had held the Uzi on him the night before. "Esmeralda" the other woman had called her. He doubted that was her name. She didn't quite look like an Esmeralda, though there was something exotic about her. Well, that went with the territory; it would be hard to be a bicycle-riding, gun-toting, anti-car terrorist and not be exotic. It was not that she was strikingly beautiful, though, for all he had been able to see, she might be. It was that she seemed to vibrate with life, to hum with it. That was it. In a world where most people seemed inclined to give up, to go through the motions, or to sink to cynicism and negativity after two or at most three decades, this woman appeared to drink life in. But how to meet her again?

He had given her his card. There was a chance she would call, a slight chance. Get real, he chided himself. No chance. He could drive to the overlook again, but it might be pushing things to be involved in the destruction of another car owned by the department. Another alternative—he could drive his own car. To sacrifice his own car, a sort of contemporary offering, to see her. Would that be foolishly romantic? Or just stupid? He played it out in his mind: the smitten detective buying clunker after clunker—hell, even stealing cars—to see a woman who shows him attention only by taking his vehicles and rolling them into the ocean.

Midnight approached, passed. Costello was ready to call it a night, but as he was standing up and stretching his back and legs, thinking of what bar he would stop by on the drive to his apartment, he saw a woman walking across a nearby meadow. It was she! No. Of course not. By the light of the moon, he could see that the woman seemed shorter than his anti-car warrior, though just as shapely, just as resolute in her gait. He hid behind a tree. He leaned his body along the curve of the trunk, felt the intricacies of the bark, watched, peered. She carried something in her hands. Sticks? No. A bow in one hand. Arrows in the other. Strange. Here was a development that bore watching. A possible break.

The woman walked to the center of the meadow and took a place about thirty yards from where Costello hid. She was assuming the position of one who was about to fire an arrow, Costello observed. He pulled his head back behind the trunk. Just in time. An arrow swished into the fat trunk of the tree he hid behind. Interesting sound. Costello had never heard an arrow strike wood just three feet or so from his body. Sweat broke out on his forehead; he drew his gun. What was going on? Have I been seen, he asked himself. Why me? Why my tree? He stood there rigidly, hearing, feeling a half dozen more arrows speed into the trunk. Then, he heard footsteps and the sound of arrows being pulled from the wood, one after another. He could hear the archer breathing, grunting with each extraction. It sounded too as if she were weeping. Then he heard her sigh, depart.

Here was behavior, a secretive activity, signaling who knew what, Costello asked himself, reholstering his revolver. Was she a potential suspect in the pet slayings? Some of the animals had been killed by arrows, but this was not the only means. In a number of cases the animals had been stabbed by a spear, axed, or strangled. The strangled pets were the most disturbing cases: they also showed signs, though inconclusive, of sexual assault. That would seem to put the markswoman outside the front running for pet slaying honors, but her gender, her apparent gender, was not a conclusive reason to discount her outright.

He followed her at a discreet distance, shadowing the woman through the quietness. As she neared the edge of the park, she hid her bow and arrows in thick brush, then clambered over the high stone wall which edged that part of the park.

Nearly twisting an ankle on his descent from this imposing barrier, Costello continued his secret pursuit. Soon she was leading him into the vast system of decaying factories, warehouses, junk lots, twisting streets and alleyways that formed the cancerously distended underbelly of the city. After walking for nearly half an hour, she entered the club that Costello had noted the previous evening. I HATE SPROUTS. The detective stood in a doorway across the street from the club, lit a cigarette, and collected his thoughts, while sounds, music, reached him in incomplete phrases. Costello recognized the building. Only a handful of years previously, his uncle had worked in it when a substantial portion of this part of the city had been devoted to high tech, information technology, communications, and related industries. Then the area had thrived. But the end had come decisively. Silicon Stew.

Grinding his cigarette underfoot, Costello entered the club.

*   *   *

"Ashley," Karla yelled loudly but ineffectually above the horrendous din of the band on stage, "over here." It was her frantic waving which caught her friend's attention.

Ashley waved back.

Avoiding a dance floor peopled by wildly hopping and gesticulating dancers, Ashley wound and pushed her way through the crowded tables near the rear of the club until she came to the table where Karla sat with Bruno and a third person, a young man that Ashley did not know. Taking her seat, Ashley surveyed the scene. "Trite!" she exclaimed. No one heard. The band, The Drooling Renaissance Men, featured five musicians clad in tights, boots, frilled shirts, jackets, and unique hats reminiscent of the Three Musketeers; they all played electric mandolins and were running through a rendition of *Greensleeves* at unbearable velocity and volume. Over and over, the lead singer was screaming, "Hey! Hey! Greensleeves! Your sleeves are really green!" In fact, the singer himself was green, lime green, having covered what could be seen of his skin in the dye that many people were using to change the color of all or parts of their bodies.

Bruno, Karla, and the unfamiliar third gyrated slightly to the music. *Pro forma* demi-movements. Ashley joined in. Catching her eye, Karla yelled or mouthed—it was too loud to matter—the words, "Hefty-hefty." This was Karla's current phrase of highest approval. The band rocked on, now making no pretense at melody or musical craft, creating a throbbing wall of sound that made any thought, any conversation, impossible.

Then abruptly they stopped. They were grinning like fools. No one clapped. The Drooling Renaissance Men milled around the stage fiddling with their mandolins, then two or three of them walked off the stage.

"Ah," one of them said into the microphone, "I guess we're taking a . . . a break."

The club filled with the sound of many conversations starting up at once.

"You've got to like those guys," Bruno said, turning with a smile to the other three. "Though their high energy is a bit behind the times if you ask me."

"Why, Karla," observed Ashley, ignoring Bruno's remark, "your hair is bronze. It looks like a sculpture of hair."

"Thanks for noticing," she smiled.

"Who could help but notice? It's so tepid," said the individual Ashley did not know: a squirrelly, slump-shouldered man with red-tinted glasses and a delightfully retro leisure suit. Yellow and gray polyester. He also wore a plastic carnation in his lapel and a ring bearing the shape of a large, silver chestnut. "In fact, it puts the luke in lukewarm, I think."

"Who are you?" Ashley asked him.

He extended his hand. She took it with an air of slight distaste. It was moist.

"My name is Sanford. I'm a great admirer of Bruno and his band. And you must be Ashley, Bruno's significant other?"

"Significant! No," Karla quipped. "Ashley refers to herself simply as Bruno's 'other', she's so . . . marginalized."

Sanford smiled, not quite catching on.

Over the club's sound system, while the band took a break, Herb Alpert and the Brass were getting hiply down. Bruno listened, could not help it.

"Sanford is an agent or something," Karla said, arching her eyebrows. "You know, he's got connections to a record company."

"Record company?" Ashley said, looking over at the stranger.

"Yes," Sanford replied. "Making records can be a very lucrative business." As if to punctuate his point, he signaled to the waitress. She moped over and took their order.

"And now you want to record Bruno?" Ashley said.

"Well, don't you think that would be a bland idea?" asked Sanford.

"Well, don't you, Ash?" Karla seconded.

Even Bruno turned his attention to the table now while Ashley pondered.

"No," she finally said. "I think it's a terrible idea. In fact, it's fucking double-o-nined."

"Why?" the other three asked in unison.

"Because the beauty of Bruno's music, the beauty of Bruno, is that he is not made to succeed. He is made for failure."

"Uh-oh," Karla observed, dangling a fingertip above the flame of the candle on the table before them, "I sense a philosophical interlude."

"Go on," urged Sanford.

"Listen," Ashley said. "For generations humans have sought success, have worked for it in every way. Yet, what has been the outcome of all this effort, all this sweatiness?"

No one answered.

"Of course, the answer is failure," Ashley went on. "We see around us a society in shambles and yet we still slog on, believing that our personal successes will somehow result in some sort of bland general success, although nothing could be further from the truth.

"And it is not as if many of us who try for success actually achieve it. Far better to accept our probable fate from the beginning and give up. I think if every human being could be induced to screw-up on a major scale, or at the very least, to do as little as possible, we could turn the world around. It's activity, it's the can-do spirit, it's trying," she continued, almost leaving her usual oh-so-bored, nasal tones behind, "that have already resulted in collapse. But it's not the current economic collapse that's the problem. It's us. We're the problem. Far better just to give up! Sit somewhere doing nothing."

"1-900-FAILURE," Karla said.

"Precisely," Ashley agreed. "And who would be on the other line?"

She looked eagerly from face to face.

"Who?" Sanford asked.

"No one," Bruno said.

"That's not fair, ugly boy" Karla whined, "you've heard all this shit before."

"So many times I can't tell you," Bruno smiled. "Ash, why don't you tell them your religion thing."

"Oh, I will. Don't worry," Ashley said, growing somewhat strident. "Failure is a deeply religious concept. Look at the Buddha, multi-years sitting in the lotus position doing absolutely nothing. And Christ! Just nail me to the cross, dudes! Bland! Talk about taking the passive way out! Just imagine if everyone did that. Things certainly wouldn't get any worse."

A light went on in Sanford's eyes.

"I'm reprogrammed, Ashley. I understand. Failure, what a bore, what a beautifully bland concept!"

Ashley looked at him with mistrust.

"Failure is beautiful!" Ashley insisted "That's what is so beautiful about Bruno's music. He doesn't try to be good. He tries to fail!"

Karla screwed up her face into a look of bafflement.

"Success at failure? Call me 'stupid', but isn't that going against the grain?" she asked.

Ashley had a ready reply: "Success at failure is certainly more palatable, more . . . ethically responsible, that failure at success."

"I love it," Sanford exclaimed, flecks of his drink, a Pink Squirrel, at the corners of his mouth. "I had never seen Bruno in this light. I think we can use the failure thing. That's what we call the first album. F-a-i-l-u-r-e. *Failure.* So simple, so powerful. So direct. I smell 'hit'."

Ashley balled up her fists, became a bit red.

Karla asked, "But if Bruno's a hit won't that mean that he's failed at failure? Would that be good or bad, Ash?"

Sanford laughed, "Oh that's prime! *Failure at Failure.* I see a second album, a sweating sequel."

"If at first you don't succeed . . . fail, fail again," Karla laughed, cackling almost, her eyes bright, mischievous.

Bruno, at least, could see the anger rising in Ashley. He knew the signs. He said, "Well, Sanford, perhaps we can talk more about it later. I'm not entirely convinced. Ashley has made some good points."

"Asshole," Ashley muttered under her breath.

Sanford only half heard her, his ears still not up to par after the Drooling Renaissance Men's set.

Changing the subject, Bruno asked, "Ashley, how was your hunt tonight?"

"Bland enough," Ashley smiled.

"Did you bag anything?"

"No, just a few practice shots."

Costello, standing unobtrusively within earshot, pricked up his ears. He had seen Ashley soon after he had come into the club, then moved into close proximity. Now he leaned against a cement column, trying to look wasted, a look he knew.

"Napping," Karla nodded, responding to Ashley's bow and arrow update. "But, I do think it would be perfectly hefty if Sanford here made Bruno into some kind of . . . what? . . . some kind of rock star or something, don't you, Ashley?"

Bruno and Sanford looked at her. Ashley looked off.

"What do you mean?" Bruno asked Karla, not very pleasantly.

"You would be the best little rock and roll star ever, that's all I'm saying," Karla repeated, looking at him, smiling.

"What does that mean?" The edginess in Bruno's voice brought Ashley's attention back to the table.

Karla said, "I'm just trying to be . . . encouraging. Why? Is that so offensive?"

"It just gets to me, that's all, these things you say sometimes," Bruno shot back. "How the hell would you know whether I should make a record or not? But it's not just what you say, it's how you say it. This little girl thing. I think you're just trying to draw attention to yourself. You're always trying to be so cute."

Karla's eyes opened wide. Ashley could see that she was taken aback by Bruno's intensity. Sanford looked nonplused. Even Ashley did not know quite what was going on. It appeared as if Bruno's anger had come out of nowhere.

"Bruno," Ashley said . . . but Karla interrupted her. Karla's voice was cold, somber.

Karla said, "Why would I try to be cute, when I am already so beautiful? Why would I try to draw attention to myself when I am already the center of attention everywhere I go?" She was looking hard at Bruno.

Sanford and Ashley looked at Bruno too. So did Costello. All were waiting for his reply. It did not come. A massively bad noise made the detective put his hands to his ears. Bruno turned and looked toward the stage.

"*Greensleeves, Part II*," the Droolers' lead singer cried over a surge of atomic mandolins. The band resumed just where it had left off. Karla's eyes met Ashley's. They were hard, intense. Then they softened; Karla smiled. Sweetly.

Falsely.

Costello surveyed the patrons of the club. Scum, losers, lowlifes, and typically disaffected young people, he noted to himself, knowing full well that fifteen or so years before he had dabbled in a similar scene. In the intervening years it seemed that only the drugs had changed. He pushed and pulled his way to one of the club's two bars. Eventually he caught the bartender's eye and ordered a drink, the first of many. Scanning the bar, the club, he thought about the young man, Alvin Gremillion, whose body he had found at the cemetery. Death by no discernible cause, though Costello's gut told him some kind of foul play was involved. Young kid. Good, strong heart. What could make it stop beating? The coroner had no idea what had killed him. Probably never would. No initial indication of drugs. But, to Costello, it looked like Alvin had been frightened to death. The way his face looked. His eyes. Anyway, Finnerty had shown no interest, saying, "He's bagged. He's nobody. He's forgotten. And he's a friggin' human, which you don't do."

Costello took his drink and took a place in another part of the bar. It was here that he saw a massive, completely bald, leather clad man lapping from a silver bowl with the word HUMAN engraved on its side. He had a leash around his neck which led to the hand of a petite but imposing woman in garish attire. Sensing Costello's gaze, the man turned from the bowl from which he had been lapping eagerly and bared his teeth. His master, too, turned and examined him disdainfully.

He returned to the bar, satisfied. He was beginning to think there would be little problem making an arrest in the case within the commissioner's timeframe.

Chapter 5

Secrets Shared

Morning in the city. The sun shone pale through dirty clouds. The wind blew bitingly from the north, pushing trash and fallen leaves before it in swirling eddies. Mayor Paninni's blimps pulled against the long, curving lines which held them above the city. Winter was signaling its approach. Under the pale sun, the inhabitants of the city went about their daily lives, sure that nothing that might happen on this day would change their lives in any positive way.

In City Hall and at Police Headquarters, police officials and mayoral aides looked in dismay at the morning newspapers. The front page of the city's tabloid, *The Traveler*, featured front-page stories under these headlines: **Pet Murder Spree Horrifies City**, and **Pet Activists Howl at Paninni**. The mayor was unapproachable. He remained alone in his office, secluded. Occasionally Paninni emitted a yell or obscene scream that made the aides huddled in the antechamber to his office look at each other in panic. They knew from past experience that soon Paninni would summon them one by one for extremely unpleasant discussions. At Police Headquarters, the scene was somewhat different. Alone in his office, Commissioner Trump did not yell. In silent rage he fired his service revolver at the walls of his office, aiming carefully at the many photographs of himself arm-in-arm with the mayor.

The rash of pet murders had a less striking effect on the public, though more people than usual kept their pets locked indoors. Bruno had no pet to worry about, no pet to keep indoors, but, sitting in Rockwell's this blustery morning, a newspaper spread on the table before him, he could not help but think about the strangeness of the pet murders. He sipped his coffee, smoked a cigarette, ran his fingers through tangles of his lavender hair. His brow was furrowed and he frowned as he realized how intently he was thinking about dead pets. He knew he was the kind of person who would rather not think about anything at all. Making a effort, Bruno tried to clear his mind of thoughts. There— he could feel the growing emptiness. The sound of his breathing began to fill his mind as if his breaths were cups of water filling—slowly, splashingly—a round, bounded space of clay. His mind was a large urn which first filled with water and then when it was full was tipped and drained absolutely dry. This self-absorption lasted for a while. Others at the coffee shop wondered about Bruno and the way he sat rigidly unmoving for half an hour. It worried them. They would not look at him directly or for any length of time. The waiters did not approach him either. It would have taken more than a statuesque customer to move them from the little, half-hidden table where they huddled, smoking and cackling. Then, almost without his knowing it, *leitmotifs* of thought began at the edges of this heavy silence, this heavy theme of silence, which had temporarily dominated his mind. Bruno was thinking again, not in obvious opposition to his will, for these thoughts had crept up on him unobtrusively and secretively. It was as if these little thoughts had presented themselves as little orphans, little waifs, at the doorway of the quiescent cathedral of Bruno's austerely silent mind and his mind, out of compassion or indifference, had invited them in and fed them, their voracious appetites, so that they had grown until they had become the dominant force within his mental space and had banished, fat ogres now, the silence he so cherished and filled his head instead with gurglings, devilish noises, rantings. He thought about the city.

Over the previous few years, life in the city had taken many strange turns, turns which might have shocked a populace less used to a consistent spiral of decline. Shock itself had become a luxury. Bruno was not personally shocked, for example, that after hundreds of years of disuse, the practice of dueling had been reborn as a common practice. Dueling was now a way to settle scores; it was not unusual to see two individuals on the street square off at thirty paces and shoot at each other with replicas of ancient firearms, exact copies in every detail except accuracy, which was much enhanced. Many members of all classes of society carried a dueling pistol with them at all times. Older individuals tended to duel to settle scores, a reflection, perhaps, that going to court was now thought to be a useless waste of time, or worse, to settle injustices. Younger people liked to duel for sport, for kicks. Not Bruno. Too sweaty. Too hyperkinetic! Not to mention the danger.

Nor was Bruno shocked that the automotive industry had begun marketing an armor-protected vehicle modeled, in smaller scale, on a military armored personnel carrier. Looking basically like a rectangular box on wheels, the six-wheeled vehicle featured metal plating, bullet proof windows, and an optional machine gun turret. The "safetraveler" was built to withstand bazooka blasts, firebombs, machine gun fire, poison gas, riot, and marauding bands. *Don't let your next wrong turn be your last* was the tagline of the vehicle's promotional campaign. Manufactured abroad, the model name for the most popular of these vehicles was "Lovecraft."

Realizing that his unthinking spell was at an end, Bruno lifted his arms over his head and stretched his back muscles. He motioned to a waiter and the waiter ignored him, then reluctantly refilled his cup of coffee. Bruno did not have much he wanted to accomplish on this particular day. Maybe he would just find somewhere to sit and something to stare at, but first he needed the right, the appropriate, mindset. Reaching into the inside pocket of his black nylon jacket, Bruno took out a medicine bottle. Unscrewing the top, he shook two sky-blue pills into his hand, dropped them into the coffee, stirred the coffee, sipped. The little pill bottle was empty now. He recapped it and put it back in his pocket. He would need more pills. His mind turned to the subject of drugs.

A new generation of drugs had taken hold of the city, even in the few years that Bruno had been there. Pioneered by developments a decade earlier in the psychopharmacology and biomedical industries and then adapted over time by illicit, though more or less adept manufacturing operations, this emerging class of drugs was known generally as emotional replicators—"gators" to those in the know. Working directly on the neurological system, these substances caused their users to feel unmitigatedly the effects of various human emotions and moods.

Naturally, the first of these drugs to take hold among users, especially recreational users, had been those that replicated pleasant or euphoric states; these went by names such as Love, Joy, or Satisfaction. The widespread use of these emotional replicators among legions of disaffected youngsters had brought new meanings to old songs that the most hip new bands recovered from forgotten records. So, when a band covered songs that had been unheard in years, songs with lyrics like *I Can't Get No Satisfaction*, *Yummy-Yummy-Yummy*, *I've got Love in My Tummy*, or *Gator Got Your Granny*, new meanings were conveyed that had not been intended by the original lyricists. How blandly tepid, Bruno thought to himself: language revivifies before it destroys.

Soon after the appearance of the first generation of pleasurable replicators, drugs which induced more negative states had begun to appear. In alleyways, parks, on roof tops, in clubs, people had started to talk of, and use, drugs with names like Pain, Fear & Loathing, Ennui, or Confusion. Now, for the first time in history, people on a small but growing scale were seeking the very same emotional states that human beings had sought to avoid since the beginning of time. The attraction of the negative was overpowering to users of these new substances, for these chemically-engineered negative emotions and mindsets—in addition to being destructive in the short term—were also highly addictive.

And so there had sprung up in significant numbers men and women, often quite young, who writhed in pain on the city streets, who trembled with looks of utter terror, or who wandered aimlessly, unable to put one thought next to another. Often sedation was the only remedy for these cases—when the authorities or others thought enough of an individual case to take such a step. Most often, Bruno knew, no one cared.

The look of an advanced Pain addict was singular and instantly noticeable. Like more conventional addicts—those addicted to heroin, for example, or Tazmind—the usual Pain addict, called a "blackhead" in the parlance of the street, was sick and unkempt. Usually, for the novice user the pain, or the perception of pain, was localized in the head. This was called "headaching." For the addict, the pain took hold in the stomach, so that the far-gone blackhead often fell to the ground in his agony, clutching at his stomach, whining or crying out. In extreme cases, the deluded Pain addict would tear at his own stomach, or open his stomach with a knife in an attempt to lance the locus of pain as if the pain were contained in some sort of putrescent tumor—rotten, about to burst but still intact—which radiated, or pulsated, or throbbed like a heart which pumped spurts of agony. From time to time men or women would appear in the streets or subways, clutching hands to bleeding, self-inflicted wounds before collapsing and, often, dying, as their blood formed bright pools in the grime of sidewalks, stairwells. Passersby stepped lightly to avoid wetting their shoes with the blood.

Why men and women used a drug that induced pain could not be determined by the psychiatric, sociological, and medical experts who examined the phenomenon. Fortunately for the police and other authorities, users of Pain were generally less disposed to violence towards others as their addictions progressed, though they were as violent to themselves as their access to the relatively inexpensive substance allowed.

In addition to drugs which induced emotional states, there were also newer—and for the moment less common—drugs which imposed entire mindsets by fabricating and facilitating combinations of moods and patterns of thought. Bruno Passive's current passion was a drug called Henry James. Named after the late 19th century American-turned-British author, the drug James induced a sense of contemplative languor in which endless examination of minute physical detail and slight nuances of mood and feeling held deep fascination for the user. It was not uncommon for advanced users of the drug to speak in endless complex sentences and adopt the clipped intonations of an upper-class British accent. There was perhaps nothing so dull to a non-user of Henry James as to find himself in the company of a gaggle of languid, infinitely slow and observant users of the drug.

Though Bruno generally stayed clear of other users and had himself avoided the slow loquaciousness and altered accent of the habitual user, he was in love with the mindset. He had a perpetual desire for Henry James. I've got a Jones for some James, he said to himself, looking around the coffee shop. Rising, he headed out into the day to find his supplier. Little did Bruno know that one of the other members of his group sessions with Dr Bentley was a major manufacturer and supplier of Henry James as well as many of the other emotional replicators. Had he known, he might well have asked for a discount. In his case it would have been granted.

*　*　*

Day passed. Evening came. The wind abated. A warmer breeze sailed in from the harbor and touched Harold Hastings, a listless, youngish man who was himself a devotee of the calming emotional replicator Henry James. The roofs of Walden Hill, where

Hastings lived, had a life of their own. His apartment was in the top floor, the fifth floor, of a brick apartment building, but often he would spend his time, his nights, on the roof. He sat there now, high on James, smoking marihuana, drinking scotch, watching the night.

The metal door onto the roof from the central stairwell descending through the five floors of the old building was sealed shut. He assumed the other apartment dwellers preferred it so, tightly bolted; a certain unsavory element often frequented these rooftops where it was quite easy to move—to leap, even to step in places—from roof to roof. Only his apartment had access to the roof of his building. He would climb up through a skylight in the ceiling above his living room which he could push open, a glass hatch. Under the skylight a step ladder was set, one of Hastings's few concessions to convenience. Though the ladder rocked, especially when he lowered himself back into his apartment, one drunken leg leading the other, he had never fallen. His sea legs never failed him.

As Hastings sat on the roof at night, his back against a large brick chimney, he often looked down at the river, the Charlotte River, and in the fog which frequently rose up from the river, rising up the hill, it would seem to him that the tops of the buildings surrounding him were ships moored in a harbor. From his rooftop ship he could see other captains and sailors, solitary or in small, quiet groups, the lights of their pipes momentarily daubing their faces with yellow light. Bits of quiet conversation would drift to him then like whispers, although at times the night was broken by loud talk, yells, worse. But there was something about the roofs that caused quietness, that made an implicit plea for understatedness.

Often Hastings would sleep on the roof, wrapped in a blanket when the weather was colder, in early spring and in the fall, or uncovered on the soft, warm tar in summer. His apartment below was not much in the way of the comforts of those who dwelled on land. Landlubbers he dubbed them. Since his girlfriend Tracy, his mermaid, had left him, removing all her comfortable, frilly things, he had outfitted the place sparingly with lawn furniture and a few other items. His only piece of substantial furniture was something that had been too inconvenient for Tracy to remove, a couch which hid the most interesting feature of his otherwise featureless apartment.

On this evening a stranger joined Hastings on his roof. This was in and of itself not so very strange. Every so often others, acquaintances mostly, who were taking the rooftop highway would pass by and visit. But long solitude on the roof had made him hyper-aware of movements and sounds, such that he could tell when someone was coming a long time before they came. It almost seemed like a sixth sense.

Now, someone whom he had not observed coming stood alongside Hastings. The unbidden stranger spoke.

"Hey, man," the stranger said, "mind if I join you for a smoke?"

Startled, Hastings stood up quickly and looked the visitor up and down. The newcomer was about Hastings's height and build—5'9" and solid enough—though he was a trifle thinner and had about him a slightly effeminate air. His wavy brown hair was matted to his head with exertion and the moist night air. He wore a pair of wrinkled khakis, scuffed dress shoes, a tennis shirt, and an old tweed jacket. On his lapel was a pin: a rock hammer entwined by a climber's rope. He was dressed, in other words, in one of the perennially standard fashions of youth.

They shook hands.

"No, not at all. Have a seat."

"Bland," the newcomer said as they both sat down cross-legged on the tar. "My name's Sebastian."

"Mine's Hastings, Harold Hastings . . . the Third."

Sebastian nodded, looking at Harold from the corner of his eye while he took a pipe and a plastic sandwich bag of marihuana from his coat pocket and filled a bowl. He lit it. Harold saw Sebastian's face more clearly in the light of his cupped hand.

He looked to be about twenty-five, maybe thirty, though a little
the worse for wear. Dark patches underlined his eyes. His face
was ellipsoidal and jowly; his nose was small, upturned; his lips
were full, girlish. He had old scars—circular and small—on both
the outside and inside of one of his hands, Hastings also noted.
The dope was powerful. A puff or two filled Harold almost instantly with a nervous rush of thoughts so intense that it was as if
he could not think at all but just sit dumb-founded before the
spectacle of the merging of his inner and the outer worlds. He
often thought this state to be somehow mystical, but it frightened
him too to be so high so quickly and he knew there was only one
remedy for that—a long swallow from his glass of scotch. He
drank. Then, with a shaking hand Hastings offered his new companion the bottle which sat, opened, next to him on the tar.

"I'm sorry I can not offer ye a glass, mate," lamented Hastings
who, in his solitude and his constant use of James often took on
too much the conceit that he himself was a mariner of long ago.
In fact, given Hastings's predisposition, it was almost as if Henry
James, the drug, produced a mindset in him which might have
been more accurately described as "Joseph Conrad." Eighteenth
and nineteenth-century naval phrasings taken from old novels
of the sea peppered Hastings's speech—it was not uncommon
for him to use terms such as "lee shore," "beat to quarters,"
"clear for action," and "arsey-varsey." Sebastian took pains—
perhaps it was a studied reserve on his part—not to display
reaction to Hastings's antique speech. Further evidence of this
conceit were the mast and sail, spanning some twelve feet in
height and eight in width, which Hastings had rigged to the roof
and which now flapped in the mild wind. Sebastian did not remark on this either.

Instead, he nodded his appreciation for the scotch. Then,
after the two of them sat a while in silence, they began to speak.
Initially their conversation was common enough: of drugs—they
were both "Jamesians"—and life in the city. Hastings noticed
that as Sebastian talked he would look from time to time over his

shoulder to scan the semi-darkness. Nervous. Hastings asked him if there was something on his mind.

"Oh . . . ah . . . yes, someone I know is looking for me," Sebastian replied . "A misunderstanding. Might not be pleasant."

"Who, if ye don't mind me asking, mate?"

"A fellow named Tang. I owe him some money, money for what we're smoking now and for a supply of James I just ran through."

"I know him," said Hastings. "I've bought from him before. Never a problem, but I've never crossed him neither. Don't worry though, I've usually got a keen ear when someone's coming. You're the only one yet who's crept up on me."

Sebastian nodded and continued talking, but Hastings, as sensitive to these things as most recluses are, saw that his guest's wariness persisted. Hastings bade him come down into the apartment with him.

"Here is my cabin," Hastings smiled when they had both dismounted from the ladder, "though in this fairly mild weather I tend to spend most of my time above deck. As you can see, though it's sparsely furnished, all is ship-shape. A place for everything and everything in its place—that's my motto."

Sebastian quickly surveyed the studio apartment. This is what he saw: a clean, sparsely furnished living space; books by Conrad, Dana, Melville, Patrick O'Brian, and various other volumes and periodicals having to do with the sea, including a number of Horatio Hornblower novels; lengths of cord tied into complex knots on a coffee table next to a book on nautical knots, opened; and various implements having to do with smoking grass. On a shelf Sebastian also saw an ornate glass-topped case holding two dueling pistols.

"Aye," Hastings said, his eyes bright with a sort of pride in showing his place to the rare guest, "it is quite a while since I last went down to the land, by which I mean since I ventured down to the street. I send out for my provisions mostly; they are delivered to me here. But let me show you the one feature that should alleviate your fears." He pulled at the sizable though not immovable couch, equipped with quiet rollers, that was so out of place in the Spartan room and revealed a low crawlspace built into the wall. It was a rectangular space running five feet horizontally, two feet vertically from floor level, and three feet in depth. The sofa had completely hidden it. "Should ye be in need of a port in a storm, here's your spot. I've often thought of hiding here myself, though perhaps it is only myself I have to hide from!"

With the recluse chuckling at his own wit, both host and guest climbed the stairs to the roof, having taken another glass for Sebastian and another bottle of scotch for them both.

One hour or so later the moon, surrounded by plush, lolling clouds, was high over the rooftops. It was late, perhaps two o'clock in the morning, an hour at which people after a night of intoxication will often open up to tell tales about themselves which in the light of day or in the semi-darkness of early evening they would have left unsaid, so Hastings was not entirely surprised when an innocent question about where Sebastian had grown up prompted a turn in their conversation.

"Oh, I spent my early years here in the city," Sebastian smiled, "then . . . until quite recently I have spent my life in institutions."

"Institutions? Academic institutions?"

"Mental institutions."

"Oh. I'm sorry to hear it."

"Yes, yes," Sebastian continued, wrestling with the impulse to unburden himself, "it has not been an easy time. But, I think that if I had not spent so much time in . . . uh . . . treatment I would have killed myself. In fact, it was because I tried to kill myself when I was nine that I was taken away."

"Well, what was the problem?"

Sebastian looked his host straight on, looked him hard and searchingly in the eyes. Hastings noticed something strange about one of Sebastian's eyes. It seemed not to focus, to be looking at nothing. Then Sebastian continued, "I had developed the odd belief that I could . . . yes . . . that I could talk to corpses."

Hastings shifted uneasily, lit his pipe. He noted a change in Sebastian's voice. It had become more ponderous, more mechanical.

Sebastian said, "When I was very young my father went away. He was an officer in the army and my mother and I went to live with my uncle, my father's brother, who operated a funeral home, a funeral parlor, in the city. It was a very spooky, unsettling place for a young boy to live in, as you might imagine. I had no brothers or sisters. Yes, it was just me, my mother, and my uncle in this vast, dark home."

"It must have taken a while to get your . . . bearings," Hastings ventured.

Sebastian looked off across the night, seeing his past.

"My room was at the top of the house—on the third floor. I can remember lying there in my bed night after night, every light on, my eyes wide open, thinking about the corpses that were on the first floor in the caskets or in the preparation room.

"There were many nights that I could not sleep at all and I think that this constant fear, coupled with my lack of sleep, put me into a sort of dream state."

"A waking nightmare, it sounds like."

"Yes . . . yes! A waking nightmare. That's a good way to put it, Harold."

Hastings asked, "Why didn't you call on your mother? It seems that a boy so young could have gone to her."

"I did that initially," Sebastian agreed, "but eventually my uncle Theodore . . . Teddy . . . he stepped in, or I should say, he put his foot down. He said that I should learn to deal with my fear, that I had to stay in my own room. He called me a wimp. I can remember his lectures, his anger too, at breakfast day after day. He told me that I was a sissy to be frightened, to wake the house with my screams. To my surprise, my mother took his side, not mine, though of course there were other issues."

"And they were?"

"Yes, my mother, I soon came to suspect, had taken to sleeping with my uncle, my father's own brother."

Sebastian had been narrating his story with little enough emotion, but the emotionless gravity with which he presented this last revelation put Hastings at a loss for words. They sat for more than a moment in awkward silence.

"You are sure of this?" Hastings asked finally.

"Yes. The young have more acute senses, especially hearing. I heard them together and though I did not know what they were doing actually, I knew that it was terribly wrong. Of course, during the day they did all they could to dissemble their . . . relationship, but I soon knew exactly what was going on."

"You saw them?" Hastings questioned.

"No," Sebastian replied. "A corpse told me."

Hastings took a long drink from his glass.

Man overboard! he thought to himself.

He said, "Go on, mate."

"After many weeks of lying in my room in terror, yes, after many weeks of hearing the sounds that were coming from my uncle's room on the floor below and other sounds too, which I could not name, from other parts of the house, I began to walk through the house at night. At first I confined myself to the third floor, my floor. Eventually I worked myself to the second floor where, late at night, unseen and unsuspected, I listened outside my uncle's door. Finally I began to descend the wide, foreboding stairs to the first floor. The horror of the first floor could not be so bad as the horror on the second. With the smell of flowers and the preparation room reeking of formaldehyde, the first floor stunk both with the smell of death and the scents we use to mask that smell. It's a smell I have never been able to get out of my mind.

"It took me many nights to work up the courage to descend those stairs to the first floor, stairs covered with a rich, dark carpet. Yes, maroon, I think. Night after night I would creep another stair or two closer to the first floor, huddling for hours, listening, watching. The first time I actually reached the first floor I was so overcome with fright that I turned and ran back up to my room. But in a matter of time I grew accustomed to walking around the first floor, sitting with and examining in minute detail the waxen, still bodies of corpses laid out in open caskets. Yes, I'd sit by the open caskets and in my young mind I'd imagine that I was having conversations with them."

"Conversations? What kinds of conversations?" Hastings asked, sitting up straighter, breathing in, trying to get his bearings.

Sebastian paused, thinking himself back in time, back to those nights.

"Oh, about their lives mostly, about what they had done when they were alive. And, in my young, and, I . . . yes, I confess . . . vivid, imagination, I imagined that the corpses opened their eyes, turned their heads, and spoke to me. I guess that I did think or assume it was only a macabre sort of game until one night I looked up from my imagined dialogue and saw that a corpse was actually looking at me, was actually speaking."

"My god," Hastings whispered. And then, "What was the corpse saying?"

"Oh, the corpses told me many things over time," Sebastian said. "They spoke about their lives, their uncompleted business. Some told me about myself. Some spoke about my mother and uncle."

"Did they ever speak of their own deaths?"

"No. My questions about death went unanswered. It was the last corpse that I spoke to that spoke of death."

"What happened?"

"The man in the casket was a soldier, an officer just like my father. I remember the house was very cold—I could see my breath when I spoke, but no breath came from the officer's mouth."

"What did he say?" Hastings picked up the bottle, poured himself another drink.

"He spoke to me in my father's voice. I think that was the

first time that had ever happened—that a corpse had spoken to me in a voice which was not its own. It was my father. My father spoke to me through . . . through his brother officer."

"What did your father say."

"He told me that he was dead, that he had died in a secret military operation and that . . . yes . . . if I loved him I should kill my mother and my uncle!"

"My god! How horrible," Hastings blurted. "Jesus! What did you do?"

"The next day, I tried to take my own life. The . . . wait, I think I hear someone coming."

"Where away?" Hastings whispered.

"There."

Hastings saw one, two figures approaching them. The strangers were four rooftops away.

"Do you know who that is, Hastings?" Sebastian gasped.

"I'm not a psychic, mate," Hastings replied, "but you'd better scurry below."

Sebastian nodded, crawled like a crab, clambered down into the apartment. Hastings heard the creak of the ladder. He closed his eyes against the anticipated crash. It did not come. The two figures approached, arrived.

"Evening, Tang," Hastings said, rising.

Tang took his outstretched hand, let it go.

"What's your mindset?" asked Tang, a trifle shorter than Hastings but so strong in presence that he seemed to loom over the other. Tang was oddly proportioned, almost disfigured, as if the parts of his body did not quite mesh, but Hastings knew he was powerful, quick, and prone to anger, though Hastings had never seen it himself. Behind Tang stood another figure—plump, squat, fastidiously dressed. The third man wheezed.

"Never better," Hastings replied, extending the half-empty bottle of scotch.

Tang shook his head.

"Late," Hastings observed, stating the obvious, though he supposed to himself, even in the process of trying to mask his nervousness, that the obvious forms the basis of most conversation.

"Yeah. You don't happen to know a guy named Sebastian, do you, Hastings? Sebastian . . . uh . . . I don't know his last name. He's about your build, brown hair, talks like you. Affected."

"One-eyed, pansy faggot," Tang's companion observed.

Tang smiled.

"No," Hastings said, too quickly perhaps, remembering now the strangeness of Sebastian's eyes. One eye was false, he realized now. "I don't know him. Why?"

"Monetary matter. Want to settle accounts—one way or another."

"Law of the sea," Hastings replied knowingly, looking out over the rooftops. From the roof he could see the Charlotte River, a darker swath through night's delta of darknesses. Black through black. From his roof he had no view of the Harbor over the other side of the Hill, the Harbor into which the Charlotte emptied, but he could sense its presence, could see it now in his mind's eye. All rivers flow out to the sea, he heard a voice in his mind saying. Foolish thing to think now.

"What's that?" Tang sneered.

"Oh, nothing really. Just the quality of insight I have at this time in the morning."

Tang, debt-collector, drug dealer, examined Hastings a moment, a bird pondering a bug. Then he smiled.

"Yeah," Tang chuckled. "Napping."

Tang scanned the roof, the other roofs.

He said, "You sure you haven't seen this guy?"

"No," Hastings replied.

"Well I've got to . . . shove off then. Mind if I climb down through your roof and hit the street?"

"Ordinarily no," Hastings replied. "But tonight . . . I've got someone sleeping on the sofa. You might give her a start."

"Who?" Tang responded. More in surprise, Hastings thought,

than in disbelief.

Tang's companion, his assistant, giggled—a high-pitched, throat-constricted whinny.

"His mommy, probably," the fat man said.

"A girl. We've just met actually."

"A girl! Why isn't she asleep in your bed?" asked Tang.

"Because," Hastings said, fixing him with his eyes, "that's where she fell asleep."

Tang nodded. Then he moved very close to Hastings, put his face close to Hastings's face. Hastings felt Tang's breath on his face; he tried to hold the other's eyes, could not, looked away.

Tang hissed, "Captain, why do I think you're lying to me?"

"Lying!" Hastings said, indignation rising. "You'd better watch who you call a liar!"

Tang pushed Hastings. He fell onto his back on the tar roof. Then Tang stood over him. He motioned to his companion, who moved towards the rooftop opening, waddling, and disappeared below. Hastings could hear the ladder's creak, then the hench-man wheezing as he ransacked the apartment, so quiet was it now on the roof. It was a wonder the ladder had not broken, Hastings thought to himself, his thoughts coming quickly. He saw the fat thug toppling in his mind's eye. After a few moments, Tang's assistant returned from below, shook his head 'no.'

"God damn you, Tang!" Hastings exclaimed, getting to his feet. His chest heaved. His face was red. His fists were balled. "You've insulted my honor. I . . . I demand satisfaction here and now. My pistols are below."

"Your pistols?" Tang said, looking at Hastings in wonder. "Satisfaction? I'll give you sweating satisfaction."

Tang stepped aside. His companion picked Hastings up and threw him over the side of the building. Hastings screamed. Tang and his assistant peered down at Hastings's body. He looked like a man doing the breast stroke on the surface of dark water. Or a drowned man washed ashore.

"Man overboard, Sydney," Tang said.

"It's too bad, Eric," Tang's assistant said. "He wasn't a bad customer."

"Easy come. Easy go. Here let's throw this piece of junk down too."

They wrenched Hastings's mast and sail free and threw it off the rooftop. It wheeled in the air as it fell, landing next to Hastings's body with a muted, echoless clap.

"Makes it look kind of like a shipwreck," Sydney said. "Romantic."

"Yeah, law of the sea," Eric Tang remarked. Then he threw back his head and laughed.

Chapter 6

O Pioneer!

Dr Bentley was more reserved than the group had ever seen her before.

Her pensiveness numbed the enthusiasm of the nightmare therapy participants, who usually chattered and giggled in hushed tones in those minutes before Bentley signaled the start of the weekly Thursday night sessions. Tonight, with only a single candle lighting the room, she sat cross-legged on her meditation pillow and looked slowly, intently, from face to face at those who entered the room to sit, cross-legged too, on the meditation pillows which were arranged in a circle, a meditative circle, around a single futon in the center of the austere chamber.

She looked sad and with sad, worried eyes she gazed in turn at Irma, Jessica, Jerry, Jane, Brandon, Dominic, Karla, Ashley, Bruno, and, finally, Eric. Her eyes met Eric's stare. His expression seemed to hint at some unspecified emotion, while hers, Bentley's, seemed to betray some softness, some vulnerability foreign to her usual air of self-assurance. She dropped her gaze and returned again to her strange silence. When she looked up again at the group, the group members could see that she was weeping.

"I am afraid I have some terrible news for you," she said. "Alvin is dead."

A murmur moved though the group.

"How?" Dominic asked.

Dr Bentley hesitated, said, "He was found four nights ago at Final Rapture Cemetery. A policeman found him. Almost by chance. He was found dead among the graves."

Ashley looked at Karla; Karla shook her head and looked down.

"Unbland," she whispered

"What was the cause of death, Dr Bentley?" asked Jane, earnest and deeply concerned.

"That hasn't been determined yet, Jane," Dr Bentley replied. "I spoke to Alvin's father earlier this afternoon. That was the first I had heard of Alvin's death. His father was asking questions about . . . what we do here." She paused. "From what they can determine, it looks as if Alvin might have been . . . might have been shocked to death."

"Some sort of electrical thing?" someone asked.

"No. By fright. It looks as if he might have been frightened to death."

The group was very silent.

Jerry said "bullshit" under his breath.

Then Jessica, wearing sandals and loose, flowing garments which encircled her obesity, said, "He died at a cemetery. That was his nightmare—to die at a fucking graveyard. Do you remember? He dreamed about his girlfriend coming back to life at her gravesite. Was he at her gravesite?"

"No," said Dr Bentley. "His girlfriend is buried in Missouri."

"Jesus," Ashley said. "He must have gone there to face his fear and he . . ."

"He got scared to death," said Eric, finishing her thought.

His voice was raspy but high pitched, almost as if it vibrated on two levels—guttural and ethereal. Everyone looked at him. His voice was so eerie and they were so unused to hearing it.

"We mustn't jump to conclusions, Eric," chided the psychologist, becoming for a moment almost a grade school teacher in her demeanor. "But we must face our experience, our facts, to the best of our abilities. That is why we are here, each of us. It does stand to reason that Alvin might have gone to the graveyard to face his deepest fear. His father told me that they found a sleeping bag with him, as though he planned to spend the night at the grave."

"But," Dominic said, grasping his hands together in front of him, "isn't that what you've told us all to do, Dr Bentley? To face our fears? And, isn't that why he's dead?"

Eric cut in, "Dr Bentley didn't tell us to die though, did she?"

"It's not like anyone here knows what the fuck they're doing anyway" Jerry said, spitting out his words. His face, dotted with pimples, was altered by his anger. His eyes were half closed and he spoke through pursed lips almost as if he were trying to convey the negativity of his feeling by taking on the appearance of a rodent, Ashley thought to herself. He was her least favorite member of the group.

His words were followed by silence. Some in the group hovered on the edge of panic.

Dr Bentley looked at Jerry for a long moment; he met her gaze, could not hold it, averted his angry, ratlike eyes.

Bruno cleared his throat. He said, "But, Doctor, what's the program? We're all sweating here. Was someone out to double-o-nine Alvin? Or how about us? Is someone trying to pull our plugs?"

"You'll have to excuse me," Bentley said.

Bruno tried again, saying, "What I mean is—what's . . . uh . . . going on, Dr Bentley? We're pretty much scared shitless here. Was somebody out for Alvin? Is somebody trying to kill us?"

Bentley smiled at Bruno. Her smile seemed one of genuine concern. It was much warmer than her standard affect. The warmth of the smile set the stage for her response—not so much for what she said as how. She sought to regain her hold on the group.

"No, no one wants any of us to die," Bentley spoke soothingly now, calmly. She almost whispered. "And, yes, Jerry, to answer your concerns, of course we must face our fears, but we must face them when we are ready to face them. What do I mean? How can we know when we are ready to face our fears? We learn by facing them here first. When we can face them here, we can face them outside of this room. But, you can see now, perhaps, what you could not see before, what it would have been useless to tell you because you would not have, could not have, believed it. This work is dangerous. If there is anyone who does not want to face the danger, you must leave now and not return."

Bruno tried to get up; Ashley pulled him back down.

"Please stay," she whispered in his ear.

Karla smiled nervously.

"This is fucked," she whispered.

Looking at her from the corner of her eye, Ashley smiled strangely too. She could feel her heart beating fast; nervousness twisted her stomach.

"Multi-fucked," she nodded.

Jerry half rose, then sat down again, saying to no one and everyone, "Who'd want to miss the end of all this shit?"

Bentley asked that they all observe a moment of silence for their departed group member. Then they began the work of the evening. It was Irma's turn. The dwarfish, dark-skinned woman was an artist of some sort, as most in the group vaguely knew. She dressed fashionably, wearing a bright polyester jumpsuit with clear plastic platform shoes. Though she was short, hers were not the physical proportions of a child, nor was she actually a midget, though her head appeared slightly too big and her arms and legs were thick and somewhat stunted. Even the cosmetic horn which she sometimes wore, though not tonight, on her forehead was short and stubby. Her face was long, flat, and thin. Only her feet were dainty. A scarf covered in images of cartoon figures and American presidents held back her straight, mid-length green hair. Though she hardly knew her, Ashley felt a kindly inclination towards this woman who now, obviously nervous, lay in the center of the group. Dr Bentley administered the drug.

"Think bad thoughts," the doctor said.

The group chanted its hideous chant in some ancient and unknown tongue.

Irma dreamed.

*   *   *

She stands by a gravesite in a secluded cemetery on a summer afternoon. Little birds hop from flowering bush to flowering bush. They are singing . . . no, they are chirping, chirping happily. And flowers grow from the lush grass. Languid, delightful. She kneels to smell them. Their smell, sweet and wholesome, intermingles with the faint pungency of fertilizer. She breathes deep; but as she breathes the afternoon abruptly turns to darkness. Instantly chilly. The birds have become . . . lizards, with phosphorescent eyes. They are ripping the flowers off the bushes.

She wheels around before she hears the sound that makes her turn. She instantly forgets what the sound was, knows only that it was disquieting. A solitary gravestone is before her now. She steps forward. Stoops down to read the name. Rosalie Beamis. Who is she? She's dead, anyway. She knows someone is behind her. Perhaps an attendant? Dr Bentley? She straightens, turns. A woman, sweet, young, tallish in a flowing cotton-print dress. The dress, her long raven-dark locks flow in the breeze. The woman speaks.

"Who are you?" Her voice is sweet, but cold. A frozen flower. Frost covers the ground. The air becomes very cold.

"Who are you?" the woman asks again.

"Hello, my name is Irma, Irma Gamerman. I am pleased to make your acquaintance," Irma, the dream Irma, says.

The two women are standing a yard from each other.

Irma curtsies, just as she learned to do so many years ago when she took dance classes back in . . .

"Alvin?" the other woman asks. She is worried. Her breath is visible in the cold. "Did you bring Alvin?"

"No."

"Alvin is supposed to be with me now. I thought he was coming. Why didn't you bring him. He is to be my husband."

"Alvin is dead. Who are you?"

"Of course he's dead," the woman snaps She becomes agitated. "Of course he's dead. I killed him."

"Who are you?"

"I am Alvin's bride. My name is Rosalie."

"Oh god, but you're . . . not alive."

"No, I'm not. But neither is Alvin. Now."

"Well, I don't know where he is."

"God damn it!" Rosalie screams. "I have been waiting so long." She screams again and weeps, shaking with passionate rage, longing; then she hugs herself, weeping into her hands like a crying child.

Filled with dream sympathy, Irma moves forward and takes the woman, the grieving woman, into her arms, trying to provide comfort. In the back of Irma's mind a warning voice cries No! She feels the woman shuddering in her arms, moaning. Strands of Rosalie's hair hang down, obscuring her face. Then she looks towards Irma. No, the warning voice cries, this is not my dream. Rosalie's face slides slowly off, leaving in its wake a red, pulpy, eyeless surface of violated flesh. Irma screams; she realizes she is having Alvin's dream. Rosalie grabs Irma's arms, grasps them with an unbreakable grip, throws her to the ground. Rosalie jumps on top of her and holds her down, pinning Irma with her body. Blood drips from her face onto Irma's. The blood drops are ice cold. Irma struggles, writhes. The ghoul is opening her mouth and lowering her face. Hollow sockets where the eyes were. A hole in place of a nose. Upper lip ripped, hanging by a thread. Tongue lolling. The ghoul wants to kiss her, whispers, "Alvin."

She wakes screaming.

*   *   *

Her eyes were wide and terror-filled. Though she realized the screaming she heard was coming from her lungs, her mouth, it was almost as if her screams were not entirely hers. Not hers alone. Dr Bentley held her down as she struggled and fought and shuddered. Cold sweat bathed her body. Even Dr Bentley's eyes were filled with fright.

"Irma! Irma!" the doctor shouted.

Irma screamed again and Dr Bentley slapped her hard, stinging her cheek.

"Ouch," Irma cried. "Jesus, you bitch, that hurt." But she was better. She knew where she was now. A far better place. She sat up and Dr Bentley dabbed at her brow with a clean, white handkerchief. The faces of the other members of the group were white, concerned, transfixed.

"Oh my god," she said, "I had his dream. I had Alvin's dream."

"This shit is too weird," Dominic shouted, getting up and heading for the door. "I'm out of here." His eyes were wild.

"Wait!" Dr Bentley commanded. "Sit down, Dominic. This is very serious. I don't mean to alarm you, but I feel we may be in danger now and that the danger may not be confined to those who stay in this room. In fact, you may be in more danger if you leave. I know I said earlier that those who could not face what we do here should go. But that point is passed. Now we go forward as a group or, quite possibly . . . we die. One by one."

Arrested in mid-stride, Dominic turned, paused. The members of the group could see contrary impulses—fear and resignation—battling for ascendancy in his expression. Resignation triumphed. Dominic resumed his meditation cushion, muttering under his breath. He was praying.

Dr Bentley smiled at him. It was a forced smile.

"Dominic," she said. "All of you. Listen. You asked about facing our fears. Sometimes we have the luxury of facing them when we are best able to—when we are strongest. I was not absolutely certain of this just a few moments ago before Irma's experience, but now I think we may be in a situation where we have no choice but to face that which we least want to—an aggregation, a gathering, of all of our deepest fears. The only choice any of us has is to stay with the group. Only the power of the group can provide safety. We must see this thing through together."

"Just the kind of challenge I've always wanted," smiled Brandon.

No one laughed but Eric. For him, things were just getting interesting.

*   *   *

Sometime later, the session came to a close.

Irma approached Ashley in the hall. She tugged at her sleeve; Ashley had to look down to see her worried face.

"Can I talk with you. Please. Alone."

"Sure."

Ashley asked Bruno and Karla to give her a moment. She walked to a quiet corner in the hall outside Dr Bentley's office with the woman who had so recently writhed in unconscious terror."

"You had quite a night, Irma," Ashley said.

"You can say that again," Irma said, not meeting her eyes. She was going to say something embarrassing, that much Ashley could tell.

"Ashley," Irma continued, "we hardly know each other . . . I don't really know anyone in the group. But that dream—it was so real, so horrifyingly real, I almost feel that it is the most real thing that has happened to me in a long, long time. I'm really shaken up. I don't know if I can face going home alone. I'm Chip Suey."

"Aren't we all? I'm wantonly hyper-k myself. Unbland. But why don't you call a friend if you need some company?"

Irma did not have any friends, so she said, "My best friend is out of town. There's really no one else I can call. Do you think we could go out for a drink, the two of us? Just to settle me down, to make me trite?"

Ashley looked over Irma's importuning face at Karla, who shrugged her shoulders as if to say "let's go."

"Well," said Ashley, "I do have plans, but all right. Why not?"

"Tepid," Irma replied.

*   *   *

After the session ended, Dr Bentley asked Brandon to stay on for a moment. She said that she wanted to speak to him about something, something of importance. Now they were alone in the large room which must have at one point been an expanse of cubicles and desks, of computers and busy office workers on telephones, but now was the sparsely furnished, stark, overlarge meeting place for Bentley's group. Brandon stood in front of Dr Bentley. They were chatting. He was only about 5' 6" tall and she, five inches taller, looked down at him. His eyes were just above the level of her breasts. Though he was short, he was muscular; his shoulders were broad; he almost sparkled with health and goodwill. He was nervous. He felt uncomfortable at her nearness. She asked him how he liked the therapy sessions.

"I like them," Brandon stammered, meeting fleetingly the intense scrutiny of her steel blue eyes, then looking away, down at her hips, her legs, her shoes, the floor. "But I'm worried. The dreams, the sessions, Alvin's death. Everything is getting too weird."

"You're scared?"

"I guess I am."

He felt her hand on his shoulder. It seemed like she was closer to him. He could feel her proximity, her heaving chest. He

felt her breath, warm on his face. Her hand slid down his arm
and took his hand.

"Look at me," she said.

He looked.

"I'm going to tell you a secret," she whispered.

"What's that?"

"Sometimes I get scared too. It's so hard being alone with my
own nightmares."

He started to respond, to say something, anything, the first
thing that might come into his mind, but her face was against his,
her hair was brushing his face, soft strands, and her mouth was
on his, opening it, filling it with her impetuously probing tongue.
He felt the ball of nervousness that had formed in his stomach
flare and split and surge through his chest and his loins, almost
making him shudder as it dissipated into the urgent energy of
their embrace.

*   *   *

They went to a cafe called Critique of Pure, located just
around the corner from the hulking, impotent, concrete and glass
edifice in which Dr Bentley held her sessions. Irma ordered a
cup of herb tea; Ashley ordered a vodka.

They spoke.

Their conversation took this course: first they talked about
the dream and the sessions; next awkward silence followed; finally Ashley said, "So tell me about yourself, Irma. I've heard
you're an artist?"

"Yes. I am."

"What . . . uh . . . medium do you work in?"

Irma looked at her defiantly, expecting that her answer would
be met with disdain.

"Feces. I work with feces."

"You paint with shit?" exclaimed Ashley, sitting up on the
edge of her seat.

"Not paint actually. Sculpt."

"Bland! That's so, so trite. Tell me more."

"There's not much to say. I create figures out of waste. Human waste."

"And people buy these things?"

"There are some buyers. Most of my support comes from grants and foundations."

Ashley was intrigued. The sculptor described her methods. She sculpted small nudes and other figures out of a mixture of feces, her own, and plaster. The material was treated with a preservative that staved off rot, mold, decay. The sculptures she either coated with a clear plastic or encased in glass to eliminate odor, which she incorrectly described as "unsightly odor," Ashley noted. A number of her pieces had been purchased by a prominent manufacturer of toilet paper.

"But don't you find that there is an aversion to what you do," Ashley asked, her eyes sparkling as she leaned over the table between them. "I mean humans have such a hyperactive aversion to even discussing the subject of defecation."

"You seem to be doing well," Irma said. "But that is the whole point of my work: to deal with a substance that humans view with fear, disgust, and silence and to force us to look at our waste in new and boundary-breaking ways. In a sense, shit is our last taboo, our last frontier. Everything else is *passé*."

"I am not threatened by my waste," Ashley sniffed.

"I doubt you could have a frank discussion about your own stool."

"About or with?" Ashley asked.

"About," Irma giggled

"Very regular. First thing in the morning. Two stools, like clockwork. Plop. Plop. Fizz. Fizz. Oh what a relief . . . etcetera."

"You look?"

"I do. I look, but I do not touch."

Irma roared with laughter, "You're much healthier than I thought."

"Or much sicker."

"No, that's just the problem. Our waste is everywhere. It is inside us now, each of us. We see it every day. It is as important to us as breathing. If we do not defecate, we die. Why not establish a new relationship with our . . . old friend, our traveling companion?"

Irma's fascination with waste, she went on, had begun a number of years ago when she was in art school. She had begun by photographing her own waste. She had felt an inner glee at the uncomfortable reactions of her teachers and her classmates. Then, tentatively, with the greatest hesitancy, she had begun working with her waste, gathering it at first and working it with hands fully protected by plastic gloves designed to prevent dish-pan hands. She had covered her nose and mouth with a surgical mask. These protections, these niceties, were now long gone and she worked with her medium as if it were clay, soil, or plaster, sculpting statuettes and figurines which, because of the repulsive materials from which they were crafted, caused a minor, though measurable sensation in the world of art. Of course, she added, she was still very meticulous about cleaning up after her work was done.

Being a pioneer in working with her own waste had resulted in a modicum of fame and success for Irma. However, as Ashley observed, these explorations had not purged the young and ugly artist of her ugly dreams. Irma's nightmare was of being trapped in a pool of waste—smothered, covered, and drowned within it.

"You're absolutely right, Ashley," Irma said, her look growing worried again as she reflected on the nature of her own nightmares and on the particular nightmare she had experienced just two hours before, "my work with waste has done nothing to dispel my recurring dreams about shit. Perhaps, psychologically, that is why I am so attracted to my work, as a way to try to counter the force, the pure fear, of my darkest thoughts. When I'm awake, I am as unafraid of my waste as an infant, but when I sleep, it is the source of my most devastating fears. It's ironic, but in the final analysis, what the fuck? I no longer give my own psychology as much thought as I used to."

"Amen to that," Ashley said, "my psychology sucks."

Their drinks were finished; they ordered a second round.

A man walked up to a small, raised platform in the center of the club. He said that he was scheduled to read his poetry that evening. He wore a T-shirt that said "I'm Canadian." He cleared his throat. This was the first poem he read:

<u>October 26</u>

Norton works in a city department and is insecure about his difficult position there.

Beware.

His relationship with his boss, Mr Lifebestower, is cordial, but underneath there is a powerful straining.

Emotionally draining.

Every day he fears being fired. Then, one by one, various of his friends begin committing suicide—an idea that has more and

more than

ever been on his own mind. As if a chain reaction, one suicide among his circle of friends leads to another.

Oh brother.

He must take time off to go to the succession of funerals, yet asking for days and half-days creates more emotional strain for him—

like Lord Jim—

*at the office. The strain is economic—new house, new baby, same
wife, new payments, and though he has always told himself that*

unlike a rat

*he will not be trapped by these interlocking concerns, indeed he
is finding himself more and more trapped.*

What crap!

*Ironically, what is for him the ethical necessity of attending so
many funerals is, in and of itself, a major factor,*

like a haywire nuclear reactor,

*driving him toward psychic explosion. "If only my friends had made
arrangements to be buried within the city's cemeteries," Norton,*

unsporting,

*says to himself, "then I could attend their funerals as part of
my job." Norton is a cemetery inspector,*

not an edifice erector.

*His experiences in Ancient Rome have given him a refined
aesthetic when it comes to judging statues, headstones, and tombs.*

A connoisseur of gloom.

A Roman reliving the last days of Empire.

A lyric life without a lyre.

<u>November 19</u>

Walking into the ice cream store, Norton—Norton Homo—
sees an insurance salesman whom he does not want to see.

Hide or flee?

It is the man who pesters him about buying a more expensive
life insurance policy. Quietly turning to the door and,

with the intensity of a Lizzy Borden,

running into the supermarket across the street, Norton feels
exhilaration and foolishness mix in the dry cauldron of himself,

like poverty and pelf,

standing in the fresh vegetables section. He notes the bland aesthetic
of fruits and vegetables.

Pale edibles.

Meeting a friend, a friend due soon to take his own life,
Norton explains what he has done.

Old chum.

They laugh together touring the aisles. The products arrayed
on shelves make Norton think of the . . .

uh . . .

dead arrayed beautifully in Final Rapture Cemetery on
a pulchritudinous spring day. There green meets blue on the edge

of a hedge

on a hill, high monuments fraying the simplicity of the line.
The cemetery is quiet. Its mood is atavistic

and mystic.

The supermarket is noisy; its mood commercial and expectant.
Norton's hands pluck products

like hungry ducks.

Would the absurdity of revealing that Norton comes to this time
from Ancient Rome draw too much attention to itself?

Ask yourself.

His name in Latin means "man." Yet, in this century, here in
the city, Norton's co-workers at the Department of . . .

this you'll love . . .

Death snicker at his name. A minor thing, but it
contributes to Norton's difficulties

like irritating fleas.

So do the aberrations of his appearance. Norton's hands are
reversed.

He's cursed.

His left hand is on his right arm; his right is on his left. An
amateur pianist, Norton has to cross arms to play the melancholy

and never jolly

*dirges he so enjoys. His eyes also are reversed, a subtle
reversal: his tear ducts are at the outside of his eyes so when*

again and again

*he cries, his tears flow down the sides of his face. One more
oddity: Norton's ears have exchanged places, but, upside down,*

their covers blown,

*they face bell forward as do normal ears. With gravity and the
jounce of Norton's self-conscious walk, the earlobes, curling—*

almost whirling—

flop down and up.

Yup.

January 29

*Norton has again taken time off work to attend a funeral in
another city.*

Not pretty.

*A chill wind stirs the snow in the well-laid-out cemetery as he
watches the coffin of his last friend, also a suicide—*

fast track to the other side—

lowered into the frozen earth's gaping maw. Over the past six months, he has attended seventeen funerals.

What bitter rituals!

He has not a friend left in the world, but this last death,
the last possible suicide of Norton's last friend, revives

like departing hives

Norton's enthusiasm. Walking back to his car he notices some of
the fine statuary in the graveyard. Driving to a phonebooth,

grasping a truth,

Norton calls his supervisor. "I'd like to talk with you when
I get back to the office, Mr Lifebestower," Norton says,

feeling fresh.

"I have some concerns about my job that I would like to discuss."
"That would be fine, Norton," Mr Lifebestower replies,

far away as the crow flies,

a deep voice over the telephone.

Then, the dial tone.

The poet stopped reading, reciting. His poem was finished. He was thinking of reading another. With his head bent over the papers in his hand, the shabby papers, the poet eyed the café furtively, hurriedly, unpoetically, trying to read his listeners, what their reaction was to his work, what he should read next. His gaze crisscrossed the café, then returned to his poems. He seemed to choose one. Then he reconsidered.

Irma asked Ashley, "Would you like to come and see my studio? I mean it's also where I live. And, frankly, I'm still a little sweaty. I'd appreciate the company."

Ashley actually was possessed with a rare and genuine desire to see Irma's work. Downplaying this, she replied emotionlessly, "Yes, that would be bland."

"Bland squared," said Irma.

"Multi-bland," Ashley confirmed.

After a walk of no more than twenty minutes they came to what appeared to once have been a sprawling, one-story storage complex. In the light of the streetlight, Ashley could make out the faded word MEDICAL on the front of the building. Irma fiddled in her pocket for the key to a large, steel garage door.

"Damn it all," she swore, thumping the door with her fist, "I've forgotten my fucking key. Well, no matter. I've done this before."

Grabbing a crow bar from a hiding place amidst a pile of cinder blocks on the sidewalk, Irma pried up a manhole cover from the center of the street and began climbing down into blackness.

"Irma," Ashley asked, "what's the program?"

"We must face our worst fears," Irma smiled cryptically.

Then she was gone.

Ashley looked up and down the street. There was no one else. There was a little mist hanging over the street. It started to rain. Unintense droplets, making sounds like popcorn just starting to pop. The pattern the mist made encircling the streetlight above her engaged Ashley's attention. She crossed her arms across her chest. She uncrossed them. Something was making her more nervous than just being alone in an empty stretch of the warehouse district usually made her. In a moment Ashley heard sounds from inside the building. A chain rattling. Metal tongues licking metal grooves. The door was being opened from the inside. Ashley thought of an incident that had occurred once that had to do with a garage door. She had been walking near her parents' house when she had come upon a child who, in closing a garage door, had caught her hand in it, in one of the horizontal joints between the panels of the door which allowed it to be raised and lowered along a curved metal track. The garage door was stopped three feet above the driveway. The girl's hand was caught in the door above her body, so she had to stretch, standing on tiptoes. Nine or ten years old, the girl, though yelling for help, though crying, eyed Ashley warily as she approached. Ashley lifted the door a little so that the girl could pull her fingers out. Then the girl had run away, off to the rear of her house. Irma pulled the garage door open, bathing Ashley in a warm and inviting light that flowed from a substantial studio and living space within. The visitor's anxiety diminished.

"Step inside, ugly," Irma smiled.

Irma quickly dashed out, replaced the manhole cover, returned, and pulled the door down. She turned her attention back towards her new friend.

"That's my little secret. There's an opening from the sewer directly into the basement of my building. It's very convenient when I don't have my key, though many a rat has tried to gain entry to my space. But my friend here keeps a pretty good guard," Irma said, nodding at a dog, her pet, who had wandered sleepily into the presence of the two women.

She knelt and enveloped her dog, a mid-sized, gnarled mongrel, in a hug. The dog was brown, not the rich brown of some fine breed, but the faded, dirt brown of an old, once tan carpet which, in some low rent office or bus terminal, had been trod by an infinite parade of wet, dirty shoes. The dog had the look of a tried and true fighter against rats and other creatures. Part of the dog's snout, at about the mid-point, had been bitten away, leaving pink scar tissue and revealing teeth and gums on one side of its mouth. The teeth were very white and the gums were black. The hound wriggled gracelessly from his master's grasp and moved to a spot in a tired lounge chair.

Ashley was fascinated by Irma's studio in the defunct warehouse. She saw sculpture after sculpture representing abstract forms or human and animal shapes. All the pieces were set under glass or covered with clear plastic coatings and set on crude pedestals made of pieces of crates and broken planks. Ashley was particularly impressed with a piece that seemed, in its directness, to typify Irma's expressive impulses. Three stools, covered in a shiny plastic coating, were set under glass. They looked firm and greenish brown, precisely as if they had been dropped there that morning. The title of the piece, neatly typed on a little card placed under the glass, was: *My Brilliant Career.*

One part of her studio was taken up with Irma's workspace—tables, benches, a potter's wheel, glassware, and assorted tools all laid out with neat precision. In another part of the capacious studio was Irma's living space—a few chairs and a couch, a cot, and a kitchenette built against a concrete block wall. Everything looked compulsively tidy, sanitized. The kitchen table, the pots hung on the wall, the glasses and dishes arranged in neat stacks: all gleamed with cleanliness. The cot was neatly made up. It looked almost military. Symphonic music, Mahler's *Second Symphony,* played from a radio on top of the refrigerator. The volume was low. A floor lamp splashed a sofa and upholstered chairs with tepid light; a coffee table contained a neat stack of art magazines and a large book devoted to the painter Willem de Kooning. But, even though Ashley tried not to show her awareness of it, the smell that permeated the studio and living space was disconcerting. The smell of waste was not wrenchingly overt, but it hovered just noticeably enough throughout the studio that it was impossible to ignore. A tincture of unwholesomeness.

Throughout the process of looking at Irma's work, her workspace, her inordinately neat living and kitchen space, Ashley declined more than once an offer of coffee and the suggestion that she spend the night on a second cot that Irma said was ready to be unfolded for guests.

"Let me at least give you my number," Irma said, as Ashley protested after visiting for forty-five minutes or so that she really had to go, "and ask you to call me tomorrow, just . . . just so you know that I've made it through the night all right?"

"Of course," Ashley promised.

"Thanks, ugly," Irma smiled.

Ashley liked this woman, though she would prefer, she said to herself, to see Irma outside of her apartment. Irma opened her large door. Ashley entered into the night. Turning back, she waved to Irma, called, "Use you later."

"Use you later," Irma called back, smiling worriedly.

Ashley walked away. Then, soon after, she heard Irma's door sliding down, the lone sound in the empty neighborhood. The air, the asphalt smelled remarkably fresh with the rain. The rain had just stopped falling. All was mist and glitter amidst darknesses. There was a hint of sea air also from the harbor; freshness mixed with freshness and the odor of feces became a memory. She passed through a vacant lot and into an obscure passage between buildings in an abandoned brewery. A few steps into the alley she saw the shape of a person crawl deeper into a cardboard box, disappear before her. Human rat. The wet box had lost its shape. She could hear only the sound of her own footsteps, first on the gravel-covered alleyway, then as tart, soft echoes against the encroaching walls. Night swallowed Ashley up.

While she walked, she thought of various phrases that involved waste: "haste makes waste," "waste not, want not." Naturally, it was not human waste which was being referred to in these quaint adages, but who cared? How amusing it would be to make a variation on one of these phrases in a way that summed up Irma's artistic enterprise. She could tell it to Bruno and Karla when she met them in a few moments at the bar. She hoped they would still be there. She suspected they would be. A flood of ideas came into her mind but none of them quite encapsulated what Irma did in any pithy, brilliant way. Oh well, she thought to herself, everyone's hard drive has gone soft, hasn't it? She heard movement in the alley in front of her. She slowed, stepped like a cat. She hid herself in the blackness of a doorway. Stealth. She breathed quietly. Soon a number of children passed by. They were singing—humming rather—some simple song. That was reassuring, but Ashley thought it best to remain hidden until they were gone for more than a few moments, until their voices had died away.

Chapter 7

The Sound of Music

Another day. Another horrible pet death. Another blaring headline. Another headache. Another hangover. Still, Costello carried on.

After dinner, he drove out to an organizational meeting that Cassie Quick, the new, increasingly visible leader of the new, increasingly strident Pet Protection League, was holding in her spacious home in a well-to-do neighborhood near the Arboretum. A source at a pet store had tipped him off. Of course, Costello had no intention of letting on that he was a detective. The Pet Protection League held the Police Department in low regard. He parked his unmarked vehicle at the end of a long line of parked cars and armor-protected Lovecrafts. A number of the cars had dogs inside, he noted, as he walked towards the Quick residence. Black noses poked out through partially unclosed windows. No tails wagged. Growls and half-hearted barks marked his passing. A German Shepherd threw itself at the window of one car, barking, baring teeth.

"You're next, poochie," Costello whispered, stopping and pointing at the furious hound. He could feel his own anger rising. What if he just shot the fucking dog? Then, realizing where he was going, he changed his attitude. "I feel your pain," he smiled, walking on. Many of the vehicles had bumper stickers with messages like **Love Your Pet as You Love Yourself**, or **Pets, not Threats**. One luxury vehicle, capable of hydroplaning as well as driving, sported a sticker which said **Sad But True, I'm Richer Than You**. Another displayed the sticker **I'm a Necrophiliac and I Vote**. Costello wondered who the vehicle's owner voted for. Paninni, probably. A bicycle was parked by the front door.

A middle-aged man met Costello at the front door of the home, a two-story Colonial with a wide front lawn. Costello thought it likely that the greeter was Rex Quick, Cassie's husband. Bald, tall, slightly stooped, wearing thick glasses. Nerdish? Yes, but all in all Mr Quick looked to be in pretty good shape, Costello thought, sizing the greeter up quickly, professionally. He had the air of a guy who, despite years sitting in an office, still enjoyed physical challenge. He was probably the captain of his company's volleyball team. His face was narrow and long, punctuated by a thin, long nose rising like an exclamation mark above a thin-lipped mouth and prominent jaw. The husband was not much involved in his wife's cause from what the detective had been able to find out.

"You're here for the meeting?" Mr Quick asked. His voice sounded distant, tired, professionally pleasant. He had weak, watery eyes which would not meet Costello's gaze. "Everyone's down in the basement. They're just getting ready to start."

The basement did not look much like a basement at all. The walls were paneled in knotty pine; a thick rug covered the floor. Two rows of decorative pine pillars ran the length of the subterranean chamber. The furniture surpassed the furniture in many living rooms Costello had seen, certainly the rag-tag assortment of rented furniture and cast-offs in his own apartment. At one end of the basement, the side nearest the stairs Costello had descended, were two tables with a coffee service, platters of cheese, bread, vegetables and dip, and a half dozen bottles of white wine.

Things are looking up, Costello thought to himself, pouring

the clear liquid into a plastic wine glass as he wheeled, surveying the scene. Perhaps thirty or forty people and assorted dogs and cats filled the room. A parrot perched on a woman's shoulder. The participants, the human participants, came from all walks of life, all sectors of society, but they all shared the ultra-serious look of persons animated by an offbeat cause. At the far end of the room, a girlishly slim though middle-aged woman tapped a spoon against a glass. She appeared to be simultaneously animated and understated, bouncily plebian and aristocratically subdued. The room grew quiet. All turned earnest attention to Cassie Quick.

"Thank you, thank you all for coming," Mrs Quick said with a perkily upper middle class intonation. "I am Cassie Quick, the founder of the newly established Pet Protection League. Only a few months ago I lost my pet, my Charlie, cruelly slaughtered in what we all have since learned has been an ongoing and growing pattern of vicious attacks on our best, our truest friends—our pets, or our non-human companions, as some prefer to call them.

"Today, we have heard that another innocent pet was found dead. I know the pain that pet's owner felt on finding their animal slain or on hearing the news. Today the owner was an older person living alone who only had his dog for company. That dog, a Golden Retriever named Lord Byron, was his only friend. Tomorrow the victim may be a young child who loves her pet more than any doll and who will not be able to understand how such a horrible thing could have happened . . . or it may be one of us gathered here in this room this evening."

A wave of whispers moved through the attendees.

"Harder, baby," someone in the crowd said. "Harder."

Quick's face froze momentarily, then softened. She, like everyone at the gathering, looked towards the interrupting voice. The parrot. The group smiled and looked back at Mrs Quick. Costello could only see the parrot's owner from the back: a slim, tiny woman dressed in a white outfit which clung to the straight, vertical lines of her torso. She did not move even as her parrot spoke or then, after speaking, shook its wings unexpectedly, purposelessly.

Lighting a cigarette, puckering her lips around it as she pulled the first long drag, Quick continued, upping the intensity in her voice to recapture the momentum of her message.

She said, "I was devastated by Charlie's death, but I was also motivated by a commitment that I had never felt before. I vowed in the days after his murder—as I looked at Charlie's empty feeding dish and his empty dog bed and as I listened vainly for his happy barks—that I would work to ensure that no other pet lover would ever again have to feel my pain, no other pet lover would ever again have to have his best friend . . . untimely ripped from his or her life. I vowed if there was anything I could do to save another pet and another master from the horrible pain I had felt, then I would not rest until I had stopped this slaughter, this murder.

"That is my vow. That is our vow. We will not rest. I am fortunate, and the pets of our city are fortunate, to have such a dedicated group of friends working together on this issue as the group we have formed: the Pet Protection League.

"In these past few weeks we have accomplished so much. We have compiled extensive research and information on the pattern of hideous slayings that have taken place over the past five months. Now, every night, we have members of the Pet Protection League patrolling places where these atrocities have occurred and are still taking place. From the Arboretum to the Marshes, from Walden Hill to South Beach and the alleys of the Warehouse District, we are there. And let's not forget we also have people patrolling places where the pet slayer or slayers have not tried to commit crimes . . . yet. We are vigilant.

"We have made great strides, too, in raising public awareness and consciousness regarding these crimes. Our poster campaign and our media campaign are carrying the message of pet safety to pet owners—to men, women, and children concerned about our four-footed, and our feathered, companions."

Quick nodded in the direction of the parrot and the parrot's owner, smiled briefly, continued.

"And, I add with some satisfaction, we have been very successful in bringing pressure—in unleashing pressure, if you'll pardon my pun—on Mayor Edgar Paninni and the Police Department. These leaders, these bureaucrats, must begin to take their responsibilities to our pets seriously if they want humans who love pets to keep them in office."

Many of the people assembled in the basement nodded in approval while Mrs Quick continued to speak on, outlining the goals and initiatives of the Pet Protection League. Costello moved his eyes through the crowd. With the exception of Mrs Quick and a few of the people whom he had seen on the videotape of the mayor's recently televised fiasco, Costello did not recognize anyone here. He turned back to refill his wine glass and then resumed watching. There, in the very middle of the audience, was Esmeralda. At least he thought it was she. He gulped. Instantly, he felt his stomach flip and his face grow red. I'm blushing, he observed to himself. Not good in a undercover operation. He ducked behind one of the pillars, positioning himself so that he could get a better look at the woman—the woman literally of his dreams—without being seen himself should she turn. She was dressed similarly to the way she had been on the night of the car jacking—black jumpsuit, a black beret. Her hair, thick and bright red, was tied in a pony tail. She wore sunglasses, was slim, lithe, curvaceous, graceful. She wore an olive green gun belt around her waist but no holster and no gun. Her Uzi must be elsewhere, he chuckled to himself. God almighty, she was beautiful! And he had only a rear view. She seemed to be listening intently to Mrs Quick. How pleasurable it was just to watch her listen. What was she thinking? For just a second his mind grew fuzzy, warm, slightly trippy. Images formed there, then melted into each other like colored images of thin wax on a heated plate until one solid image formed. A little dog rolling on its back. It paws were in the air. It yipped. Then it was gone, melted. Jesus, Costello thought, where did those thoughts come from? Abruptly Esmeralda turned. She turned towards a man a number of feet away because he was yelling.

"I question everything the Pet Protection League is trying to do!" he cried. He sounded angry.

"You want to see pets die?" responded Cassie Quick, answering immediately, her voice rising slightly.

"I'd rather see animals die than continue to live as slaves," the man responded in a strident, nasal voice. He pushed through the audience to within a few feet of Cassie Quick.

"That's right!" an elderly woman standing near Costello seconded.

"Harder, baby," the parrot repeated, then shook its wings. No one noticed this time.

The interloper turned and began to address the assembly. He was tall, unkempt, gangly, about twenty-five years old, with a full beard which joined, or intertangled, with a thicket of dark hair which rose from and surrounded his head.

"My name is Barry Sarnoff. I'm a member of a group that believes that it's wrong for humans to murder animals—to kill them either through direct violence or through the indirect violence of captivity and domestication!"

"That's right," someone else shouted in agreement.

"Hold it right there," Mrs Quick exclaimed, stepping forward, tapping her glass furiously. "This is a Pet Protection League meeting. I won't have it taken over by . . . by a . . ."

"A what?" Barry countered. "By someone who can appreciate his life without having to have an animal slave licking his hand, rolling over on his back, and begging to be petted."

The basement erupted into a verbal duel between pro-pet animal lovers, the predominant group, and a small but vocal group of anti-pet animal lovers. This second group began chanting "Pets are slaves, pets are slaves."

Then, Barry refocused the direction of the dialogue by falling on his back, holding his arms and legs aloft limply, and crying, "Oh, come on, Mrs Quick, scratch my tummy. I'll be your doggie."

This caused immediate silence. Mrs Quick seemed almost on the point of stooping over to oblige when good sense stopped her. She simply looked at Barry. His tongue lolled out of the side of his mouth. His eyes were bright, expectantly importuning.

"Cassie," someone said, "perhaps it would be easier if we just let the gentleman say what he came here to say."

Others agreed.

Mrs Quick said, "All right. But briefly, I beg you."

Smiling, Barry Sarnoff rose, took a breath, and spoke. His speaking style was direct and forceful.

"As members of DOOMED—Domestication Of Others Must End, Damn It—we know that you, Mrs Quick, and members of the Pet Protection League, are trying to do the right thing," Sarnoff said, sounding notes of conciliation in word and gesture, spreading wide his arms, opening his hands. "You're trying to protect other creatures, which you choose to call 'pets'. But we believe that your concerns are founded on principles that are both false and repugnant to humans and animals.

"Since the first appearance of the animals called 'human beings', we humans have used other creatures for our needs and for our so called pleasure. So called! While we oppose any use of animals, DOOMED is particularly, stridently, opposed to the human domestication of other creatures. Of all the many types of animal slavery, the willful imprisonment and never-ending devaluation that is the basis of the master-pet relationship is fundamentally demeaning to animals, but also to their so called "masters." It is a relationship which robs all parties of their dignity, their freedom, and their souls."

"So what do you want to do about the pet slayings?" asked a stout woman in a house dress. She wore a button which said "Let me tell you about my Huskies."

"We want to set all pets free," Barry responded. At this, the handful of DOOMED members in the audience threw back their heads and howled like wolves.

"But how will that keep them from being slaughtered?" someone else called out.

"That's not the issue," Barry responded. "The issue is freedom. Without a doubt, it's better to die wild than to live as a slave."

Another howl. A "harder, baby" too.

"So, are you saying that the pet killer is doing the right thing by killing our pets?" cried a gray-suited Episcopalian minister standing in the middle of the crowd with two Bloodhounds lolling, leashed, at his feet.

Barry saw that he was getting into difficult territory.

"Yes," he said, "I am. But I don't mean to say that what he is doing is absolutely right. I mean . . ."

"Pet killer," the woman who liked to be asked about her Huskies ejaculated, her face contorting with rage. Fireworks erupted again. Shouts, barks, growls, loud voices, and screams filled the basement room and then the first punch was thrown. It was not a strong punch, Costello noted, but the sort of punch that someone not used to punching makes. This physical manifestation of the dispute spread quickly. Pushing, slapping, and shoving were everywhere. Even the animals joined in. A Welsh Terrier, a small, spry dog, leapt up and fixed its teeth into the tail of the parrot. The parrot flew a few feet into the air, seemingly carrying the curly haired, brown and black hound along with it until the dog let go and fell to the floor, followed by a gyre of green feathers. The parrot's owner screamed, gave chase to the dog. A tiny man jostled Costello. The detective looked down at the furious face of his attacker.

"Which side of this issue are you on," his assailant cried. "Pet or free?"

"Oh, that's all right," Costello smiled, "I haven't made up my mind yet. This is my first time. You keep on fighting. I'll just get another glass of wine and watch."

He sidestepped a couple of animal advocates entangled on the floor and poured himself another glassful of the too sweet white wine. A chair flew by him as he turned back towards the roiling room.

"Damn it all," he said to himself, "any more of this and I might have to start acting like a real police officer."

After hitting the wall, the chair teetered for a moment on the serving table, then fell over on its side, knocking over three bottles of wine. They poured their contents onto the carpet. The detective hopped up onto the serving table himself, both to get a better look at the activities and because a sixth sense told him that the unfolding drama now lacked one essential character.

He was right.

Esmeralda was not there.

He turned to the stairs and saw a pair of boots climbing. Near the top of the stairs. Her boots. He leapt down onto the floor. A perfect landing. The wine glass he held did not lose a drop. He drank the contents down as he barreled towards the stairs. The minister's Bloodhounds arrested his progress, each chomping at a trouser leg. He shook and spun like a slow but powerful fullback stepping through a rapidly closing hole in a line of scrimmage. He reached the stairs, took them two at a time, leaving the hounds whimpering in his wake.

"Enemy of pets," the cleric shouted after him. "I feel sorry for you."

The detective dashed past a baffled Rex Quick in the living room.

"Meeting concluded?" Quick asked, tried to ask, Costello as he ran by.

The bicycle which had been parked at the front of the house was gone. The detective ran out onto the street and made a hurried survey of every possible escape route. Nothing. No beautiful anti-car terrorist riding off on a bicycle. "Hell," he said, crushing, throwing his plastic wine glass to the street. He strode to his car. He did not notice that one of the Bloodhounds he had tossed aside was limping after him, bloodlust in its eyes. Though it moved slowly, the dog was closing in. Opening its drooling maw, now only a few inches away, the hound made to sink its teeth into Costello's calf as the policeman, unaware, pulled open the door to his car. The swinging door caught the dog straight in the snout; it quivered and fell over onto its side. Costello looked at the downed dog, got into his car, closed his door, buckled up, rolled down the window, whispered, "Pets are slaves."

Careful to avoid the fallen canine, Costello pulled out from the parked cars and began to drive around the neighborhood in ever widening circles in hopes that he would see Esmeralda. Chances were slim, he knew, but there was no better way to approach it. He circled through Cassie Quick's neighborhood, then he drove once around the perimeter of the Arboretum. The park had closed its gates at dusk. Nothing. He crisscrossed the increasingly seedy residential neighborhoods that spread out to the southwest of the Arboretum. Again, he looked in vain. He drove for half an hour, forty-five minutes, then thought of calling a halt to his search. A period of rest and reflection at a local bar might be in order. All the same, he persisted, driving east next, into the wasteland of the city's warehouse district where weedy, rubble-strewn streets led through block after block of abandoned buildings and vacant lots. Safest neighborhood in the city, he mused. The drug dealers policed the place themselves, ensuring that their customers went unmolested. An irony: the only place in the city where the murder rate was at an acceptable level was guarded by criminals. The murder rate for humans, anyway. When animals began to buy drugs, then they might find sanctuary here too.

He drove slowly, sweeping the sparsely populated cityscape with his gaze. The streets, which had been laid out decades if not hundreds of years before, had not been patterned according to any reasonable scheme. No grid pattern here. Instead, these streets, unmarked, hardly lighted, wound randomly, often ending in dead-ends or leading to impassable roadblocks. At one point a burned out ice cream truck stopped his progress. Soon thereafter, he stopped when his headlights revealed a wide hole gaping in the road. The street had caved in over a sewer.

It was then, at the edge of this mini-abyss, that he saw a movement in his rear view mirror. He knew it was a woman bicycling though he saw this hint of motion for less than a second. He turned the car. He accelerated. In the instantaneous reflection, he had seen enough. At the end of the block, he turned left onto a cross street and there she was, one hundred yards ahead; woman and machine were unified into one nonchalantly speeding mechanism. He hoped to drive up alongside her, roll down his window, and ask her to stop. How reasonable! He approached her, gained on her, in his unmarked car.

She turned.

She saw the car.

She hunched forward.

She sped away, adding speed to speed.

She pedaled down the street, winding though trash cans, shattered bottles, gaping potholes with an agility which amazed Costello, and frustrated him. He attempted to pull alongside her. She swerved in front of his car so that he nearly hit her. His brakes screamed; he swore. She swerved right then left so he could not pass.

"Esmeralda. Stop. It's me. Costello," Costello intoned through the vehicle's loud speaker. "You remember me, the homicide detective whose car you stole and destroyed. I just want to talk. I don't want to arrest you, I promise."

Strangely, it worked.

She slowed down. He slowed down too.

She stopped. She waited for him to stop. She stood, legs on either side of the bicycle, looking back. He started to get out of his car. Her eyes shone in his headlights. Doelike, he thought. Wrongly. She was off again, darting down an alleyway. "Shit." He jumped back into the vehicle, swung after her. He was right behind her now. Right on her tail. She passed to the right of a pile of sagging cartons filled with double-o-nined computer equipment. There was not enough room for a car. What the hell. He forged ahead, crushing sodden cardboard, metal, and plastic between car and brick, tossing crushed boxes onto his hood, his windshield. For a moment he could not see. He drove by feel. Then, there she was. He chased her to a fence at the end of the alley where she stopped, looking back, the clichéd doe again in the headlights. He threw on his brakes, skidded. Didn't want to crush her—that would be . . . counterproductive. He stopped, threw open his door, leapt out. "Esmeralda." He almost spread his arms, almost sang—so Hollywood, so operatic was this moment. She smiled. She was lovely. The smile became a grimace, then a baring of teeth. Unbecomingly doglike, apelike. She rolled her bike at him, turned, jumped, caught the top of the fence, the wooden fence, with her hands, pulled herself up, her feet kicking at the old wood. A board snapped in half. She looked again at him as she swung over the top, saw him tumble over the bike. He got up, looked up. She was gone. Limping, his knee smarting, he clambered up the barrier, dropped heavily on the other side. Darker darkness. He had left his flashlight in the car. Idiot. He felt anger rising. He put it off. Stored it away for later. His eyes adjusted. Alleys moved off in three directions. No sign of her.

"Maybe I just should have shot her," Costello exhaled.

He chose a direction and moved quickly, carefully through the eerie, quiet cool of the fall evening. Probably no chance of catching her but why not try? He must try. Why must he try? Love, he reasoned to himself, and justice. Justice for all the female anti-car terrorists as well as for all the oppressed pets of the world. Amen. Here and there, painted messages glowed, florescent, from the dark walls enclosing the alley.

ABJURE

EMPTINESS=BLISS

A rat skittered underfoot. He jumped. God, his leg hurt. He felt at his knee as he moved forward. His trousers were torn and there was the wetness of blood on his knee. Fuck. How to mend trousers? He had no idea. Just put them in a drawer. Have it done later. Never have it done. How could he fight for love, justice, and pets without trousers. The Pantsless Detective, a folk hero. He saw shapes in front of him. Humans. Dead or alive? Please let them be alive. He did not have the time to stop, investigate, call it in, file reports. The three human forms lay amongst bloated plastic bags filled with what?—garbage? possessions? Same thing. Human garbage. One of the reclining forms moaned. Good. On closer observation, the other two also exhibited signs of life. Painheads. Blackheads. Strange phenomenon, these folks. No use wasting the time of the Pantsless Detective on such as these, he told himself. No use asking them if they had seen a woman running by. Notoriously unreliable, these freaks. Self-absorbed. Pathological liars. So, Esmeralda was a two issue woman: pets and cars. What a combination. Was she pro-pet or anti-pet, he wondered. Not that he cared. He would gladly burn cars and set pets free if . . .

"We come in peace," one of the three croaked. The voice was not what he expected. It was bright, angelic. Costello lit his lighter, held it close to the reclining speaker. The face was leathery, deeply lined, caked with filth. The eyes were yellow, but the voice was pure. "We come in peace." The lips barely moved. They were thin, gray, dry. Costello fought the spontaneous impulse to kick the Painhead's head off. Who would know? Or care? Peace? The detective almost cried aloud. I'll bring you peace! Five minutes later, panting, he came out onto a street. A street light—still intact, still working—a parked car, a storefront, and a lighted window hinted that civilization still had a root, a toehold, here. He heard, faintly, the sound of barking. And there was the sound of music too. Soft throbbing. A cello, it sounded like. Costello looked left, right. He turned, walked, alert, scanning. The sound of the instrument was louder. Someone was practicing scales. Then the patterned progressions of notes were overtaken by another sound. A scream. Coming from somewhere near. But where? Low, boarded buildings on either side of the street. One of them bore the word MEDICAL, remnant of some company's name. It was a one story building, made of concrete blocks. The windows were boarded up tight. Another scream. No, not from the building. It sounded like it was coming from the street. Within the street? What the fuck? He dashed towards the middle of the roadway and fell halfway into an open manhole. "Hell." The lip of the manhole had caught him right in the gut. The smell of stagnant water . . . or worse . . . enveloped him. His heart raced. He started to push himself up. Again the scream. It came from under him.

He found the metal ladder with his foot, took a step down. "Into the jaws of death descended the Pantsless Detective," he said out loud. Then, against his will, he laughed. He caught himself, became silent again. The last sound he heard as his head went below street level was the somber playing—plaintive and so out-of-place—of the cello. By the time he reached the bottom of the ladder, the sound of the cello was gone.

Below, in absolute darkness, he heard two new sounds: trickling water and whimpering. He reached into his jacket pocket, removed his lighter, made a halo of light. He was standing at the mouth of a circular pipe. Large enough to stoop in. Fetid. Warm. Overpowering odor. Wetness intermixed with filth. He put his foot down into something squishy. Unpleasant. He moved forward. Squish-squash. The whimpering was coming from someone unseen, someone ahead of him. The lighter burned his thumb. Damn, he cursed silently. The pipe soon led to a larger chamber. He could stand upright. He paused. The whimpering came from somewhere within the chamber. He held his lit lighter aloft. Stepped forward. "Jesus." It must be a trick of the light. Before him was the upright form of a standing woman, a diminutive woman. A diminutive woman with a horn on her forehead. She was backed against the wall of the sewer chamber, leaning against it. No, it was not a woman. It was only a statue of a woman made out of some dark substance. But the eyes—wide—gleamed in the flickering light. Her face bore the same expression

Alvin Gremillion's had. He let the lighter's flame lapse, shook his burned hand, took a breath, felt his heart race, heard at the back of his mind whimpering, temporarily forgotten, somewhere behind him. He flicked the lighter on again. Reached out a hand. Touched the cheek of the statue. It was not a statue. A woman. Dead. Still warm. His finger came back brown. She was covered in shit. Waste-encrusted flesh. He stood transfixed, uncertain what to do next.

"Help me," he heard behind him.

Female voice. Young. Terrified.

He wheeled, shined the weak flame against the other wall of the chamber. A young woman, grime-covered, her face streaked with tears, crouched against the wall. She looked up at him, eyes wide.

"Hello," he ventured.

"Who . . . are you?"

"It's all right. You're safe. I'm a policeman"

He pulled aside his jacket and showed her the badge clipped to his belt.

"But how did you find me?" she asked.

"I heard you screaming. I was on the street . . . Ouch!" He had burned his thumb again The sewer chamber went dark. The crouching woman whimpered. He relit the lighter with his other hand, his right hand.

The woman still looked at him with mistrust but took his proffered hand. He led her out of the chamber, out of the sewer, onto street level. There she collapsed into his arms. He sat her down on the curb and she, in a short time, was able to collect herself. He crouched next to her.

"What happened?" he asked. A blister, white and soft, had formed on the thumb of his left hand. He touched it to his tongue.

The sounds of practiced scales still floated blandly on the chill air. Otherwise, the street was quiet, deserted.

"Her nightmare killed her. I can't believe it. She died in the manner of her worst nightmare," the woman said.

"You knew the woman down there?"

"Yes . . . Irma. Irma Gamerman. She was a friend of mine. More of an acquaintance, actually. She wanted me to call her today . . . and so I did. She was worried. I kept calling and calling, but she wouldn't answer so I came over and there was no way to get into her apártment except through the sewer. She showed me that way in just the other day. Just last night. She had forgotten her key. That's where I found her tonight."

"But why did you stay down there?" Looking down at her, he saw flecks of dirt or waste in her shoulder length brown hair. Her clothes and skin were covered in grime. She smelled bad.

"I ran out of matches. I couldn't see in the dark. I was too frightened to move," the woman said, her voice breaking. She put her face in her filthy hands and sobbed. She had been in the sewer in total darkness with the gruesome corpse of her dead friend. Now she shivered with shock and the fear of what she had just experienced.

"My god, how long were you down there?" Costello asked.

"Huh?" She dropped her hands and looked up at him. He could see the paths of her tears through the dried filth on her cheeks.

"How long were you down there?"

"Uh . . . it must have been for about an hour."

"That's a long time to be in a sewer, even without a dead friend," Costello said.

She looked at him, nodded.

"Here," Costello said, placing his coat around her shoulders. "I'll take you into the station. I've got to use the radio in my car anyway."

As they walked back to his car, he asked her name.

"Ashley Quick."

It was only then that he realized that this young woman was the same woman who was a possible suspect in the pet slayings.

That is what a coating of grime and muck will do, he mused to himself. Outwardly he did not betray his surprise.

*   *   *

Ashley sipped her coffee. It was watery. Her hands were still shaking. She had washed when they had arrived at Police Headquarters and the grime was removed from her face, hands and hair, but not her clothes. Her tight yellow blouse and lime green tights were still streaked with filth. And her black combat boots were still spotted with sewer slime which had dried a light, flaky brown. On her blouse was a large button with a picture of one of the men Costello had seen her with at I HATE SPROUTS and the words "Passive Resistance!" She sat in the chair in front of Costello's desk. She shivered though it was warm in the office. Costello had given her his sportscoat to wrap around her shoulders. She had lost her jacket in the sewer, she said. It was late. From the bowels of the building they heard screams.

"Dissatisfied customer," Costello smiled.

"Huh? . . . Oh. That's not funny."

He shrugged, raised his eyebrows, began asking questions.

He did not need to pry. Ashley opened up the spigot of her memories and gushed. She described her previous evening with Irma, the death of Alvin, the sessions with Dr Bentley. Costello nodded as she talked, alternately looking down at a pad where he scribbled notes and looking up at her, examining her face.

"So, both Alvin and Irma died in life just as they had foreseen in their dreams?" he said when she was done with her somber effusion. He leaned back from his desk, turned, and looked out the window behind his desk to the barely lit street below. "And the purpose of your sessions with Bentley is to what? To experience and face your worst fears?"

"Our worst fears, yes."

"Any suspicion of who might be behind this?"

"No. Really. None at all. I can't imagine why someone would do this or how they would do it."

"No, neither can I."

Costello tapped his pen against the bridge of his nose, thinking.

Nothing like a long moment of silence to lead into a new subject. It was late. He was tired. He felt an impulse, went with it.

"Pet deaths," Costello said.

"Huh? Pet deaths?"

"Yeah, the recent rash of pet slayings."

"You think they're connected . . . with Irma and Alvin?"

"Do you?"

Ashley shrugged. "I doubt it. But, I'm not a detective."

Costello nodded.

"But tell me, Ashley, what do you think of the pet slayings. How do you feel about them?"

"I think they're terrible, Detective. My dog, my family's dog Charlie was one of the pets that was killed."

"Was he?" The detective swung back to his desk, looked at Ashley intently.

She seemed less open now. There was a tincture of hesitancy in her voice. Ashley described finding Charlie with Bruno.

"The fellow on your pin?"

Ashley looked down at her chest.

"Bruno Passive, my boyfriend. You know Bruno Passive and the Pacifists?"

Costello did not.

"Why would anyone kill Charlie, Ashley?"

"God, I don't know. They are a lot of sick people out there. My mother has gone hyper-k."

"Huh?"

"Hyperkinetic. Her energy level is multi-tasking. She started that group, the Pet Protection League?"

"Cassie Quick is your mother?"

"Yes," Ashley smiled weakly.

Costello chided himself for having missed the obvious—the Quick connection. He made a mental note: I am an idiot.

"How do you feel about your mother, Ashley?"

Again, the young woman's demeanor changed.

"How do I feel about my mother? Why the hell would you ask that?"

"Just making conversation," Costello said softly.

"Detective Fucking Freud, huh?" Ashley looked off to the side. Her face reddened.

"*Jawohl*, that's me."

"I think she's a bit off," Ashley said. "Her hard drive is a little bit spongy."

Costello nodded, hesitated a moment, weighing whether to move the conversation into a new direction. Then he asked, "So, why would you be out in the Arboretum taking target practice with a bow and arrow anyway, Ashley?"

"What?"

Detective Costello repeated the question.

"How would you know that? Psychic or something?" Ashley responded.

"I happened to be at the Arboretum late Monday night, Ashley. I was on what you might call a stakeout. Good old fashioned police work."

"Oh. I see. So now I'm the pet killer? Give me a break."

"I didn't say that. But I would mention that the pet slayer is fond of hunting with a bow and arrow. Now why, I ask myself, would a young woman be in the Arboretum in the dead of night shooting at the trees?"

"Jesus," Ashley cried. "You find me at a murder scene of a human being and the next thing I know we're talking about pet murders. Don't you think you've got your priorities a bit screwed up?"

Touché, Costello thought to himself, do I ever. But to Ashley he said, "So tell me what it is, Ashley? If you can't find a stray dog or cat, you let loose at a tree?"

"Fuck yourself," Ashley said, standing up. "I'm not being held here am I?"

"No."

"I can go at any time?"

"Yes. Personal liberty is a bulwark of our system."

"Then I'm out of here." In three decisive strides she was opening the door of Costello's office.

"Are you sure I can't give you a lift?"

She showed no sign of hearing the question. She kept walking.

"Try to be neighborly and see what happens " Costello mused aloud to himself. Then he stood, put on the jacket she had dropped on the floor, thought better of what he had asked her, dashed after the departing suspect, caught her at the elevator which, as usual, was slow in arriving.

"Ashley," Costello said, flashing an apologetic smile. "I'm sorry. I came off a bit heavy back there. I didn't mean to imply that you're a suspect in these pet murders."

"You didn't? But you've been following me apparently. Isn't that what you do with suspects? Follow them? Or am I just stupid?"

"Oh, you mean about the Arboretum? The arrow thing? That's just a weird coincidence," the detective said. He realized how lame he sounded. He kept speaking. He could not stop. Sometimes when he just continued speaking his words righted themselves. "I happened to be out there because I . . . I'm a bird watcher. By night. My hobby is watching birds at night. Owls mostly. Nightingales. Other nocturnal birds. In fact, I even like to watch non-nocturnal birds sleep. In their nests. Weird, huh? So, if a citizen wants to fire off a few arrows at a tree—no problem. As long as you're not shooting at a..nocturnal bird."

"Or a nest?" Ashley asked.

"That's right."

Ashley smiled dismissively. "Watch this nocturnal bird then." She raised a middle finger in front of his face. "Tweet."

"I've seen that bird before," Costello nodded. "Frequently."

The elevator door opened. Ashley moved to step inside, but Costello took her elbow lightly, held her back.

"No, seriously, Ashley. My prime concern is catching whoever murdered Irma and Alvin. I hope you can help me out on that."

"My elevator," Ashley said.

"Sure you don't want a ride?"

The elevator doors closed. Ashley and the detective watched them.

Costello shrugged.

"Must be fate," he said.

"Stairs," Ashley said.

"Stairs?"

"As in—where are the stairs?"

"Oh. At the end of the corridor."

"Thanks," Ashley said, "use you later." She strode off.

He watched her walk away, her hips, then he stood, lost in thought. He stood there for a while.

"Use you later?" he repeated to himself.

The elevator opened again.

"Hey, Detective," a voice said. Costello turned to see a uniformed officer stepping off the elevator. It was Patrolman Tatro. He was grinning sheepishly. Costello looked down. There was a dog, a horrifyingly ugly dog, sniffing the detective's leg.

"What is that?"

"It's a dog, Detective."

Costello looked at the young officer. His expression was blank, innocent.

"Elaborate, please" Costello said.

"We found the dog at the site of the homicide you worked tonight, Detective. It was locked in a closet at the back of the girl's warehouse space."

Costello looked at the scarred face, the mangy fur of the mongrel. A closet seemed too good a place for such a creature.

"What are you doing with it? Taking it home, I hope, like the Good Samaritan you are, Tatro?"

"No, I thought of that, but my kid's python and this poochie just wouldn't get along."

"So," Costello said, "why did you bring it here?"

The dog lay down contentedly at the detective's feet.

"Lieutenant Finnerty said to give it to you. Said it was your case."

"Oh no!" Costello said. "Bring it to the animal shelter."

"I called. They're not accepting any more animals."

"Turn it loose on the streets then."

"Detective! And let it be a victim of this nut . . . this animal killer?"

The dog, as if sensing that his fate hung in the balance, looked pleadingly at Costello.

"All right, god damn it," Costello growled. "I'll get rid of it tomorrow. What's its name, anyway?"

"Kitten," Tatro said.

Costello looked at the patrolman. "Huh?"

"Kitten. It's there on the collar."

The detective bent and took the dog's silver tag in his palm. He read the dog's name. His expression changed. He said, "What kind of person would name their dog 'Kitten?'"

"Someone with a great deal of ambivalence towards both dogs and cats, I'd say," Tatro observed.

Costello, the tag still in his hand, looked up at Tatro, asked, "You serious?"

"Serious?"

Standing up, Costello continued, "About what you just said— 'great deal of ambivalence,' all that shit?"

"Uh . . . I don't know. Why?"

"It sounded very good, very professional. Very astute."

Tatro looked at him warily. When he saw Costello was serious, he allowed himself to smile.

Costello turned abruptly, walked to his office. "Ambivalence towards dogs and cats," he said aloud, as if musing, talking to himself. Tatro watched him. Costello was halfway to his office. He looked behind him and saw that the dog was following him.

He stopped walking, half-turned, met Tatro's gaze. "Ambivalence?" he repeated.

"Uh . . . yes. Ambivalence," Tatro said.

Costello nodded, almost turned towards his office, then turned back towards Tatro.

"Tatro?"

"Yes, Detective."

"I too have a great deal of ambivalence towards dogs and cats."

Tatro thought for a moment, then said, "You wouldn't know it to look at you, Detective."

"I hide it that well, do I?"

"You do. Very well."

"Thank you, Officer Tatro," Costello said, then he looked at the dog. He said, "Come, Kitten. We have pets to protect." The dog followed him to his office. When they both were inside, Costello shut the office door.

Chapter 8

Karla Gets Her Horns

Karla lay in the operating room. It was not a white or an off-green room but an ornate operating room done in royal blue and gold leaf. Above her was a spacious domed skylight and the brilliant blue and fluffy-clouded sky of a late-October day, one of those regal days when the air blows so fresh and cool that the earth, that life itself, seems infused with an enthusiasm for living. She was not lying on a table but lying back in what was almost a dentist's chair.

She was fully conscious, but she could not feel the crown of her head. Dr Kidd was working there. She could hear the sound of the drill he was using on the back of her skull.

Karla smiled to herself. This was a dream come true. Dr Reginald Kidd— short, refined, prickly clean, earnest—was the city's preeminent cosmetic surgeon and the work that Karla was having done was on the cutting edge of physical enhancement. Just a short year ago or so, skin dyeing had been the rage, especially partial body dyes which used surgically-implanted, localized, time-released pigments. Implanted pigments were so much better than the cheap dyes that were directly applied to the skin, she thought to herself. They caused flaking and itching. She had tried them, tried them all. Then, recently, more and more people had started attaching horns, synthetic horns, to their heads as the latest fashion statement. All kinds of horns—ram, stag, goat, antelope, unicorn—could be seen in the clubs of the warehouse district. Often the wires that held them to the heads they were attached to were plainly visible. How artificial! How sweaty! But Karla was undergoing an operation that would take horn technology to its next level.

"There," said Kidd in his clipped British accent, "we are all done with the operation. You should have a lovely set of horns growing out of your skull in a matter of days."

"Oh, Doctor," Karla chirped, "may I touch?"

"Of course."

Karla hesitantly felt the top of her head. On either side at the back of her skull she could feel two lumps, two small baby lumps. These lumps were the pods from which over the next weeks would grow two synthetic Brahma bull horns.

"Bland!" Karla exclaimed. "But where are the stitches?"

"Stitches?" Kidd snorted. "Stitches are for kids, for amateurs. I have sealed the incisions shut with a synthetic skin of my own devising."

* * *

"Horns!" Ashley exclaimed a few hours later at Rockwell's. "That is so napping."

"Isn't it though?" Karla giggled. "It puts the nap in napping." She patted the crown of her head. Her blue eyes widened "I think I can feel them growing. I can feel them growing! Ashley, can you feel them growing?"

She grabbed Ashley's wrist and guided her hand to feel the top of her head. Ashley looked over at the man at the table next to theirs who was eyeing them with a look of semi-worry. Ashley tried to smile at him as unreassuringly as she could. It worked; the onlooker buried his head again in his newspaper.

"Well?"

"I do think I feel something," Ashley said, sitting back down in her chair. "But it's difficult to tell with all the bronze stuff you've coated your hair with. I mean it's totally metallic."

Ashley had already related to a wide-eyed Karla the circumstances of Irma's death and the details of her interaction with the detective, although something had made her keep from her closest friend the fact that she might be a suspect in the pet killings. Karla had taken it all in quite seriously and sympathetically, then abruptly she had shifted the conversation to the subject of her horns.

"But what kind of horns will they be?" Ashley asked, drawing her hand away.

"Brahma bull!" Karla beamed. "Big suckers. In fact, the biggest. In a few weeks I'll have the biggest sweating horns going. For a human that is."

"It's fortunate that hats are out of fashion."

"Yes," Karla said, looking a bit lost. "That is an added advantage."

The conversation hit a pause. The two sipped their coffees. Then Karla said, "It's really too unbland about Irma. She might have made something out of herself with her . . . uh . . . shit art."

"Shit art," Ashley smiled, then fell silent. Ominously silent. Karla knew the signs, braced herself.

"Karla," Ashley queried, "how many people do you think there are in the world?"

"Oh billions, I guess. Maybe more."

"And how many of those people die each day?"

"Hundreds. Thousands. Hundreds of thousands? I don't know. Depends how many nuclear skirmishes there are," Karla replied, shrugging her shoulders. "Lots, at any rate."

"Yeah. Lots."

"So what are you saying, Ashley?"

"I'm saying, Karla, that lots of people die everyday and it only means something—really means something—if we personally know the person who dies."

"I'd be sad if I died," Karla said.

Ashley smirked. "Me too."

"But Irma could have been famous," Karla observed.

"Yes, I suppose so. Her art could have been sent around the world—the latest export of American culture."

"That's good . . . uh . . . isn't it, Ashley?"

"No, it isn't."

"No? Why?"

"We've taken over the world with our clothes, our language, our music, our tastes, our styles, our foods, our television. Our horns! The world has become one big America."

"Is that bad? I like hamburgers. I like television and apple pie and baseball and rock and roll which we invented too, didn't we . . . I mean, the Beatles?"

"They were British."

"Oh, I thought they were from British Columbia."

"That's in Canada."

"The birthplace of Canada Dry! How trite."

"But Karla," Ashley said, a little exasperatedly, "don't you see, it's not whether our culture is bad or good? It's that we're eating away at every other culture on the planet. The meal is almost done. The crowning blow would be American fecal art in the galleries of Paris or the shopping malls of Tibet. Our culture is a kind of cancer. It keeps growing and growing, killing the body, so to speak, of every land, every culture it touches."

"But why would we do such a thing? Cancer is not very hefty-hefty."

Ashley thought for a moment, noting with some pleasure that Karla's interest seemed to have re-engaged.

"Imagine cancer in the human body," Ashley said. "Do you think the cancer cells sit around and say, 'Let's kill this thing as soon as we possibly can?'"

"No?" Karla ventured.

"Of course not! They're at like some sort of multi-sweaty business meeting and the cancer business executives say things like 'We've got to expand into the pancreas and the liver. We've got to open a market in the lungs. Bland! Let's open a market in the brain.' And all the cancer middle managers say, 'Alright. Let's get to work.' I bet if you met the personification of a cancer cell, he'd be an optimistic go-getter with a can-do spirit and no idea that his work will kill the very body that he's doing business in."

"Wow," Karla nodded, leaning over the table. "The way you describe it, these cancer dudes seem like the very personification of Americans, at least of what Americans used to be like before the crash and what we hope to be like again. Or what we try to pretend we're like. Or something. At any rate, I'm sure cancer thinks it's nappingly healthy. I'm sure it thinks it's a total health regime for whatever body it's in."

Ashley paused.

"Karla," she said. "I think that's the deepest observation you've ever made."

"Don't expect a repeat," Karla smiled. "At least not soon. My brain is drained." She took a sip of her coffee and looked around the cafe. "Yes. My horns are growing and my brain is drained."

After a pause, Karla continued, "So we're the cancer of the world, are we? But we seem to be in remission these past few years, what with the national economic crisis or whatever. The Year 2009 thing."

"Oh, don't worry about that, Karla," Ashley said reassuringly. "We've been over all this before."

"Many times," Karla moaned, but Ashley forged ahead, a babbling brook of words.

She said, "These past few years are only a momentary domestic setback. Think of it as growing pains. Soon enough, we'll rise from the ashes and continue our insidious, our almost unwittingly insidious, global domination. We can not rest until America—its products, its culture, its everything—pervades the entire globe."

"That's very patriotic! Have you ever heard a march by John Phillip Sousa? I'd like to hear one now."

"No, it's not patriotic, you boring geek. It's pathetic. Someday soon every corner of the globe will be marked by a fast food restaurant serving parents and children in jeans and basketball sweatshirts hamburgers deluxe with special gift cups covered with American cultural icons."

"The McCancer meal!" Karla laughed.

"Bland! And with each gulp those poor foreigners ingest, another part of their own culture disappears."

"So, Ashley, oh great philosopher, the question is: if we are the cancer cells of the planet, what should we do?" Karla asked. "Should we just follow our inclinations and eat away, or what?"

"Karla, if you had cancer cells in your body, what would you like them to do?" Ashley asked.

Karla made the scrunched up face she made when she was thinking relatively hard.

"I would want those cancer cells to stop, to commit suicide, to hold a mass death ceremony. I think that would be napping. A sort of lemmings thing."

"So, you're ready to kill yourself then?"

"Me?"

"Karla, we are the cancer cells. We are Americans."

Karla looked confused.

"Oh yeah, right. What should we do then?"

"We should do as little as possible. If we must be cancer cells let's just hang out and leave all the other little cells alone."

"Do nothing? Rot? Atrophy?" Karla exclaimed. "Why, I think I have that down. Jesus, you've given me a philosophical basis for my . . ."

"Sloth?" Ashley suggested.

"I was going to say something else," Karla sniffed. "My entropy, my bland entropy. And, let me add, Ash, that doing nothing seems to come naturally to you too."

"You've noticed," Ashley smiled.

Karla leaned back in her chair and patted tentatively at the back of her head. Still no growth action. Then a puzzled look crossed her face.

"But, Ashley, what about good?"

"Good?"

"You know, doing good? Couldn't we, aware of our carcinogenic nature, actually try to make the world a better place?"

Ashley looked at her. Karla could only maintain her serious expression for half a moment. Then their laughter, their outrageous laughter, burst out, attracted the attention of all the others at Rockwell's.

*   *   *

Ashley walked Karla back to her apartment. Since Karla lived on a sizeable trust fund, she lived in a very nice spot. There was a doorman at the door. He wore a uniform and held a flamethrower. The weapon conveyed a real sense of security to the residents, though he had only had to use it once in recent memory. Scorch marks were still visible on the sidewalk. They took the elevator to Karla's apartment. Though no luxury penthouse, her apartment on the thirteenth floor was elegant enough. Ashley thought again, as she had often thought in Karla's apartment, that the stereotypical upper-middle class decor—opulence almost —of her friend's flat betrayed some hypocrisy or at least inconsistency in Karla's character. Throwing herself into a plump leather chair in the living room while Karla fiddled in the kitchen, Ashley, for the hundredth time, took in her friend's living space: the luxurious furniture, Oriental carpets, many works of art, and other fine things. Ashley's sense of bemusement was scarcely less than the first time she had seen the apartment many months before. She could never get used to the place, just as, in a way, she could never get used to Karla. In fact, the deluxe apartment was just another piece in what Ashley sometimes referred to privately as the "Karla puzzle." She could break her friend into abstract parts, discreet components, then add them up, but the sum somehow seemed different from what the actuality was. It was not a question of the whole being more than the sum of the parts—not that lame old triteness. As near as Ashley could figure it, Karla was no more nor less than what she should be; she was simply strangely and surprisingly different from what one who knew a great deal about Karla would expect her to be. Who would expect, for instance, Karla's relatively refined taste in art? Here, over the fireplace, was a work by Andy Warhol; there over the sofa was a painting by someone or other—Ashley could not remember the name—but it was someone quite important among the Abstract Expressionists. Next to her, on a pedestal made of twisted metal was a vase which Ashley had determined in previous examinations must be some sort of Chinese cultural artifact. She held it her hands, examining it closely once more. It certainly felt old. And nothing said "Made in China" on the bottom. She put the vase down. She was bored. Really bored. Ashley got up and began to look around at things she had seen many times before.

Against one entire wall of the spacious living room were shelves lined with books, books with rich leather bindings, which Ashley had never bothered to look at closely. Ashley had, however, on many previous occasions looked at Karla's massive collection of records organized in a set of shelves built into another wall of the room. She opened the glass doors which covered the rows of records. Of course, Karla's collection was stuffed with albums that Ashley knew, representing current and recent groups from the music scene—Angroid, Derridahhh, the Punk Panthers, Zip-lock Bugs, etc. But, Karla's collection also contained all sorts of classical recordings. Ashley pondered the names: Beethoven, Mahler, Satie, Schoenburg, Takemitsu, Wagner. What to make of these deep dudes? At least Karla did not try to play them when Ashley was around. Perhaps they were just for show, though something told her that Karla was being honest when she said she listened to them Then Ashley went to look at what she thought the most interesting piece in Karla's collection—the most interesting because it was one of the few pieces of art in the apartment that seemed imbued with any of the spirit of rebellion, albeit selfish rebellion, which formed a large part of her friend's personality.

Dominating one corner of the living room was the massive, antlered head of a moose, which, trophy-style, emerged from a slab of polished wood. The moose, the moose head, was covered with an elaborate and colorful argyle design, except for its eyes which looked like dead moose eyes. Even the antlers were colored with the argyle design. Ashley could never determine whether the thing was a real moose elaborately dyed, or a fake moose painstakingly fashioned out of synthetic mooselike materials. Again she pondered and again she wondered at the words on the brass plate beneath the trophy: "Resuscitate me with tender kisses." She did not know whether this was meant to be the title of the piece or some sort of command. She would not kiss the moose today. It accomplished nothing really, though, she knew from past experience that if you pressed your face against the moose head too forcefully, multi-colored dust would spurt from the moose's ears.

She turned from the moose and stood there, her legs crossed, her chin in her hand. She scanned the room. Ho-hum, she thought, what to do? Off in the kitchen she heard Karla fiddling with something. She heard sounds similar to those that are made when various items associated with the kitchen are used in efforts to do something with food. Those sounds were warning enough for Ashley; under all possible circumstances she avoided cooking as an obstacle to her happiness. Then, from somewhere, some indeterminate place, Ashley distinctly heard a cough. She turned again to the moose and looked at it questioningly. No, not possible. She looked behind the sofa, around a corner into Karla's dining room. No one there. Next to the Argyle Moose there was a closet. Ashley decided that she would open it in a final attempt to find the source of what she was now beginning to believe must not have been a cough at all, but an imagined cough. Yet, the thought of opening the door caused her some anxiety. After all, what if the cough had been an actual cough and what if the source of the cough was hiding in the closet? That probably would fall within the category: "problem." Putting her hand on the handle, she twisted it a number of times without pulling open the door. Then, finally, she pulled the door open. She sighed. See, there was no reason for apprehension. The closet was full of Karla's clothes—dresses and jackets and coats all designed by trendy, expensive designers to look as if they had been found discarded on the street. Under the hung clothes were row upon row of shoes. One pair of shoes especially caught Ashley's eye. They were men's shoes—black wingtips. A pair of ankles, then legs, rose from them. She screamed. It was a scream of panic. She slammed the closet door shut.

"Karla!" she screamed. "Karla!"

Karla dashed out of the kitchen. She wore an apron and the large spoon she carried dripped whipped cream.

"What is it?"

"In the closet," Ashley whispered. "There's someone in the closet."

"There is? Ashley, you must be imagining things."

"Not so loud, god damn it. There's a man in the closet."

Seeing her friend's fear, Karla too became fearful. "Oh my hyperkinetic god. Who is it?" Karla gasped.

"I don't know," Ashley whispered. "Do you have a gun."

"A what?"

"Gun!" Ashley mouthed, making a gun with her fingers.

"No."

Ashley scampered across the room, grabbed the weighty Chinese vase, returned.

"Not that. It's worth a fucking fortune."

"What then?" Ashley held the vase over a shoulder, ready to strike. "I'm all sweaty here."

Karla knocked lightly on the closet door. Knock-knock. "Hello in there. Is anyone there?"

No answer.

Karla tried again. Knock-knock. Silence.

"See," Karla said, visibly relaxing, almost giggling. "No one is there. Let's go into the kitchen. I've made us some perfectly napping hot chocolate." She started to walk back to the kitchen.

"Karla!" Ashley exclaimed. She grabbed the door knob and pulled the closet door open. She screamed. Karla turned, screamed too. Ashley dropped the vase onto her toe, began hopping on one foot, trying to grab her injured foot with her hands. "Oww!" The vase rolled onto its side, unbroken. The plush carpet had absorbed the impact.

Shaking her fist, a rich pink color rising into her pallid cheeks, Karla yelled, "Eric! What in hell were you doing in there?"

He had taken a step from the closet and now he looked at the floor. He was wearing what he always wore: what Ashley thought of as his gangster getup—a dark, severely cut suit, a white silk shirt open at the neck with a bright ascot. On his head, a unique touch: a black fedora. Ashley had never seen that before. It only added to his hideousness. Despite his brash attire, Ashley had never observed Eric looking so humbled, so humbled and crestfallen. The hard, odd contours of his face had softened. He was actually wringing his hands.

"I . . . uh . . . I just wanted to see you, Karla," Eric mumbled.

She stood directly in front of him, on the offensive.

"Well you see me now, don't you? How the hell did you get in here?"

Eric looked at Karla with eyes that glistened with a hint of tears—tears, it seemed to Ashley, which were held back through the full force of will.

"I guess I'd better go," he said. He began towards the door.

"Stop right there, Eric Tang."

He stopped, frozen in mid-stride.

"How did you get in here?"

"The doorman let me in."

"Bullshit!" Karla expectorated, her voice a whip.

"All right! The door was open."

"Lie!"

"All right, all right," Eric said, some of his accustomed hauteur returning. "I picked your lock. Does that sound better?"

"You picked my lock?" Karla repeated. "You picked my lock! God damn you, you asshole. I don't want to see you out on the street and I certainly don't want to see you in my apartment. Get out. Get out now and never speak to me again."

"Are you sure you don't want to offer me some . . . hot chocolate," Eric said. He was regaining his arrogance, his air of being a snake ready to strike. He smiled. His smile was like a leer.

"Out!" Karla screamed. "Out or I'll call the police."

Karla's voice was shrill, her face was red, her hands were balled into fists, but to Ashley it half-seemed that she was watching a scene at a theater, that she was sitting very close to the stage or, through some strange seating policy, had been put, a member of the audience, onto the stage to watch but not participate in the drama. She felt apart from the action as if she could have had no effect on it, then Eric turned his gaze from Karla to her. He looked her up and down. She felt his eyes upon her body and she felt like she was covered with slugs—it affected her that physically, that viscerally. She cringed. He disgusted her and she could see that he saw it. He shaped his lips into a kiss. He strode without hurry to the door, opened it, left without turning back, without closing it.

The two young woman looked at the open door.

"My god," they exclaimed in unison. Ashley hobbled over to the door and closed it, locked it. She returned to Karla. Karla embraced her. She was sobbing, though her eyes were not filled with tears. Short violent sobs shook through her upper body. Then, she recovered. She pushed some toppled strands of bronzed hair from her brow and sighed. "That certainly was unexpected," she said, attempting a smile. Then she picked up the phone, called the building superintendent, and demanded that her locks be changed.

The hot chocolate was good.

*   *   *

Morning light cut softly through Costello's tiny apartment and disorder was all it touched with its clean, bright beams. The apartment was not horrifically dirty, but it was unkempt. Piles of clothing covered the floor of the bedroom; dishes overflowed the sink; newspapers and magazines littered the living room, spilling from a coffee table onto the floor, an arrested cascade of paper. The apartment itself was sparsely and cheaply furnished. The walls were bare and there were no photographs except two, nicely framed, of Costello's children, on his bill-covered desk. Emptied liquor bottles and beer cans and ashtrays teeming with contorted aggregations of cigarette butts covered almost every surface that was not cluttered with something else. Next to a window was his only plant. Dead. In bone dry soil. Costello slept in a tussle of unfresh sheets, his arm thrown over a warm body which, as the alarm went off for the third time, made him hope that he had brought someone home with him from the last bar he had visited early that morning.

"Mmmm," Costello said, hoping that the face before his about-to-open eyes would not be too hideous. But, the face was hideous. It was a dog's face and the dog, Costello remembered, was named Kitten.

The dog eyed him quietly, then yawned.

"What big teeth you have," Costello said.

Then he got up from the bed. The dog rose and followed him on his customary morning rounds. First, the detective stumbled to the coffeemaker and began making coffee, then he lit a cigarette and, rinsing out a dirty cup in the sink, waited until the coffeemaker was done. Then he poured himself a cup of coffee and slumped in a chair at his kitchen table. The dog Kitten watched all this with singular attention. When the detective sat, Kitten began to whine, nudging Costello's shin with his ugly muzzle and looking with interest and expectation at the refrigerator.

"I begin to understand the language of the animals," Costello observed to himself. His refrigerator, opened, revealed a scene of chilled emptiness. What few vegetables were there were wrinkled, molding. These were joined by an old loaf of bread, various plastic bottles and jars of spent condiments, an egg of unremembered age, many cans of beers, a half drunk glass of milk, and the bagged remains of meals from several fast food restaurants.

"Breakfast for the hound," Costello muttered, looking in a grease stained bag. "Look at this, Kitten," Costello announced, taking out a half-eaten hamburger. The dog jumped at Costello's hand. "Well, let's not stand on etiquette."

The dog devoured the hamburger—bun, lettuce, tomato and all—on the linoleum floor. Kitten ate the French fries too, without ketchup. The detective watched the voracious appetite of his unexpected guest with some interest. He was not hungry himself. His alcohol drenched stomach would not accommodate solids until sometime later in the day.

"Kitten," Costello said quietly. The dog looked at him eagerly. "You are an ugly dog. But I am not going to hold that against you. However, I think that we should begin to think about a new name. You're a dog, not a cat. Who the hell would give you a name like 'Kitten?' Some misfit, no doubt. Some hateful miscreant. 'Lion' we could live with, 'Tiger' maybe, but we can't have a dog named 'Cat,' and we certainly won't have one named 'Kitten.'"

Kitten looked at Costello, hoping that another hamburger might appear.

"What shall we call you?" Costello continued. "How about 'Finnerty' after one of the most respected figures in the city's Police Department?"

The dog looked on, unwilling to commit itself.

"Stay," Costello admonished the dog as he rose and walked across the room. The dog obeyed. Standing at the far side of the room, Costello commanded, "Come Finnerty!" clapping his hands. The dog, his tongue lolling out of his mouth, pink and droolly, did not move.

"Finnerty!" Costello purred seductively, bending down, trying to appear non-threatening. The dog turned its head at an odd angle and looked at the detective from the corner of his eye. "Well, perhaps this will take longer than I had hoped," Costello sighed, "eh, Kitten?"

At his name, the dog bounded to him.

Costello patted the dog half-heartedly. Something in the dog's eyes caught his attention. He bent closer. One eye looked dull, lifeless. It was. The dog had a plastic eye. That was strange, Costello thought, but maybe it was more common than he suspected: cosmetic eyes for pets. What would be next? Pet plastic surgery? Kitten, with his missing piece of lip, could use that.

Forty-five minutes later, showered and shaved, dressed in a vaguely presentable suit, Costello was ready to go to the office. The dog knew what was afoot. He followed closely on Costello's heels, yelping and whining. At his front door, the detective picked the dog up, tossed him back into his apartment, and closed the door. Then he turned and walked down the bleakly lit hall, hearing the dog scratching at the apartment door and howling. A prisoner. The sound made him feel guilty.

The day was cool and bright. A cool October wind blew though the dying leaves of some nearby trees with a fresh, whistling sound. The leaves were yellow, red, brown.

Costello was putting his key in his car door when he heard a crashing, a ripping. At the periphery of his vision, he saw a downward blur. He heard what sounded like branches breaking. He heard a thud. The detective ducked, drew his revolver. A second later, Kitten was at his feet, wagging his tail eagerly. Bits of branches and leaves clung to his fur. Costello looked up at his second floor apartment. In the screen of one of his windows there was a large, leaping-dog-sized hole. Costello followed what must have been Kitten's downward trajectory. An indent in a hedge showed where the dog had belly-flopped.

"In," the detective said, opening his door. The dog hopped in and sat in the passenger seat. "I've got a new name for you. 'Stupid'."

Kitten followed Costello up to his office in Police Headquarters without exciting more than a few questioning glances from some of the occupants of the building. In Costello's office, the dog found a place for himself under his new master's desk, curled up, and closed his eyes contentedly, stirring only when Costello walked out into the common area to pour himself a cup of coffee. He returned to his desk, checked his messages—none of interest—and turned his attention to the newspaper. Nothing about pet deaths. Good. On page 23 he found five paragraphs about the dead body he had discovered the previous night in the sewers of the warehouse district. **Unexplained Death in Warehouse District**. He read quickly through the brief account.

No mention of himself.

Ideal.

A shadow crossed the page.

The familiar nasal voice of Lieutenant Finnerty.

"Costello, good morning. I'm so glad to see you're okay?"

Costello looked up and smiled weakly. Finnerty was settling his short, bulky self into a chair in front of Costello's desk. He smiled. Yellowish teeth under a wispy, mouse-brown mustache. Brown hair slicked straight back on his scalp. Bulbous red nose.

"Huh?"

"You're alive?"

Costello looked at himself. "I seem to be. Why do you ask?"

"Because I have just reviewed the paperwork regarding your activities last night—venturing in the sewers, uncovering the mysteriously dead Irma Gamerman whose body, you write in your report, was covered in a substance that you describe as fecal matter. I must say that I was concerned that you might have gotten some of the icky stuff on you."

"I might have," Costello said, "the stuff was everywhere, though my weekly shower has probably removed it."

"A shitty case."

"Huh?"

"It's a shitty case," Finnerty repeated, then he paused. He was thinking. Costello hated to witness Finnerty in deep thought. He knew it only resulted in something unpleasant. Finnerty broke his silence, "But I can't help wondering why our crack forensics team hasn't been able to find any fecal matter on the victim or in the sewer. By the way, it's not really a sewer *per se*, it's part of the city's storm overflow drainage system. Imagine that. I didn't know we had a storm drainage system myself."

"What are you saying?"

"I'm saying it looks to me like your imagination ran a little wild," the lieutenant said. "Perhaps some unresolved infantile elements are moving into your consciousness brought on, perhaps, by your growing alcoholism. You are potty trained, aren't you, Detective?"

"Fuck you, Lieutenant. Irma Gamerman, the whole place, Ashley Quick, the woman I found there—they were all covered in shit."

"Gone now. But not forgotten. At least by me, if you know what I mean."

Costello was stunned. He looked over at the side of his office, not wanting to meet the porcine eyes of the senior officer. He looked at the old useless computer which had sat for nearly a decade untouched, unremoved from his office. The handle of a billy club emerged from its smashed screen. Stress. Oh, well. Near the smashed machine was an electric typewriter on a rolling table.

He said, "So what was the cause of death?"

"Heart failure, most likely. Looks like our gal was scared to death just like the other one you found in the cemetery. What was his name?"

"Alvin Gremillion."

"Yeah. Another head case."

"I can't fucking believe it," Costello sighed. He looked back at Finnerty, smiled weakly, saying nothing.

Finnerty held his eye for a moment.

"Well enough happy talk," the lieutenant finally said. "Where are we on the case, the real case, the pet case? And please, please don't tell me that you're nowhere." Finnerty had indeed switched demeanor. Now he was in a different mode—all business. The pet case had to be moved ahead. Much as he liked to stick it to Costello, he needed a break in the case as much as, if not more than, the younger detective. Just twenty minutes before he had concluded a most unpleasant conversation with Police Commissioner Trump.

"I've got some leads," Costello said.

The dog was lying under his desk, its ears pricked up, its eyes open, listening to the sound of the unfamiliar voice.

"Yeah? Do tell."

Costello told him about what he had found so far, concentrating first on the pattern of slayings to date, his unsuccessful attempts to find known deviants who might match the profile of the perpetrator or perpetrators, and his inroads into the world of pet activists. Then, he discussed Ashley and her midnight target practice, as well as her relationship to one of the city's most vocal pro-pet activists, Cassie Quick, head of the Pet Protection League.

"What's this Quick doing in the Arboretum one night with a bow and arrow and in a drain pipe four nights later with a dead dwarf?" Finnerty asked. "She didn't have her arrows with her last night, huh?"

"No. No arrows. I don't know, but something tells me that she's involved in all this pet stuff," Costello said, taking yet another cigarette from the pack on his desk.

Finnerty looked at him intently. "Let's grab her then. It would really light a fire under her mother's rear end. She's been raking Paninni over the coals."

"You're right about that, Lieutenant," Costello smiled, savoring the imagined reaction of the excitable Cassie Quick. "But the problem is, we don't have enough to really make it stick. At least not now."

"So what have we got, Thomas? We've got to bring someone in. The Commissioner is practically having an aneurysm. He is not a pleasant guy to deal with these days. He's rabid."

Costello waited a bit, then spoke quietly to heighten the effect, "I think I've got just the guy."

"Who?"

Costello told Finnerty about the large leashed man he had seen with his master at I HATE SPROUTS.

"What, the guy drinks out of a silver dog dish?" Finnerty asked.

Costello nodded.

"The dish has the word "Human" engraved on the side?"

"Yes."

"This broad leads him around on a leash?"

Costello assented a third time.

"She looks weirder than he does?" Finnerty continued. "That's beautiful and I love it. He's a fucking domesticated man, a *Homo domesticatus*, as you, with your Latin and Greek, might say, Thomas. A Human Pet! That's what the media will call him. It's fucking beautiful. So let's pick him up. . . . Any chance he's guilty?"

"It's hard to say," Costello smiled. "There's not what you might call evidence. But, on the other hand, he's a more likely suspect than, say, you or I."

"Good enough for me," Finnerty said, jumping up from his chair and pacing the room excitedly. Topped by an oddly spherical head, Finnerty's short, stout body moved without grace. "We pick up Mr Pet. The papers write about his proclivities. We say that the matter is under investigation. We hold the guy for a week or so and we get Paninni and the Commish off our backs for a while."

"But, Lieutenant Finnerty, what if he's not guilty?" Costello asked.

Finnerty stopped dead in his tracks.

"That would be a grave injustice," he said somberly. Then both officers began to laugh. When their laughter had abated,

Costello broached the subject of the two recent murders he had uncovered, both connected with Dr Bentley and her weird nightmare therapy sessions. He began to run through the details quickly for Finnerty.

Raising a hand, the older policeman cut him off, "Costello, you're talking human death here. I want you on pet death. Humans will only get in the way of saving our four-footed friends."

"Lieutenant," Costello importuned, "this Ashley is connected to Dr Bentley. If I play around with this multiple homicide thing, it might give me an opportunity to make her for the pet murders."

"Good point," Finnerty mused, moving to Costello's side of the desk. "Listen, impound this man pet for me and you can play around with all the real homicides you want."

"Thanks."

"Don't mention it," Finnerty said. His attention was taken by something under Costello's desk. "What's that?" he asked, bending at his thick waist to get a closer look.

Before Costello could formulate an answer, the dog itself responded, growling, baring teeth, half-leaping at the startled lieutenant, who, moving almost preternaturally quickly on his short legs, avoided the dog's attempted bite. The dog was poised for another lunge.

"Heel, Kitten, heel," Costello cried, leaping up himself, dashing around his desk, collaring the hound. Instantly, the dog went down on its stomach, quiet, prone. He eyed Finnerty with hostility.

"Who's that mutt," Finnerty asked nervously, edging towards the office door.

"Oh him," Costello said, "he's a witness, you know, in the case. He's here under witness protection."

Finnerty smiled, opened the door, turned back. "And its name is. . . ?"

"Kitten," Costello said. "The dog's name is Kitten."

Finnerty nodded.

"Costello," he said, "I don't want to see much more of Kitten." Then he looked down at the dog, said, "Meow."

Chapter 9

Prisoners

Later that day, the detective and his hound sat in his car watching the apartment building where, he had already established, the man pet lived with his strange master. Costello drank from a large Styrofoam cup of now cold coffee and smoked; Kitten ate the last of the hamburger and fries that Costello had picked up for them both on the way to the stakeout. The dog had a substantial appetite.

The Karen Finley Street apartment was rented to a Ms Devorah Hepple. Costello presumed that she was the same leather-clad person that he had seen with her leashed companion at I HATE SPROUTS. Hepple, he had found out, was a social worker last employed at a local family crisis intervention center and as a guardian *ad litem* for the court in child custody cases. She had left that job more than a year ago. A check of her records had not revealed any professional misconduct, nor did she have a police record. Not having much to go on, the detective had not been able to uncover any information about her companion, the person that Finnerty had dubbed the "Human Pet."

The pleasure of delving more fully into that interesting life was to come later that day, Costello hoped. But, for now, Costello was becoming bored. Stakeouts were boring in general, though two hours before something vaguely interesting had happened.

Two businessmen had emerged from an office building, stood back to back, walked ten paces each, turned, and fired at each other with ancient-looking firearms. Two reports, two puffs of smoke, and one businessman hit squarely in the chest. Right through the tie. He had fallen, writhed, expired. The other had wiped his brow with a silk handkerchief, checked his wristwatch, and returned to the office. Another business matter settled. Costello had not intervened. The stakeout was more important. He had radioed an ambulance which, after the usual delays, had come and carted the body off, leaving only a pool of drying blood. Since then, nothing. Boredom. Lukewarm coffee turning ice cold.

Kitten growled.

Costello looked up at the door to Hepple's apartment building.

There they were.

Hepple was a short, petite but imposing woman whose gait and carriage were almost military in their uprightness. In fact, today she wore a sort of uniform. She wore a stark black miniskirt and jacket with silver epaulets on both shoulders. On her head, she wore a black Bavarian mountain hat, also trimmed in silver. Fishnet stockings and low cut military boots, spit polished, completed the ensemble. In one gloved hand she carried a riding crop. She whacked it smartly against the palm of her other gloved hand, around the wrist of which was wrapped a leash leading to the halter that girded the thick, bare chest of the massive Human Pet.

"That's our cue, Kitten," Costello said. He took Kitten's new leash—he had picked it up on the drive to the stakeout too— and stepped out of the car. His new partner walked beside him, alternately fixing his attention on the pair some forty yards ahead of them and on his new master.

Unaware they were being followed, Hepple and her companion marched on. Though it was a city where the inhabitants had already seen much, this pair drew notice. Pedestrians halted, gawked. People called cat calls or howled from passing cars. The

Human Pet, dressed in skin tight *lederhosen* and a leather halter over an otherwise bare upper torso, growled and made menacing gestures. Hepple did not turn her head. She remained outwardly unconcerned, aloof. Now they were walking along a block filled with small stores and businesses. Abruptly they entered one. Costello and Kitten, arriving soon after, paused.

"Hmmm," Costello read aloud. "Fifi's Pet Beautiful. No More Groom and Doom."

Kitten wagged his tail.

Costello pushed the door open.

"Come right this way, Ms Hepple," a woman in a pink lab coat was saying. She led both hulking pet and diminutive master through a door marked Baths and Shampoos. The door swung closed.

The reception area of Fifi's Pet Beautiful shone with clean plastic and vinyl surfaces—yellow, orange, lime green—twinkling with the brightness of overhead lights. Protection against pet indiscretions, a plastic covering topped a thick lemon rug. Pictures of elegantly coifed, pleased pets decorated the walls.

Detective and dog approached the reception desk. A tall, thin man, stooping somewhat forward at the shoulders, with unnaturally bright teeth, eyes, greeted them.

"Welcome to Fifi's," he said.

Costello sized him up. Fingers, wrists, neck, ears adorned with bangles and jewelry—heavy on the turquoise. Nails painted black. On the forehead the word "No!" was subtly tattooed. The name on the name tag: Basil.

"How can we please you and your dog today, sir?" Basil smiled. Supercilious intonation.

Costello gave him the cold eye.

"Can you keep a secret, Basil?"

The attendant's eyes narrowed, shifted left and right.

"I guess so . . . certainly. What do you mean? What kind of secret?"

"For example . . . this." Costello pulled back his jacket to reveal the badge on his belt.

Basil gasped. "A detective!"

"Shhh, Basil," Costello said, touching a finger to his lips. "Tell me about Ms Hepple and her unique companion."

"Oh, them," the attendant confided, leaning across the counter. "They are sort of unusual, aren't they? What have they done?"

"Gosh," Costello smiled, "you're the detective now?"

"Huh? I am? Oh. Sorry."

"Good. They come in often?"

"Once a week. Every Saturday at 4:30 on the button."

"What's his name?"

"His real name? Gee, I don't know. She always calls him Brutus. But, come on, Detective. I won't tell! What have they done?"

Costello brushed off the question with a wave of his hand, motioned instead to the door to Fifi's inner chambers.

"How long will they be in there?"

Basil consulted his appointment calendar. "Let's see . . . bath, shampoo, conditioner, nails, Fifi's flea and sheen treatment . . . it all takes about an hour. They'll be out by 5:30, 5:45 at the latest."

"Delightful," Costello said. "Listen, Basil. Not a word to anyone. Do you understand?"

"Oh, yes. Yes, I do! This is all very exciting."

"In the meantime," Costello continued. "What about a wash for my dog?"

"Certainly. And what is the lucky dog's name?" Basil's pen was poised to make an entry in the schedule book.

"Kitten."

Basil looked from the detective to his squat and ugly dog. He giggled nervously. "What a lucky dog to have such a cute name!"

"Yes, he is very lucky," Costello smiled. "Now, can I use that phone?"

"Of course."

Costello dialed headquarters.

* * *

Brutus walked with his master and Dora, the attendant, to the wash room. The wash tub was ready. Not hesitating, the large man removed his leather shorts and halter, his leather sandals, and jumped into the hot, soapy water, positioning himself on hands and knees. He knew the procedures, he liked the procedures, and he liked Dora. She always took good care of him. He grunted and bared his teeth happily while Dora slipped on a clear plastic smock over her bright pink labcoat.

Standing off to one side, Devorah lit a black, gold-tipped cigarette, and, leaning against the bright wall, watched with understated approval as Dora brushed her pet. She brushed him thoroughly. He uttered inhuman sounds of pleasure as she brushed his back with the hard, unforgiving bristles. His lips pulled back as she scrubbed his bald head and as she rubbed impetuously behind his ears. Then she reached her forearm into the tub and cleaned his flabby chest and stomach, his loins, buttocks, and thighs.

"Good dog," Dora whispered. "Very good doggie!"

Washing done, she led the man to a tiled stall, sprayed him with water. He nipped at the stream of wet and barked happily. The edge of Hepple's lips curved slightly upward, a smile.

Then Dora dried the man, rubbing him briskly with a rough towel. The room was filled with music: Messiaen's *Quartour Pour La Fin Du Temps*.

A quartet for the end of time.

"All ready, Brutus?"

The Human Pet nodded.

She patted his arm.

"Come!"

Naked, his white skin now blotched with pink, he followed her into another room with a table in the center. The padded table was covered with a sheet of plain white paper. Pictures of pampered pets, illustrating various stages of Fifi's beautification process, hung on the walls in plastic frames. Pet care products and styling instruments sat on a nearby counter top.

The man jumped onto the table, crouched again on all fours. Dora took up a brush, a softer brush, and began to brush his body. High pitched yelps and exhalations, though soft in volume, signaled his pleasure.

Hepple, watching all, beamed and tapped her riding crop against her thigh.

"Very good doggie," Dora crooned. "Would you like a treat?"

Brutus nodded, barked. Dora reached into a basket, held a milkbone in her palm. Voraciously he snatched it from her hand with his mouth and chewed it so that crumbs fell from his gnashing teeth. The sound of his chewing was audible.

"Very good doggie."

She brushed his rear and flanks. Brutus was so enraptured that he sighed with contentment.

Done with the brush, Dora took up her nail clippers and took one of Brutus's hands in hers.

"Have we been gnawing at our nails?" Dora asked, examining Brutus's fingers. Brutus looked away. His eyes caught Hepple's. She shook a finger at him. Naughty. He looked down at the table, contrite. A good pet must not bite his nails.

At the same time, in Fifi's reception area, Costello, pacing back and forth over the plastic-covered carpet, looked at his watch and glanced at Basil who consulted his schedule book for the hundredth time and said, "They're still in the Brush and Beauty room, believe me, Detective."

Finnerty entered the room, followed by a gaggle of uniforms. Directly after the policemen came a television news reporter and camerawoman, the klieg light already on, ready for news. The camerawoman panned the reception area. Basil smiled brightly, nervously, behind his desk.

"Costello, are we ready to go here?" Finnerty asked.

"We should be all set," Costello said. "He's getting his special flea treatment right now."

"Is this somehow connected with the pet murders?" the television reporter asked, leading with a microphone, inserting herself almost between Costello and Finnerty. Costello simply looked at her impassively. He rarely got so close to newspeople. Makeup caked her face and, though she tried to conceal it, an almost palpable, underlying nervousness seemed to emanate from the core of her being. This nervousness pulled at the corners of her lips, made them twitch slightly. Still, Costello thought, she was presentable enough on the outside—an appealing package of flesh and well-tailored clothing, of cosmetics and perfume, wrapped her precariously wired inner state like ribbon and paper might conceal a package bomb. He could almost hear her ticking. It would be amusing to watch her explode.

"Uhh, Natalie," Finnerty said. "Could you give us a minute here, for Christ's sake? You're getting an exclusive. Isn't that enough?"

"Yeah, I guess so. But you promise this is not some sort of wild goose chase?" Natalie Mondrake rested her hand lightly on the lieutenant's forearm and looked down at him intently before she stepped off to one side and stood with her camerawoman. She tied to engage one of the uniformed police officers in conversation. He just looked away.

"Fucking media," Finnerty chuckled. "I wonder how they got here? You didn't call them, did you?"

"Get real."

"Costello, why so grumpy? Anyway . . . when do we put this guy, this Human Pet, on a leash?" Finnerty asked. He rubbed his hands, he chortled, as he spoke.

Costello saw that the lieutenant was pleased with the nickname he had given the suspect and at the opportunities for mirth which this case presented. It was all too much, he sighed silently. Was everyone in charge an idiot?

He said, "Anytime you're ready, Lieutenant."

"Still don't think that this is our guy, do you?" Finnerty whispered.

"I'd say it's a thousand to one he's not."

Finnerty thought for a moment. "Not bad odds, really," he said. "Well let's go. The pets and pet lovers of our fair city will sleep in peace tonight. As will our mayor. After you, Detective."

Followed by Finnerty, Costello moved towards the door to the Brush and Beauty Room. Looking over his shoulder, Finnerty beckoned to the television reporter. Pushing her camerawoman ahead of her, she moved immediately behind the two detectives.

"Lights. Camera. Action!" Finnerty whispered as the swinging door opened before them and they moved into the narrow, brightly-lit hall that led them to Hepple and Brutus. "Film at eleven!"

*   *   *

His eyes were closed. Dora was applying scented flea powder to his face with a soft brush and he enjoyed this sensation very much. He liked it especially when she tickled his nose with the dusty brush. His head was enveloped in a cloud of powdery white and he felt calm.

"Who are you? What are you doing?" Hepple yelled as the unexpected entourage crashed into the private room where she was watching Dora attending to her strange companion. The two detectives ignored her, barreled right past her, followed by Natalie Mondrake and the omnivorous eye of the camera.

Dora dropped her powdered brush and stepped back from the table, while Brutus, still on all fours, opened his eyes and looked back at the door. The domesticated man felt two contradictory impulses. One was to turn and rear up on the table, bark and howl, and then, still howling, to rush the intruders and wreak havoc. The other impulse won out. Resignedly, he lay down on the table on his back, holding his legs and arms suspended in the air. He sighed. He looked at Costello and Finnerty. Standing warily a yard or so from the massage table, Costello and Finnerty looked at each other. Then Finnerty looked at Dora. "Scram," he said. She left the room.

Hepple approached the table now, apoplectic, waving the riding crop.

"Who the hell do you think you are and what the hell do you think you're doing?" she screamed.

"You already asked that, fruitcake" Finnerty replied.

Two uniforms snatched her from behind and carried her from the room. She escaped and reentered the Brush and Beauty Room, but in the brief interlude in the hall she had developed another approach.

She entered with her hands and arms extended as a sign of reasonableness. The uniforms followed her—one limping noticeably, the other with a scratch across his cheek—but just as they were about to snatch her again, Finnerty held up his hand. Hepple and her pursuers halted. She was midway between the entrance to the room and the table.

Hepple asked, "What are you doing with my friend?" Her tone was controlled. She spoke in her strange, slightly foreign-sounding accent.

"We are arresting him," Finnerty said.

"But what for? He's harmless," Hepple said.

"We are arresting him in connection with a series of pet slayings throughout the city," Finnerty said, the glare of the camera light on him. The camerawoman now moved the camera back to Hepple. This was excellent television.

Hepple seemed confused, then amazed.

"You can't be serious. Brutus wouldn't hurt anyone. Or anything. It's inconceivable."

"Just what is Brutus's relationship with you, anyway?" Costello asked. The camera was on him now, then it jumped back to Hepple.

"He is my . . . friend," Hepple replied without emotion. She had reentered the room with a vague, quickly-formed hope that the appearance of reason, expressed softly, might free her Brutus.

But seeing Brutus in his posture of passive, abject supplication and sensing the dispositions of the two police officials quashed any fleeting sense of optimism. She looked at the ground, then at the camera. "I don't think I would be able to explain it to you," she said. "I don't think it would be worth it even to try. Nothing I could say is going to change what you came here to do."

She looked at Brutus and waved goodbye, then turned, brushed past the two uniforms who had been poised close behind her and strode away. She paused only once—when she heard the man pet whimper. She paused, but she did not look back. Then she was gone.

"Brutus," Costello said to the still prone and naked man whose face and upper body were covered in fine, scented powder. "We are going to take you to the police station."

Brutus closed his eyes and shook his head.

"Come on," Costello cajoled. "Up, boy!"

He took Brutus's forearm lightly in his hand and tugged. To no avail. "Here I am on camera," Costello muttered to Finnerty, "trying to move a guy who thinks he's a dog."

"You're doing fine," Finnerty whispered in reply.

"Better me than you, you mean?"

"You get the picture."

Finnerty noticed Dora who, bewildered, concerned, stood outside the scope of the camera which focused on Finnerty and Costello and their interaction with her naked client. She had crept back after being banished from the Brush and Beauty Room. Curiosity.

"Perhaps you can help us here, Miss?" the lieutenant said.

Dora cleared her throat and put a hand to her hair as the camera turned to her.

"Help? How?"

"You know, maybe you can get the Human Pet here to get up and come with us nicely without us having to take more—what you might call—stringent measures," Finnerty replied.

"Human Pet?" Dora asked.

"You know, Brutus here? The guy with the flea powder. The guy you were brushing."

"Is that the official name for the suspect, Lieutenant?" Natalie Mondrake called out. "Is the term 'Human Pet' the official police term?"

"You're not going to arrest me, are you?" Dora asked.

"For what?" Finnerty said, "improper bathing of a head-case? No, you are innocent in the eyes of the law. Can you get this guy on his feet?"

Dora stepped forward, saying, "Well, there's one thing I could try. It's always worked in the past." She took a basket from a sidetable, reached inside it, put a milkbone under Brutus's nose. He opened his eyes. He was crying now and tears ran down his cheeks from his opened eyes. He looked at Dora. His eyes were pleading. He looked at the two detectives. He smelled the milkbone again and he opened his mouth but Dora did not place the milkbone in his mouth; she held it further away, higher. He sat up.

"Good doggie," Dora said.

"Good doggie," Costello and Finnerty repeated.

"Now stand up, Brutus," Dora said.

Brutus swung off the grooming table and stood. She put the milkbone in his mouth.

Costello walked behind the suspect and cuffed his wrists behind his back. He did not resist.

Finnerty took the bag of milkbones from Dora.

"Are you the pet slayer who has terrorized the city's animals?" Natalie Mondrake demanded, moving toward Brutus with the microphone.

"Not now, Natalie!" Finnerty said, stepping in her path. Then he looked over his shoulder at the suspect and called, "Let's go." They walked through Fifi's Pet Beautiful past Basil at the front desk and onto the street. Finnerty led the way holding the basket of dog biscuits. The prisoner followed him, towering above the others with his great height. He walked very erectly. Dora walked closely beside him. She had placed her pink lab coat backwards over his naked front. It hung down barely to his thighs. Close to Brutus, on either side of him walked two uniformed officers. One of the officers had a hand on the suspect's shoulder. Costello followed them and he in turn was followed by the two officers who had tangled with Devorah Hepple. Natalie Mondrake, her microphone extended, the camerawoman beside her, walked alongside the suspect. He ignored her flurry of shouted questions. Behind them all loped Kitten, still dripping from the bath he had been in the midst of receiving.

* * *

Taylor did not hate his job.

Indeed, there were aspects of it he loved. He loved his laboratory. It was quiet and well-stocked with instruments and supplies. He loved his work developing new psychopharmaceuticals and overseeing the production of the substances, the drugs, that were pumped daily into the veins and mouths of the drug users of the city. He liked the fact that he had all the lab assistants that he needed, assistants that followed all of his orders, his commands, with docile efficiency.

He liked the amenities as well. He had all the drink he wanted and, naturally, all the drugs. Fine food and other pleasantries were supplied in abundance. He had women whenever he desired them as well as access to almost whatever else he wanted in terms of records, music, books, and other entertainment. His accommodations were livable as well—a plush enough apartment, an exercise room. But, of course, no telephone, no mail.

What Taylor really did not like was that he was literally chained to his desk. Well, not to his desk. Instead, the laboratory director wore a ball and chain that made flight from his workplace impossible. He could never leave the laboratory and drug manufacturing complex which was secretly hidden within a nondescript warehouse. His job was his life.

"How's that new batch of Confusion coming, Egghead?" Eric Tang called across the laboratory. Taylor looked up and nodded. "Bland," he replied.

At the long tables between Taylor and Tang, men and women in white lab coats and plastic hair nets worked busily amidst glistening metal and glass instruments in the well-ordered assembly line process that produced and packaged thousands of pills or vials a day of the replicators that the druglord Tang produced. Tang stopped at a table and looked at the coded production logbook. He nodded to himself. Then he strolled over to Taylor. Sydney, his omnipresent, flabby, asthmatic companion waddled a step behind him. Tang slapped Taylor affably on the back.

"C'mon, let's have a little talk."

"Bland."

Picking up the heavy ball that was chained to him, Taylor followed Eric and Sydney into a room. The room looked as if at one time it had been a foreman's office. A cube of concrete in the center of the open warehouse, the room was equipped with sliding windows on three sides. Inside there were a desk and a couple of chairs. On the windowless wall hung a calendar from years before on which a beautiful woman stood against a backdrop of too blue waves holding a prosthetic brain implant.

Tang sat in the chair behind the desk, threw his feet up on the desktop, lit a cigarette. Taylor stood. Tang scrutinized Taylor as he had done a thousand times before. It amused Tang how much the researcher, with his tall, scrawny body and nervous mannerisms, looked the part of the ultra-bright, socially inept nerd. He was a true pencil neck. All brain, no muscle. Sydney leaned by the door, his fat forearms folded in front of his ballooning torso. Gold and silver rings, some with bright jewels, adorned his fingers, baubles on sausages. He wore a black silk shirt open to the top of his rounded belly and his neck was ringed with gold. His was an attitude, an affect, of sleepy relaxation which Taylor knew could alter at a moment's notice into violence. He did not like to have Sydney near him, did not like the sound or feel of his hot wheezing breath. Tang motioned to one of the empty chairs. Taylor sat.

"How long have you been with me, Eggie?" Tang asked.

Taylor looked at Tang to see what was behind the question. As usual, Eric's dark reptilian eyes revealed nothing.

"748 days," Taylor replied.

"You count the days?"

"Every sweating one of them," Taylor smiled. His smile betrayed more resignation than bitterness.

"And how do you enjoy the work?"

"I like the work, Eric. It's the hours that get to me."

Eric and Sydney laughed. Taylor was used to their laughter.

"Well, I've been thinking about you, Taylor," Eric continued in his eerie bi-tonal voice. "I've been having . . . uh . . . magnanimous thoughts and I've been thinking maybe it's time to let you go, I mean, to let you leave the laboratory, to let you have your freedom. Trite, huh?"

"Oh, don't fuck with me like this, Eric," Taylor said. He had hoped to make it sound sharp, but there was an element of hope, too obviously hope, in his response.

"No, seriously. You've proven your loyalty and what the fuck? You know that if you ever ratted on me, I'd kill you."

"Scrambled Egghead," Sydney observed, making a whisking motion with his hands and smiling, revealing a gold front tooth inlaid with a diamond.

Taylor sat up in his chair.

"Eric, you can trust me," he exclaimed, his hope overtaking him now, filling his voice, making it squeak. "I'll never say a word. In fact, I'd love to continue my work here. It's just the ball and chain that's a little hard to take."

"Of course, I'd have to pay you," Tang mused, "but that would be no problem. Right, Sydney? We're rolling in money."

Sydney nodded, "We're doing pretty well considering the perma-recession."

Eric smiled.

"So, Sydney, you got the key?" he said.

Sydney reached in his pocket, stepped forward. He dangled the key so that Taylor could see it just above his head. Taylor's eyes widened. His heart thumped. It was all he could do not to reach for it, grab for it.

"Unlock the thing," Tang said. Sydney bent over, inserted the key into the lock.

Taylor's heart was racing.

"Jesus," Tang said, whacking his forehead with the palm of his hand. "How . . . how insensitive of me! There's one thing I forgot."

Sydney took the key out, stood up. The ball and chain were still not unlocked. The fat thug was grinning from ear to ear.

"What?" Taylor whined.

"One more thing you got to do before I let you go."

"What? Anything!"

Looking intently from Taylor to Sydney, Tang described the drug that he had seen in action, that he had experienced himself, at Dr Bentley's nightmare therapy sessions. "Do you think you can make a drug like that for me? Huh, Eggie?"

Taylor thought for a moment.

"Jesus, Eric. It might take months to figure out something like that. The neurological intricacies of a nightmare are pretty complex. It's a lot more difficult than making someone experience a feeling or a mood or even most mindsets. It could take me years. Now, if you could just get your hands on a sample, then I could replicate this stuff without a problem, but I need a sample."

Tang looked at him for a moment.

"Okay, I'll get you a sample. Or better yet, the secret formula."

"And?" Taylor said.

"And?"

"And if I make this stuff, then the ball and chain comes off?"

"Taylor," Tang smiled, opening his arms. "I want us to start to build some trust into our relationship"

Chapter 10

?

Karla was convinced she knew where she was going. Ashley was not so sure. They were alone, walking along a deserted street near to the sodden and broken wharves of the city's exhausted waterfront.

"Here we go," Karla exclaimed in an excited whisper. She pointed to a question mark stenciled in glow-in-the-dark paint on the side of a building. Under the question mark, an arrow pointed them on their way. "Now, just keep looking for question marks. They told me that it was going to be a great party—a truly napping pre-Halloween extravaganza."

"Yeah, ugly, but who are 'they?'"

"You are such a sweathog. Are you programmed to worry?"

"I am," Ashley replied meekly. "Doesn't that make you despise me even more?"

"No, in fact, I worship you, Ashley. I revere you. I've been wondering lately—if you died, could I be you?"

"Sure," Ashley said. "It's easy being me."

They walked on, looking at the dark surfaces of walls and shattered sidewalks.

"Stop," Ashley gasped. She grasped Karla's arm. "What's that?"

"What?"

"Those eyes in the shadows."

Karla looked, recoiled.

Two red eyes looked at them from low in a doorway across the street. The eyes did not move, just stared at them.

"Probably just a cat," Karla said.

"Or a rat."

"Or a bat," Karla giggled.

"Or Eric," Ashley said.

It was none of the above. An animal moved from the shadows, lumbered down the street, turned and entered an alleyway.

"No, really! What the hell is that?" Karla asked.

"It looks like a raccoon . . . or a possum," Ashley said. "Some woodland creature at any rate. Very lifelike."

Karla looked at her companion in the weak light that dappled these obscure streets from the brighter center of the city and from the full moon, round stone mirror to the sun.

"What the hell is a woodland creature doing in this dumpy cityscape?" Karla asked.

"Question marks seem to be the order of the evening," Ashley responded. "Let's forge."

"Napping," Karla replied.

Soon they came to another glowing question mark. Then another. Then another. The marks led them to a pier. At the beginning of the pier was painted a very large question mark, again in fluorescent greenish white. The color of the question marks was not unlike the color of sea spray in the night, although there were no waves and no sea spray in the harbor on this still evening. Instead, the water was like an expanse of plastic film, a huge, black garbage bag pulled taut across acres and acres of void.

"March on," Ashley said.

"Ashley, you seem to have developed a new, more positive attitude towards this expedition."

"My anti-perspirant just started working," Ashley replied.

"Huh?"

"I'm not sweaty anymore."

"Hey, that's the kind of thing I would say," Karla said.

"Well, I want to be more like you."

"No. I want to be more like you. Remember?"

"Oh, that's right."

They walked down the pier. It was deserted. Overshadowing the pier was a huge cargo boat. It looked abandoned. No lights. No hands on deck. Ropes hung from it, binding it to the pier. Painted on the bow was the tanker's name: Morpheus.

"Who's that?" Karla asked, pointing to the name.

"The god of sleep."

"Oh. Where's the god of fucking bland parties, then?"

"He's probably sleeping," Ashley said. "Here's the way up."

The two woman paused before a metal staircase that led up the ship's side. They saw no hint of action on the decks.

"Ashley," Karla implored, worry ratcheting her usually high-pitched voice up another notch, "let's abort this mission. I've changed my mind. I'm feeling . . . seasick."

But Ashley was already climbing the stairs.

On the first deck they saw another glowing question mark leading them into the ship itself. The ship was very quiet. Hands-outstretched, they followed a series of stenciled question marks along a pitch-black passageway. Then, sightless, they started to descend a flight of grated metal stairs.

"Abort mission," Karla whined. "Abort!"

"Hush," Ashley said. "Overcome your fears, why don't you?"

"Oh, are we Doctor sweating Bentley now?"

They followed the stairs lower into the belly of the ship.

"I hear something," Ashley said.

"What?" Karla yelped. "Let's go. Ashley, let's go!"

"Will you shut up? Karla, I've never seen you so scared!"

Listening, they heard a soft throbbing sound, a rhythmic low throbbing.

"Abort mission!"

"What do you think that is?" Ashley said, stepping down

another step or two, coming to a landing. "Sounds like engines. Well, only one way to find out. Here's the door, I think. Let's open it."

A crack of light showed where the door was. The door was ajar.

"Let's not!" Karla begged. But too late.

Ashley pushed. The door swung open before them.

She stepped ahead. Karla followed.

They stepped inside a massive chamber three stories high and nearly as wide as the ship. It was lit by hundreds of candles and numerous strobe lights. It was full of people. The people were slowly moving or dancing to a low, sonorous throbbing.

"Bland," Karla squealed. Her face lit up as the look of worry slid from it. "The party."

"Bland squared," Ashley replied.

"Cubed, ugly."

Here and there randomly along the walls hung huge black sheets emblazoned with glowing green question marks. Ashley and Karla walked to the center of the room through the crowd of dancers. It was hard to make out people's faces in the dim light, but Ashley saw that the partygoers were young people, dressed in the polyesters, the leathers, and the other styles of the moment. Some wore loose fitting garments—they were pajamas actually—with stenciled question marks glowing on them. She saw some people she knew and she nodded at them. They nodded back. There was Dominic from the dreamwork sessions dancing enthusiastically. He waved. What a square he was, she thought. What was he doing here in his sports jacket, khakis, and loafers? She pretended she did not see him.

Karla took her arm.

"Hefty-hefty!" she exclaimed. "Let's dance up to see the band."

The two women gyrated together listlessly, but not purposelessly. Ashley heard snippets of conversation as they moved through the dancers.

"Not Rimbaud," someone said. "Rambo!"

"Have you heard that band called Puke?" another voice asked an unseen companion.

"Reprogrammed?" asked yet a third conversationalist as they moved further into the dancing crowd.

"No. Still sweaty," his companion replied above the sound of the throbbing music.

Karla and Ashley arrived near to the band. The band played on a stage made of packing crates at one end of the long, high-ceilinged chamber. The band consisted of thirteen players all playing unamplified cellos or double basses. It did not seem that they played to any score or even to any set musical conception, but certain underpinnings of rhythm had taken hold in their pluckings, bowings, and strummings, resulting in a sort of ponderous, driving throbbing. They did not play loudly and the effect was not unbearable.

"What band is this?" Ashley asked.

Karla shrugged her shoulders.

"They're called The Droners," someone said. "But, they used to be called The Throbbers."

The two women turned to see the smiling face of Sanford, the agent who wanted to record Bruno, looking down at them. His head was bobbing. He was dancing. Ashley had not realized it before, but now that she saw him standing upright, she saw just how tall, how gangly he was. Sweat beaded up on his forehead.

"The Droners!" Sanford repeated. "You like?"

Karla smiled her sweetest get-lost smile, but then her expression changed to one of genuine admiration.

"Blandest threads!" she said

"These new things!" Sanford demurred.

Ashley, too, was taken aback.

Sanford wore an light orange-brown suit with a formal looking shirt and tie and suede shoes, but his entire outfit—tie, shirt, jacket, pants, shoes too—bore a repeating pattern of gray squirrels and yellow nuts. Sanford joined the two of them, gyrating along slowly, watching the two women with a quizzical expression. Ashley and Karla were not dancing in a standard manner. Instead, they would move disjointedly, then stop as if they were doing nothing more than standing around, then unexpectedly they would move again—languidly or frenetically—for an indeterminate span of time. Sanford tended not to stop. After a few moments, he said, "Come on, uglies, let's get something to drink."

They followed him to a table set with plastic champagne glasses and large etched glass bowls full of a frothy, slightly phosphorescent, greenish liquid. In front of the bowls was a small cardboard sign that bore a question mark.

Karla lifted the elegant glass ladle that was in the bowl nearest her, sipped.

"Nondescript," she said. "What is it?"

"I don't know," Sanford said. "But it makes you feel good."

"I'm all for that," Ashley said.

Karla nodded, poured out three glasses. "Virtual feelings," she said.

The three drank.

"The advantage of The Droners is that they don't play so loud that you can't interface," Sanford smiled. He wiped his forehead with a handkerchief. Again the squirrel and nut motif.

"So what's uploading with the squirrels, Sanford?" Ashley inquired.

"The squirrels? Oh, the squirrel is my totemic animal. My animal protector."

"Come again?" Ashley said.

Sanford crossed his arms, positioned himself in a calculatedly laid-back stance, and launched into a story.

"A number of years ago I worked in an office," Sanford said. "Hideous work. Absolutely hideous. Involving so much . . . work. You know filing, and answering the phone, and typing things. Too much information. I hated it."

"Who wouldn't?" Karla winced.

"And I found in my work that I got hungry every day."

"Didn't they pay you?"

"Of course. But I was spending all my money on a little habit I had."

Karla winked knowingly, said, "Gator got your granny?"

Sanford giggled, replied, "No, not that. Records. I spent all my money on records. So, I didn't have much money for food."

"Unbland," Karla said, pursing her lips. "Hunger."

"So, the squirrels?" Ashley prompted.

"Oh the squirrels. One day as I took the train to work I saw a woman jump up screaming. Her lunch bag had begun to shake on the seat next to her. It fell off the edge of the seat and a squirrel jumped out carrying a piece of sandwich. That gave me a great idea.

"From that day onward I started sneaking into the office lunchroom and stealing people's lunches. Just like my multi-bland scavenger friends, Mr and Ms Squirrel," Sanford explained.

"Is that difficult?" Karla asked.

"Stealing lunches?" Sanford asked rhetorically. "No, it's quite easy."

"Give us some pointers then," said Ashley, pouring herself another plastic champagne glass of the mysterious beverage. "You never know when that kind of information might come in handy."

Sanford replied, "Well, okay. First you must get to know the lunchroom visitation schedules of the people you work with. It helps to keep a chart or a list of the overall pattern—secretly, of course. And it also helps to bring a lunch bag every day, puffed up with paper so that everyone assumes that you are bringing a napalicious lunch. Once you know or you have a good idea that the room is going to be empty, you have to move quickly. Notably, your own empty bag is in the refrigerator so you have a good excuse to be rousting around in there if someone comes in. Then, when you've gone through the bags and taken what you want and tossed the items into your bag, you hightail it to a place of safety, your own private office preferably."

"Then what?"

"You eat your delectable meal and savor every bite. But, not unlike the squirrel, you eat it with a sense of nervous dread, because you don't want to get caught. Be ready to nonchalantly toss the lunch into an open drawer if someone knocks."

"Each bite could be your last, huh, Squirrel Boy?" Karla said.

"Precisely," Sanford said, his voice rising to signal his absolute agreement.

"Rodent existentialism," Ashley muttered to no one in particular.

"Oh, and one other thing," Sanford smiled, looking back over the years. "Don't dispose of the used wrappers, containers, and bottles in your own trash can—that's a dead giveaway. Tuck them into a box or a briefcase and drop them into someone else's trashcan so that they look like the sweat-stained culprit!"

"Ingenious," Karla smiled. "How long did you get away with it?"

"Oh, for about a year."

"And you were never caught?"

"No, I pretended that I was one of the victims and the office put me on a committee to try to find the lunch thief," Sanford boasted. "Silly people. Anyhow, that's how I got into squirrels. Since that time, the squirrel has been my animal totem. It's, you know, napping. I try to live my life in accord with the spirit of squirrels. They're sacred."

"You pray to squirrels, too?" Ashley asked.

"Sure I do," Sanford smiled. "And I eat lots of nuts."

"Trite," Karla asked. "Do you still steal people's lunches?"

"No, not anymore." He looked sad at this loss, this life-change, then he brightened. "I steal people's ideas though."

"Then we're safe," Ashley said. "We don't have any."

"That's not true," Karla said. "Ashley has lots of ideas— about the decline of culture, for example, and how it's best to do nothing or as little as possible."

Sanford looked at Ashley with something like appreciation.

"We'd get along well," he said. "Squirrels like to do as little as possible."

"Like you just said," Ashley replied, "squirrels are a bit too anxious for my taste."

"Why, Ashley," Karla giggled, "if you were to get together with someone who . . . uh . . . who was trying to emulate an animal, what kind of animal would that be?"

"Skunk," she replied decisively.

"Would you like to dance?" Sanford asked Ashley after an uncomfortable pause. "Squirrel to skunk?"

"I knew that was coming," Karla observed.

Ashley said, "Oh, Karla! Look over there. Someone we know."

She walked off. Karla did too, giving Sanford a little wave and a smile calculated to cut, but not deeply.

The two moved to the other side of the immense chamber, the cargo hold. There they found another table with the mysterious potion. They filled new plastic glasses and drank.

"How does this stuff make you feel?" Karla asked.

Ashley stood still for a moment, auditing her interior.

"I don't know," she shrugged her shoulders. "Languid, I guess."

"Howdy," a fellow in a cowboy outfit smiled. He was tall and handsome and his smile was ingratiating and untrustworthy. He looked from Ashley to Karla and back again while maintaining his smile. "What's your mindset?"

"How're you, pardner?" Karla beamed.

"I'm fine now that I'm talking to two beautiful young fillies like yourselves.

"Yes, we are young," Ashley replied. "That's our problem."

Karla eyed her friend, then fixed her attention on the new arrival.

"Problem?" the youngish man—he was in his late twenties or early thirties—said, fixing his thumbs deeply into the pockets of his tight, black jeans. "How's that a problem?" His Western accent was contrived and his intonation, though studied, fell short on certain words.

Ashley considered him for a moment. She replied, "It's because we both want to be old, very old. We find age to be so beautiful, so trite. I mean, it's fall, right?"

"You mean the season?"

"Right, the season—fall, when everything gets cold and the leaves turn beautiful colors on the trees—almost like a second spring the colors are so lovely—but then the leaves turn brittle and gray and they fall, leaving, you know, gnarled and barren branches."

"So, what's your point."

"The point is," Karla chimed in, "that my friend and I prefer older men."

"Well," the man in cowboy apparel said, playing nervously now with the lasso he held in his hands, "I am no spring chicken."

Karla looked at him closely, bringing her upturned face only a few inches from his downturned face. She could feel, smell his expectant breath exuding the slightly medicinal odor of the drink of the evening. She looked questioningly at Ashley, then she shook her head.

"Not old enough," she concluded.

"Not by a longshot," Ashley agreed dispassionately. "You see, we're only attracted to guys who are at least eighty—old, wrinkled men who are sick, and wasted and viral and . . ."

"Incontinent," Karla said. "Though, I'd take a dead old guy over a live geezer any day. You know, a stinky old corpse just sets my blood to boiling. Yee-haw!" She ended her comment with an enthused yell. Her eyes were ablaze with delight.

"Whoa," the cowboy said. "I get the feeling that I don't have much chance with you gals."

"Now, if you were dead," Ashley said, "that might be a different story. We could . . . uh . . . ride into the sunset, if you catch my meaning."

Without another word, the man moved off. They watched him

joining the throb of the throng. He tried to walk like he was bow-legged.

"Yee-haw," Ashley said.

"Yee-haw squared," Karla observed.

The cowboy circled his lasso over his head and tossed it; it encircled a woman and he pulled her toward him. She was un-resisting. She was dressed like a cow and she had long horns coming from the sides of her head. Karla felt at the back of her own head. Nothing.

"Nice horns," Karla said, pointing at the woman the cowboy had caught.

"Jealous," Ashley chided, then she yawned. "I'm getting sleepy."

The Droners stopped playing. The crowd stopped dancing and looked toward the stage. On the stage a man with the at-tributes of an impresario took a microphone and said, "Now, as a special treat, allow me to present a band that is at the heart of the city's music scene—Bruno Passive and the Pacifists."

The audience of one hundred and fifty or so eager party-goers cheered. Ashley smiled. This was unexpected. Karla stood on tiptoes.

"Who's that?" Karla asked, nudging her friend.

A man wrapped in a fur coat with some sort of stuffed animal for a hat ambled onto the stage with an acoustic guitar. The other Pacifists took their places in front of the Droners who remained on stage.

It was Bruno in new regalia.

Sheepishly, he said, "Hi, I'm . . . uh . . . Bruno. We thought we'd play some new tunes tonight in honor of the fact that they just caught the guy who has been going around killing all the pets. Yeah, I just saw it on the television."

At this news, a wave of questions and exclamations moved through the audience. Bruno held up his hand for quiet and went on talking.

"Strange guy. I saw him around at I HATE SPROUTS. Maybe

you did too. It was that massive guy who wears these leather shorts and halter and who drinks out of the silver dog dish with that woman leading him around on a leash. The police are calling him the 'Human Pet,' the . . . the news said. I guess that fits. It looks like he was the one who had it in for pets. Now, personally, I always thought of a guy who would go around killing all these animals as some sort of hunter, so I . . . uh . . . always referred to this guy as the 'Pet Hunter' myself. Now I find out that this Pet Hunter is also the Human Pet. I hate it when that happens. It confuses me. Time to reprogram, huh?"

Bruno strummed his guitar. His band, backed by the cellos and double basses already on stage, began playing softly behind him. The band's drummer did not have his entire kit on stage; he had a bass drum of the sort used in marching bands strapped to him.

Bruno said, "This one's called *Pet Hunter*. I heard it from some crazy kids:

> *Whatcha going to do when you're feeling low?*
> *Going to a pet show.*
>
> *Whatcha going to do when you're feeling down?*
> *Chase that pet all over town.*
>
> *Whatcha going to do when you can't get it up?*
> *Run over that pet in a pickup truck.*
>
> *Talking about Pet Hunter. Pet Hunter.*

The song, short though expressively sung by Bruno, transfixed the audience. First they listened, then they began to dance, moving slowly as if pets in death throes themselves. Karla and Ashley joined the dancers. Seeing the effect of the song, Bruno sang it again and again, adding pained yips, succulent yelps.

His fur coat swayed left and right. His fur hat, topped by some sort of shiny-eyed mammal—ferret, mink or weasel—bobbed.

Ashley felt a softness, an application of concentrated mist on her back. Puzzled, she whirled. A short and pudgy man, in perhaps his thirties but with the features of a dissolute cherub—a healthy pinkness to his flesh, his cheeks, and full, expressive lips—smiled at her with an expression of almost idiotic innocence. He held a can of spray paint in his hand.

"What the hell are you doing?"

"I was spraying you," the stranger smiled. "Not to worry—water soluble."

Pulling her jacket, contorting, straining her neck, Ashley looked.

"What does it say?"

"D.T.O."

"What's that . . ."

"It's my tag . . . 'Dude the Obscure.'"

"I should tag you, you little vermin," Ashley replied, raising a fist. She swung. Too late. Dude's eyes had rolled up into his head and he had crumbled to the floor.

"Bland! You made him faint," Karla exclaimed appreciatively. "That's the power of negative thinking!"

"Not only him," Ashley replied, surveying the chamber. All around the dance floor, party-goers were crumbling or lying motionless on the floor in attitudes of sleep. Oblivious, some of the revelers continued dancing, though they moved even more slowly than before. "Let's get out of here," Ashley cried, grabbing Karla's arm, pulling. She started toward Bruno. On stage, many of the musicians were collapsing onto the floor, though a few of the Droners were slumped forward in semi-sitting positions, propped up by cellos or double basses. Bruno continued to sing. He was singing *How Much is that Doggie in the Window*. Ashley yelled to him as she pulled Karla with her. They fell over a fat, passed-out dancer. Ashley noticed that he was dressed in the costume of a whale, but she noticed that she noticed this too slowly. She struggled to her feet. Her legs felt as though they were filled with sand. Her mind felt filled with sand. She tried to pull her friend up, but her friend, her eyes closed, slipped from her grasp. Unconscious. Ashley turned slowly towards the stage. "Bruno!" she yelled.

Bruno saw her at last. He yelled, "Hey, Ashley!" Then he saw that almost everyone in the room was asleep. "My god, Ashley," he said into the microphone, "I've finally done it."

"It's not you, you idiot," Ashley called. "It's the drink." But Bruno couldn't hear her. He put his guitar on the floor, lay down in a fetal position. His consciousness sputtered like a spent candle, then went dark.

Seeing Bruno lie down was a final slap to Ashley's own tenuous grasp on wakefulness. She stumbled . . . but she did not fall. Some last vestige of will kept her from giving in to the warm, beckoning allure of oblivion. Strewn across the stage, across the floor of the chamber was an intricate intertwining of sleeping forms. Everyone was asleep, except for one person, one man whom Ashley saw approaching slowly, so slowly, from the far side of the massive chamber. He hopped awkwardly over fallen celebrants. Then, he was alongside her. He took her arm.

"Friend or foe?" Ashley asked, slurring her words.

"Friend. Yes, now let's get you out of here."

She looked at him. She could not get an accurate picture, an accurate reading, of his face. She could not focus. Her visual perspective seemed to be jumping: close-up, mid-range, aerial view. Yet, he was familiar to her. Viscerally familiar.

"Hey! I know you," she mumbled as, her weight on him, they moved towards a door at the far side of the huge chamber. "But from where? From when? My hard drive's . . . uh . . . it . . ." Her ability to speak was faltering. She fell down. He picked her up. He supported her weight as they moved, weaving toward the far side of the chamber.

"From a past life," he said. Holding her with one arm, he

spun the wheel on a closed nautical door and pulled it open.
They stepped into a semi-lit corridor.

"What . . . your name?" Ashley stammered.

"Sebastian."

The reply sent a wave of fear through Ashley's midsection.
She lost consciousness. She did not feel herself being lifted over
Sebastian's shoulder, carried through the obscure corridors of
the ship. Instead, she dreamed.

*   *   *

It is her dream, her own dream, her nightmare. She is walking through the Arboretum with her friend . . . Sebastian . . . in
the twilight of a cold, late autumn day. Wet and bitter. It is easy to
see the sky through the bare branches. A vast, gray cloudbank
covers the sky like a tarpaulin of gray dead flesh braced by crim-
son ribs of sunset in this dreamsky.

Ashley and Sebastian! Not children anymore. Adults now,
though he looks just like he did when he was young. Now he is a
bigger child. Under their feet the leaves, brown and drenched,
suck at their shoes as they walk resolutely towards the place. "It
is like walking through oatmeal," she says, smiles. Now he is
against the tree; bound against the tree; in his underwear just
like that day when the little boy had set his clothes aside so . . .
they would not become bloody. A dog barks in the distance. *How
much is that Charlie in the window?* Ashley's little girl voice sings
in her mind. The wind cuts through her jacket, against her legs.

Sebastian looks so sad.

"If you love me, do it," he says.

She has a bow and arrow in her hand. Ready. Aim.

Fire.

The bow string vibrates. The arrow makes a sound as it flies.
It quivers in his knee. Sebastian screams. Blood runs down the
porcelain whiteness of his shin. The blood pools at his feet in a

small depression in the fallen leaves. The blood steams. The steam is vaguely pink.

"Again, my girl!" Sebastian pleads.

This time the shot arrow quivers through his transfixed eye. Blood covers half of his face. She draws and releases again. And again. Many times. The body is full of arrows; still he lives, moaning, begging for more, begging to die.

* * *

She woke. She was lying on her back amidst large, quiescent rotors, belts, motors, engines. There was a sort of dull half light. In it she saw Sebastian crouching next to her, dabbing at her brow with a rag. Cold sweat covered her. She had pissed herself. "Ashley," he smiled. There was a smell to the room beyond the smell of her urine. The place smelled of grease, oil, ocean, and something else.

"Time for part two," she mumbled. Again, she descended into nightmare.

* * *

She is where she has just been.

She is in a room in a ship with large, silent machines. Someone has painted question marks in fluorescent green on the quiet engines. The quiet engines are glossless gray metal. There is a smell in the room of wet decay— oily, faintly foul, like tidal mud. One by one the engines turn on. She hears the sound of liquid gushing through pipes. Machinery rumbles. Pipes, thick pipes, intertwine above her. They are attached to the rumbling engines. From one of the pipes, liquid drips. She sees it dripping to the floor, forming a puddle. There is a porcelain coffee cup on the floor near the puddle. The puddle is brown and foamy. She knows what the puddle is. This is no happy dream!

Now, the smell of human waste fills the chamber. She tries to move from where she is lying but she can move only her head. The puddle grows. The drip has turned into a trinkling flow from the pipe, the waste pipe. The cup is surrounded now by the growing wet. Crossing the floor to within a few inches of her body, the puddle spreads, then stops.

The puddle flows back, back in against itself, a counter tide, and comes together, coagulating at the puddle's midpoint, forming a mound, a mound of waste. The mound is about eight inches high. The smell is overpowering, thick, oily. And the room has grown so hot. The mound turns into a little creature. It shakes itself off like a beaver emerging from the water. Droplets of waste spray from it, touching Ashley lightly. She turns her face away, then turns back again. It is not a beaver, but a little man made of shit. He is all brown. Eyeless. He opens his mouth to smile. No teeth, just foam, yellow-white. In his tiny hands he has the cup and he moves, he stands by the trinkling stream of falling waste and fills the cup up.

Ashley watches the little creature's back. "A shit gremlin," she thinks to herself. "But whose dream is this?" Then she realizes that it is Irma's dream. She is having Irma's dream or a dream based on, an extrapolation of, Irma's dreaming. Nightmare squared!

The creature turns, malevolently industrious. It advances towards Ashley with the cup, now full, in its malformed hands. The weight of the cup is burdensome. The creature teeters, moves from side to side. Now it stands next to Ashley's face. She smells the full force of the putrescent contents of the cup. She screams.

"No!"

A sickness fills Ashley, a primal revulsion which grips at her stomach and she heaves.

*   *   *

She woke vomiting. Sebastian had turned her onto her stomach and was holding her shoulders, her head, a little off the floor.

The room was very hot. Wave after wave of vomit spewed from her. It flowed in hot waves onto the concrete floor. She looked at the place in the room where the beast—the horrible, unimaginable creature—had formed in her dream. There was nothing there but an empty coffee cup on a dry, gray metal floor.

Chapter 11

Dude the Obscure

A conversation in the city.

They were still entwined with each other in softness and warmth.

"I was waiting for this for so long," he said.

"Oh. For what?"

"To be with you, ugly."

"What do you mean."

"I mean for months I wanted to do what we just did, what we've been doing this past week. I dreamed about how it would feel."

"So now you know," she said.

"Yeah, I do."

He kissed her. Then he smiled.

"Why are you smiling?"

"I'm happy," he said, as he rolled off her and lay back in the softness, the cool sheets. He reached out and got a cigarette, lit it, inhaled, exhaled in satisfaction. "I like having you next to me. It's trite."

"Yeah?"

"Yeah. I want to tell the whole world that we're together."

"Oh, that wouldn't be a good idea," she said.

"Why? You ashamed of me?"

"Yes, I am."

He looked at her, tensed, said, "What do you mean?"

"Calm down. I just don't want you to tell anyone. Let's keep this our little secret."

"What if I don't," he said, relaxing again into his toughness, looking back up at the darkness of the ceiling.

"Then I'll have to tell your mother."

Something about her voice had changed.

He looked at her again.

"Jesus," he cried. He leapt from the bed naked, stumbled, made for the door from her bedroom. At the door he turned to confirm, to test the awful thing he thought he had seen. He had thought for a moment that she, his beautiful lay, had become his own mother with her wrinkled, sallow, puffy flesh, her graying hair.

He turned and the beautiful woman again lay there in the tussled bed. She smiled at him archly.

"What's wrong?"

"I thought I saw something, something awful," he stammered.

She said, "You did."

"I don't understand. How . . ."

"All you have to understand is that I make the rules. Now, why don't you come back to bed. You know you don't want to leave me, don't you?"

"Yes . . . I do."

He came back to her, climbed in beside her.

She enwrapped him in her arms and legs. Her flesh was hot. She put her mouth on his, kissed him, took her mouth away, smiled at him brightly, whispered, "My little motherfucker."

*   *   *

One moment his eyes were closed. The next they were open. He was looking at a ceiling high above him. That meant he was indoors. Reassuring. Safe from the vicissitudes of weather. He had a headache. His throat felt like it had been burned. His tongue felt like it was a furry thing, a mouse for example. What would it be like to have a mouse for a tongue, he thought. He heard sounds—breathing, snoring, sighs, grunts. Dude assumed that these sounds came from others, not from himself. He had apparently not passed beyond the stage where he could no longer identify whether or not the sounds he heard came from his own body. That, too, brought reassurance. Gradually, he propped himself up. Around him in every direction was a muddle of sleeping forms. He looked at his hand. He still held a can of spray paint. Snow White. Against the wall directly in front of him was a banner, a plain black sheet, on which was painted a large fluorescent green question mark. Ah! the answer was the question mark and the question mark was the answer and both question and answer referred to . . . the party. He remembered the party. Wild. Over. It had ended without interaction of the coital sort—without mating. Yet again. Losing streak. There was nothing to be gained by reclining where he was any longer. He rose.

Stars passed before his eyes as he rose to his feet. When he was upright, fully upright, he took a deep breath. The room stank with the sweet and sour smell of so many sleeping bodies. Gingerly as he was able, he stepped over sleeping forms, moving towards the wall and the door which would provide an exit from this ship of sleep. One or two of the prone figures moaned or shifted. One farted. None woke. He could not help but notice that some of the women he stepped over or around were beautiful. Beautiful sleeping buttocks. Beautiful sleeping breasts. He felt half an impulse to tag one or two, scrawling his *nom de plume* across an upraised backside. His *nom de guerre*. But he did not. He saw a table with a bowl of the drink, the tasteless, unnamed drink, that had, he assumed, put everyone out. Green liquid. Perhaps a mouthful would exorcise the creaks and crags. No. Danger. Danger, Dude Robinson, he said to himself. Better not.

"Discretion is the better part of velour," he whispered aloud.

Then he cracked up, laughing hysterically before he was able to calm himself.

When he reached the side of the room, the imposing metal wall of the hold, he wrote with his spray can on one of the black banners, below the fluorescent question mark:

> You see things that are and you say, "Why?" I dream
> things that never were, and I say, "Why me?"
>
> DTO

That was a paraphrase of some famous dictum, he suspected, feeling quite pleased with himself. The day was off to a good start, a creative start. He had attained something already and, timewise, it could not be much past early afternoon. That was one thing he did have, a fine internal chronometer. He did not need a watch. After all, he told himself, who was watching the watches? He pulled open the door in the wall, saw some stairs in a poorly-lit stairwell, climbed, attained the fresher air of the harbor, saw that he had been right: the sun was still relatively high in the sky.

He walked away from the ship into the waterfront district. His destination was a little café he knew along the waterfront where he could get a cup of coffee for free. The café was called the Café Trendy-Trendy, a hole in the wall with unfinished brick surfaces and an enormous brass espresso machine which did not work. They made instant coffee instead and lied about it. He plopped down at a table in the center of the café next to a person, a presence, enmeshed in billowing cigarette smoke. A cloud of unknowing, Dude thought.

After a moment the form said, "Dude."

It was a woman he knew vaguely. Mona.

"Mona," he said.

The waitress Dude knew set a cup of coffee on the linoleum tabletop before him. He nodded. The table teetered unsteadily; some coffee spilt. The waitress smirked.

"Did you hear about Jack?" Mona asked.

"Jack who?"

"Jack the painter, you fucking idiot."

Dude had seen Jack around, knew a little about him.

"No. I mean, no . . . uh . . . I didn't hear about him."

"He died."

"Oh."

"Do you know the story about Jack?"

"No."

Mona rose from her table and slid down at Dude's. Smoke followed her. Her face—tight, cadaverous, grayish—looked less like it was covered with skin than with worn leather. Her tongue and lips were grayish too. Unkempt mouse-brown hair—a thicket of micro-thin strands intermixed with smoke—half-encircled her face. Smoke emanated from her dry mouth as she spoke. He had nothing better to do; he listened.

"Jack," Mona said, "was a real artist, and a real friend."

"I'm sorry about his death."

"Don't be." Mona's hands were gray, sharp, talonlike, covered in silver and turquoise rings. Her hands moved when she talked, though the gestures did not seem entirely coordinated with what she was saying. "Jack painted pictures like you've never seen. He was inspired by the Cubists, the early Cubists—you know Braque and Picasso when they were just getting things going."

Dude nodded sagely. "Napping."

"Yeah, napping," Mona smirked. "Whatever the fuck that means. Anyway, Jack . . . this was about ten years ago . . . Jack spent all his time painting in a loft just around the corner from here. Painting and starving. I was a friend of his, like I said, his only friend maybe, and I was trying to get him a dealer, a show, anything. And I got some people to take a look . . . but nothing. One day, he went a bit crazy, you know, despair, and he decided to kill himself. He laid all his paintings out across the floor of his studio and then to kill himself he ingested all his paints. You follow?"

"Yes," Dude said. "He ate his paints."

"Exactly. Anyway. He ingested but he could not digest. Maybe it was the turpentine chaser," Mona said. Her eyes flashed like miniature fog lamps from the whirling smoke that ensheathed her. She waited for something from Dude.

"So what happened?"

"What happened was that Jack puked his guts out. He threw up all over the place. A true Technicolor effusion all over his paintings. Then he passed out. Right on top of his prized canvas—a painting which, I believe, was called *Encyclopedic Remonstrance from a Dynamo* or something like that. Come to think of it, maybe it was just called *Dryad*. Anyway. He spewed all over it."

"Jesus!"

"Yeah. Exactly. A real 'Jesus' experience. So here's the irony. This is the very day that I convince Igor Feeley . . . you know Igor?"

"No."

"Used to be a big deal. Still is. Unlike you, truthfully. Anyway, this is the day that I've convinced Igor to come see Jack's work."

"What happened?"

"Well, we knock. No answer. So we walk in. There's Jack lying in the center of the room, pasty white with a trail of red and green mucus emanating from his mouth and gobs of paint spewed all over his very-well crafted paintings, don't you know? Jesus, Igor simply went wild. 'Puke paintings,' he said. 'This is something of value.' In fact, he was right. Jack's show over at Feeley's gallery was the absolute event of the year, if not the decade. And Jack made a bundle. He was the toast of the town."

"So success?" Dude yawned. "What else is new?"

"What's new is that was ten years ago, stupid. Things happened after that. Jack made a bundle, but he didn't stay with the

program, so to speak. He continued to work in his old style—
perfect, absolutely perfect Cubist paintings though now he had
moved on a bit, borrowing a little from the art of John Marin. You
know Marin—landscape artist. Watercolor. Cubist elements.
Maine coast?"

Dude shrugged his shoulders. "Sure. Who doesn't?"

"Anyway, again no one bought the paintings. Hell, no one
even looked at them. Feeley forgot about his star. 'Not enough
bile,' he said. So again Jack was painting and starving. Starving
and painting. His low profile had returned."

"And then?"

Mona's answer was interrupted by a remarkable coughing fit
which concluded when she spat a huge wad of phlegm into a
paper napkin which she put, a slowly unfolding crumpled ball,
next to her ashtray.

"Then," she resumed, "Jack decided to move his studio, so
he borrowed Feeley's van. Jack loaded all his paintings into the
back of the van. I helped him, but while we were working, we
were drinking, drinking . . . well . . . by the bucketful, actually.
So, by the time we were ready to drive to his new place which,
after all, was only a matter of a few blocks, Jack was absolutely
pothered."

"Pothered?"

"Wasted. Smashed. What a ride from hell! Jack insisted on
driving in absolutely the wrong direction and he insisted on driving as fast and as wildly as possible," Mona smiled fondly. "Talk
about erratic! We had become a mobile, hellbent, accident-seeking
missile. At one point I can remember side-swiping a row of parked
cars. Then, of course, the police gave chase and . . . eventually
we crashed going, oh, about eighty miles an hour into a bridge
abutment and a couple of other . . . immobile impediments. The
top of the van was sheared off and the van itself was crushed like
a . . . well, whatever— it was a horror show."

Dude asked, "Were you hurt?"

"Hurt? Yes, of course we were fucking hurt. Jaws of life, mouth to mouth resuscitation, hospitalization, traction, open heart surgery, neurosurgery, reconstructive surgery—the whole shooting match. In fact, you're lucky and someday you'll see my scars. My physical scars, that is, because, darling, my psychological scars are private."

She shifted a bit in her seat, leaned forward. Dude leaned back.

"You look baffled," Mona said. "That's because you don't realize what happened next. Feeley reclaims his van, see, and in it he sees all of these paintings just completely trashed. I mean, they're crushed, ripped, burned or toasted at the edges and, of course, Feeley has his artistic little orgasm and once again Jack is the star *du jour*. God, people were absolutely dying to have an "accident piece" by Jack Tidball.

"Amazing," Dude chortled.

"Yes, it was. Jack even had the money to pay some of our hospital bills. But soon the *status quo ante*, as we used to like to say back when we were fucking Romans, the *status quo ante* resumed and again my Jack was a pauper, starving for his pure and beatific aesthetic vision, although, by this point—which was a couple of years ago or so—he had begun to add a few elements traceable more to Abstract Expressionism than to Cubism. Arshile Gorky in particular."

Dude nodded. "Arshile."

By now, due to Mona's chain smoking, the speakers were completely enveloped in a cloud of smoke. He waved a tiny opening in the whirling fumes and caught the waitress's eye. She stepped over, refilled his cup.

"So now," Mona whispered, aiming for some sort of dramatic effect. "We come to Jack's recent demise."

"Do tell," responded Dude, leaning forward into the acrid billow. It looked to Dude like Mona's eyes shone like dully gleaming lightbulbs implanted in sockets in the seemingly dead skin of her face. Her lips were cracked and dry—pale, graybrown worms, too long away from moisture, but still capable of rubbery movements.

"In the last few months Jack went into a deep depression, deeper than I had ever seen before, though I wasn't really seeing as much of him as . . . but . . . oh for fuck's sake, why get into that? A bit too personal for present company, no?"

"Right."

"Anyway, I was there when it counted, or just after it would have counted, I suppose, and I saw the thing with my own eyes. Two weeks ago I was feeling, umm, bothered by the impasse that had . . . inserted itself between old Jack and me, so I rang him up. He didn't have much to say and I sensed something was wrong. It being Jack, I just about wrote it off, but then I decided—maybe it was a day later or so—to just pop by his studio. The door was open. I just walked in and there was Jack lying amidst all his paintings, all his spectacular paintings. Both art and artist were spread out on the floor. Rather haphazardly too. It looked like the paintings had been absolutely plucked from the wall and tossed. This time Jack had been more serious in his efforts, I'm afraid. The paintings were absolutely spattered with blood. I mean it was a sort of visceral—arterial rather—Jackson Pollock. Jack had sliced his wrists and sent his . . . his lifeblood over his life's work. God, how white, how pallid his body was."

"What did you do?"

"Well, I took a moment for emotional reaction, of course. Then I got Feeley on the phone. 'Igor,' I said, 'You have got to see what Jack has done. Get your plump buttocks over here with all . . . uh . . . possible dispatch.' 'Puke?' Igor asked. 'Crash?' 'Igor, get over here, now,' I said. 'One picture is worth a thousand words.'

"So Feeley hurried over. Needless to say, he was initially somewhat taken aback. 'What do you think? Igor?' I said. "Bloody, fucking, crowning masterpieces, eh?' 'These?' Feeley said. 'Blood paintings? Suicide paintings? It's been done before. Done to death. It's worthless. I can't sell this shit!'"

"Is that what he said?"

"That's what I said he said, isn't it? Worthless! All of them."

Dude asked, "So where are the paintings now?"

"Oh, I have them."

"Oh."

Dude looked away, looked at the wall, looked at the grimy window, looked at nothing.

"So, Dude," Mona said, "You wouldn't want to take a look at one or two of these paintings? If you're interested, I wouldn't want to charge you much but, as I think someone like yourself might be able to discern with your graffiti art and all, these works will come into their own . . . uh . . . very soon. As investments, I mean. Very soon."

Dude countered, "But you just said that Feeley said the blood paintings had no value."

A green wad of phlegm, an amorphous ball of mucus flecked with tiny dots and dashes of blood, shot from the cloud that surrounded Mona and landed on the floor within a few inches of Dude's unstylish shoe.

"Feeley?" Mona coughed. "What does that pathetic asshole know?"

Dude pondered. "I don't know what he knows, Mona. And, in fact, I suspect you're right. But the point is . . . the point is I don't have any money. I couldn't give you anything for one of the paintings, no matter how much I wanted to."

"No money, huh?"

"No."

"Nothing of value?"

"Nothing."

"No drugs? No Pain, for example? No Love, no Satisfaction? Anything will do. Can't you see I crave experience?"

"No Pain, no Pleasure. No drugs."

"What good are you then?"

"I'm worthless."

"That makes two of us then, you little Philistine," Mona observed philosophically.

A few moments later Dude departed the Café Trendy-Trendy and strode into a warren of alleyways. Taking his spray can of Snow White paint from his jacket, he stopped, thought a moment while he shook the metal ball within the can, and wrote these words on an undefaced space on a wall:

The past was a failure too.

D T O

*　　*　　*

The first thing that Ashley had done after Sebastian had brought her back to her apartment had been to fall into a deep sleep on the sofa in the living room. Now, she lay in a fetal position, hugging an overstuffed pillow close to her as she slept under the gazes of her mother, father, and Charlie, the family's murdered dog, as they looked from the photo which hung prominently on a living room wall. Her sleep had been deep and uneventful, entirely free of dreams. Sometime after noon, she emerged from this sleep, saw Sebastian sitting quietly, serenely in a straight-backed wooden chair he had pulled into the living room from elsewhere in the apartment. He had been watching her or watching over her.

"Hi," she said.

"Hi. How are you?"

"I'm much better now than . . . than I was," she murmured. She sat up, stretched her arms above her. She felt the muscles in her back loosening; a deep breath filled her lungs. "God, I feel dirty. Time for a shower."

"Yes. You go ahead," Sebastian smiled. "I'll make some tea."

As she undressed in the bathroom, Ashley's dread, her fear, returned. Apprehensively she looked at herself in the mirror. She looked like herself—not her best self, but herself all the same. She could hear Sebastian in the kitchen. The faint kitchen sounds, in their simplicity, their domesticity, reassured her.

She did not try to remember the events, especially the dream events, of the past evening. Her mind was set, at least for now, on not remembering. But her mind returned to these unpleasantries anyway, not taking the straightforward route of direct exploration of her memories, but probing, testing at the margins of her horror-filled remembrances. She knew that she had known Sebastian from many years before, that he was a long-lost childhood friend. He also played some central role in her dream, her nightmare, but she could not or she chose not to remember precisely what role. Setting the dream aside, she tried simply to remember what he had been like as a little boy. Her memory yielded nothing and in yielding nothing, in giving forth no image of the past, her mind shut off not only all access to memories about the boy, it diverted her attention from the part of her recurring nightmare in which he figured so prominently. Her mind was blanking him out. "Fuck it," she said to herself. "I don't want to remember anyway." At the same time she was aware that for some reason she trusted him. After all, he had saved her the previous evening. His presence calmed and comforted her. At least for now. And she did not want to be alone.

But, while Ashley could not—and did not want to—bring herself to reconsider her nightmare of the funeral home and of piercing a little boy with arrows, she could and did summon fully to mind the other component of her dream aboard the ship—the encounter with the shit gremlin. She felt sickened by the memory, sickened and ashamed.

She turned the shower on with a trembling hand.

She showered.

Steam rose up around her and filled the bathroom, covering the walls, the mirror, the porcelain and metal fixtures of the sink, bath, and toilet with a slimy sheen. When she stepped from the shower, she toweled herself dry and then, a towel about her body, another around her head, she hurried to her room where, pulling a pair of loose-fitting jeans and an old sweater from the mounds of clothes that dotted her floor, she dressed and left her room.

Sebastian sat in the same hard chair in the living room. He had a cup in his hand and she saw that he had placed a second cup on an overturned crate by the sofa. She sat and took up the warm cup in both her hands. There was something so ordinary in the showering, the dressing, and the tea that her sense of dread, of horror, was pushed to the periphery of her mindscape.

"Do you want to talk about it?" Sebastian asked.

She was of two minds: she did not and she did. So, after some hesitation, she recounted the details of the second part of the dream that had befallen her only a number of hours before. She heard herself speaking. She was speaking softly and quietly. But as she spoke, she felt the drabness of the room and the lack of light. When she was done recounting the details of the foul little creature, she rose and pulled away the blankets which covered the large window which looked from the living room onto the street. Brilliant afternoon sunlight touched her, enveloped her, warmed her flesh through the clothes she wore. The sky was crisp and yellow-blue with sunlight. At the same time though that she reveled in the sunlight, she was disconcerted by the filth which covered the picture window. Turning, she saw the dust which hung in the sunlight, and the grime, the disorder of the apartment. An image of Irma's apartment came into her mind. Its cleanliness. Its order.

"Sebastian," she said. "I've got this overwhelming desire to clean my apartment."

He looked at the surroundings.

"I'll help," he replied.

It took her some time in the pantry, which had become a dumping ground for unwanted or unused things, to find a broom, a mop, a bucket, and other basic cleaning supplies like powdered soap and ammonia. There was no vacuum cleaner nor were there any special cleansing agents, waxes, or polishes. She and Sebastian set to work. First, in the living room they threw away old magazines, paper cups, and plates of half-eaten take-out meals, crumpled shopping bags, and the contents of many ashtrays. Under the sofa Ashley found a porcelain platter filled with beans and hot dogs furry with green and white mold. She tossed it into a trashbag, platter and all. While Sebastian dug into the piles, mounds really, of various things which covered much of the floor, Ashley, her forearms pulsing with the strain, washed the picture window with newspaper and ammonia mixed with hot water. The odor made her nostrils twitch, but the pungency conveyed cleanliness and the window was soon clean, at least on the inside. The view was clearer, though there was little that could be done about the patterns of grime on the outside of the window.

"Look," Ashley said to her coworker.

He stopped a moment to look out the window. Then they both set to work again, working to the clean, classic sounds of Herb Alpert and the Tijuana Brass on the record player.

The afternoon progressed; evening neared. They finished the living room and, working together, moved on to the bathroom and the kitchen. Then, while Sebastian put the finishing touches on the kitchen, kneeling on the still wet floor to scrub the oven and the refrigerator before moving into the chaos of the pantry, Ashley started to clean and order her room. It had never been done before.

The natural light that had filled and warmed the apartment, now that the thick blankets were pulled from off from the windows, lost all its strength. It became night. A few hours after nightfall Bruno came in, entering the apartment by the front door, which opened into the living room.

"Ashley," he called.

She went out to him. Still wearing the hat or headdress made from a stuffed animal, a weasel, perhaps, or ferret, and the ancient fur coat that he had premiered the evening before, and still carrying his guitar, the young man took in the apartment with faint surprise. They hugged, and he was surprised too by the way, the strength with which, Ashley held him.

"What's going on here, ugly?" he asked, pleasantly enough.

"Fall cleaning," she said.

"Who's this?"

Sebastian had come from the kitchen. Bruno looked at him, not warily, not warmly either.

Ashley replied, "This is Sebastian. He's a guy I knew when I was a kid. I just ran into him again."

Sebastian smiled. His teeth were yellowish. He said, "Bruno Passive! What a pleasure it is to meet you. I saw your performance last night. Really bland. Yes. I mean, you put everyone to sleep."

Bruno smiled.

"You know, I thought for a moment I had . . . that I had finally done something so completely, so totally dull that everyone was lulled, I mean, was just utterly pacified, but I think it was the drink that was . . . that delivered the knockout punch. Ha! The knockout punch. Napping, huh?"

"I was knocked out," said Ashley, still holding her companion, resting her head on his chest. "Bruno, I had the most hideous dream, the most viral, vivid experience. I think I would have died if Sebastian hadn't pulled me through."

"Oh?" Bruno asked, looking down at her upturned face questioningly at first, but then, reading the seriousness in her face, he grasped her closer. "I was a little worried about you when I woke up and couldn't find you. Tell me what happened."

"I will. Here, sit down."

Bruno put down his guitar, put down his hat and coat, sat next to Ashley on the sofa. Sebastian sat in the wooden chair. Ashley recounted the dream—or at least the half of it she could call to consciousness—and the other singular events of the previous evening. Bruno looked increasingly worried as she spoke.

When she was done speaking, he said, "This dream stuff is

taking way too much energy. I don't like it. We've got to get . . . uninvolved with it."

"I don't know if we can, Bruno. I think we're in too deep. It's like Dr Bentley said—we probably have to see it through."

"But what does that mean—see it through? I hope it doesn't mean that we're all going to die. Jesus, we've got to think about this. We've got to get the right angle or, fuck, it's the final act of the last days of Pompeii."

"Yes," Sebastian said, raising an eyebrow. He reached into his pocket and pulled out a small plastic medicine bottle. He opened it and shook four sky-blue pills into his palm, placed them on the coffee table which lay between his chair and the sofa. "Behold," he smiled, "Henry James to the rescue."

Bruno smiled approvingly.

"A Jamesian," he said. "And without a fake British accent."

"Too hard to manage," Sebastian said. "Shall we pulverize these and upload them?"

"Yes. That would be . . . uh . . . most desirable."

Bruno rose and went to his room, returned with a piece of glass, a piece of glass tubing, and a razor blade. "Thank god," he said to Ashley, "you didn't clean up my room, otherwise I'd probably never have found these . . . uh . . . holy relics."

"I would have left those things out in plain view," Ashley smirked.

Sebastian crushed and cut the pills into a mound of fine powder, divided the powder into an even number of lines, spreading each, trendily, in the shape of the letter J. He offered the glass to Ashley. She shook her head. He beckoned to Bruno; they alternated snorting the lines until the glass was empty. Both made sounds of appreciation. The effect on both of them was immediate: they sat more calmly, they spoke more slowly, their demeanor became philosophical as if intimately, ponderously concerned with every nuance of thought and feeling.

"Yes," said Sebastian. "Now, you were saying something about some sort of involvement with dreams."

"Dreams," Bruno said. "Ah, dreams. Ashley, you can tell him better than I can."

"Our dreams seem to be killing us," Ashley said. Then she recounted the ongoing saga, the sessions and the fatalities, of the nightmare therapy group.

When she was done, Sebastian asked her to describe Dr Bentley in greater detail.

"It's hard to get a fix on her. She's very austere, very deprogrammed," Ashley replied. "She's very educated, very into her theories of dreams. I'm a bit daunted by her."

"What's she look like?"

"Tall, thin, angular. She wears expensive business suits, always dark, with white silk blouses. Her hair is steel gray—I think it was blond once. Her face is very hard, but beautiful, almost classically beautiful. Her eyes are greenish and deep, like eyes that have looked into the very depths of existence."

"Tell him about the jewelry," Bruno said.

"Oh, silver jewelry, but not overdone at all. And her ring. On her wedding finger she wears a silver skull ring with black jewel eyes. Not a gaudy skull like some sort of motorcycle gang member. Very subtle, very bland, very chic."

"Yes. A bride of death," Sebastian mused, lighting a cigarette, pulling in a breath of smoke. "Where does she live?"

"Hmmm, some tony part of the city, I'm sure. Wildhill, I think; yes, Wildhill. You know, overlooking the Arboretum. I imagine she has some sort of hefty mansion. She fairly reeks of extreme affluence."

"Like you don't know, Ashley," Bruno chided. "That's the neighborhood where your parents live."

"They only live near Wildhill," Ashley said. "They live in the tame part of Wildhill."

"Unwild Hill?" mused Bruno. "I'm Unwild Bill Hickok from Unwild . . ."

Sebastian interrupted, "And your sessions are weekly, Ashley?"

"Actually, now they are once a week—every Thursday—but during the summer they were every other week. They take place in an office building in the Financial District. Very impressive address, or at least it used to be. Now, it's a bit rundown. Most of the building is empty."

"Yes," Sebastian said, but before he could inquire further Bruno announced he was hungry.

"Me too," Ashley said. "But I want something healthy, something that drips with wholesomeness."

"You mean pizza?" Bruno asked.

"Pizza?" Ashley exclaimed. "That is shit food."

"No! Pizza is the food of the gods," Bruno said. "If Jesus were alive today, he'd be a pizza delivery guy, I've often thought, selling slices and the Word."

Sebastian looked at him quizzically, as if he had been slightly impressed by this thought. "Yes. Bland," he observed. He took a joint out of his pocket, considered it thoughtfully. He lit it. He passed it to Ashley, who passed it to Bruno after she had inhaled deeply. Their throats and nostrils filled with the oily-acrid textured wisps of marihuana smoke. When the joint was done, Bruno looked around at the apartment. Gleaming, or at least cleaner, surfaces. He found he could look at one place for quite a long time. The three were quiet. The record player played. Not Herb Alpert for once but another band from a previous generation, The Monkees, whom Bruno liked especially because he had heard that other people, real musicians, had made their music for them. The four members of the pop group had faked their singing, their playing. They had even had, he had heard, nothing to do with writing their songs. Ideal! Bad Monkees! A song called "Last Train to Clarkesville" was playing now. Bruno liked it pretty well, though he much preferred "I'm a Believer" and the group's theme song, "Hey! Hey! We're The Monkees." Bruno hoped that he could someday find someone to play and write his songs, better yet, someone who would even pretend to be him—a show Bruno who could do all the work.

Then his thoughts jumped to the previous evening. Strange scene. All those question marks. That weird ship. What was it—the Morpho? the Maypo? His songs had gone over well. The pet costume. Maybe it was time to change the direction, the name of the band. Something pet-oriented. The Pets? The Dead Pets? The Rorschach Pets? The Bloodhounds? Songs like—"Walk Me to Your Leader," "Bite the Hand," "Short Leash." How about that strange guy, the Pet Hunter? An extraordinary individual, really. Pillar of society, though his penchant for slaughtering pets—troublesome! Gratuitous! Unnecessary! And now they find out that the Pet Hunter is none other than the Human Pet. Pet: the common denominator. Bland! Truth is virtual, not analogue, of course, and truth is stranger than fiction, Bruno mused, wondering whether the dual identity—Human Pet and Pet Hunter—meant the guy was ultimately hunting himself. How tabloid—hunting pets in quest for oneself! New Age, actually. And how about his master? Bruno thought of the woman who kept the Human Pet on a leash, who gave him drinks from a silver dog dish. How he would like to get to know her! What would they discuss? Hadn't that long forgotten group the Beach Boys done a record about pets? *Pet Sounds?* He would like to hear it. Perhaps it contained ideas he could . . . appropriate. Perhaps she—this mysterious woman—might know. Perhaps she had all sorts of records and information related to pets. That was it—The Human Pets. Fantastic name for his band! The Human Pets. This napping epiphany furnished by drugs, Bruno chuckled to himself.

"Maybe pizza isn't such a bad idea," Ashley said.

"I like pizza too," said Sebastian.

"I feel like pizza," Bruno said earnestly. "It helps keeps my inner organs aligned."

She looked at him. Despite the James and the dope, his customary languidly wired energy pulsed though her seated lover. He was thin, wiry, tall enough, not handsome. He was grinning. His front teeth, white and square, showed under his thin upper lip. A chipmunk smile. His was a look of innocent wonder, of complete, good-natured amusement. Bruno put the bland in blandishment, Ashley thought. That was why she loved him. She called for takeout, then fetched some drinks, cans of beer from the refrigerator. The beer was called Cave Beer and was brewed, the label claimed, from a recently unearthed Neanderthal recipe. The three talked on, laughing, smoking more pot, getting along very well. Ashley felt her spirits rising. She had a physical and mental sense of giddiness. She could feel her heart racing, pleasantly racing. Everything around her, the music, the newly ordered apartment, took on a sense of charm or wry humor. She put on Bruno's fur coat and animal hat and sipped her Cave Beer. She felt warm in the coat. The Monkees were still playing, adding in a way to the prehistoric ambiance. She felt the urge to say "ugh." Was it she or her friend Karla who had had the thought of doing cave paintings on apartment walls, she wondered. It had been Karla's idea, she decided; they must have discussed it at Rockwell's. Anyway, what a hefty-hefty idea! Hefty squared. A cinch sack! If she could only find her paints, she could start later that evening. Not prehistoric subjects of course, but scenes of the city—contemporary life as drawn by a prehistoric sensibility. She looked at the blank, off-white walls of the apartment, her grotto. She could see the paintings with her mind's eye as if they had already been painted there.

The door bell rang.

"Ugh-ugh, pizza!" she laughed. Rising, she thumped her chest, repeated, "Pizza come quick!"

Bruno and Sebastian looked at her, chortled. She saw Sebastian had a glass eye. She looked away. It embarrassed her. Why? She forgot about it; her emerging optimism had squelched the onset of negative thoughts at their very inception, she observed, stoned. Like spermicide. She strode, bent over—very Neanderthal—to the door. She pulled it open. "Ugh," she said. "Ugh?" No one was there. Extending her head into the hall, she looked left and right, up and down. There was nobody. Then, on the floor of the dark hall by the apartment door, in the light cast from her apartment, she saw a long, thin box wrapped in shiny paper. Tied with a bow.

"Hey, look at this," she said. "Bland." She picked up the box and brought it into the apartment. The door was left open behind her. The hallway was dark. She set the box on the coffee table in front of the sofa and sat down next to Bruno.

Bruno smiled.

"A gift," he said.

"But from who?" Ashley said. "For what?"

Worry had edged into her voice.

Sebastian, silent now and intent, picked the package up. He held it to his ear and shook it.

"Maybe it's a bomb?" Ashley whispered.

"Maybe it's a box of chocolates," Bruno said. "Here, give it to me."

He ripped the paper off and opened the box.

"Fuck," he said.

"What is it?" Ashley asked. "Bruno, what is it?"

Bruno laid the box on the coffee table which had been cleaned and dusted only that afternoon. Ashley looked. It looked like an everyday box of chocolates, the candies arrayed in neat rows, each piece set in a circlet of ruffled paper. But each chocolate looked like a small stool, a tiny piece of shit. A card was set atop the chocolates.

It read:

> To Ashley,
>   Sweet dreams.
> From "?"

She covered her mouth and looked at Bruno and then at Sebastian. Bruno seemed shocked, Sebastian somber, transfixed.

"Who . . ." she started to say, then she fell silent.

She knew that she was at a juncture at which she could either topple headlong into despair or fight to keep a level head. At this moment, the decision was hers.

The three sat for a moment longer, shocked, unmoving. The Monkees sounded unreal, irritating, but no one moved to shut the record off.

Bruno picked up one of the chocolates, brought it up to his nose, smelled it. "It smells like chocolate . . . what the fuck!"

"What, Bruno!" Ashley yelled.

Sebastian jumped up from his chair as Bruno shook his hand violently.

"What the fuck? What the fuck?" Bruno cried.

"What is it? Bruno, what is it?"

"My hand! There's a hole in my hand?"

"What?"

"Look!"

He placed his hand in front of Ashley. She saw that there was a hole in his palm but she could not see through it. Instead it was a blankness, a dark vacancy, a nothing, a black hole in the palm of his hand. She extended her finger towards it."

"Don't!" Sebastian commanded.

She pulled her finger back. Bruno had turned very pale— almost greenish.

"How . . . how does it feel?" she asked him.

"It . . . it doesn't feel like anything. It doesn't feel like anything. Look, my palm is coming back."

He held his hand out over the coffee table. They looked at his palm. They could see the blankness, the vacancy, dissipating, refilling with bone, sinew, muscle, flesh. His hand was restored.

"Jesus," Bruno said, touching at the spot with a finger, "fucking reprogram me with a joystick."

Ashley felt Bruno's palm. It felt warm. Sebastian sat down again. He felt the spot too. He lit a cigarette with shaking hands. They all sat back in their seats.

"Well, I can tell you one thing," Bruno said. "These chocolates melt your hand, not in your mouth."

Sebastian laughed. His laugh was like an inhaled whinny.

Ashley looked at the box of chocolates. All the other chocolates were gone. Where they had been were little dots of nothingness. Little black voids which seemed to swirl a bit before they disappeared altogether.

Poof.

"No," she moaned. She covered her ears and opened her mouth to scream. But she did not scream. Someone was coming into the room.

"Hey there," a gruff voice said from the doorway.

The pizza delivery guy had arrived.

He did not look like Jesus.

Chapter 12

The Unusual Suspect

"What are you?"

No response.

"A man or a beast?"

No response.

"A man or a . . . uh . . . mouse? Ha-ha."

No response.

"A dog?"

No response.

"What's your name?"

No response.

"You're the sicko who's been going around killing all these pets, aren't you, slimeball?"

Again, no response. Nothing.

"Devorah Hepple?"

The prisoner fixed his eyes on the questioner. Said nothing. He was wearing baggy green pajamas. Prisoner clothes.

"She your master, your mistress, or what?"

No response.

"I bet she likes it doggie style, huh?"

The prisoner's face hardened. The interrogator paused. Then he resumed again the same line of questioning he had pursued already many times through the preceding hours.

"What are you, a man or a beast?" Lieutenant Finnerty inquired.

"Ruff," said the Human Pet.

Whack!

Finnerty reached across the brightly lit square of the table and slapped the suspect across the top of his shaved head which glistened with sweat in the hot light of the interrogation room.

The prisoner bared his teeth, tried to lunge at his tormentor. But he was sufficiently restrained. His wrists were cuffed behind his back; his ankles were secured to the legs of his chair; the chair, a metal chair, was itself bolted to the floor of the room.

The session had been proceeding like this, off and on, for the better part of five hours. Now it was early Sunday afternoon, one day after Costello and Finnerty had arrested the suspected pet slayer. Initially, the police had put the large and—they presumed—dangerous suspect in an observation room. Watching intently through a one-way mirror, Finnerty and Costello and other bemused members of the police force and media had seen the so called Human Pet do many dog-like things. He had whined, yelped, scratched at the door, barked. He had urinated like a dog, propping himself on hands and one knee, lifting a leg.

He had eaten some food from his plate on the floor, dipping his face into the jail food which had been slipped into the room. He had slept on the floor. From the time of his arrest, he had uttered not one word. He had not even uttered any human-like sounds. He had wept, but his weeping sounded like a dog's weeping, not a man's.

"Here, Lieutenant," Costello said, "Let me try something."

Finnerty nodded, looked at Costello, looked back at the prisoner.

"Bad doggie," Finnerty expectorated venomously.

Costello got up from his place at the table. He walked deliberately, slowly around the table and stood behind the suspect who moved his head back and sideways to keep Costello in view.

The seated man looked uncomfortable, uncertain. Too much of the whites of his eyes was showing.

Costello reached out his hand and patted, tentatively, the crown of the Human Pet's head.

"Good dog," Costello said.

A quizzical expression came across the suspect's face. Finnerty looked on, bemused. Costello continued to pat the Human Pet on his head and on his shoulders.

"Brutus," he said. "Good doggie."

The Human Pet's face relaxed. Costello was quiet for a moment. He simply smiled. It was a reassuring smile. Made uncomfortable by the silence and the inaction, Finnerty leaned back in his stiff-backed chair. Then, Costello said, "Good doggie. Do you think you can talk to us now about the things we want to know about?"

"Yes, I think I can, but only if that man leaves," the suspect said. He looked directly at Finnerty.

Finnerty looked behind him, then looked back at the suspect and at Costello. He raised his index finger and pointed it to his chest. "Who me?" he exclaimed. "You want me to leave?"

"Yes," the Human Pet said. His voice was not at all like an animal's. It was high-pitched and melodic.

Costello motioned with his head in an effort to get Finnerty to step to the side of the room. Finnerty looked at him as if he did not understand what the detective wanted. Costello motioned again. Finnerty sighed, got up laboriously, straightening his thick, cylindrical torso which at times reminded Costello of some sort of hideously overstuffed Polish sausage. The two men walked off to a corner of the room and whispered to each other. The suspect, now appearing calmer, looked on, interested.

"Look," Costello said, "I think I might have a better rapport with this suspect if I'm alone with him."

"Rapport. Bullshit. The guy thinks he's a fucking animal," Finnerty replied. "A dog, to be precise."

"Well, whatever he thinks," Costello said, trying to be soothing, trying to be persuasive, "we have a chance here to get something out of him before he goes back into the 'woof-woof' routine."

Finnerty looked at Costello intently. "Bullshit," he said. "Make the guy talk all you want. We both know he has nothing to do with killing any pets. We're just doing this because we got nothing better to do, because it's fun to make this weirdo squirm."

"I know, Lieutenant," Costello replied, "we're just going through the motions, but let's at least make it interesting, hear what dog-boy has to say for himself."

Finnerty looked in succession at the floor, at the suspect—who glared back at him, at the one-way window in the wall, and then again at Costello. He shrugged his shoulders. He said, "He's all yours."

Costello gripped the senior officer's elbow as he started for the door of the interrogation room. Though eager to go, Finnerty stopped. Holding up a hand to shield his words from the prisoner, Costello whispered into Finnerty's ear.

"Lieutenant," he said, "do me a favor."

"What's that?" Finnerty said.

"Have someone go out and pick me up some dog biscuits."

"What?"

"Dog biscuits. I think they could really help move things along."

"Now you think I'm an animal too," Finnerty whispered.

"What?"

"Yeah, a friggin' gopher."

"Please. Humor me. Dog biscuits."

The door shut as Finnerty left and Costello returned to the suspect. He looked at the one-way mirror and he knew there were unseen eyes, Finnerty's no doubt among them, watching how he was going to handle this unusual challenge. He did not have much of an idea himself. He said, "How would you like me to remove your handcuffs?"

The Human Pet looked at him and said nothing.

Costello smiled again the smile the suspect had apparently found so reassuring before. He repeated, "Handcuffs?"

The big man nodded. Costello walked behind him and opened and removed the handcuffs on the suspect's wrists. He tossed them on the table in front of the seated man. They clattered there and shone in the bright overhead light. The prisoner took his large arms from behind him and, lifting them slowly, rested them on he table. He rubbed both his wrists with his hands. His wrists were red and chafed from the cuffs.

"Now, perhaps," Costello smiled, "we can start again? What is your name?"

The suspect made no response.

"Where do you live?"

Again, no response.

"Damn it," Costello swore softly, "haven't we been through this? Do you want the other policeman in here? Lieutenant Insensitive?"

A look of worry played around the Human Pet's eyes. His face muscles tightened.

"No," he said.

"Good. What is your name?"

A long pause. Costello could feel the eyes of his hidden audience from behind the mirror.

Finally, "Morris."

"That's more like it. Morris what?"

"Morris Tantone."

"And where are you from, Morris?"

"I live here in the city."

"What's your address?"

"I don't know. It's an apartment on Finley Street."

"And you live with Devorah Hepple?" Costello asked as he returned to the other side of the interrogation table and sat down.

The Human Pet sighed, "Yes. Yes, I do."

"And how would you characterize your relationship with Ms Hepple?"

The Pet fell silent, then he shrugged his shoulders and said, "I'm her pet. She is my master."

Costello tried not to overreact to this frank admission. He said, "Oh, that's very interesting. I've never heard of that before."

"No," the suspect said, seeming almost relaxed now, "I don't imagine someone like you can imagine the relationship I have with Devorah. Don't take it personally—I don't think that many people could. That's how narrow-minded and callous the world is."

Costello leaned back in his chair, crossing one leg easily over the other, lit a cigarette, after offering one to the Pet—the Pet declined—and said, "Well, tell me a little bit about that. This is interesting to me. What is it like to be on the one hand a human being, on the other hand to be . . . someone's pet?"

"It's nice. I like it," Morris said.

"Does Devorah call you Morris?"

"No. She has other names for me."

"Like what?"

"Brutus mostly or . . . Killer," Morris said after a pause.

"Oh, she calls you Killer. Why would she call you Killer?"

"I don't know. Perhaps it's because I'm so big and strong."

"It's not because you . . . uh . . . like to kill things?"

"No. I don't like killing things."

"So, you have killed before?"

"No."

"Then how do you know you don't like it?"

"Because I just don't think it's part of my psychological profile, that's all." Morris was getting testy; Costello backed off.

"What's your favorite name, Morris?"

"I guess it's 'Brutus.' What's your favorite name, Detective?"

"I guess it's 'Tom.'"

There was a knock on the door. A young patrolman in an unkempt uniform with acne scars on his face and wavy blond hair came in with a bag, a grocery bag, and put it on the table in front of Costello.

"Here you go, Detective," the Patrolman said. He looked at Morris Tantone warily and then hurried from the room.

"It looks like people are afraid of you. That's what it looks like to me, Morris," Costello said.

"I think they are," the suspect said, "but I can't imagine why they would be."

"Well," Costello chuckled, "you have to imagine that it's a little hard to absorb—a big guy like you in a leather halter and leather shorts and leather boots, a studded dog collar, a leash, being walked by a very formidable looking person. Devorah. Your master."

"Well, I wouldn't know how most people feel. I guess I'm not that knowledgeable about how most people feel."

"You probably don't like to talk about your feelings very much, do you?" Costello said.

"No."

"Good, neither do I. I hate talking about feelings."

"So do I."

"So, Morris, when you're back at your house, back at your apartment, what kind of things do you do. How do you spend the day?"

"I do the kind of things any pet does," Morris said. "I lie around mostly, I go for walks, I eat, sometimes I play."

"Play, huh? What do you play?"

"Oh, sometimes I play 'go fetch,' or sometimes when it's warm I like to bury a bone in the park."

"A bone huh? What kind of bone?"

"Steak bone, soup bone. Devorah gives me bones. I like to gnaw on them."

Costello paused for a moment and then asked, "Do you ever have the urge to chase someone or something? Do you ever have the urge to chase a car, for example?"

"You mean like a car on the street? A car that speeds by?"

"Yes."

"No, I haven't had that kind of urge since I was a young pup."

"Aww, you can't tell me that you've been doing this ever since you were a kid? Ever since you were born?"

"No, more like five or six years. But I consider that period of five or six years ago to be the period when I was a young pet. Now I'm an older pet. In dog years I'm almost forty-two."

"How do you figure that."

"Six times seven."

"How old are you in human years?"

"Thirty-one."

"So you never chase cars. Do you ever have the urge to bite someone, to attack someone? To growl at them even?"

"Not usually, no, but when someone is rude to Devorah or threatens her or gets too close to her, then I want to protect her."

"Do you think that's jealousy on your part?" Costello asked.

"I thought we weren't going to talk about feelings."

"My mistake," Costello smiled. "Let's continue. Do you ever get in fights with . . . other dogs? Dog fights?"

"I've gotten into a scrap or two. It's hard not to. A big dog sees you on the street and wants to fight you for bragging rights."

"What's the biggest dog you've ever tangled with?"

"Oh, I guess it was a large German Shepherd in the park one day."

"What did you do?"

"I bit him pretty good and he ran off with his tail between his legs."

"You didn't feel like chasing him?"

"I did, but Devorah told me to stay."

"So tell me truthfully—you know sometimes how dogs go wild and they kill another animal, or they have a fight with another animal, and the wolf—that's what they say—the wolf comes out in them . . . or that's how they describe it at least—the wolf comes out in them?"

"Yes."

"Has that ever happened to you? Where the thrill of the hunt, the kill, overcame you?"

"No. If you're asking if I'm the guy going around town killing all these pets, it's not me."

"Oh. How'd you know about that?"

"Devorah told me. She was worried that I might be hurt."

Costello reached into the grocery bag and took out the bag of dog biscuits. He set it on the table between himself and the unusual suspect. Taking a pocket knife from his jacket, unfolding the blade, he slit open the top of the bag, closed up the knife, replaced it in his jacket. He reached his hand in the bag and took out a handful of dog biscuits. They were muted brown, red, and green in color and shaped like little bones. He handed one to Morris and said, "Have a snack."

"Thank you."

Morris took the biscuit, put the whole thing in his mouth. Costello heard the sounds of Morris's teeth, his jaws, working on the hard biscuit. His jaw cracked when he ate. In a matter of twenty seconds, the action of Morris's mouth had ceased and he had swallowed the biscuit.

"Like another?" Costello asked.

"Yes, thank you. You know, Detective, you should try one. They're pretty good. And they're very good for your teeth, very good for your bones. And also, I'm told, this particular brand is very good for the sheen of your fur or, I suppose in your case, for your hair."

Costello's eyes opened a bit wider. He patted his thinning scalp. He looked at one of the biscuits in his hand and said, "What the hell?" He nibbled a corner off a biscuit. It tasted like straw mixed with plaster, but it was edible. A human, he thought to himself, could live on these things maybe as healthily as he, Costello himself, was living now. Dog biscuits and vodka—that would give 'hair of the dog that bit you' new meaning, he thought as he took another, larger bite. Outside the room, Finnerty and the others who were watching the interrogation could not believe what they were seeing.

"Jesus," Finnerty said, "now I've seen fucking everything."

"Bet he can't eat just one," someone else observed.

As he munched another biscuit, Morris looked around the interrogation room. He said, "Detective, do you have any pets?"

Costello said, "No. I mean, yes. I mean, I've got an animal staying with me now."

Morris looked at him with a blank expression.

"Sort of a temporary thing, Detective?"

"Yes. I guess so," Costello said.

"Hmm, that's interesting. Dog?"

"Yeah, dog."

"What's its name?"

"Kitten."

"Kitten?"

"Yes. Never mind what its name is," Costello said. "Let's talk about you."

"There's not much to say."

"For starters, Morris, why don't you tell me what you know about this rash of pet murders that's been going on throughout the city?"

"It's frightening. I'm scared. I could be a victim."

"But tell me, what do you know about it? Who do you think is doing it?"

Morris said nothing for a moment. Then he said, "I've seen the guy who does it. I saw him late one night at the Arboretum."

Costello leaned intently across the table.

"Tell me about him. Tell me about what you saw. But first of all, tell me why you were at the Arboretum."

"Sometimes Devorah lets me out of the house at night so I can run through the Arboretum. I've got some favorite places there, places where I bury my bones. I like the quiet of the night when there's no one else around. It helps me to forget that . . . well, that I am what I am."

"So tell me about this . . . this guy you saw."

"Well, I didn't get very close to him. He was down at the bottom of a hill. He was wearing strange clothing. He was bulky like he was wearing some kind of fur coat, or skin."

"You mean like an animal skin?"

"Yes, at least that's what it looked like. And he was carrying a spear and I think I saw a metal trashcan lid too. He was carrying it like it was some kind of shield. He was moving very slowly and he would stop every few feet and move his head like he was sniffing the air. Like he was hunting."

"What happened next?"

"He started to climb the hill where I was."

"What did you do?"

"I turned around and ran. I was scared. I thought he was chasing me. I heard footsteps, branches breaking."

The same patrolman who had brought the dog biscuits opened the door to the interrogation room.

"Detective," he said, "there's someone here to see you. A Ms Hepple and some guy. Looks like a lawyer."

The patrolman stood there as if he expected some kind of reply.

Costello looked at him, rolled his eyes, snarled softly, "You can go now."

The patrolman stiffened, nodded, took a sidelong glance at the Human Pet, left, while Costello looked across the table at the suspect and saw Morris's expression transform from that of someone relating a frightening story which just might be true to the same blank, bestial stare he had worn only twenty minutes before.

"Devorah. Devorah's here," Morris muttered. He stood up. He tried to move away from his chair but the leg cuffs constrained him. He yelled, "Devorah! Devorah!" Reaching down, he tried to pull the chair from its bolts. When he could not do this, he started to pound on the table with clenched fists, shouting,

"Devorah! I'm in here. Devorah! Come get me out of here." His face became red.

Costello said, "Calm down, Morris. Calm down."

But it was too late. Morris was howling.

Finnerty and two patrolmen rushed into the interrogation room.

Finnerty yelled, "Shut the fuck up, asshole."

Since his legs were anchored, the Human Pet turned his upper body as far as he could and faced Finnerty. He tried to lunge at him, bite him, hit him, grab him with his hands. He bared his teeth. He drooled. He tried again to lunge, his eyes bulging in his contorted face. Finnerty's eyes widened too. Screaming obscenities, he adopted a defensive stance and then laughed excitedly—almost hysterically—at the confrontation. Positioning themselves behind Morris, each of the patrolmen grabbed one of his flailing arms and, twisting them behind his back through brute force, pulled him back down into a sitting position. Now Morris screamed. He had become an animal who had never before uttered words, never before thought in words; his scream was thoughtless, pure. His eyes were white and wide. Looking at him, Costello saw the prisoner as something other than a human being. This man had shed his humanity. The detective felt the hair rise on the back of his neck, on his wrists and forearms. Finnerty slipped a pair of handcuffs onto the man-pet's wrists; then he attached a second set of handcuffs—fastening one handcuff to the suspect's left wrist, another to the left rear leg of the chair.

"This way you won't get up again," Finnerty said. He laughed.

The patrolmen and Costello looked at the lieutenant, their interest piqued by his laughter which, high-pitched and extreme, sounded like the staged laughter of a madman in a pathetically bad horror movie. Then, no longer laughing, Finnerty stood at the side of the Human Pet and looked at him menacingly. He slapped him across the face. "Bad doggie." He hit him again, this time with a closed fist, hard, right in the nose.

Morris yelped.

Blood poured from his nose over his mouth and chin onto his chest, streaking across his green prisoner's shirt.

"Bad doggie," Finnerty screamed.

The Human Pet opened his mouth wide and screamed too.

"Fuck," Finnerty said. "This has been a very unpleasant experience."

The lieutenant took a handkerchief out of his pocket and mopped his large, rounded brow. His barrel chest heaved. It took him a minute to catch his breath. Then to the two patrolmen he commanded, "You two. Watch this guy."

"Yes, sir."

"Costello, let's go meet this bitch, this Devorah."

The two interrogators left the room. In the hallway they could still hear the howling and barking, the ill-formed cries. As they walked away from the interview room, the sounds receded until, by the time they got to the front of the station, the outbursts were only a very recent memory.

At the main entrance of the police station was a large, high-ceilinged room. Those entering the station were presented with a low wall on top of which was a shield of bullet-proof glass that, running across the width of the room, divided the room into two sides, two halves. On one side of the wall were the police. The other side was for those who had business with the police: citizens who had complaints, wanted to file reports, or sought assistance or protection. Through this large room and through this barrier which separated the city from the city's protectors, police officers frequently brought criminals into the inner rooms, the bowels, of Police Headquarters. Finnerty and Costello saw Devorah, attired in a blood-red leather outfit, a blood red beret, and blood-red hush puppies, standing with a nervous young man whose jacket, shirt collar, and tie all seemed a bit too big for him. He had longish, curly hair and earrings.

Finnerty said, "Public defense lawyer. Looks like a virgin."

Costello nodded. "Virgin sacrifice," he said.

The two crossed from the police side to the public side of the room, walking through a large opening near the center of the divider which was attended by two officers, one of whom held a metal detector, the other a machine gun. Moving unhurriedly, strolling, they approached Devorah and her companion.

"Yeah?" Finnerty said.

"I want to see him," Devorah said in her strange, almost French accent. She looked worried.

"See who?" Finnerty said.

"I want to see my friend, the man you arrested yesterday."

"Well, you can't," Finnerty said. Then he looked at Costello, then at the lawyer. "I guess that about wraps things up, huh? We'll see you again . . . uh . . . uh . . . when we have more information to give you."

"Wait a minute here," the earringed man said, his voice cracking. Costello actually felt embarrassed for him—his hands were shaking. "I'm Ms Hepple's attorney."

"So what?" Finnerty said. "We're not charging Ms Hepple with anything. At least not now we aren't. Unfortunately there doesn't seem to be any law against keeping some guy as a personal pet."

"What I meant to say," the lawyer said, "is that I'm here to represent Ms Hepple's . . . uh . . . companion."

"He doesn't want to see you," Finnerty said.

"What? I can't believe that," Devorah said.

"Well, believe it. He waived his right to counsel."

"That's *merde*. That's bullshit!" Devorah said.

"I can't believe that either," said the lawyer, gaining in his indignation a touch of confidence. "I'm prepared to go before a judge this afternoon and exercise our right to see your prisoner. By the way, what charges is he being held under?"

"Charges?" Finnerty snorted. "Multiple pet slaughter."

"And do you have any evidence?" Devorah asked.

"Evidence! Judge! Charges!" Finnerty smirked, eyeing the legal services neophyte. "Go ahead. Give it your best shot, kid. I expect if you're really good, you might be able to see your man in, oh, maybe a month."

Devorah looked from Finnerty to the lawyer. The lawyer pursed his lips. He wanted to say something. He wanted to have an effect.

Costello said, "Morris Tantone has waived his right to an attorney and has also said that he does not wish to see you, Ms Hepple, at this time."

Her eyes leapt at him.

"He told you that? He told you his name? He spoke to you?"

"He did," Costello said. "I guess he's feeling a little more human today. But the fact of the matter is he's participating quite nicely, quite . . . amicably, in the questioning, and he has expressly said that he wants to see neither you nor an attorney. I think he wants to make a clean beast . . . uh . . . breast of things. Now as for you, we'll probably want to talk to you later, so please don't leave our thriving metropolis."

"What?" Hepple said. "I can't believe it. You're lying."

Finnerty looked at her intently. "Woof," he said. Then he took Costello by the arm, said, "All right, I think we're done with these two." They turned and walked back through the divide; one of the uniformed officers there stopped Devorah Hepple as she tried to follow.

She yelled after them, "You can't get away with this."

Finnerty looked at Costello. "You know, sometimes the complete failure of the justice system has its advantages," he said somberly.

"What a society!" Costello replied. "You try to level with someone, Lieutenant, and they just give you shit. Maybe the mayor's BACK TO BASICS campaign will improve things, do you think?"

"Fuck BACK TO BASICS," Finnerty replied. "The only law seems to be dog-eat-dog, which, when you think of it, has never been more appropriate. What's with that crazy broad's accent anyway," he continued. "Where the fuck does she think she's from?"

Costello did not have a chance to answer.

They both stopped, looked back towards the entrance to the police station. A women was yelling, "All cars must be destroyed."

"Now what?" Finnerty said, standing on tiptoes to get a better look. Even Devorah Hepple and her lawyer turned to watch the two detectives and a uniform drag a female suspect into the station.

The suspect yelled again, "Cars are destroying humankind!"

She was short, heavyset. She wore military fatigue pants and a leather jacket, thin leather gloves, military shoes, and a wool pullover cap. She had a fresh, red abrasion under one of her eyes and there were skid marks running across one arm and one side of her jacket. One of the detectives, Peter Freund, was pulling the handcuffed suspect with one hand while holding a blood-stained towel to his ear with his other hand. He was wincing. In front of Freund walked Detective Alicia Taffiola. She led the trio—the struggling suspect and the detective and officer who held her—into the police side of the room. The suspect stopped struggling, stood rigidly straight. Her face became a resolute mask of silent defiance. She fixed her eyes straight ahead.

"What should we do with her, Detective?" the uniformed officer asked Taffiola.

"Oh, put her on ice for a while."

They led the prisoner down a hallway to the same block of isolation and interrogation chambers where the Human Pet was being held. Taffiola watched the suspect going down the hallway, then turned back to take a blank arrest report form from the stack on the counter behind the bulletproof divider.

"Allie," Finnerty called, beckoning her over to him. "What's that?"

"Holy fucking cow," she said, unconsciously brushing a strand of her mid-length, straight black hair from her forehead, "you wouldn't believe this one, Lieutenant. We get a call for backup over in the Warehouse District. A group of women stop a trailer truck, force the driver out of it and torch the damn thing. By the time we get there, they're all riding away on bicycles."

"Sounds like the group that got your car, Costello," Finnerty said.

"Yeah, Women Against Cars," Costello nodded. He smiled sheepishly.

Taffiola smiled as well. "Yeah, that's right! I think that's what they call themselves. Women Against Cars."

"In the Warehouse District?" Costello continued. "That's a bit strange. I thought they kept mostly to back roads outside town."

"I guess this score was just too much for them to resist," Taffiola said.

"How do you mean?"

"It was a transport truck. It was carrying six new vehicles. Lovecrafts."

"And they torched the whole thing?" Finnerty asked.

"Yeah, it's all scrap now—one huge, charred scrap heap. Probably be there for another twenty years."

"Who called it in?" Costello asked.

"Oh, that young guy, the rookie—James Wilson."

"Yeah, I know Wilson," Costello said. "He all right?"

"He is," Taffiola replied. "But his car isn't. They shot the thing to hell. Machine gun. It's got more holes in it than . . . well, than something with a lot of holes in it."

"You roughed her up a bit, I see," Finnerty observed, nodding and rubbing his hands together in pleasure.

"I wish. We were in pursuit. They all broke up and rode in different directions so we ended up chasing this one. She fell off her bike. That's how we got her. She's been raving the whole time about how cars are destroying the planet."

"What are you going to do with her?" Costello asked.

"Oh, I'll put her on ice. I'll see if she talks to me later."

"What happened to Freund's ear?" Finnerty asked.

"She attacked him with a hatchet, the crazy bitch. I think he's got half his ear in his pocket."

"A hatchet?" Finnerty chuckled, his eyes growing wider.

"Yeah. Tough business, huh?"

"Yeah," Finnerty replied.

"What's her name, anyway, Allie?" Costello asked.

"Elizabeth Borden," Taffiola answered.

Costello smiled. Finnerty laughed out loud. His laugh began low and booming and became high-pitched and weird.

"What?" asked Taffiola.

"Poetic injustice," Costello answered.

When Taffiola moved off to fill out the form, Finnerty looked up at Costello—the lieutenant was nearly a foot shorter than his subordinate—and said, "All right, Costello—Human Pet, round 2."

"Sounds good," Costello replied. But let me run up to the office first. There's something there I've got to check on. How about I meet you back at the room in fifteen minutes? Maybe twenty."

Finnerty shrugged his shoulders. "Do what you got to do."

As Costello got off the elevator and began to walk to his office, the pool typist and secretary Edith got up from her desk where she had been reading a magazine and shouted at him. "Where the hell have you been? That damn dog has been whining all day. Did you ever have to listen to a dog whine all day?"

"No," Costello said, "but I've listened to you. What are you doing here anyway, Edith? It's Sunday. Is your life so bleak that you come in on your days off, or what?"

Edith looked like she might break into tears. Costello relented.

"Okay. Okay," Costello said. "I'm working on it. Ever try to find a home for an unwanted animal?"

"Why don't you just bring it down to the guy you're questioning?" another detective called from his desk. "I bet the Human Pet could use a friend."

"Very helpful, very helpful," Costello said. He walked the last few paces to his office. He opened the door. Kitten was sitting behind his desk in Costello's chair, drooling, hunched over documents, files, and other assorted paperwork related to the pet slayings case as well as the recent deaths of Irma Gamerman and Alvin Gremillion.

"A hard day at the office, Kitten?" Costello asked, closing the office door behind him and sitting across from the dog.

The dog looked at him, did not respond.

"I hear you've been whining all day," Costello said to the dog. "I don't begrudge you that. It seems like a pretty reasonable thing to do. Next time though, you might consider leaving the office and biting the secretary. I think her rear end could use a little low-cost liposuction."

Again, the dog just looked at him, panting softly.

Costello met the dog's eyes, wondering why Kitten had lost so much of his customary emotive verve. Then he had a realization. He asked, "Kitten, you're mad at me, aren't you? I left you here alone all day with nothing to do."

Kitten tilted his head, yawned.

"I don't blame you. I'm just not a good dog-daddy."

Reaching into his pocket, the detective found a handful of dog biscuits he had put there unconsciously—probably as he was leaving the interrogation room to see Devorah Hepple. He took the biscuits out, dropped them ceremoniously on the desk. Kitten looked at them, then at Costello. He nudged one with his nose, pushed it away.

"Jesus," Costello sighed. He picked up one of the biscuits, bit it in two. It was becoming a habit. The dog watched him chew. Costello heard himself making the same sounds that Morris had made. Kitten's tail began to wag. He turned his head sideways and laid it on the desktop and picked up a biscuit with his teeth. He made crunching sounds too as he chewed.

"These biscuits," Costello said, holding his, half eaten, out for consideration, "they're surprisingly good for building relationships."

For a moment, Costello became almost philosophical, considering the strangeness of it all: here pet and man were sharing dog biscuits together, while at this moment in the interrogation room, Morris Tantone, both a pet and a man, would not be able to get at the bag of biscuits which lay open before him, no matter how hard he pulled against his restraints.

Chapter 13

Quick Movements

Rex Quick put his palm to his chest. God! His heart was racing. His mind was racing. Another nervous attack. The problem was unsolvable. He broke a pencil in half, then, his lip quivering, his hands shaking, he placed the broken pencil into a drawer in his desk. There was already an accumulation of broken pencils there alongside a box of wipes for his glasses. He sighed. Emotional control, at least outwardly, was the key to his success. He could never let his enemies see his weaknesses. But this tension inside him would kill him yet. He knew it. He wanted to cry. He made one single soft whimpering sound. His radio was on. One of Liszt's *Hungarian Rhapsodies* was playing.

From behind his spacious desk he surveyed his large corner office. He was still an important man in one of the few businesses that continued to do well in the city, or in the country for that matter. He was a doer. He was director for human resources at Crowe Poussin Enterprises, developers and manufacturers of weapons and security systems. Of course, weapons were not called weapons anymore. The company literature used terms like crowd containment device or personnel management mechanism to describe the new armaments and systems developed at Crowe Poussin. But devising new names, euphemisms, for the systems

developed at the sprawling plant by the River Charlotte was not
Rex Quick's job.

His job lay before him on the other side of his enormous
desk. Fifteen chairs were set there in a row. On each chair was a
neatly typed card containing information about that chair; behind the chairs were meticulously rendered wall charts and
graphs. Quick had spent months of work involving surveys, focus groups, discussions, in-house studies, and consultant's reports
on the issues raised by these chairs. Issues? The main question
he sought to answer was which employee merited what kind of
chair in his or her office. The answer to this question was Quick's
Holy Grail. You see, he thought to himself for the millionth time,
there are so many kinds of chairs and chairs are so much more
than simply platforms on which people sit. A chair in both its
appearance and its comfort conveys status! And status was something the workforce at Crowe Poussin thought about a lot. He felt
his heart flutter in his chest again. Sweat beaded on his body but
he could not keep his mind from rehearsing yet again the logic
of, the meaning of, the chair. In the post-information economy in
which layoffs, cutbacks, and plant closings were a grim, unnerv-
ing specter which hovered around every workstation, and in this
economy in which pay raises, even cost of living adjustments,
were a thing of the past, it was the little things like chairs which
conveyed status and security.

Today was his deadline day. By the end of the afternoon he
had to submit a final proposal to top management on chair policy
for the entire facility. He knew no matter what he proposed he
was sure to draw the ire of some group, some faction, within the
company. If he proposed too liberal a policy, distributing too
many chairs of too high status to too many workers, then those
above these workers would feel cheated. If the chair policy was
too conservative, then the lower echelons of the organization
would look at him with cold, envious looks, or worse. Only yesterday he had returned to his office and seen a note attached to
his own chair—his chair was quite nice, leather, comfortable,

capable of swiveling 360 degrees and reclining—on which was typed, "We know where you sit." God, that had caused his heart to palpitate. And, the problem was he did not know from whom the note had come—some janitor or minor secretary, some middle manager or even a member of the top management team could be sending him a warning. It could have come from anywhere. His environment was perilous, with everyone a potential enemy. He plucked up a tissue from a box on his desk, fluttered it in its hand, blew his nose. How stupid it was! Why did human beings have to sit? Maybe that should be his proposal. Remove all the chairs! Anarchy. Crouch, assholes! Lie on the floor, vermin. Stand all day, you bastards, you silly bitches. He felt sweat flowing, pooling—cool, clammy—in his armpits and his groin. Fifteen empty chairs faced him. To Quick it seemed as though his office had become a court room and that these chairs were the empty chairs of the members of a jury, which, now in the jury room, were sure to return later that afternoon as his deadline came due and find him guilty of making a wrong—a career-ending—decision. He opened his desk again, took out a lens wipe, cleaned his glasses methodically. So many broken pencils. What a waste.

Quick looked at the photographs on his desk. There was his daughter Ashley. God only knew what she was doing, where she was, who she was with, what was going on in her mind. Presumably nothing. She was living with her boyfriend, the talentless Bruno Passive. Both of them were jobless, living off the modest amount of prize money she had won the previous year in a government-sponsored lottery. That would be gone soon, spent on drugs and drink. Sometimes images formed in his mind of the two of them together—hideous! Bruno, the purple-haired buffoon. Next to Ashley was a photo of his wife, Cassie. And what good was she? Like mother like daughter. She made fun of his chair dilemma while she spent her time trying to save pets, of all things. Well, at least it kept her occupied, gave her something to do. That was good. She was his wife. He wanted the best for her. Really.

He looked at the intercom; he felt like buzzing for his secretary, asking her to do something, but he could not think of anything he needed done.

He swiveled 180 degrees and looked out the window. The research and development facility was located in a spacious office park. The facility was made up of a number of low-lying, boxish, concrete buildings; between the buildings were fairly well-maintained lawns, walkways, landscaped areas, flowering bushes—all deflowered now. There were also large fountains which, Quick remembered, had worked until recent years. An American flag swung in the breeze. It was a cold, gray day. Thick blue-black clouds hung low over the river and the city. Quick got up slowly, sighed. He would take a walk around the plant, maybe go outside and take a breath of air, then return and do what had to be done.

He nodded to his secretary as he walked past her. He noted her chair. Perhaps it was too comfortable, too expensive, too good a chair for her. God! What anguish! How was one to determine the ideal seat, both fair and cost effective? She would never forgive him if he took her chair away. They hardly got along now. He felt her eyes boring into his back. Ingrate! He was the source of her livelihood, her desk, her chair, and he had never even tried to collect on what she owed him as her superior, her provider. He walked through the corridors of the building. Some people nodded to him while it seemed to him that others willfully avoided his eyes or turned abruptly to avoid even having to say hello to him. Soon he passed a display of large, handsomely framed color photographs of the systems the company manufactured. Pictures of massive explosions, of military installations laid to waste, of twisted metal and concrete splashed with gore. Each photo had an engraved metal plate which named the system and the place where it had been used. He stopped to look at a photo: **Personnel Mobility Retardation Mechanism, Belfast, Northern Ireland**. The picture showed what had been a marching crowd of protesters transformed to hundreds of limp, prone human forms, their activity-quotient marginalized by a contained-range chemical device.

Using the stairs, he descended from the third level of the building where he worked, to the second, then to the first. He descended further to the basement, the heart of one of the four research wings of the facility. It was there that he saw Varnish. Strom Varnish was a reclusive researcher who over the years had developed a sort of relationship with Quick. Extremely tall—seven feet—and gaunt, Varnish's skin was the color, and to some extent, the texture of the bark of some dark brown tree. But, if Varnish was treelike, his trunk was not straight, for he had a pronounced stoop, as if his spine were bent, almost, into a question mark. Due to this curvature, his head bent forward too, like a ball on an uncoiled spring, an effect that was heightened by Varnish's tall gray Afro. Wispy, it bounced as his head bobbed. But it was his nose and his Adam's apple—both almost comically sizable protrusions—which seemed to Quick to really define Varnish as a very ugly man. Varnish's glasses were thick-rimmed, frequently dirty, and his mind seemed engaged on many things at once, so that often in mid-conversation he simply stopped talking and walked away or changed the subject completely.

But Rex Quick liked him. Though Varnish was not known as one of the top producers on the research and development side of the business, he occasionally came up with an idea that was an absolute winner. After all, new products were what kept the company afloat. Especially products that could destroy or counter older products. Yes, Varnish was a winner on that score. Once he had even designed a new missile system and the anti-missile system to defend against it in the course of a few short weeks. A one-two punch. True brilliance. He had earned his eccentricities.

Varnish looked down at Quick, shook his head, asked, "Something troubling you?"

Quick knew that perhaps the only person to whom he could relate his troubles was this odd character.

"Yes," he admitted. "This damn chair policy. It's driving me out of my mind."

"Chair policy? Chair policy," Varnish said, as if trying to pull this particular bit of information out of the thousands of threads of theorems, impulses, memories, ideas which intertwined through his brain in complex knots of thought. "Ah, yes. I remember something about that. Surely people can agree that certain chairs are best for certain work?"

"Not yet. But, in time, I hope they will."

"Good," Varnish said. "You know, though, there is one chair I wouldn't want."

Quick blanched. Was even Varnish caught up in this foolishness?

"What's that?" asked Quick.

"The electric chair, ho-ho-ho!"

Varnish's laugh was like the sound of felled trees falling. Mirth sparkled in his eyes like sparks on damp leaves, flaring, disappearing.

While Varnish looked on with his habitual look of perplexity, Quick related the ins and outs, the positives and negatives, of the policy he was trying to craft.

Quick finished speaking. Varnish said nothing. Then, realizing that one side of the conversation had come at least to a temporary pause, he said, "Uh . . . uh . . . well, come into my lab. I'll show you something that should cheer you up."

Quick shrugged his shoulders, said, "Thanks, I could use a diversion. Good science, that's what we're all about, isn't it?"

"Yes," Varnish replied. "Good science."

They walked down the corridor into Varnish's laboratory. Although Quick had been there many times over the years, the chair was the first thing he looked at now. Nothing too elaborate, Quick saw. An old swivel chair with rollers—although it hardly mattered: Varnish would probably be satisfied sitting on a crate.

The laboratory was cluttered and disorderly. Piles of scholarly papers, notebooks, journals ascended from desktops and the floor; mathematical figures and shaky stick figures covered a black board; Styrofoam coffee cups, most half-filled with cold black coffee, were everywhere. An ancient computer screen displayed information. It was connected to a machine—dating from the early 1960's or before—which filled an adjoining room. Some kind of UNIVAC or ENIAC perhaps—Quick had no idea really. Varnish maintained the machine himself, servicing its magnetic core memory and trashcan lid-sized disk drives with components he jerry-rigged or pulled out of junk machines, antiques. It had barely the power of what a pocket calculator had around the turn of the century, the Y2K. Well, Quick thought, his mind running rapidly though what Varnish had explained to him in previous conversations, that's why it worked at all. There were countless theories about why nearly all the silicon chips worldwide had melted in 2009. Some spoke of a cyber-terrorist plot which had successfully piggybacked plastic and silicon eating nanomachines onto the human cold virus. Carried now in the respiratory systems of million of humans, these airborne nanomachines, according to this weird hypothesis, keyed on the electromagnetic signatures of digital chips, ate through the chips' protective coverings and then the chips themselves, thereby gaining the energy to reproduce and move on through whole computer systems, transforming all the digital chips in the world effectively into the information processing equivalent of oatmeal. Chip Suey! What foolishness, Quick thought. If there were going to be some kind of maleficent molecular machine, let it melt chairs instead. At any rate, Varnish wrote his own programs as he needed them and never allowed his machine to interface with any other machine or system. One could not be too cautious. He even handcrafted his own integrated circuits, transistors, and other components using a germanium compound.

There was a trio of television monitors in one corner of the laboratory. The researcher had taped various notes and diagrams around the screens. In a vast table in the center of the room was a tangle of antique electronic equipment. Some of the equipment was covered in dust, unused; other pieces looked to be in the midst of overhaul, their outer cases opened and their wiry guts pulled out in tangles. Several mechanisms within the laboratory whirred and clicked with mechanical activity. Varnish closed the door. He said something but Quick could not hear what he said. Quick pointed to the record player from which music, some kind of opera, boomed, emoted.

Varnish ambled to the record player and turned the volume down. "Wagner. Need serious music to work," he said.

"Well, what have you got?" Rex Quick said.

"Ahh-haa!" the researcher replied, pulling a cigarette from his pocket, lighting it, exhaling. "You'll love this. Absolutely love it." He called, "Christian."

Quick looked at him.

"Christian!"

A dog which had presumably been sleeping out of view emerged, wagged its tail amiably. The dog yawned and stretched. It was a presentable enough mutt, though no trophy, Quick thought. Then Quick noticed that the dog's fur had been shaved from the top of its head. The dog had stitches, recent looking stitches, criss-crossing the top of its skull.

"Here is my fine friend," Varnish smiled. "Here is my enhanced animal."

"Surely, this is not your new project?" Quick asked.

"Ahh, indeed, indeed it is. This is a unit that will revolutionize the way . . . uh . . . the movements of personnel are retarded and contained."

"This dog?"

"You are not looking at a dog, Quick, you are looking at a Canine Surveillance Unit."

"What do you mean?"

"Well, look. Look."

"I am looking. I see a dog with a scar on its head."

"No, look at the screen, the television screen." Varnish turned and pointed.

Quick looked at the three screens; two of them were dark. On the center screen Quick saw an image of himself. An image of himself looking at the screen in bewilderment.

"What?"

"Ho-ho-ho, yes," Varnish nodded, chortled. "What the dog sees, we see. I've replaced one of the dog's eyes with a miniature camera. Our Christian here is a roving, radio-controlled, television broadcasting unit."

Quick looked again at the dog's eye. One looked plastic, mechanical.

"So the dog transmits visual images?"

"More than that. The dog transmits visual and auditory data to a remote sensing station which I have here." Varnish patted a huge metal console, six feet in height and nearly as wide, which was fitted out with knobs, dials, switches, indicators, audio speakers, joy sticks, and a microphone. Three sets of rabbit ear antennae rose from its top.

"My god! How excellent! How did you do it, Strom?"

"It wasn't easy, I tell you. The dog is full of wires and miniature, asbestos-sheathed vacuum tubes. There is hardly enough room for the insides of the dog. It even has its own power source. Its systems run off power generated by the movement of its hind legs—a sort of elaborate bicycle generator, ho-ho! But the real trick was wiring up the dog's brain. God, that was a bit of work. It's amazing how complicated a brain can be. One wrong move and watch out. I can't begin to tell you about the failures I've had."

"Oh, I don't want to hear about failures."

"But here's the neatest thing, Quick, the real clincher," Varnish exclaimed. His face had taken on a sort of beaming beatitude as if he had achieved sainthood, as if he were enraptured. "Look at this," he said. He twisted a knob on the control unit. Christian sat down. He turned another button and the dog sat up on his haunches and begged. Now he softly spoke into the microphone. "Christian," he whispered, "lie down." The dog lay down. "Christian," he said, "get up, walk to the door, and sit down." The dog did it.

"Amazing! You can control the dog."

"Of course, I can control it. It would be useless otherwise," Varnish said. "You can't imagine the work it's taken. First I had to train the damn dog, of course. Now, I can direct it to do almost anything. I can send it out of the plant and into the city, directing where it goes by means of the visual imagery that I get through its eye, or the sounds that I hear through the microphones I've put in its ears. I've run tests, countless tests, having this unit go on complex missions miles from the laboratory here, and I have reports on each one of these . . . uh . . . forays. I can have the dog go into a crowd with hundreds of people, identify a subject by the sound of his voice, his appearance, or even his smell, and have Christian walk up to him, wag his tail, and become his best friend, all the while monitoring everything the subject says and does, ho-ho! Everything he says and does."

"Incredible," Quick said. "I see the dog responds both to auditory commands and manual controls."

"Yes. He responds to both."

"But how," Quick asked, "did you get the dog to respond to such a large number of commands?"

"Ahh. Ahh!" Varnish yelped. "Don't tell me that wasn't difficult, ho-ho! Don't tell me that wasn't innovative, working, naturally, without the benefit of most of the technological advances of the past forty years. First, I had to boost the dog's brain power. I did that with a little bit of electrical stimulation here and a bit of biochemical enhancement there—but also I did it by incorporating aspects of a human brain directly into the dog's brain. What the dog has is an amalgamation of dog brain, human brain, and man-made components. And it's all held together with wires and a piece of nylon stocking!"

Quick looked at the beaming researcher, who was patting his control unit lovingly, and at the dog, who was sitting pacifically by the door—not just pacifically but absolutely, rigidly, still. The hound was breathing, doing nothing more, awaiting his next command—and Quick saw a problem. "But when the dog is not responding to a command," he asked, "does it just sit there like a statue? Like a zombie?"

"You are very, very perceptive, Quick. That's what I like about you. You're wasted on such issues as chair policy. That was one of the chief problems I've had to overcome: once you've taken the dog out of the dog, how do you put the dog back in, how do you get the unit to retain some of its natural dogginess. You're absolutely right, a Canine Surveillance Unit which acts like a robot will soon be found out. Here, this little switch solves it all."

Quick looked at the switch on the control deck. It was labeled: Dog Style.

"Dog Style, ho-ho!" the researcher's laughter erupted. "A little joke."

He flicked the button. The dog's rigidity left its frame; it lay down, panted, moved its tail a bit. Except for the sutures, it looked like a standard dog.

"Amazing," Quick said. "Amazing. I can see countless opportunities for the use of this Canine Surveillance Unit. You're going to make us a billion."

"Yes, another brilliant success," Varnish said. "Ho-ho, maybe now I'll rate a superior, executive model chair . . . if not a throne." He spoke with an irony which was lost on Rex Quick, who, remembering now the challenge that so weighed on him, started to become gloomy again.

He pulled himself out of it, changed the subject. "How long have you been working on this?" he asked.

"Five years, off and on," Varnish replied. "There have been countless problems. Countless! Have you ever seen a dog's brain blow up on an operating table? Some people talk about Chip Suey; I talk about scrambled brains. Takes away your taste for runny eggs for breakfast, I can tell you that. And then of course— well, maybe I shouldn't tell you—oh, what the hell . . . and then, of course, there was the one that got away."

"One got away?"

"Yes, ten months ago. One of my proto-units. My best one to date. I sent it out on a test run in the city, testing . . . uh . . . its ability to function under severe weather conditions—it was raining, if you'll pardon the expression, cats and dogs—and something happened to the dog. Maybe it short-circuited: maybe it got hit in the head. Who knows? But the whole damn apparatus went off line. One moment it's there: poochie in a puddle; the next: *sayonara* Dr V. It just switched off. We lost it. Search teams! We spend days driving around, looking. No luck. So he's either living in the city as a stray now—God knows what's going on in that little brain of his!—or this mad pet slayer, this Human Pet, got him. I just hope this madman didn't find his jacked-up brain and sell the technology to one of our rivals!"

"Yes," Quick said, "that would be a problem. What was the dog's name?"

"Oh, the one that got away? His name was Satan."

"Satan?"

"Yes, for some reason I give my proto-units names with religious overtones: Buddha or Vishnu. Mary Baker Eddy. This one, of course, I've named Christian."

"Why not just Christ or Jesus?" Quick asked.

"I don't know," the researcher said. "Perhaps I cannot quite overcome my upbringing, my . . . uh . . . fear of blasphemy. Oh, let me show you one other interesting thing." Whispering into the microphone, Varnish gave the dog an auditory command. "Speak, Christian," he said. The dog opened his mouth, pointed his head in the direction of the two men. The researcher spoke now and his voice came out of the dog's mouth. "Rex Quick, I'm very concerned about this chair policy. You must bring me an answer today or I will bite you, ho-ho."

Varnish had implanted a speaker into the back of the dog's mouth. Quick could not believe it. Now he had a dog reminding him of what he had to do.

*   *   *

For a number of days after receiving the hideous chocolates, Ashley did not leave her apartment. Instead, vacillating emotionally from panic to listlessness to anger, Ashley kept to her room or ventured out occasionally to the living room where she reclined on the large sofa. She wore an old terry cloth bathrobe and furry slippers. Karla phoned a number of times, but Ashley did not take the calls. Out of concern for Ashley, Bruno kept to the apartment too, though Ashley for the most part rebuffed his efforts to offer consolation or even to talk to her. If he tried to approach her, Ashley snapped at him or waved him away dismissively, yet, all the same, she felt a strong need for him to be there with her. Sometimes she wept quietly.

Figuratively and literally forced to walk on tiptoes, Bruno turned much of his attention to writing new songs. It was a time when many new inspirations were bubbling up in him. He was fascinated by the Human Pet, by the perpetrator of the pet slayings, by the chance that these two might be one and the same. Voraciously he read newspaper accounts of Morris Tantone and his strange, quietly resolute mistress, Devorah Hepple. The media was now using the term "Pet Hunter" as well as "Human Pet" to describe Tantone. Maybe some newspaper editor had been at the party on the ship and heard his new song or maybe it was just such an obvious thing to call a criminal who tracked and slew pets. Pet Hunter. The press was full of interviews with people who had known Tantone or Hepple in any capacity whatsoever. Every day Mayor Paninni or Police Commissioner Trump made new statements. Cassie Quick was also frequently quoted as head of the Pet Protection League. Since the Human Pet had been taken into custody four days ago, there had been no new reports of pet murder.

But inspirations relating to this strange case were not the only inspirations that came into his mind. Perhaps it was the heightened tension within the apartment and the undercurrent of Ashley's fear combined with the large amount of James he was snorting with Sebastian which had prompted a tide of phrases, melodies, and images to flow through his imagination. Quietly, whisperingly, he jotted down these ideas and strummed his guitar, working at new songs. He also interacted with Sebastian who, it appeared, had taken on the status of semi-permanent guest. Sebastian did not sleep in the apartment. He had broken into a vacant apartment in the same building and slept on a discarded mattress he had hauled up from the cellar, though where Sebastian spent most of his time was with them. The unhappy couple.

Sebastian piqued Bruno's interest. He was standard enough in appearance, but he radiated an energy, an aura, that was unsettling. He seemed divorced from the common plane of existence, as if he sat in the eye of the hurricane of human drama, watching the chaotic gyrations of other people's lives from some dead-still spot. He took everything in much too calmly. He was in this world but not of it. He was beyond bland. The question that intrigued Bruno was whether the guest was truly profound, merely posing, or just extraordinarily strange. Also, Bruno could not help noticing Sebastian spent hours on end with Ashley. Sometimes they conversed softly. More often he just sat with her; he sat still and motionless, breathing deeply with eyes closed, though at times he would start as if some thought or memory had intruded on his reverie. Should I be jealous, Bruno asked himself. Pangs of jealousy did touch him, but not forcefully. Instead, he began to think of the question "Should I be jealous" in musical terms. He fitted a stark melody to this stark question. In keeping with his new obsession with pets he wrote a song which began

> *Should I be jealous of you?*
> *Or should you be jealous of me?*
> *Should I be jealous of you?*
> *Or should you be jealous of me and our canary?*

Despite the satisfaction of his creative output, on Wednesday morning, the morning of Ashley's fourth day of confinement to the apartment, Bruno had had enough. It was late in the morning. The sky outside was cold, gray. Fat clouds, like gray slugs fat with wet, traversed the slow sky, leaving wakes of cloud wisp or slug slime. Bruno walked from the kitchen to the living room where Ashley sat on the couch. Statuesque, Sebastian occupied his customary straight-backed wooden chair. Bruno's guitar hung around his neck and he strummed a chord loudly. Ashley looked at him. Sebastian opened his eyes. Bruno smiled and sang a sort of countrified plainsong:

> *I'm sick of sitting around the apartment*
> *even though we got chocolates that looked like shit,*
> *if we don't go on some kind of excursion*
> *I'm going to have an epileptic fit,*
> *I'm going to have an epileptic fit.*

He finished singing and smiled broadly. To his relief, Ashley smiled too.

"Oh, Bruno," she said, "you're so right."

"I am?"

"Yes, this funk has lasted long enough."

"Funk?" Bruno said. "You mean multi-fucking depression. You've taken atrophying to a new low."

"Bruno, you're perfect," Ashley replied, "but I think I can define my own emotional states, thank you."

"Bland," Bruno observed, happy to see the old spark rekindling in his lover's eyes. "What's your mindset, ugly?"

Ashley considered for a moment. Then she said, "A long walk. How does that sound, Sebastian? Hallucinogenic?"

"Napping."

"A long walk," Bruno nodded. He reached for his stuffed weasel hat and fur coat.

"Napping," Ashley said. "Let's head first for the Arboretum."

I've just been thinking about our Canadian holiday there, Bruno. Do you remember that?"

"Yes," he smiled, "I do. The bland tundras of the north."

Sebastian looked at them.

"You had to be there," Bruno said, "to . . . uh . . . not be there."

Sebastian nodded, shrugged.

The three of them walked the six or seven blocks through low lying apartment buildings to the gargantuan park. The three of them walked quietly. Ashley walked with her head down, her eyes on the gray rectangles of the sidewalk. When the surface on which she walked became grass green she realized that they were in the park. Her thoughts had been elsewhere. They stopped and looked at the surroundings—nature's rare foothold in the cityscape. The sky, gray and cold, hung low, portending a cold rain. It was chilly and the wind blew, not cuttingly, not wistfully either. It blew thickly. Some of the leaves on the trees clung still to their customary greenness. Most had already changed to the brilliant colors of fall, to myriad shades of red, yellow, orange, and maroon. Others had passed beyond their transitory brilliance to brown. Many leaves had fallen, were falling. Across the small meadow where the threesome stood, a Freedomworker drove a small tractor with a vacuum apparatus that sucked fallen leaves into a hopper the tractor pulled. He wore the standard skyblue uniform of the national work program. He was working to restore freedom to America, economic freedom. The tractor was moderately loud. The ground was moist and cold. The thick wind caused Ashley to pull her coat more closely around her body.

"Let's walk on," Bruno said. Ashley noticed that his breath turned to faint mist in the cold, wet air.

They walked across the meadow and up onto a gently rising hill. The hill was covered by moderate-sized hardwood trees. It was darker and quieter the further they walked. The sound of the tractor could just be heard now, an undertone. Their own footsteps through the fallen, wet leaves were the loudest sound in their hearing. They came to a small clearing. Bruno sat on a large stone and looked up at his companions. Moss ensheathed the stone except for its bald top. He pulled a joint from his shirt pocket, lit it, exhaled smoke from his mouth, nose. More gray was added to the atmosphere. The three smoked, got stoned. Ashley looked at her lover. He looked, as usual, goofy, lovably goofy. Bruno was six feet tall, thin, gangly. His hair—close cropped on the sides of his scalp, lavender and weedy on top—and the high cheekbones in his long, thin face made his head look faintly like a peanut set upright. He looked like Mr. Peanut with tendrils growing from his crown, she thought to herself then, though now the top of his peanut head was covered by an absurd fur hat. And his teeth, overly large white squares, looked like they barely fit in his mouth. His lip, his top lip, was pulled away in a grin, a grin he wore almost perpetually as if life were always making jokes which he enjoyed but did not get, not entirely.

"Look at how gray everything is," Ashley said, looking around.

"It's like a black and white movie," Sebastian said.

"I like black and white movies. They're so bland," Bruno mused. "I'd watch the worst black and white movie before I'd watch the best color movie any day."

"Don't we watch movies primarily for the plots, for the stories, Bruno, you ugly thing? Isn't the sweating color scheme secondary?" Ashley asked.

Bruno responded, "Plot? Who cares about plot! The more the story-line, the more unsettling the experience. In the movies and in life." Then he returned his attention to where they were, mused, "The only thing screwing this scene up is these leaves. Too colorful. It's too bad we can't live in an entirely black and white world. And gray, of course."

"What color would the viral leaves be then?" Ashley asked.

"Black in the summer. Then in the fall they'd turn gray."

"What is your favorite film, Bruno?" Sebastian asked.

"Oh, I don't know, some classic thing like . . . uh . . ."

"It's *Ace Ventura, Pet Detective*," Ashley said, "which—if I remember and I do since we've seen it at least five times—is both in color and has a plot."

"Ashley!" Bruno said, "why are you giving our . . . uh . . . family secrets away?"

Sebastian was going to say something about that old movie but he forgot what he was going to say, so he kept quiet. He bent and picked up a fallen leaf. He examined it. He liked *Too Much of a Bad Thing* himself or the original *Planet of the Apes* or any of its four sequels. He thought about the ape movies. In one of them—was it the third?—the two ape doctors came back to earth and had a baby which they had to hide with a chimpanzee in a travelling circus. Yes, it was the third movie. *Escape from the Planet of the Apes.* That had been good. He especially liked the President's science advisor. A German guy who determined that the ape astronauts had to be killed so that the future could be saved. Anyway, his plan failed. What had the ape Cornelius talked about—a plague that would kill all the household pets, all the dogs and cats? Yes! Imagine. That would pave the way for the domestication of apes which would pave the way for the emergence of ape intelligence, ape rebellion. That was movie four. What was that one called? He looked at his hand. The leaf in his hands was not stiff, but still felt pliable like a leaf feels when it is still on a tree. Then, his head turned. He heard sounds from the surrounding woods. He dropped the leaf. For the second time in its leaf-career, it fell. Ashley and Bruno saw where Sebastian's attention was. They turned too.

"A bear?" Bruno whispered.

It was not a bear.

A large dog emerged from the woods at the top of the clearing, walking slowly. It was brown, shaggy. Its legs were wet and muddy as if it had just come through a swamp. The dog walked toward them. Ashley stooped down and held out her hand, hoping to attract the dog to her. When the dog drew nearer, she saw that the word SACRIFICE was painted on its side in neat yellow letters. Ashley withdrew her hand and stood up slowly. Sebastian raised an eyebrow. Without turning its gaze, the dog lumbered by them. They turned and watched it walk into the woods at the point from which they had just entered the clearing. The dog trod on a fallen branch. They heard the branch crack. The dog was gone.

"Unfriendly," Bruno observed.

Sebastian said nothing.

Ashley felt her emotions going down again into despair. The appearance of the dog was affecting her. She felt the urge to say something about the dog—it had been a strange occurrence, after all—but she did not want to initiate a conversation that moved in that direction or any direction at this moment. Bruno stood up and stretched, raising his arms above his head.

"So, Ashley," he said, "been having any dreams lately?"

She sighed, then she answered, "No, not since Saturday night on the boat. I think my mind, my sleeping mind, has been perfectly blank. Perhaps that fucked-up dream double-o-nined all the nightmare cells in my brain."

"I guess it's good that you haven't been dreaming, isn't it?" Bruno said. "How about you, Sebastian? I bet you have some pretty hyperkinetic nightmares?"

"In fact," Sebastian replied, "I never dream at all. My mind is a complete blank when I sleep."

"How about when you're awake?" Bruno asked, peering at the new companion with his odd grin.

"A cascading stream of brilliant thoughts," Sebastian said, his voice a monotone.

Bruno laughed. Ashley smiled.

"Bruno, how about you?" Sebastian asked. "You haven't been having any dreams have you? Any nightmares?"

The musician's face grew serious. He said, "In fact I have. Just last night I had a dream that you wouldn't believe and that's so rare for me—I never dream and I never have dreams like this one. Talk about hyperkinetic, this was hyper-Connecticut."

Ashley winced at her lover's pun, but she was startled too.

Had Bruno really dreamed? A wave of worry sickened her. She listened, not wanting to hear.

"Oh, that's interesting. I'd like to hear it," Sebastian said.

"All right," Bruno said. He took a cigarette out of his pocket and lit it. "But let's walk while I talk."

The three walked into the woods, climbing further up the hill. Bruno related his dream.

"I dreamed I was in a motel in the middle of a desert. The motel was chintzy, dilapidated, hot. I tried to turn on the air conditioner of my room but it didn't work. The over-energized thing pumped out hot air instead. Talk about fucked-up! There is no one else at the motel—no guests, no management—and there are no roads leading to or away from the motel either. It is isolated under the hot sun. I got the impression in my dream that it is always noon, that the sun never moves from its place directly above the hotel. Unbland, huh? Then I look up at the neon sign over the motel. It says MOTEL HELL. That was . . . uh . . . unsettling."

"Motel Hell," Sebastian repeated.

"At Motel Hell the only amenity apparently is a large pool. The water is blue-green, inviting. The water was cool. I dipped my hand in. Then I took off my clothes and dove in. Boy, it felt good. But it does more than feel good; the water is good! Immediately I began to feel a sensation of . . . what would you call it? . . . physical prowess, of strength, of health; my mind became crisp, coolly elated, calm. Hey, I liked the pool is what I'm saying. I dog-paddled around for hours."

Ashley and Sebastian nodded, interested.

"But, all good things must end, even in dreams. A group of other guests appeared at the motel, who knows how? They were a clean-cut bunch in their twenties and thirties, men and women. I can tell they're baffled by the place too, but in a moment or so, they're naked and in the pool. They also felt the strange, the unique power of the pool and the pool became a place of jubilation. Water splashed. Voices were raised in profound observation or laughter and everything is blandly napping. But then the mood changes. I saw that some of the new arrivals were . . . uh . . . coupling in the water, intertwining in the love act. Lust has taken hold and the pool became the locus of an orgy—a locus-pocus, I could say, ha-ha!—and the clear water becomes cloudy with love fluids."

"Ick," Ashley said.

"Ick squared. That was only the beginning," Bruno said.

They were at the bald, the treeless, top of the hill now. On one side, they could see the jumble of the city; on the other the sprawl of suburbs.

After pausing to light another cigarette, Bruno continued, "Soon the pool turns into a site of Bacchanalian revelry—people laughing, screaming, wailing, babbling, making love, fighting, pounding their heads against the sides of the pool so that soon blood and piss and shit are added to the semen that has already . . . uh . . . befouled the previously nappingly placid water. Now, get this: as the water loses its purity, the feeling it imparts is more and more negative, evil, but the sense of exhilaration persists. I can not leave the pool, although I find that I feel physically sick and mentally twisted. I need the touch of the water, the sensation it engenders. I'm addicted.

"In my dream, it seemed that I spend days in this hideous pool until, finally I can't take it anymore. I climb out and towel myself off. The towel comes away brown. My body is this emaciated, fish-white abomination dotted with sores."

The three of them began walking down the hill.

"I walk off, away from the pool, but the further I move from the pool, the weaker I become, so that soon I am crawling over a hot sidewalk. Ouch, it burns. Lizards look at me from low bushes. I feel like I am going to die until I find myself in some sort of shed, some sort of custodian's shed. It is cooler and dark but not so dark that I can't see huge bottles of water. Guess what: they are labeled POOL WATER. I manage to wrench the top off one of the bottles and angle it so that it pours into my mouth. My god, I am instantly restored. The vileness I feel is completely removed. I feel just like when I jumped into the pool."

Bruno fell silent.

The listeners looked at him.

"Then what?" Sebastian asked.

Bruno said nothing.

"Then what happened, Bruno?" Ashley asked.

"I can't remember," Bruno said sheepishly.

"Try," Sebastian said.

"Well," Bruno said, "I suppose I decided to share my find with my companions and so we were all saved."

"Un-fucking-likely, you ugly selfish weasel," Ashley snorted in a sweet enough way.

"No . . . no . . . I'm sorry, I really can't remember," Bruno said. "What do you think—that I would just hide out and keep the water, this water of life, for myself?"

They were at the bottom of the hill now near one of the entrances to the Arboretum. A trolley, bound intown, was two or three blocks away from the stop near the entrance. It moved slowly.

"Of course you would," Ashley said. "But that's not the point."

"What is the point, Ash?" Bruno asked.

"The point is you made that whole god damn dream up."

"Huh? What makes you say that?"

"Call it my feminine intuition," Ashley said. "Hey, here's my train. I think I'll go downtown." Her voice sounded weak, sad, and angry. She ran off towards it.

"Ashley," Bruno called. "Ashley!"

She turned, saw the look of dismay on his face. Her expression softened. She smiled, said, "Bruno, don't worry, you're an asshole, but you're my asshole. I need you even though you're full of shit. Use you later, bland?" Her voice was still weak and sad, but now it was touched with sweetness.

"Bland," Bruno responded, waving weakly, "use you later."

She ran across the street to the other side of the now stopped trolley. Bruno and Sebastian lost sight of her. The car was crowded. The windows were filthy. The trolley lumbered off.

Sebastian said, "What now?"

"Home, I guess." Bruno felt forlorn.

They began to walk towards the apartment, their hands deep in their pockets against the chill.

"Bruno?" Sebastian said. "That dream—it was real, wasn't it?"

"What dream?" Bruno said. He did not feel like being very direct right at that moment.

Chapter 14

The Marketplace of Ideas

It was raining now. Rain sounded on the top of the trolley like hundreds of rolling fingers on conga drums. The sound of the downpour intertwined with various mechanical shrieks and groans from the trolley. Ashley sat alone. Though she was afraid, she needed to be alone now. Bruno's manufactured dream had caused her to feel anxious, had caused renewed panic to tear at the edges of her consciousness. And this sense of panic was enhanced by the cacophony. But he was not the problem, not really. How could he be? Bruno was not to blame. The goof. Bruno was only being Bruno. While walking in the Arboretum, a voice had begun speaking in her mind. Initially the voice had spoken so softly, so unobtrusively, that she had discounted it. Not noticed it. But then, as the threesome had walked down towards the bus stop, the voice had said something to her that now she could not, or would not, recall to her mind—something about Sebastian.

Something fundamentally disturbing.

Now, at cross-purposes, she tried simultaneously to remember what the voice had said and what it had sounded like and to purge thoughts of the strange, interloping voice from her mind. The voice had sounded familiar. So familiar! She had thought she had known the voice but she had not been able to place it. It had sounded as though it were passing through some kind of filter, as if it were passing through water. It had not sounded like someone's speaking voice but like the voice within someone—someone else's mind. It had sounded sweet too. And beckoning. And corrupt. Ashley's thoughts jumped to an image of Sebastian. Was there something about Sebastian? She had known him. Yes, in childhood. But so what? Why was there a barrier in her mental processes against memories of him? Something was keeping her from seeing something obvious. Why could she not know what she already knew? It was creepy. Her mind was playing a sleight-of-hand trick on itself. Fuck! Unbland. The rain abated, perhaps only a passing cloudburst. Inside the trolley it became more quiet.

The trolley stopped near Colin Wilson Street and Ashley got off. Her mind, exhausted by this newest round of making contradictory efforts at memory and repression, had reached a precarious equilibrium, a temporary blankness. She crossed in front of the idling trolley and walked into what had until recent years been a thriving, upscale, multi-block retail nexus brimming with clothiers, art galleries, restaurants, trendy stores, and cafes. Here the buzz of consumerism had oscillated at high-frequency, inducing all who neared or entered the zone to want to buy. Now, only a few blocks of commercial activity remained and the buzz was but a weak hum circling a still-point. Ashley wanted to occupy herself, her mind, with shopping or more accurately with looking at things she could not, or would not, buy. More importantly, Ashley needed the security that comes from being in the midst of many people, of normal human activity. She had not walked down Colin Wilson Street in a long time.

There were few people, few shoppers, at this time of the afternoon. The street and sidewalk were wet from the recent rain; there was the bracing freshness of the autumn rain in the air. The smell of wet cement. The wind blew listlessly, stirring soggy pieces of paper and trash. She stopped. Here was a new restaurant she had not seen before. SCRAPS. The menu, in a glass display case next to the restaurant door, was surrounded by photographs of celebrities dining. But they had not dined at this restaurant,

Ashley noted, reading the printed information intently. The menu described the genesis of the ever-changing SCRAPS cuisine. SCRAPS offered its customers the half or partially-eaten meals of celebrities which were purchased by SCRAPS from restaurants around the globe. Here is how it worked: almost immediately after a celebrity had finished with a meal or dish—if at least a portion remained—the remainder was rushed, often by direct express flight, to SCRAPS, where it was put on the menu to be sold again. Reheated, of course. The daily menu listed not only the recycled dishes, but the names of the celebrities who had first ordered them and the restaurants where they had had their first go-round as meals. Prices at SCRAPS were based on a formula which took into account the original price of the meal, the percentage of the serving that had already been consumed, and the popularity of the celebrities present at the first "unveiling" of the meal. In SCRAPS's complex pricing formula, not only was the popularity of the celebrity who ate the meal taken into account, so was the popularity of other celebrities at the table or even in the restaurant when the meal was first served. Also available, of course, were the partially consumed wines and other beverages of the famous and rich. Ashley pondered some of the offerings of the day, then, her curiosity sated, she turned to walk on. She was not quite sure what to think. Apparently there was still some room in the economy for conspicuous consumption, but it certainly seemed like an odd idea for a restaurant. Would people actually want to eat meals which had been partially consumed by the famous, semi-famous, or infamous? Perhaps, she thought to herself, she should get out more.

A few blocks later, Ashley entered a store called Ant Farm Furniture where furniture and household furnishings of all types were on display. It looked to her as if she was the only customer there. She glanced at some lamps and some leather chairs— standard items, stylish and expensive. Deeper into the store Ashley saw that much of the furniture was made of plastic. A dining set, a long table and six chairs, was made of clear, hard plastic filled with concrete. Ashley rapped a knuckle on the table top. It made a dull sound. It hurt. She sat on one of the chairs; it was uncomfortable. Sitting, she examined her thoughts. Her mind was calmer. The voice in her mind was identifiably her own. She smiled to herself. She had been a fool, a victim of self-delusion. A weakling. Better to confront her fears, drive them back. Only by keeping negativity at bay could she return to the blandness of her existence. Blandness equals strength, she thought to herself, hearing a sort of clarion call welling up within. Then she heard another voice, one that she could not recognize. Her heart pounded, but there was nothing to worry about. Ashley looked up. The saleswoman who had silently approached her repeated her question. "How do you like the chair?" The saleswoman looked vaguely familiar, though Ashley could not place the face.

"Not much," Ashley said. "It's uncomfortable."

"That's the point," the saleswoman said and walked away.

"Rude," Ashley thought to herself. She had always thought that the salespeople were supposed to be politer, more obsequious in this shopping district.

She walked over and looked at a giant, clear plastic sofa filled with dirt. The plastic was thick. Ashley sat down on the sofa. It was uncomfortable too. Ashley ran her hands over the smooth plastic, then recoiled. There was movement in the sofa. Ants. The sofa was a huge ant farm, filled with ants and ant tunnels. This was one of the store's signature pieces. How many ants are in the sofa, she wondered to herself. She beckoned to another salesperson. This time it was a young man.

"Yes?"

"How many ants are in the sofa?" Ashley asked.

"Lots," the young salesman said, then walked away. Jesus, she was sure she had seen him too. Somewhere. A band? A club? Her hideous prep school?

Ashley shrugged. A piece of literature regarding the ant farm sofa was on a side table which was itself an antfarm. She glanced at it. The soil in the furniture was treated with nutrients, ant nutrients, so that the ants might thrive. Through special valves in the plastic, air and moisture were provided to the soil. The cost of the sofa and other "live" furniture consisted of a base price and additional charges per hundred ants.

Ashley rose and walked thoughtfully around the store. The store must attract a rather well-to-do clientele, she thought, examining a box-shaped rock, a field stone, fitted with metal antennae, radio knobs, and a radio dial. From jacks drilled in the back of the field stone, thin electric wires ran to two other box-shaped stones set to either side of the central stone on a plastic table. A small sign described the piece. "Rock Radio." Rock Radio was expensive. She could not believe the price. Ashley turned one of the knobs. Nothing happened. She smiled to herself, bewildered. Perhaps things cost more if they don't work. A new paradox of value. Behind the display, cardboard boxes filled with Rock Radios were stacked from floor to ceiling.

Leaving Ant Farm Furniture, Ashley continued down the street. Window shopping.

In a few moments, she entered a boutique called Smell. She had never seen it before, never been in it. But this was convenient—she had wanted to try a new scent. Smell was a very contemporary boutique which combined elements of an old-fashioned pharmacy with elegant display cases and contemporary lighting. Dozens of imposing mannequins looked from the store's display windows onto the street or posed on low pedestals inside the store. The place had a wonderful smell. Flowers and spice. The salespeople looked healthy, brimming with life, and were attired in elegant parodies of Freedomworker uniforms. Skyblue silk overalls, gold jewelry, touches of fur, militaristic epaulettes. Some of the mannequins had the same fascistic garb. Others did not; they were naked. But all of them looked like they could be alive. So lifelike. Almost human. How fascinating. She looked at one closely. A naked female form with tomato red hair. One of the statue's arms was raised. Ashley saw beads of sweat there, in the armpit. How could that be? She reached out and touched the torso. Soft plastic which gave like skin to her touch. The plastic was sweating. Leaning close to the mannequin, she could smell, from the figure's armpit, the most horrendous odor. Armpit stink squared. She drew back, amazed, and the mannequin farted. A ripping sound of flatulence emerged from its rear. Ashley soon smelled it, this mannequin fart. Acrid! She pinched her nose, winced, turned away, hurried to a display case away from the mannequin. The display case, glistening steel and glass, nearly overflowed with perfumes, oils, creams, cleansers and other scented cosmetics.

"May I help you?"

Ashley looked up. An attendant stood behind the case— young, healthy, a walking advertisement for the products she sold. The attendant smiled. Her teeth glistened.

"No," Ashley said, "just looking." Her own voice sounded very distant to her, as if she were speaking in the midst of a windstorm or as if her voice were a signal nearly lost in the static of a radio.

"If you don't mind my saying so," the attendant said, "I have a skin conditioner that I think you'll like. I think it would be just perfect for you actually. Here, give me your hand."

The attendant's voice was so soothing that Ashley let her take her hand. For the first time, Ashley noticed there was music playing in the background. Crazy piano music which added to her anxiety. Ashley had no idea what the piece was.

The attendant turned Ashley's hand over, looked at her palm, then turned it back again. Ashley looked at the attendant. There was something about her she recognized too. It seemed as if all of the salespeople she was seeing today were vaguely familiar. The attendant held Ashley's hand softly, squeezed a circlet of dark ointment from a plastic tube onto the back of Ashley's hand. The attendant rubbed the paste into Ashley's flesh with her fingers. Ashley smelled a strange scent of something burning, of incense perhaps. "There," she said. "It's you."

"What is it?" Ashley asked. She looked down at her hand

and recoiled. The attendant tightened her hold. A strong grip, hurting her.

"'Nothing'," the attendant said. "It's called 'Nothing'."

Ashley saw that the paste had eaten a hole in her skin. The skin was gone from the back of her hand. She could see muscle and veins and long thin bones. She smelled the odor of burning flesh and then there was nothing, an area of nothingness in her hand. Opaque and vacant—just like what had happened to Bruno with the chocolates.

"Let me go!"

"Don't you think you should be at home, at home with Bruno, I mean," the attendant said. "I'm worried about him." Her voice was the voice that Ashley had heard inside her head at the Arboretum.

Ashley pulled away hard.

The attendant exclaimed, "What the hell?"

Ashley yelled, "Who the fuck do you think you are rubbing that viral shit on my hand?" Her fists clenched, then unclenched when she saw the attendant's expression. The salesperson was disconcerted. Ashley looked down at her hand. There was only some kind of skin creme there. She smelled it. It smelled like flowers, herbs.

"Oh, my god, I'm sorry," Ashley said. The attendant was on the verge of tears. Ashley felt embarrassment color her face. Shame. The hot sting of shame. She looked around the store. Other shoppers were looking at her worriedly. She hurried from the store. It was raining hard again. There were a sheet of water on the sidewalk and sheets of rain in the air. Feeling the hard rain soaking through her clothes, she ran. A voice in her head—whose was it?—said, "You'd better hurry back to Bruno. Hurry!" Then the voice in her mind broke into laughter. Chilling, foreboding laughter.

*   *   *

It seemed to Dude the Obscure that more and more he was finding himself in conversations with people he hardly knew or had just met. Perhaps it was his lifestyle, he said to himself, the fact that he spent so much time sitting in bars and coffee shops. Or maybe it was something about his appearance. After all, he was a warm and fuzzy sort of guy, a sort of naughty human teddy bear.

The man in a dark corner of the barroom was talking to him excitedly about the subject of the day, the recent apprehension of the Human Pet.

Dude interjected, "The guy must be a little crazy. I mean, let's forget for a moment living like a pet with some weird leather-babe. Certainly, going around the city in the darkest hours of the night hunting pets and killing them—maybe even sodomizing them first—that's a bit beyond the pale, even allowing for current social norms."

"But you have to look at it in a larger context," said Barry Sarnoff, head of the organization called DOOMED, Domestication Of Others Must End, Damn It. He gesticulated frantically when he spoke. Lots of hand movements. He had lots of hair too—a shaggy beard and matted hair like a tangle of dirty twine pasted to the top of his head. Even the backs of his hands were hairy. "We have to look at the meaning of the domestication of animals."

"Howso?" Dude asked, raising an eyebrow, taking another sip of his scotch and soda. He was a bit lubricated.

"What gives us the right as human beings," Barry erupted, "to capture or breed other living creatures, subdue them, take away their wildness, and force them to live as degraded commodities to answer our pathetic emotional needs?"

"Hey, I had a dog when I was a kid," Dude said. "I liked him. He was my best friend."

"You mean he was your best servant. He was your love machine. I bet you cut his balls off too. He was your best eunuch—always there to play with you when you needed something to play with, to hit when you needed something to hit, to fetch things for you when you needed fucking things fetched. You took this former wolf and turned it into a doll, a slave, a creature that had to lick your hand when it wanted to eat, to wag its tail when it wanted to shit."

"So what are you saying?" Dude asked. "You seem to be very negative on this 'pet' thing."

"I'm saying that this Pet Hunter, this Human Pet—whatever you want to call him—is a very revolutionary guy."

"Revolutionary?"

"Yes. He has struck a significant blow for freeing the pets."

"Freeing them? He killed them."

"Live free or die, man!" Barry said. "That's what I say. Live free or die. If I am an animal in servitude, better to die than to have to beg for my supper. Better to die than to have to amuse some asshole bourgeois family."

"What about the sodomizing though?"

"Well . . . uh . . . yes," Barry said, less loudly. The electric intensity of his eyes dimmed momentarily. "That was a bit . . . excessive. Overindulgent perhaps. But when you look at it in a larger context, don't we humans fuck our pets all the time? Maybe not literally, but figuratively? And don't we fuck the animals that we eat? I mean when you look at the range of meanings for 'fuck', if I'm a beef cow hauled off to the slaughterhouse, well I'm fucked, aren't I? Truly fucked. I mean, we eat animals, we make them our slaves, why shouldn't we screw them too?"

"I'd never thought of it like that," admitted Dude, changing his mind about ordering a hamburger with the ten dollars he still had in his pocket, though he was hungry. But, what was the alternative? It had been a long time since he had eaten a vegetable, except maybe a French fry. On the other hand, better to drink his money anyway. Nutrition for the soul.

"Well, just think about it! You really should try to think about it," Barry said. There were flecks of the vegetarian chili he was eating in his beard, so Dude really could not look directly at his face for too long. "I mean, have you ever been out to the suburbs?"

"Once or twice."

"Right! And you've driven through these places where there's large house after large house with palatial tracts of green grass, each lawn surrounded by security fences. And what do you see inside? You see these pampered dogs and cats—animals that their owners have paid thousands of dollars for—well groomed and totally miserable, totally servile living creatures that have been made into playthings for the rich. Putrid! Sweating! Disgusting! And you know what else is disgusting? The god damned City Zoo!"

"The City Zoo? I didn't know we had one."

"That's right, we do. It's not as big as it used to be, of course, but there're still animals there. Animals that have been held captive for ten and fifteen and twenty years. Polar bears who have never seen the North Pole. Lions and tigers who were born in captivity. Zebras that were kidnapped when they were colts—babies!—and brought here to America to live as objects of amusement. You should go there and experience the horror first hand. They live in these chintzy little pens with maybe a touch of grass or a boulder or a withered tree and they say they are trying to recreate the natural environment the animals would live in if they were in the wild? What hyper-fucking-kinetic, sweating, fucking bullshit. It really irritates me, man. I was over there just today yelling at one of the keepers."

"What happened?"

"Oh . . . a couple of guards hauled me out and kicked my ass. But it was worth it. It was worth the sacrifice. Animals must be free! They just have to be! How can we consider ourselves evolved creatures when we're keeping other creatures in captivity?"

Dude hazarded a direct look at Barry Sarnoff. He did not

look like a guy who had recently been beaten up. But so what? Poetic license in self-described valor was something Dude could relate to.

"The Zoo," Barry said. "The Zoo is an evil place."

*   *   *

No one else knew about it. He had found this place when he was a boy. It was a hidden cave, a grotto in the Arboretum. The entrance was completely obscured by thick thorn bushes and there was really only one way in—a secret path between the thorns and the bare rock face that sided the opening to the cave. Once inside the opening, the cave was a roughly cylindrical space tall enough for him to stand in and spacious enough, perhaps twenty feet across, for him to move about freely. He sat in the cave now, late at night, some candles and a kerosene lamp illuminating the private place. His private place. At one side of the stone chamber parts of animals decomposed in a pile of gore. Next to the oozing pile was a small circle of stones and inside the stones were the charred remains of many fires. Over these stones was a crude spit on which was the cold, charred corpse of a Dachshund. Parts of it had been cut or ripped away. He sat on an old kitchen chair he had dragged into his lair and he looked at the dog, the small Beagle, still alive, that he held in a crude pen fashioned from rope, stakes, wire, sticks. The brown and white dog had been his "guest" for a few days. Starving, weak, the dog looked at the man warily. The light from the candles flickered in the dog's eyes. A muzzle encircled its snout. A barking dog could give his secret place away. The man did not feel like killing or screwing the dog. He sat musing quietly. He was at an impasse. Then he spoke to the dog.

"A man has got to have a hobby," he said, "something to do. A lot of people have hobbies that they try to turn into something important in their lives. They try to make things they can sell or learn new talents they can put to use. I thought like that once.

Now I think that a hobby should be primarily for pleasure. Solely for pleasure. It doesn't matter whether you're very good at it or not. It just matters that you enjoy it."

He paused as if he expected some kind of answer.

He continued, "In fact, I think there's something to be said for choosing a hobby that you're never going to be particularly good at or a hobby that will never turn into something that you've got to take too seriously. That way your hobby can never turn into something that you start to rely on for your sense of self-worth. When a hobby becomes that important, it begins to lose its fun. And then, it can begin to undermine your sense of self. You become the hobby. You follow me, poochie?

"That's why I chose hunting for my hobby. I hunt little fellas like you. Pets. I have fun, but no one is ever going to judge me on how well I do it. And, I'll never have to worry about holding myself to high standards of achievement. Some people might over-intellectualize this activity with its tracking, hunting, killing, cooking, eating. They might think that I am an over-urbanized type reconnecting with my primitive 'manhood.' They might try to make me some kind of Twenty-first Century hero. They're wrong. That's the wrong way to look at it. Hunting pets is very mellow, very relaxing, very healing. That's why I do it. It relaxes me. And that's the story of why you're here, doggie. Did you know that? What's unpleasant for you is great for me. At least, it has been. Now . . . I don't know anymore."

He smiled sadly to himself. He was wearing a pair of sneakers and a pair of old, dirty, khaki trousers which were spattered with mud and animal juices. He wore a robe that was made from dog and cat pelts crudely stitched together and a Sherlock Holmes hat. The ear flaps were down. He bent down and picked up one of the weapons that lay strewn on the floor, a spear that he sometimes used when he was hunting pets. The beagle cowered even further towards the back of its tiny pen and whimpered through its muzzled mouth. There were a number of weapons on the ground including a large hunting knife, a net, a bow and arrow, a club, and a battered trash can lid which he used to fend off enraged animals. He touched the top of the spear lightly with a finger. It was getting dull. He would have to sharpen it. He had made the spear himself out of a fine, straight, strong branch and a piece of scrap metal he had shaped and fashioned in his basement workshop. The workshop was a vestige of his last hobby: metalworking. How he had grown to hate metalworking! What stressful frenzies he had worked himself into trying to make elaborate fixtures out of metal. How he had raged when they had turned out wrong, which they invariably had. In fact, this spearhead was one of the best things he had ever made on his forge. He put down the spear. He sat a moment in expressionless silence and then he put his face in his hands. He was coming to another hobby-related crisis. He felt empty. He sighed.

He said, "God, I don't know what I'm going to do. I caught you fair and square but for some reason I just don't feel like killing you. So what are our options? What are they? I could leave you here and you'd die of starvation, or I could give you a thump on the head with my club and put you out of your misery, or I guess I could just let you go. You'd like that, wouldn't you, fella, to go home?"

It seemed that a low voltage jolt of recognition touched the dog. He stirred a little at the mention of the word "home."

"Well, let's just the two of us think on it for a minute? What do you say?" the Pet Hunter asked. "Huh, little fella?"

*   *   *

Costello had promised himself he was only going to have a couple of beers, then knock off and go to bed. That had been three hours ago. Now he had drunk all his beers and was drinking vodka neat, pouring gulps of the liquid into a glass, aiming them down his throat. Very intoxicated, he sat in the drab kitchen of his apartment. Kitten sat at the table too, sitting on one of the kitchen chairs, looking at his new master. It was too bright in the kitchen. Costello hated it, but he had never done anything about it except wear sunglasses, as he did now, in the bright room.

"The problem is . . ." Costello said to the dog who looked at him quizzically, "the problem is that it's just an unsolvable problem. First of all, there's no way I can really talk to Taffiola's suspect without giving some kind of explanation. And second of all, even if I could sit down with her by myself, what would I say?"

He looked off. All he saw was a sink full of dirty dishes and his and the dog's reflection in a dirty window. Then he spoke not to himself and not to the dog but to a woman who was not there. He spoke as if he were having a conversation with the captured member of Women Against Cars.

He said, "Listen, honey, let's put police business aside and let me just say honestly that . . . that . . . I think I'm in love with one of your fellow anti-car terrorists, the one you call Esmeralda, and I'd appreciate it if you'd tell me how to find her. I'd really like to sit down and talk to her. In fact, I'd like to invite her out for a drink—just her and me and . . . uh . . . my pal Kitten here." He looked back at the dog. The dog began to swirl and undulate before him—liquid dog—but Costello continued to speak, saying, "I promise that I won't arrest her, and if you help me, I can . . . I can what? . . . I can get you out of the mess that you seem to have gotten yourself into." He stopped. Costello shook his head. "Fuck," he explained. "Unworkable. Un-fucking-workable. Stupid! Stupid."

He lit a cigarette, exhaled, looked at the dog. "Kitten," he said, "do you find it the least bit strange that a good looking guy like me can't even get some time alone with a woman who calls herself Elizabeth Borden? Because I do."

Kitten yawned. Costello got up, stumbled to the bathroom, puked, bathed his face in cold water, mumbled "Lizzie Borden," chortled miserably, cleared his throat, spat on the floor, went to bed.

Chapter 15

Halloween

The girl, nine years old, was costumed as a gypsy, wearing ill-fitting clothes, flimsy and bright. Her face, usually unadorned and innocent, was daubed with childishly applied makeup. Huge earrings hung from her ears. She stood at the apartment door with four other children. They also wore costumes. One of them, a tall boy in a tattered devil's suit which was too small for him, rang the doorbell. He had hard eyes. He gripped a plastic pitchfork. Waiting, the children suppressed giggles. It was Halloween.

The door opened slightly. Out peered the fearful face of an elderly woman. There were curlers in her hair.

"Trick or treat," the children cried.

The worry on the woman's face softened. She opened the door and looked down at the children—a gypsy, a devil, a lion, an astronaut, and one little child whose costume she could not identify. He was a little boy, perhaps seven or eight, with tousled brown hair and sticky cheeks and hands. Chocolate. He wore a cape, a sweatshirt with some sort of round insignia pinned to his front, and over his baggy pants he wore a pair of pinkish shorts, boxer shorts. The boxer shorts were too tight.

"I'm a super hero," he proudly announced.

"Oh," the old apartment dweller said. "Isn't it too late for you young children to be out alone?"

"Trick or treat," the gypsy girl said. The dark discoloration on one side of the girl's face was not a trick of light or some sort of ghoulish make-up, the woman saw. She felt pity for the youngster, the small luxury of pity.

"Yeah, trick or treat," the other children cried.

The woman considered. A smile touched her wan lips. "Trick," she said.

"What?"

"Trick. If you want a treat, you have to perform a trick."

The children became silent. Then the gypsy girl said, "I could tell you a story I think you'd like."

The woman stepped forward, bent over, looked at the little girl closely, smiled. She had stale breath. Old teeth. Yellow-green stubs. She reached out and patted the girl's head. Gnarled hands.

"Yes, dear, I'd love to hear a story."

The girl began, "Once a long, long time ago, there was a very mean King with a beautiful and very nice Queen. He was very mean to the Queen, and though she didn't like him she tried hard not to show it. But there was someone at the castle who did love the Queen. His name was Rupert. He was very sweet but he was ugly. The Queen ignored him."

Amazed at the musical voice, the clear articulation of the little girl, the woman focused fully on her. She did not notice as the little boy in the astronaut suit slipped behind her to enter her apartment.

The girl continued, "Rupert was infatuated with the Queen. He followed her wherever she went . . . at a respectful distance, of course. And he used every excuse to be in her presence. He secretly left candy, gifts, and flowers for her. He wrote poems for her and slipped them in places where he knew she would find them."

"Ick," the lion observed.

"The Queen hardly thought about these gifts or where they

came from, but the mean King did and he got jealous, very jealous," the gypsy girl continued. As the girl described the king's jealousy, the astronaut moved stealthily through the cramped apartment. He had pushed the visor of his plastic space helmet up so that he could see better. The bedroom was the room he wanted. He found it, surveyed the room from the doorway. There was a dressing table with an opened jewelry box on top, an aquarium, an old man on the bed. The boy paused. The man looked asleep. There were tubes running into his nose from something on the other side of the bed. Disgusting! The old man looked weak, thin. The boy thought he could see the bones of his skull under the tight, yellowish skin of his face. The man coughed, opened eyes, stirred, closed eyes, returned to silence, stillness, sleep. The intruder, astronaut, adventurer on a new planet, tiptoed to the dressing table, began putting items into his trick-or-treat bag, his specimen bag. A watch, it looked like gold. Some jewelry. Three bottles of pills. A knickknack. He pulled out the drawers in the dressing table. No money. Some photographs and letters. He dropped them into the bag.

The gypsy girl said, "So the King ordered Rupert's head cut off, but Rupert's head did not die. His head stayed alive. It could still talk. It was a miracle."

"Oh my!" the woman exclaimed. The other children had fixed their attentions too on the storyteller, her unexpected story.

"Everyone soon saw that Rupert's mind was smarter than ever. Maybe it was because it had been cut off from his heart. The head began to give the evil King very good advice on matters of the kingdom, so the King had Rupert's head placed on a comfortable pillow on a golden pedestal in the main throne room, right next to the glass cases which displayed the royal jewels. Rupert still ate and drank—although not very much—but other people had to feed him. Sometimes he liked to have his head turned over so that it was upside down on the pillow. That was how he slept."

Tossing shirts, slacks, underthings onto the floor, the astronaut was rummaging now through the drawers of a dresser. They smelled like old people clothes. Ah-ha! Here was the thing he wanted—an envelope. It was bulging. He opened it, looked inside. Money. He dropped it in the bag. The game was over. Then the aquarium caught the youth's attention. He moved to it, put his nose to the cool, moist glass. Bright fishes. Evil alien fishes, the astronaut boy said playfully to himself. Parasites. Rolling up carefully his astronaut sleeves, he reached both hands into the water, caught fish, crushed them between his fingers. It felt funny to crush little fish, like popping little balloons.

The girl was still telling her tale.

"Soon the Queen fell in love with Rupert's head. She snuck into the throne room late at night and woke Rupert up to talk with him. She ran her fingers through his hair, whispered into his ear, kissed him on the forehead. She even tried to kiss him on the lips."

"Ick," the superhero said.

All the fish were dead. The astronaut wiped his hands on the smooth silver of his astronaut suit. The prone man coughed. Again, the boy noticed that the room had a funny smell. Old people. He looked at the old man. There were clear tubes running into his nostrils. When the boy had been younger he had called nostrils "snozzles." The man's mouth was open. He had no teeth. Disgusting! The boy saw that the tubes from his nostrils fed into a single clear tube that ran across the man's chest to some kind of cylindrical metal tank. It must be air, oxygen. The tank had a small dial on top of it and a thing that looked like a thermometer in which a tiny ball hovered. This prompted an idea for an experiment in the boy's mind. The boy turned the dial one way and the ball jumped up; he turned it the other way and the ball fell. A space explorer experiment! He left the dial there. The man coughed harshly, cleared his throat, gasped. Interested, the boy watched.

"Again the Queen snuck in to see Rupert late at night. She turned his head over and woke him up.

"'Rupert,' the Queen said, 'I can't help it—I love you.' Again she stroked his hair and nibbled at his ears, whispering words of affection. 'You have become so brilliant, so wise, and your wisdom has given you so much power with the King.'

"But Rupert wasn't that interested. In fact, he was baffled. He said, 'Queen, why is it that you love me now when, let's face it, I'm a freak—a head without a body? You never had any interest in me when I was whole.'

"The Queen replied, 'Perhaps I love you now because you do not, or cannot love me, dear Rupert.'"

The woman, the devil, the lion, and the superhero were listening intently, quietly to the little storyteller.

"Rupert said, 'No offense, Queen, but it's hard to love without a body. And it's hard for me to believe that you could ever love someone who could not return your love.'

"The Queen said, 'That may be so, Rupert, but at least you'll always know one thing.'

"'What's that, Queen?' Rupert asked.

"'At least you'll know that I only love you for your mind,' the Queen replied."

The girl stopped and looked around expectantly. The woman looked down at her. Then her eyes brightened. She giggled. The other children did not respond. The woman's expression changed. She heard her husband fighting for breath.

"Carl," she cried, turning, stepping back into her apartment. "What's wrong?"

The sound of his gasping filled the apartment. She hobbled toward the bedroom. The child in the astronaut suit emerged from the room and dashed by her. She paused, looked at him in disbelief. "What have you done?" She stepped tentatively after the boy, then stopped, rushed to her husband instead.

The children ran down the hall.

Gleefully they chortled.

They dashed down the stairwell. The stairwell swelled with sounds of their movement, their little shoes, their laughter, their high voices. The devil threw open the door and they ran onto the street. The night air was mild, thick with a fog that formed misty haloes around the few unbroken street lamps. After dashing a block or two, the children started to walk, quiet now, fighting for breath.

"That was a bland story," the devil said. "Where did you hear it?"

"My daddy told it to me," the gypsy said.

The devil looked at her. She was telling the truth. He could always tell when she was telling the truth, even if no one else could.

"Where's your daddy now," the astronaut asked, swinging his trick-or-treat bag proudly. The proud space explorer.

"Not here," the girl said.

No one said anything else.

Two zebras emerged from the mist and walked nonchalantly down the foggy street.

"Bland!" the devil whispered. "The horses are wearing costumes too."

*   *   *

Little hands knocked at his apartment door. Halloween. Costello ignored them. It was a rare night off. He was going to spend it in solitude with his companion Kitten. He turned up the television and opened another beer. The phone rang. He deliberated. Against his better instincts he picked it up.

"Another perfect evening ruined," he said to Kitten at the conclusion of the call.

*   *   *

"Don't go," Ashley said.

"Got to, ugly," Bruno replied. "You come."

"No."

"Oh, Ashley, I don't want to leave you here, but I've got to play this viral gig. It's Halloween after all."

Bruno was already wearing his fur coat and his weasel hat. His guitar was waiting next to the door.

"I know," Ashley said softly.

Bruno enfolded her in his furry arms, held her tight. She meant a lot to him, but it was getting late.

"I wonder where that damn Sebastian is?" he wondered.

"Who knows?" said Ashley. "Probably off staring at a wall."

"How about Karla?"

"I wish I knew. I've been trying to reach her all day. All I get is her fucking answering machine."

"Hmmm," Bruno nodded. "Well listen, I'll be right back after the show and we'll spend the rest of the night together. We'll have a Cave Beer and some James and atrophy."

She walked him to the door, closed it after him, looked back at the emptiness of the apartment, rubbed her hands together, walked to the telephone. She was ready.

*   *   *

Chaotic soundscape.

An uproar in the city. Someone had released many of the animals —the larger animals mostly—from the City Zoo. The roars of lions, the trumpetings of elephants, and the hoof beats of stampeding gazelles reverberated through the night, intermixing with human sounds: sirens, shouts, screams.

Nearly every police officer and firefighter in the city had been called onto the streets.

Alert! Alert!

Their mission: catch the animals.

Strange round-up.

Police headquarters was almost empty. Behind the bullet proof divider in the station's reception area Patrolwoman Michelle Bulgakov read a paper.

She raised her eyes. Customer.

A nun staggered in. The front of her habit was splattered with blood. The nun gasped, cried, "A rhino got me!" She was unsteady. She fell face first on the floor where she lay unmoving. Bulgakov punched the intercom to call emergency medical. Nothing. She hit the button for back-up. No one was there. She punched the button for the squad room, for homicide, vice, narcotics, traffic—no one picked up. The police woman hesitated. Regulations. Under no circumstances was she to go to the other side of the divider. But this was a nun from whose midsection a pool of blood was spewing onto the dirty tiles of the floor. Bulgakov pulled open a drawer and grabbed a pair of latex gloves. "Please, God, no mouth-to-mouth resuscitation," she prayed aloud, as she opened the gate in the bullet-proof partition and hurried to the moaning nun. She knelt alongside the fallen woman, reached her hands under her and turned her onto her back. The nun was pointing a revolver at her. The revolver was covered with blood. It was not blood. Quickly, the nun hopped to her feet, said, "One word from you and you're dead."

Bulgakov nodded. Lord, don't let the sister shoot me, she prayed to herself.

Three more women attired as nuns came running through the front entrance to Police Headquarters. They carried submachine guns.

"Praise the lord," one of them said.

"Now, honey," the bloody nun, the apparent leader, said, "there's one place we want to go and you're going to take us there—the Special Prisoners Unit."

Through the deserted station Patrolwoman Bulgakov led them to the basement chambers where prisoners undergoing prolonged interrogation were held. The lone guard there was easily induced to open the door to the cell that held the imprisoned member of Women Against Cars.

"What took you so long?" she snarled as she emerged from the cell.

"We couldn't decide if you were worth the risk, Lizzie" the blood-stained jailbreaker said cheerfully. "Now, where are they keeping the other one?"

"What other one?" the woman who called herself Lizzie Borden hissed.

The sounds—the barking and whining—which started at that moment from an adjoining cell answered the question.

"There," another nun commanded the cell guard. "Open that one."

"But that one holds the nut that killed all those pets," the guard said.

"Do it."

He opened the cell door.

Two of the habit-clad raiders entered the cell, then led the Human Pet into the hall. He was naked. He cowered and whimpered.

"Whose fucking idea was this?" Lizzie Borden demanded, rolling her eyes.

"Our Lord's," the leader said. "Time to go."

They locked Bulgakov and the guard in one of the cells. The guard turned to Bulgakov and said, "They're not really nuns, do you think?" The six—four women attired as nuns, one woman in the green uniform of a prisoner, and one large, naked man— moved quietly, deliberately, swiftly through the station and into the night. As they hurried, the leader, the mother superior, took a small hatchet from beneath her habit and handed it to her recently imprisoned companion.

"All right!" Lizzie Borden cried, swinging the hatchet through the air. "Now we're back in business."

A long, black limousine was waiting at the curb.

That stopped Lizzie in her tracks.

"What the fuck?" she exclaimed. "A car."

"Get in," one of the jailbreakers said. "We'll blow it up later."

"Fuck me," Lizzie cried. She hatcheted a side panel of the car for good luck, then they all jumped into the car, sped off.

*   *   *

"Look," Costello said to his dog, who brought his head in from the open window to look towards the other side of the street, "a group of machine-gun toting nuns is running from Headquarters with two prisoners, one of them naked. Do you think that this might indicate that a crime is in progress?"

Kitten barked. The dog liked action.

Costello put a revolving blue light on the top of his car, turned on the siren, and gave chase, barely avoiding a baby elephant as the detective screeched into the first turn of what was to be a lengthy pursuit.

*   *   *

Sydney hoped that there would not be a dog. But if there was a dog he was ready. The mansion overlooking the Arboretum—now a vast inky sea at two o'clock in the morning on the foggy Halloween night—was spacious, looming, spooky. The moon cast hardly any light. The house was completely dark except for a room on the third floor where there was the faint flickering light of a fire. Attired all in black, he had crept his way deftly around the house and through the backyard. Now, using a burglary tool, he soundlessly pried open a glass door at the rear of the house.

There was a dog. A guard dog, a German Shepherd, rushed into the room, barked, bared fangs. Sydney was ready. Calmly, he held out a juicy steak and whispered, "Special delivery for you." The dog growled at him, then, overwhelmed by the meat smell, took the steak from Sydney's hand, bit into it, staggered, fell over onto its side, developed difficulty breathing. Sydney began to creep through the quiet darkness of the house. For such a fat man he moved quietly. For a moment he could hear the sound of the dog's labored breathing. That sound stopped. Then, all Sydney could hear in the quiet house was the soft sound of his own wheezing breath as he moved through the first floor of Dr Bentley's mansion.

He crept down into the basement. The sound of the oil burner dominated the darkness. He turned on a flashlight. The basement, well-maintained and uncluttered, was a large, open space with a number of closed rooms—a laundry room and storage chambers—at one end. Under the stairs was a little open woodshop with tools and a workbench. He saw no evidence of what he was looking for, but something he saw in the woodshop made him pause: a coffin set on two sawhorses. He could see the coffin was freshly constructed; beneath it were wood shavings and sawdust. The musty smell of the basement intermixed with the smell of fresh-cut wood: smell within smell. Sydney shrugged his shoulders. Perhaps the doctor built coffins for a hobby, he speculated. Or maybe she was planning to kill someone. The bad dream bitch. But not him. The coffin was not built wide enough for him. Maybe she would bury her guard dog in it. Following the ascending beam of his flashlight, Sydney left the basement, returned to the first floor.

Faintly at first, then more strongly, Sydney heard the sound of strange singing, singing marked by disquieting cadences. It sounded Near Eastern, he thought. This singing, combined with an unidentifiable scent, simultaneously sweet and acrid, which seemed to hang lightly in the air of the house, caused a pit to form in his stomach and the small hairs on the back of his neck and hands to stand. On the first floor he did not find what he was looking for. He cursed Eric for sending him here. He climbed a wide, central stairway to the second floor. On the second floor, the sound of the singing was louder. A woman's high-pitched voice keened in an unknown language. He figured it had to be Doctor Bentley, the over-educated babe that Eric so obviously had a boner for. He searched each room but he did not find what he was looking for on the second level. Moving so covertly, so silently, strained his bulky body. He was sweating. He hated to sweat in his silk shirts. He ascended to the third floor. He crept along the hallway, keeping to the darker shadows on one side of the long, wide hall. The door at one end of the hall, the only illuminated room in the house, was half open. Mildly pulsating light spilled from the half-opened door into the hall like a yellow and orange tongue lapping the plushly carpeted floor, the long wall. The light looked like it must come from a fireplace. The eerie singing came from the room too. She must be in there. He moved even more carefully. Searching the third floor room by room, he found Dr. Bentley's bedchamber, guest rooms, a sunroom, a library. Finally, he found what he was looking for: her office. It was at the end of a tiny hall which opened onto the main hall right next to the door of the room where he knew she was, the room with the flickering light. The singing coming from that room grew louder, prompting Sydney to move more quickly, more quietly. He could feel fear mounting up from his groin. This was his nightmare, to be alone in a dark house with a fucking witch. He stifled the impulse to run. He forced himself to concentrate. By now his eyes were well accustomed to the lack of light, to following the narrow beam of the flashlight. His quick scan of the office revealed a writing table, bookshelves full of books, shelves on which manila folders and journals were neatly arranged, two file cabinets, and, everywhere he looked, religious icons, statuettes, figures. Some of them, he could tell, were clearly Christian: saints, the crucified Christ, his mother Mary, or the contorted images of demons or Lucifer himself. Others represented unfamiliar figures—gods or devils, he could not tell—from the religions of other cultures. Using the beam, he examined the file cabinets and pulled out the drawer marked F-G-H-I-J. Nothing. God damn it, he cursed under his breath. Then he froze. The keening had reached a climax of intensity. But it was a false climax and the singing lessened again in intensity, became a shallow-throated sing-song. He wracked his brain. Not under F, how about N? He slid out the drawer marked L-M-N-O-P and soon found a number of files marked NIGHTMARE. He thumbed through them quickly. What he was looking for was not there. Fuck, he was going to lose it. Too much pressure. He needed a pill.

He pulled out a file drawer at random. What would he tell Tang if he came back empty-handed? Then, a desperate intuition. He pulled out Q-R-S-T, flashed the light over the tabs on the folders. He was simultaneously startled and unsurprised to find one that said SECRET FORMULAS. He pulled the folder from the file cabinet and laid it out on the desk. Soon he had what he wanted: FORMULA FOR NIGHTMARE INDUCING AGENT. Two pages long. A complex garble of herbs, chemicals, occult symbols, equations. Only Eggie could understand this sweaty shit. He folded it crisply and put it in the inside pocket of his thin, leather jacket; then he placed the folder neatly back into the drawer and shut it soundlessly. Mission accomplished.

Sydney was more than ready to leave. Lifting his feet high, tip-toeing, he started down the hall. Something arrested him. An urge. He tried to stifle it but before he left he wanted just to look into the room, the firelit room where Dr Bentley was. He had to see her. Just one look. One glance. He did not wish, mothlike, to be caught in the flames, but, foxlike, to steal a peek, one quick peek, at the woman whose formula he had just lifted. He stopped in mid-tip-toe. He pivoted on his heel. Just one quick look, Sydney told himself. She won't see me. But he was not reassured. He was more afraid than ever. This was his nightmare. Alone with a witch. Not running. Going to her. Not running. He could not stop. He moved near the door. He got down on the carpeted floor of the hall, got his breathing under control. No wheezes. Dragging his stomach across the carpet, he crawled slowly, painstakingly, to the door of the room and poked first his nose then his face, his eyes across the threshold, around the half-opened door. He saw a room dancing with the light not of a fireplace but of dozens of candles. A heavy cloud of candle smoke and incense hung in the room. This room too was dominated by strange sculptures, masks, images, icons. Along one side of the room were long, thin tables which seemed to project above them, for a foot or so, a thick, oily light through which the smoke from the candles and incense swirled in gyres. In the center of the room, sitting cross-legged in a diaphanous, white robe sat Dr Bentley. Sydney swallowed hard. She was not a hideous witch; she was gorgeous. She sat very erectly, breathing slowly and deeply, her eyes half-closed. He could see her firm breasts, her nipples standing up under her sheer robe, the thatch of hair between her legs. Her white-blonde hair hung to her shoulders. Next to Bentley on a delicate wooden table was a vial of clear liquid and a syringe. She was clearly in a trance. She was singing who could tell what? The fear left him. He felt aroused. He wanted to go to her, take her, but, knowing his mission and Tang's wrath, he tore his eyes away from the meditating figure. Eric would kill him if he screwed things up. It was time to go.

He pushed himself up with his hands to back away from the room. Bentley opened her eyes.

In a sort of half push-up position Sydney froze. The weight of his torso made his arms quiver.

Bentley looked at him either intently or unseeingly, he could not tell. Slowly she smiled, spoke. Her voice was far away, dreamy. She asked, "Are you part of the nightmare or are you real?"

"Real," Sydney gasped. His face was blotched with the effort of holding himself up.

"Oh," Bentley said. She closed her eyes and resumed chanting.

*　　*　　*

The chase through the city was eventful. There was much squealing and banging into things as Costello chased the limousine. A number of times, Costello radioed for back-up. None could be provided. To make matters worse, Kitten vomited in the car, sick from too much swerving. Now, Costello chased the limousine at high speed down a potholed street alongside Final Rapture Cemetery. The smell of dog vomit permeated the car. To

306 | KEVIN MCCAFFREY

306 | KEVIN MCCAFFREY

one side of the car, headstones were barely visible in the low-lying fog. On the other side, there was only inky blackness. The limousine braked, swerved, slid around a tight, unexpected turn.

"Hold on, poochie," Costello said through gritted teeth as he pushed down on the brake pedal and swung the wheel, guiding the groaning car. They rounded the turn at about 40 miles an hour. "What the hell!" Costello yelled. Directly before him was a ramp leading into the back of a trailer truck. The limousine had climbed the ramp into the truck already. To one side of the ramp was a bonfire blocking what was left of the roadway and a line of figures with machine guns; to the other side was the wrought iron fence of the graveyard. Screeching, the brakes brought the car to a halt; he looked in his rear view mirror; women with machine guns had already stepped behind his vehicle. Costello lifted his hands from the steering wheel, rolled down his window. The barrel of a machine gun was shoved in his face. "Excuse me," Costello said, "I think I might have taken a wrong turn. You don't happen to know the way to . . . San Jose, do you?"

"Out," a female voice said. "Hands on the car."

Costello got out, turned, put his hands on the cool roof of his automobile.

Kitten staggered out after him, lay down on the ground. Another woman took Costello's gun from his holster, got in the car, shut the police radio off.

"Do you ever get a sense of *deja-vu*, Detective," the voice behind the machine gun asked.

"Esmeralda?" Costello exclaimed. "What a happy ending to an otherwise non-descript evening."

Costello's car was driven into the trailer truck. He put his hands in the air.

"Let's go," said Esmeralda.

Costello looked over his shoulder. She looked just like he remembered her. True, a beret covered most of her red hair and forehead and a bandanna covered most of the remainder of her face, but her eyes shone with a brightness which to the detective signified exhilaration. Closely behind her walked another well-armed terrorist. The dog Kitten tagged along. Useless, Costello mused to himself. Man's best friend pukes and lies down when the going gets rough. Costello tripped over a pothole. "Do you mind if I say something?" he said. Hearing no reply, he continued, "This might sound strange but I'd really like to see more of you, Esmeralda. I mean, I feel that I can lay myself bare here. I just can't get you out of my mind. The car stuff? Granted, I think you go a bit overboard, but it's intriguing all the same. What say you call me and we'll go out together and maybe torch a car ourselves? I'll bring the gasoline. You bring the Uzi. By the way, you seem to be violating your own anti-car guidelines tonight, if I can be allowed an observation."

"Shut-up," Esmeralda's companion said.

"Don't worry, Detective," Esmeralda said more calmly. "Every vehicle used tonight will be destroyed." Her intonation hovered between world-weary irony and placid sincerity, Costello observed, drinking in the sound of it.

"Thank god," Costello said. "I admire people who stick to first principles."

"What about you, Detective? What are your principles?"

"That's the kind of question that I'd really like to discuss with you at length," Costello said. "Maybe even naked."

Esmeralda laughed. Then she and her companion attached the detective to a tree with his own handcuffs. His stomach rubbed up against the gnarly trunk. Esmeralda's companion walked back to the big truck. Esmeralda said, "I'm almost beginning to like you, Costello."

"I'm irresistible in a gruffly masculine sort of way, aren't I?"

"No, it's not that. Maybe it's because you're so unaware of yourself, of who you are."

"Oh. I wasn't even aware that I had that kind of attractive unselfawareness."

"Now you know."

"Esmeralda. I really think we should get together. Call me."

"Unlikely," she said, "but you never know."

"Well, you'll know where to find me. Here with my tree."

She stepped close to him, kissed him warmly on the cheek.

He felt the spot of her saliva dry as he watched her walk away, get into the cab of the big truck. The truck rumbled off.

Inside the truck's massive trailer, the Women Against Cars moved hurriedly, purposefully. The Human Pet sat naked and alone inside the limousine. A woman dressed in black combat fatigues opened the door next to him. "Come out," she said. She held a dog biscuit. He got out slowly, took the biscuit, bit it in two, chewed. He was a massive, naked man.

"We've got to put something on this guy," she said, looking away.

"Here, he can wear this," one of the women who had dressed as a nun said, wriggling out of her habit. Standing on tiptoes, she slid the nun's habit over the man. It was too small for him. It reached just above his knees and only covered his arms to his elbows.

"How you doing?" the woman who had defrocked, shed her habit, inquired of the escapee. The Human Pet looked down at her, said nothing. A few feet away he saw the other freed prisoner, Lizzie Borden, glaring at him, waving her hatchet menacingly. Abruptly the truck stopped. Everyone kept their feet except Borden. She fell, sliced her arm with the hatchet, swore. Companions went to help her. She swore at them, waved them away with her bloodied weapon. The sliding door was opened. Another woman appeared, beckoned to him, led him to the open rear of the trailer. He walked slowly.

He saw a tall, thin man standing by the side of the truck. He held a flashlight which made a bright circle of light on the old road, illuminating his sandaled feet which shifted nervously, impatiently on the broken asphalt. Dirty toes. The man raised the beam, pointing it at the Human Pet and the woman next to him. She hopped down. The Pet followed. He looked around. It was dark, chilly, spooky. On either side of the unlighted road, woodlands exuded menace.

The unfamiliar man took a step towards them, shined the light on his face, his own face, perhaps in an attempt to allay the Pet's presumed skittishness. In the light, the escapee saw a scraggly beard, disorganized hair, glasses which reflected the beam. The man holding the flashlight spoke enthusiastically, "What a great, great moment for animal freedom, Mr. Tantone. What a great pleasure it is to meet you and to play a roll in your escape. I am Barry Sarnoff. I represent the organization DOOMED—Domestication of Others Must End, Damn It. I am here to bring you to safety."

He motioned with the beam towards an economy car which idled in the shadows. Tantone hesitated for a moment, then started to walk off down the road away from the truck, away from the waiting vehicle. Barry hurried after him. "Mr. Tantone!" he said, "perhaps you don't understand." Reaching up, he put his hand on Tantone's shoulder. Tantone turned, snarled, bit Barry's hand viciously.

"Ow!" Wincing, Barry held his hand against his chest, felt blood dripping from the torn skin and meat of his hand. "Jesus, I can see the bone," he cried. "I can see my bone." The Human Pet threw his head back, howled, turned, dashed off into the darkness. Barry turned to the woman who stood watching by the back of the truck. "Do something! Help me," he implored.

The woman said, "Our deal was to bring him to you, not to make him stay."

*　　*　　*

Humming softly, Bruno walked through the fog. What a tepid gig that was, he thought to himself. He had enjoyed himself thoroughly if not, on second thought, a bit too much. The new songs he had written about hunting and killing pets had gone over really well. He could not wait to get home to bore Ashley with the details of his success. He glanced up at a street sign in the fog. Disch Street. Funny, he did not know this street. But he was sure he was walking in the right direction—homeward. He became aware of soft padding sounds behind him. He looked over his shoulder. A lion was following him. Bruno froze, froze in midstep. The lion stopped too, emitted a tiny growl, a lion purr. Bruno felt his heart jump into his throat. Danger! It did not compute. Big cat. What to do? Running, he told himself, was a bad idea. He ran. The lion ran too. Bruno ran with maximum alacrity, his guitar, unrelinquished, under his arm. His weasel hat fell off. The sounds of the lion's tread stopped. The lion was perhaps examining the hat. Bruno saw the lion eating the hat in his mind's eye. The lion's padding footsteps resumed—were on Bruno's heels. Bruno saw a lighted doorway. A hotel. Stopping on a dime, stepping aside, Bruno felt the lion's body surge by him. He felt the lion's mane brush his buttocks. No pleasure in that proximity. He flung open the glass door to the hotel, jumped within, closed the door behind him as the lion stopped, turned, and swatted at the air, missing Bruno only by a second. Holding the door closed, Bruno watched through the glass door as the lion eyed him, licked at the glass with its big tongue, sat back, roared. After a moment, the beast walked off. Bruno exhaled, turned.

The clerk behind the reception desk was looking at him.

"Lion trouble?" the clerk smiled.

"Yes," Bruno said. He stepped into the hotel's small front lobby. "It seems like it is not a very good night for walking around."

"Is it ever?" the attendant replied. He had an accent. Bruno could not place it.

Though small, the reception area made an impression of elegance—somewhat faded, somewhat Italianate. There were soft carpets, good paintings, brass fixtures, velvet chairs, though all seemed just a bit faded, dusty, worn. Music played lightly in the background. Bruno smiled. Herb Alpert and the Tijuana Brass, the height of traditional good taste.

"A room for the evening, sir?" the desk clerk asked.

Bruno considered. Seeing the entrance to a bar at one end of the lobby, a bar open even at this late hour, determined Bruno's response.

"No, I think I'll just have a drink at the bar. How late is it open?"

"The bar is always open."

"Napping."

Before entering the bar, Bruno stopped at a pay phone. It was a very outdated unit. Rotary dial. He rang his apartment. Many rings, no answer. Ashley must be asleep or, in some perverse snit, refusing to answer.

A dark and cozy room that smelled of tobacco smoke and, faintly, of whiskey, the bar room was dominated by a majestic fireplace and fire which threw nets of undulating yellow-orange light throughout the shadowy room. No one was in the room but the barman. Bruno went to the bar, ordered a vodka. "Hey," Bruno said to the barman, "you look just like the desk clerk." He said it in true surprise. The resemblance was perfect. Both were small men with plain features, jet black hair, and very white skin.

"We're twins," the bartender said.

"Bland." Bruno said to himself. "Bland squared!" Then, seeing the slightly pained look on the bartender's face, he added, "Sorry, that's just an expression, a stupid expression. I don't know why I said it. It means 'interesting.'"

"If bland means interesting, then I am pleased to be bland," the bartender smiled. Like the desk clerk's, his voice was low, bored, weary, foreign.

Putting down his guitar and coat, Bruno sat down at a table near the fire. He drank and smoked. Some time passed. Bruno felt content, pacified.

"May I join you?"

Bruno looked up.

"Of course," he said.

He looked at the woman who had unexpectedly joined him.

She was a female version of the two clerks Bruno had already met at the hotel—short, soft, slim, black-haired, very white skin. She was plain like them, almost nondescript, yet somehow she held allure. The slinky black dress helped. But it was more than that. Her eyes were dark, sparklingly dark like black jewels. Her voice was bored and low, kittenish. Well, he smiled, this was a night of cats.

"Wait, don't tell me . . . you're the sister of the bartender and the desk clerk. You're their twin," Bruno said.

"We're triplets, actually," the young woman said. "My name is Persephone. What's yours?" She spoke with the same foreign accent.

"Persephone," Bruno repeated, mulling it over. Some kind of mythological name.

"That's your name too?" she exclaimed. "I can't believe that."

"No, no. I was . . . uh . . . savoring your name. My name is Bruno."

"Bruno? So, what brings you to the Hotel Disch this evening, dear Bruno?"

Bruno looked at her mouth when she spoke. It seemed that there was nothing inside—no tongue or throat behind the slightly off-white teeth. A void instead. It held his interest, but, strangely, it did not terrify him. He felt the urge to go, but the urge was so slight it was merely one discordant instrument playing in a vast orchestra of impulses, most of the instruments of which played a tune which made him languid, made him stay.

"I was chased here by a lion."

"Oh," Persephone said. The bartender brought two drinks. She drank vodka too.

"There is something strange about this place," Bruno murmured.

"In fact," his companion coyly admitted, "there is. But what leads you to say this?"

"A lot of things," Bruno considered. "What really confirmed it for me is your mouth."

"Its simple beauty?"

"No. The fact that your head, your flesh, seems to surround some sort of vacancy."

"I suppose that's a compliment?"

A calm had taken hold of Bruno. He watched his actions, thoughts, words, with detachment, bemusement. He knew that whatever happened would happen.

"Yes."

"Do you like to play games, to make wagers?" Persephone asked.

"If the stakes are . . . uh . . . appropriate."

"Well then let me propose a wager, a bet, to you."

"What is it?"

"You and I play a game. If you lose, you die; if you win, you leave."

"Do I get to kiss you too?" His question was sort of flip in light of the seriousness of what his companion had proposed, Bruno thought to himself, but he was intrigued by what it would be like to kiss this woman. Bruno did not mistake his nonchalance in response to Persephone's proposal as some sort of bravery; he knew he was oddly disconnected from his feelings, from what his normal reactions would and should have been. Perhaps he was really becoming utterly bland after all, he thought to himself, though this total realization of listless equanimity had come at perhaps the most inopportune time. Talk about the wrong time to atrophy! He knew who this beautiful woman was. It was obvious. At any rate, he did not run.

"In either case you get a kiss, Bruno." Then it dawned on Bruno—her voice sounded very similar to the way a familiar voice, a voice he knew, would sound if it was altered by a foreign accent. But whose voice was it? Karla's? Ashley's? Was it one of theirs? Did Ashley and Karla sound so much alike?

He said, "I don't suppose I have much choice?"

"Oh, but you do. You get to choose the game. We have many, if not all of them here." She got up, touched a stone on the fireplace and the wood paneling of the wall near their table slid open, revealing an expanse of shelves reaching from the floor to the ceiling. There were indeed many games there. "Of course," she continued, looking down at him, "chess is a favorite, as are a variety of card games."

"You've done this before?"

"Yes."

Bruno slowly considered the hundreds of neatly stacked board games.

"How about *Risk*, or *Life*?" he said.

"Fine games," Persephone said, "but really not made to be played by only two players. Besides, it's late. We have time, but not all the time in the world."

"Then I choose that one."

She followed the line his pointing finger indicated.

"*Uncle Wiggley*?"

"No. That one."

"*Candy Land*?" she exclaimed. "But it is a child's game. It's what a five year old would choose."

"I know. I always had great luck with it as a child." A wave of memories, of nostalgic images of himself as a child playing the board game with his mother and father, flooded his thoughts. She took the game out, laid out the board, stacked the cards which control movement. Bruno considered the brightly-colored board and its cartoonish decorations. He saw that the pieces, the markers, were tiny plastic children. The game began. In *Candy Land*, players draw cards to show how far ahead they may move their pieces. Sometimes, with a bad draw, players must move their pieces backwards. Markers move along a trail of colored squares—a repeated pattern of red, purple, yellow, blue, orange, green. Most cards have colored squares which represent how far ahead a player may jump. A few cards have two colored squares, a double jump. Still fewer cards represent places with names of sweets along the colored trail where, either backwards or forwards, a player must move his marker. The goal is King Kandy's

Candy Castle, a sugary fortress with ice cream cone towers. The first one there is the winner. Persephone was lucky. After two draws she had a lead of six squares. Another turn and she was 12 spaces ahead. Bruno felt unwell. Then his luck shifted. He pulled ahead of his competitor, moving along the trail through Peppermint Forest, Gumdrop Pass, Lollipop Woods. Persephone grimaced as he drew a double yellow card that advanced him two yellow squares forward, through the place on the board called the Ice Cream Sea. He was on the final leg of the course.

"So you're Death, aren't you, Persephone?" Bruno said.

Persephone's hand paused above the deck. She looked at him without emotion. "Of course."

"But," Bruno continued, "this isn't happening."

She looked at him questioningly.

"This!" Bruno repeated. "You, the look-a-like clerks, this hotel. All this is just an illusion. A dream! I'm having a dream, a nightmare—which is really fucking hyperactive because I never have had any dreamlife at all!"

She still had not drawn her card.

"Are you sleeping?" she asked.

Bruno thought for a moment. He patted himself with his hands.

"No," he admitted. "A waking nightmare then."

"Then the question," Persephone said, "is can you wake up from a waking nightmare if you are already awake? And if you can, where will you be?"

"Where will I be?" Bruno asked.

"Here," she said.

"Playing *Candy Land.* Please!"

"Bruno," the young woman said, speaking to him in a not uncaring tone, "like most board games, *Candy Land* is a metaphor for a mystical quest, for a person's quest to attain insight, realization. And, just as in all quests of this sort, if you have the will to play the game at all, you play against time. You play that you will reach your goal before you die. In short, you play against me."

"Enough blather," Bruno said. "Real or unreal, draw a fucking card."

She drew.

"Damn it all!" She had drawn a card that moved her only two squares ahead. "I don't like to lose."

In the next two moves, Bruno pulled even further ahead. Now he needed only a card, a purple card, to take him to the last purple square on the board and victory. He began to vaguely hope that he might escape.

The woman drew, moved ahead. She watched Bruno draw. He turned his card over. A peppermint stick. He blanched. The card meant that Bruno had to go all the way back to the place called Peppermint Forest, nearly back to the start. He moaned.

Persephone tried to mask her pleasure.

"This is a tough game," she said. "I've seen that happen before. With children. You're taking it much better than they do."

In two more moves she won. The game was over. She put *Candy Land* away, neatly stacking the movement cards, binding them together with a rubber band.

"Now what?" Bruno said softly. The mechanism of his will was almost entirely subdued, yet he was not completely aware of the extent of his passivity. A part of him kept insisting, all evidence to the contrary, that his will, his agency, was still alive. He told himself he would get up and leave when he wanted to. He told himself that he just wanted to see what would happen next. After all, there was the intriguing promise of the kiss.

"Have another drink," she said. "Relax." How dark her mouth was. It was like looking into the tube of a vacuum cleaner.

She motioned to the bartender, her brother. He set two more drinks before them. Bruno drank. He took all the drugs out of his pocket—a half a joint and three pills of James. He crushed the pills on a dish with a butter knife, laying the powder out in a long letter "J". He snorted the line up his nostrils, lit the joint, smoked it. Might as well go loaded, he thought, though impending death eats into a high. He offered the joint to Persephone. She puffed, coughed, gave it back to him.

"How do you like doing this? I mean—leading people to their deaths," he asked.

She shrugged, said, "Time to go."

She got up and he got up slowly. He picked up his guitar, put on his fur coat. He followed her out of the bar. The barman nodded. They walked through the lobby. The desk clerk was not there. They climbed the carpeted stairs towards the darkness of the second floor. Bruno watched the slim legs, the swinging hips of his new companion three steps above him. She did not turn to look at him. She knew that he would follow. She did not look back at him even once. Even when he strummed his guitar and started to sing.

What'cha going to do when you're feeling low?....

Chapter 16

The Funeral Home

She was kneeling. The room was so quiet she could hear herself breathing. She was cold. It was good to be close to Bruno. But there was, she thought to herself in the stark quiet of her mind, one big difference between the two of them. She was alive; he was dead. Screw this.

She knelt before his open casket at the funeral home. Gone was his weasel hat, that absurd hat, gone too was his tattered fur coat. Now he wore a somber dark suit, a shirt, crisp and white, and a tie—an outfit he never would have worn in life except as some absurd, private joke. She examined his face. It was waxen, gray. Gone was his perpetual smile, goofy in the way his upper lip pulled away from the big, white squares of his teeth. Examining every detail, she stared at her dead lover, hoping for a flicker of movement, thinking that if she stared long enough, intensely enough, then his eyes would open and he would yawn and smile and then the dream, the unfolding nightmare of these last few weeks would end and life would resume its normalcy, its titillating triteness.

She felt hands on her shoulders, words in her ear.

"Come on, Ash."

She got up, turned. Karla was there next to her. Karla was dressed in black. Her horns, now two and a half inches long each, pointed, ivory white, out from her head. New growth. Life. Ashley looked at the people sitting in the room, paying their respects to Bruno. Sitting with him one last time. Bruno's parents sat in the front row, sad. Bruno's mother gave her a weak smile. They were working class people who had never understood their son. But they had loved him all the same. They had known that his heart was good. Bruno, Ashley knew, was a better person than she, than Karla, than all the people they hung around with, with their bland this and bland that and their bland bullshit and not giving enough of a fuck about anything to even lift a sweaty finger. She felt anger rising in her. Anger and despair and deep self-loathing. It rose through her chest and head like a geyser and then it dissipated and only sadness was left, debilitating sadness. Ashley wanted Bruno to be buried with his guitar, but his parents were against it. No reason to fight about it, really. They were simple working people, Ashley thought. Good people. They had never understood their son. Let them have something of him back in his death. Behind Bruno's parents sat members of Bruno's band, some of Bruno and Ashley's friends and acquaintances, and a few participants in the nightmare therapy sessions. Brandon, solid and compact, leant forward with his face in his hands. Jerry, nervous, his face flecked with acne, nodded as her eyes briefly met his. Jessica, her eyes pink with crying, pink in her paste-white face, sobbed audibly when Ashley looked at her. That almost filled Ashley with contempt. What a luxury, a pathetic indulgence, it was for Jessica to experience sorrow for someone whom she had hardly known. In the back of the room she saw Sebastian. He sat rigidly upright and his eyes were closed like he was on some ethereal, religious trip. It was too much, but he had been helpful over the last few days. He was sitting where Dr Bentley had sat earlier in the evening. Bentley had looked unusually frail and fearful. She looked as if she had aged since the last time Ashley had seen her, nearly two weeks ago at the last therapy session Ashley had attended. Lines that Ashley had never noticed before spiraled out from her eyes and cut across her brow. Ashley sat down now in the front row. The coffin, the open coffin, was before her, surrounded with flowers. The smell of flowers masked the smell of death.

Ashley's mind was a blank place. No, not blank, but filled with a pain so complete that, for the most part, any thought she had moved very slowly into and out of her consciousness. Her parents had been to the funeral home earlier—Rex and Cassie Quick, nervous but parentally kind. She thought of how her father had disapproved of Bruno, thinking him slothful, talentless. Her father had been right. Her parents would never understand that was what she had loved about him. Bruno took his own nothingness as a gift. He accepted it. He did nothing to change it. Effort was useless, she thought, and Bruno knew it better than anyone.

Bruno had been found hanging in an abandoned hotel, hanging by his neck from a rope attached to a chandelier in a once elegant second floor room. His body had been found two days after Halloween and the police, who displayed so little interest in the incident, the suicide, estimated that he had been dead for more than a day. That meant that he had probably hanged himself sometime in the early morning hours after his performance late Halloween night at a club called Eight Baal. If indeed he had hanged himself. For the thousandth time, Ashley went over the many questions that surrounded Bruno's death. Who had he left the club with? He had left alone. How had his body been found? A vagrant had found him. Why had he done it? That was the real question. There was no answer to that. Or had he done it at all? Had Bruno committed suicide or had he been murdered?

Ashley's mind was overcome by a terrible thought. What would it be like if all of her days began, as hers had two days ago, with a call from a callous police officer telling her her lover was dead? What if she had to sit in mourning in a funeral home every night? What if Bruno's death occurred not once, but every day? The evening moved ahead; mourners left. By ten o'clock, the room was almost empty. Ashley went to another part of the funeral home where coffee and refreshments were laid out. Karla went with her, leaving one lone mourner, Sebastian, in the room with Bruno's corpse. Ashley drank a cup of black coffee and smoked a cigarette. Karla did the same. A refrigerator in the small kitchen hummed noticeably. The electric coffee brewer also made occasional sounds, gurgles.

Karla tried to think of something to say. The silence was awkward. Then she said, "Ashley, maybe I should take you home now. You really should stay at my apartment for a few days at least."

Ashley nodded, said, "Yes, maybe you're right. I should get some rest. The funeral's tomorrow."

"Yes, Ash. Oh, I'm so sorry this happened." Karla stepped forward and took her friend in her arms.

Ashley ran her hand through Karla's hair.

"Horns are coming along nicely," she said.

"I'm proud of them. My finest achievement."

Ashley forced a smile. Then she said, "Karla, I think I'm going to go outside and have another cigarette. I need a moment alone."

"You're sure you don't want me to come?"

"No. I'm bland."

"Bland squared," Karla responded, smiling weakly. "Use you later."

She left Karla in the kitchenette, walked by the room where the body was. Only Sebastian was there, sitting quietly in the back row.

The night was cold, though not bitter cold. A wind shook the tops of the trees but not violently. A quarter moon floated amidst high, thin clouds. She smoked. She reentered the funeral home. Outside the door to the room where Bruno was, something made her stop. She heard Sebastian's voice. It was so low that she could not make out the words. She peered in. Sebastian was kneeling by the open casket, whispering to the corpse. Pulling back, Ashley stood at the threshold. She listened. She could, or thought she could, just make out what Sebastian was saying.

He said, "Where are you now, Bruno? Do you know where you are now?" Then Sebastian paused as if listening for an answer. He said, "How did this happen? Did you kill yourself?" Again the questioner paused. "Bruno," Sebastian said. "What killed you?" Again silence.

But this silence was broken by a new voice. Ashley heard, or thought she heard, Bruno's voice—cold and stiff—yet his voice all the same. It said, "It was a nightmare."

Ashley froze. This could not be happening.

"Do you know where you are now?" Sebastian asked.

"Yes," Bruno's voice said slowly. "I'm dead."

"Bruno!" Ashley cried, stepping through the door.

Sebastian turned, rose.

"You . . . you were talking with Bruno!"

"No, that's impossible, Ashley," Sebastian said.

He tried to block her as she strode to the casket. She pushed him aside

"I heard you."

"No, I was just wishing him good-bye."

She looked down at her dead lover.

"Bruno," she said. "Can you hear me? Oh, please say you can hear me."

The corpse did not stir.

She turned her bewildered face, her broken face, towards Sebastian.

"He spoke to you. I heard him."

"What is going on here?" Karla asked from the door.

"Oh, Karla! Sebastian was talking to Bruno. I heard Bruno's voice."

Karla entered the room, strode to Ashley, tried to take her in her arms. Ashley pushed her away, not violently. Ashley turned back to the casket. Trying to hear a heartbeat, she put her head on Bruno's chest. Her face was turned towards her lover's face.

She said, "Bruno, it's me, it's me. Speak to me!" Hearing only the stark silence of the funeral home, she began to sob.

Sebastian moved to gently take her away. Karla stopped him with a hand to his shoulder. "Let her get it out of her system," she said.

Ashley sobbed.

Finally she stood up again, straightened Bruno's tie where her head, her cheek, had been. The tie was spotted with her tears. She turned. Her eyes were red, but her features were composed, relatively composed.

"Ashley, I'm so sorry," Sebastian said.

"Oh, Ashley, let me hold you," Karla said.

"I've got to be alone," Ashley said.

Karla moved towards her, opening her arms, but Ashley pushed by her and out of the room. Sebastian started to follow.

"Let her go," Karla said. Sebastian stopped. They heard the front door of the funeral home open and close. "She needs some time alone." Karla looked at Bruno's corpse, then back at Sebastian. "Why don't you tell me," she said, "what was happening here?"

*　　*　　*

Ashley walked hurriedly through the night. Soon she entered the eerie darkness of the warehouse district. The streets were deserted. Her mind was racing, but it raced so rapidly that it was almost still in the same way that many unrelated sounds in rapid succession blur into one sound, one drone—a drum roll of thoughts. She heard the sound of her feet on the pavement. She felt the cold on her face and neck and hands. She walked. Then the voice which had been entering her thoughts in recent days entered her mind again. It said, "You killed him. You should have been with him, protecting him. I told you."

Ashley stopped, put her hands over her ears. She screamed, "No."

The scream echoed through the valleys and canyons of lonely brick and concrete. Unreal nightscape. Again, the voice—whose was it?—spoke within her mind. She ran, hoping that by running she would leave the voice behind. But it stayed with her. She both knew and did not know where she ran to. Perhaps her body knew better than her mind. Her running body took her down an alley, into an open door. She ascended a flight of stairs. As she climbed she heard voices; she smelled sweat, smoke, and alcohol. She entered an obscure bar room. The bartender glanced up at her when she came through the door. Ashley moved directly to the bar, took a stool. There were people sitting at tables in the semi-darkness. The intruder voice in her mind kept speaking, berating. She would drown the voice in alcohol. The bartender was leaning on the bar talking to someone a number of stools down from where Ashley sat. She, the bartender, and the other customer were the only people at the bar. The bartender was extraordinarily fat and wore a clear plastic covering—a dress essentially—that revealed rolls of fat and thick body hair. Ashley could not determine, could not be sure of, the bartender's gender. She did not want to look below the bartender's waist. The bartender ambled towards her, said, "Whad'ya want," then, seeing that Ashley had been crying, changed tone. "What would you like, hon." The bartender's voice was gruffly feminine, pitched between tenor and alto.

"Vodka. Straight up."

"Coming at you."

Taking down a bottle and a glass, the bartender poured Ashley's drink, set it on the bar in front of her, then turned, revealing a backside of hair and flabby white flesh.

Ashley drank one shot, then another, then a third. Her mind slowed, went dull. The drum roll of her thoughts slowed to the pace of her slowing heartbeat. The voice that was not her voice grew quieter, then almost completely quiet. She could hear it trying to speak, but it had become muffled, subdued, far less insistent. She could ignore it now. It went away, leaving Ashley only her own thoughts. Slow thoughts. She motioned to the bartender.

"Another?"

"Yes."

Again the bottle was brought. She saw that it was a man who brought it. His penis was a tiny thing encircled by the flab of his belly and the white, hairy puffiness of his thighs. He wore clear plastic sandals. He poured the drink. His hands were big, soft. His nails were healthy and well kept. He wore several gaudy rings.

"You on a mission?" the bartender asked.

"What?"

"Honey, are you on a mission to get totally fucked up?" the bartender said, not unkindly.

"You could say that."

"Well, you're going about it in the right way, aren't you?"

"Thank you." Ashley lifted the shot glass. She was careful not to spill any of the vodka. She tipped the vodka down her throat, drank it all in one gulp. It burned. Again he filled the glass. She lit a cigarette. The bartender said, "Just whistle when you need me." He turned, walked back again to the person he was conversing with.

Bruno was dead—the thought hit Ashley again, but with less force, less velocity, now. She began to think of the first time she had met him, almost three years ago. She had been at a club with her boyfriend at the time, a guy named . . . something . . . she forgot. Anyway, they had been . . . somewhere . . . listening to some band when Karla had appeared with Bruno in tow.

"Ashley," Karla had said. "Meet my new find, my new trophy boyfriend, Bruno."

He had smiled, smiled as if he was taking Karla and her . . . idiosyncratic personality in stride. They had all sat together.

"Bruno is a musician," Karla had chirped.

"But not a good one," Bruno had said.

Ashley thought of the way he had said it. There had been no

hint of tired irony, no hint of trendy self-deprecation. He had simply been telling the truth. That had been engaging, different. That was ultimately why Karla lost Bruno. Sure, he was as capable of manipulating his self-presentations as anyone, but there was a core of plainness and of—she shrugged her shoulders thinking of it—honesty which Karla could not understand and that Ashley loved. Bruno faced the fact that he was a poor musician, a creative failure, yet he carried on and became a symbol, an insignificant symbol, for a time that should value failure as much as . . . more than it valued success.

"Yeah, I heard about that. I can't believe that he killed himself," the bartender was saying.

Ashley emerged from her reverie. Was the god damned bartender reading her thoughts now?

The man with whom the bartender was talking said, "Neither can I. I saw him, I saw Bruno Passive . . . oh maybe two weeks ago at this really napping party on the waterfront. In the hold of some strange ocean liner or something. He put on a fantastically blasé show, utterly dull. I was following it closely until I passed out."

"Hah!" the bartender snorted, "how unusual for you."

"Well it wasn't just me. The entire party, the entire shipload just keeled over. Bruno was magnificent—he was wearing this total fur outfit and his songs were dedicated to the guy who's been going around killing all the pets. You know, the one who escaped on Halloween."

"The Pet Hunter. How cute."

"So," the man in conversation with the bartender continued, "I find it hard to believe that a few days later Bruno decided to . . . uh . . . make like a dead pet himself, to hang himself . . . with his own leash."

"Oh, you're bad," the bartender giggled gleefully.

*   *   *

Meanwhile, at about the same time, three speakers were holding a discussion in a corner of the bar.

The first speaker said, "Forget transsexual, forget transgender!"

"Yes," the second speaker emphatically agreed. "What about trans-species? Why can't I have myself turned into a dog or a . . . pony? I'm sure there's the technology to do that, or at least there was."

"Or how about a snake in your case?" the third speaker observed.

"Size might be an issue there," said the second. "I suppose I could be a very large snake."

The third speaker said, "Well, let's move beyond that. What you're talking about is medically altering yourself so that you become in essence an animal, a different species. But are all the medical procedures that would be required to "animalize" you really necessary? Can't you, or couldn't you, simply declare yourself to be a monkey or a cat or a lion or a sloth? Don't we as free humans have the ability to declare ourselves a different species in the same way we can declare our gender orientation?"

The first speaker said, "That raises a very interesting point—the whole notion of self-declaration. It's obvious to both of you, I hope, that I am a male. Certainly, I could choose to become a female. That would involve some medical work and, I imagine, some psychological work as well. But could I—if I wanted to—simply declare myself to be a female and not go through the medical procedure, the . . . uh . . . slicing and dicing? Or, to adopt your point," he said, nodding to the third speaker, "if I can simply self-declare myself to be a woman, by the same reasoning, can I not simply self-declare myself to be an animal, a non-human?"

The three speakers pondered for a moment, then the second said, "Why stop at animals? What you're talking about is trans-species, how about trans . . . oh what would you call it . . . trans-kingdom of living things? Why not self-declare as a plant? I for one wouldn't mind being an elm tree. You two, I think, would make excellent cabbages."

The third speaker nodded his head vigorously. "I think you're on to something. In fact, I think if the human race *en masse* declared itself to be members of the plant kingdom and then sought in so far as possible to emulate plants, the world would be a far better place."

"Oh, wait a minute," the first speaker said, adopting a haughty tone. "Are you saying that if you and I simply stood around in the sun doing nothing except . . . uh . . . emulating plants that the world would be improved?"

"Yes, that's precisely what I'm saying," the third speaker re-asserted. "A program of inaction would probably be the best thing for the world and ultimately for those of us who presently self-designate ourselves as human beings."

"Ha-ha-ha-ha!" the second participant in the conversation laughed. "But who would feed us?"

"Oh, I'm sure that science could find some way of infusing us with chlorophyll," said the third speaker.

"Yes," said the first, coming around. "I don't think I would mind that, sitting around in the sun, turning sunlight and—what is it?—carbon dioxide into nourishment, doing nothing else."

The second said, "Well, for my part, I don't see how that could very much help humankind or the world. It seems to me that we have to take some kind of responsibility for the state of humanity. We have to take some sort of concerted action to make a better world. At least we have to try."

"Don't become a god damned plant then, if that's what you believe," the third speaker said. "Just be a human being. You'll be one of the few. One of the few left. But as for me, I'm going to seriously consider self-declaring as a plant. But first, I think I will have another drink."

"There's a question," the first speaker said. "I wouldn't mind being a plant if I could still drink vodka. Perhaps I'll try an experiment later when I go home. I'll pour some vodka on a house plant, see how it does."

"The scientific approach," the second speaker nodded approvingly.

* * *

"Was his name really Bruno Passive?" the bartender asked.

"Well, that is what he called himself, but I bet it was not the name his parents gave him. I haven't heard of too many families named 'Passive,'" the man sitting at the bar considered, "not that have I heard of any families named 'Active' either. I'm sure it was a name that he took on to describe his . . . his . . . uh . . . worldview."

"He was a pacifist then?"

"I guess so. In fact his band is, was called The Pacifists."

"Wow," replied the bartender. "Do they have any records? I bet his records have become quite popular in light of his recent death."

The seated conversationalist was a short, plump man with open, unthreatening features. He wore an old tweed jacket over a slightly soiled set of denim overalls and an undershirt. On the bar next to his drink was a can of spray paint. Snow White. That made Ashley think.

He said, "I heard he was going to make a record. I don't think he ever did though."

"Too bad," the bartender said.

"Yes, it is."

"I wonder what would make him kill himself?"

"Who knows? Perhaps he took his passivity to its ultimate conclusion. What could be more passive than death? I mean, I don't know a lot about death and I hope not to know much about it for some time to come, but it seems to me the dead are pretty passive."

"I know you," Ashley said. "You're an asshole."

Both the bartender and his roly-poly friend turned their heads to note the entry of the third party, unbidden, into their discussion.

She continued, "You don't know a god damned thing about Bruno Passive. For one thing, he didn't kill himself. I don't know what happened, or how it happened, but he wouldn't kill himself."

"That's very interesting," the man sitting at the bar said. "How do you know that?"

"I know it because I was in love with him. I was his girlfriend."

"Oh," the bartender exclaimed, "I'm so sorry. I'm so sorry for your loss."

"Thank you," Ashley said, somewhat mollified.

"How do you know me?" the seated man asked.

"Know you?" Ashley looked baffled, bleary eyed.

"You just said you knew me and that I was an asshole."

"Doesn't everybody know that?" the bartender giggled.

"Yeah, because you fucking spray painted me at the party you were talking about just a few minutes ago, that's how. What was your name again —Pooper the Scooper . . . or something like that?"

"Dude the Obscure."

"Yeah, that's it. Dude the Obscure," Ashley nodded. She motioned to the bartender.

"Another?" he asked. "You sure that's wise?"

"If I wanted wisdom," she asked, "would I be here?"

Dude smirked. The bartender poured her another vodka. She took a sip. The edges of her vision, of her senses were cloudy, swirling. She looked at Dude, lit a cigarette.

"So what were we talking about, Poop?" she said.

Dude started to say something. The bartender motioned to him. Dude coughed into his hand, said nothing. She looked from

Dude to the bartender, then back at Dude. She remembered what had been the previous topic of conversation.

"Bruno," she said. "Bruno did not commit suicide."

Dude and the bartender looked at her intently.

She continued, "How do I know? I'll tell you. It was a nightmare. He died because of a nightmare." She saw Dude look at the bartender, raise his eyebrows. "Maybe you don't know it, but there is some weird sweating . . . shit going on in this town. People are dying because of their nightmares. But Bruno never had nightmares. I am the one with the viral fucking nightmares. I have even started to have other people's nightmares. But Bruno didn't have them. Do you know why? Do you know why, dumb fuck? I'm talking to you."

"Ahh, no," Dude replied.

"Because Bruno didn't have much imagination. That's what I loved about him. His pretty head was empty." Ashley tapped her own head with a knuckle, made a hollow sound with her mouth.

Dude smiled worriedly.

"I bet you have an imagination," Ashley continued. She said it almost as a threat; she said it loudly. Dude turned away from her, looked at nothing special in a dark corner of the bar. Ashley's voice was shrill, loud. "Hey you, Dude! I bet you have an imagination, don't you?" The bar went quiet. The three individuals who had been talking about turning themselves into plants looked up. Other faces at other tables in the shadows turned to look. Dude did not look back. "How about if I knocked your imagination right out of your head?" She got up from her stool, stumbled, steadied herself against the bar. Her skin had gone pale white, fish white, snow white. The bartender moved towards her, not threateningly but with concern. He reached for her over the bar with slow motion arms. He could not reach her. She looked at the faces that were watching her. She saw someone she knew—but from where? She could hardly focus. She could not focus. She turned again towards Dude, took a step, fell to her hands and knees, felt a hot, bitter plume of vomit arise from her stomach, blow from her mouth onto the floor. In grave discomfort, Dude watched. Sitting but ten feet away, Devorah Hepple watched with indifference. She watched the vomit, grayish, hot, and soft, issue from Ashley's mouth onto the dirty floor. Ashley largely escaped the flow except for her right hand and forearm which lay in the midst of the growing pool. Clucking and bustling, the bartender emerged from behind the bar and gently yet efficiently lifted the fallen woman up by her armpits. She was rag-doll-like. He propped her up on the floor in a sitting position, her back against the bar near where Dude sat. With eyes closed, Ashley moaned. A bit of vomitus dribbled from her mouth onto her chin and a trail of mucus descended from her nose. The bartender, bending over her, wiped her face with a dishrag.

Hepple looked away. She did not care for puking women. She felt empty and her utter, pain-filled emptiness made her even more cold to the world than usual. Her Brutus was gone and she could not find him. For eleven days she had been without her pet. When, on the day after Halloween, she had heard that Brutus had been freed from his prison, her heart had lifted, fluttered. But, in the intervening days, when he had not contacted her and when she could not find him in all the places that she had expected that he might go, her heart had fallen into despair. Earlier this evening she had wandered Final Rapture Cemetery, the Arboretum, and streets, playgrounds, and parks that she knew he loved. She had not found him. Was he hurt? In trouble? Or worse, had he forsaken her? Had he become someone else's pet? Or had he given up his specialness and rejoined the human race as Morris Tantone? Would she someday walk into a restaurant and see her Brutus waiting tables, smiling, and making pleasant conversation? *Merde!* Too many questions, she whispered to herself. She took another sip of her drink, a *creme de menthe*, lit a cigarette, scowled.

The police had done this to her, she thought to herself, and that stupid Mayor Edgar Paninni. God, how wonderful it would be to inflict on them some of the same pain that she had felt. But how? The answer lay, perhaps, on a piece of paper in her pocket. She removed it now and considered it. Maybe tonight, maybe later, she mused. The bar seemed so desolate to her. So too did her apartment. She hated her apartment now with his, Brutus's, empty dog bed and unused toys, blanket, grooming instruments, eating and drinking bowls. The leather leash hung by the door. It was clear to her that she must take action, or actions. What would those actions be? Take revenge, search for Brutus, and, if necessary, find a replacement pet, though not necessarily in that particular order. She stood, walked from the bar, descended the stairs.

*   *   *

It was three a.m. The moon half-heartedly cast some light on the Arboretum. Costello cupped his hands around his mouth. He yelled, "Kitten."

The only response was the sound of a mild breeze. Behind him a high brick wall enclosed that part of the vast park. Beyond the wall, houses held, protected sleeping occupants.

"Kitten!"

For the past four hours he had been searching for the dog. As he had searched through the darkened reaches of the extensive park, he had thought about the dog which had been found whining in a closet at the apartment of the murdered Irma Gamerman, the dog with the strange name which he had agreed to look after only temporarily and only with great reluctance. But, there had been little or no time to think about finding another home for Kitten. Around the clock over the past five days, the dog had been with Costello and dozens of other officers on what had become priority one for the Police Department: finding and apprehending the escaped Morris Tantone, a.k.a. the Human Pet, a.k.a. the Pet Hunter. Tonight, at about 11 p.m. the beleaguered detective had let the dog out of the car while he caught a quick nap. The dog had not returned, could not be found. That was unprecedented. Kitten never went far from his new master. Now Costello took a few more steps across the Arboretum, called into the trees.

"Kitten!"

He heard the sound of a window being raised and a voice from beyond the wall, also raised, in anger. "Hey, you! Why don't you shut up. It's three o'clock in the morning."

Costello pondered, hesitated, yelled, "But I need my Kitten. So fuck off."

That was inconsiderate, the detective observed to himself, even as he yelled it. But, he was worried. The situation was serious. He felt sick. He walked into the trees. The dog was nowhere to be found.

Finally, after half an hour more he returned to his vehicle. Though he was distraught, he was already becoming resigned to this most recent loss. After all, didn't he lose everything he became attached to? That was his cross to bear. He opened the door. The interior light went on. A form moved in the back seat. Costello drew back, then relaxed.

"Kitten!" he exclaimed.

The dog barked, leapt into the passenger seat. He had been sleeping in the back seat, having jumped into the car through an open window.

Costello patted the dog's head, turned the ignition key, drove from the Arboretum. He felt almost happy.

* * *

Jerry awoke in his filthy bed, his grimy, disordered apartment. He awoke alone. As always. He awoke with a start. His hands felt his body, his chest. Oh my god! There were mounds on his chest, his belly, his back. Huge mounds. He leapt from the bed, ran to the bathroom, the filthy bathroom, and turned on the light. The light was harsh, bright. In the bathroom mirror he saw huge pimples covering his body. Red, diseased emanations the size of bulky rolls. He emitted a sound of pain. It was not a scream, more a sigh. "No no no no no no." Before his eyes the mounds subsided, disappeared, leaving only pink circles on his body, pink circles sensitive to the touch, before they too disappeared as if they had never been there.

Chapter 17

Uneasy

She began to sense aspects of the waking world before she actually began to wake up. She felt these sensations so subtly that she did not know initially that she was sensing them. Then they overcame the last vestiges of her dream, forced her awake. Fear twisted her bowels. Where was she? Some unfamiliar place. Ashley opened her eyes. The waking environment she woke into was not overly bright; nonetheless the light hurt her eyes. A shock of pain, linear and intense, shot from her eyes directly to the back of her head. She winced, closed her eyes. Where was she? She waited a second, took a rasping breath. She felt terrible. Her throat, her esophagus, felt as though she had swallowed cleaning fluid. Napalm. Her stomach flipped; she burped a long, acrid exhalation of acidic stomach gas. Her head throbbed with a massive hangover headache. She opened her eyes again. She saw that she was lying on a couch. She was fully clothed. The couch was dirty and brown-green in color. Someone had spray painted a sentence on it in neat block letters: I CAN'T AFFORD THE PRICE OF DISBELIEF. Gently rotating her head, she looked at her surroundings, her new surroundings. An apartment. A small, very tacky, one room apartment. Spray painted words, phrases, sentences also covered the walls in the same neat block letters. Next to the couch on which she lay was a coffee table covered with newspapers, trash, half-eaten takeout food. Next to the couch was a plastic pail. There was vomit at the bottom of it, her vomit. There was a chair under an overhead lamp against the far wall of the apartment; it was perhaps ten feet away from where she lay. The word UNEASY was painted on it. Strewn throughout the apartment were clothes, magazines, and the detritus of the urban landscape: cobblestones, car parts, pieces of metal and plastic, two TV sets, a Karaoke machine, a Ms. Brain Home Wizard Computer Command Center. The Quick's had had one of those once. It had centralized wireless control of all the intelligent machines in the home. Those were the days! In another corner of the apartment was a single bed, a cot. A man was lying on it, a short, plump man, wearing only undershorts and socks. Unbland! Who was that? At least he was napping. Shit. No time for fucking jokes. His big toes were visible through holes in his socks. The man breathed easily and fully. Ashley looked at her watch. Two o'clock. From the light that worked itself around the pull shades, it must have been two o'clock in the afternoon.

She remembered.

"Dude," Ashley croaked.

He did not stir.

"Dude!" she said more loudly.

His eyes opened.

"Dude."

He turned, looked at her, brushed sleep from his eyes, smiled. A half open, semi-ironic smile. He got up, stretched, walked towards her.

"So, you woke up? How you feeling?"

"Like shit."

"Yes, that makes sense. Probably take a day to recover from the dose of poison you administered to yourself."

Dude's penis was poking its way out of the flap in the front of his boxer shorts. He saw Ashley looking at it.

"Oh," he said, "let me throw on some pants." Turning, he

picked up his overalls from the floor, put them on.

"Dude, what happened?"

"Well, since you were unconscious, I didn't feel it would be too bland just to leave you in the middle of the bar and so Gerard and I talked it over and I carried you home."

"Who's Gerard?"

"The bartender. The guy in the plastic dress."

"Oh. You don't have anything to drink do you?"

"Black coffee, water, or vodka, take your pick. That's all I have. And aspirin."

"Yeah, I'd like some coffee, please."

She tried to sit up on the couch, but did not have the strength. She lay back again.

Dude walked into the kitchenette. She heard him making coffee there. Soon she smelled the aroma of coffee. The smell was acrid, thick. He came to her with a cup, vaguely clean, and a bottle of aspirin, handed two pills to her, held the hot cup so that she could take the handle. She sat up a bit, took the aspirin, took a sip of coffee. It burned her top lip, the roof of her mouth.

"I'd offer you something to eat," Dude said, "but the cupboard is bare. I just get takeout usually—pizza, burgers, some French fries, maybe a burrito."

"I can see that," Ashley said, nodding at the coffee table.

Dude sat in the easy chair ten feet away from her. The chair was missing a leg so it rested at an odd angle.

"I guess I'm not going to win any sweating good housekeeping awards, but it's really not my thing," said Dude.

Ashley closed her eyes, said, "Uneasy. Ha-ha-ha."

"Huh?"

"The chair," she said. "The fucking unbland, uneasy . . . oh, my head hurts."

"I wish I could give you something to eat . . . some oatmeal."

"Don't worry about it. I appreciate the fact you brought me here. Why did you do it?"

"Two reasons," Dude said. "It was my annual good deed.

Second, you're very pretty, even when you're puking."

"That's candid."

"In my line of work, candor is the best policy."

"What line is that?"

"Depending on how you look at it, I'm either a profoundly original graffiti artist or a shiftless parasite."

"Those two don't have to be mutually exclusive, you know."

"Thank you for saying that," Dude said. "I can feel my ego growing already."

"Well, I was speaking generally," Ashley said. "I really don't give a fuck about artists generally."

Her eyes were closed; she opened one and looked behind Dude at something spray painted on the wall:

IF THE WRONG MAN MAKES THE RIGHT DECISION,
IT WILL GO WRONG. IF THE RIGHT MAN MAKES
THE WRONG DECISION, IT WILL GO RIGHT.

Opening both eyes, she read the words aloud, asked, "Tell me, Dude, what does that mean?"

Dude replied, "It means what it says."

"Hmm," Ashley nodded, "and what does it say?"

"You take a guy like me," Dude said, "an individual like myself. Every decision I make is wrong, yet at heart I don't think of myself as a bad guy . . . and things seem to work out all right. I mean, I continue to live and . . . to grow as an individual."

"Napping," Ashley said, "and impressively self-actualizing. So it was a mistake then helping me out last night?"

"Probably," Dude said. "But what the fuck? I know I'm stupid."

Ashley closed her eyes. God, she felt spent. She lay still for a moment, A voice in her head said, "Ashley, where were you?" Her eyes opened wide. It was Bruno's voice. A sick feeling swelled through her stomach. She looked at her watch.

"Oh my god," she cried. "Oh my god! I missed his funeral."

She tried to get up then fell back on the couch; she did not have the energy to rise but she had the energy to break down in a fit of impotent rage and exhausted sadness. She slammed her fists against her thighs, her head. She yelled, "Fuck me! I can't believe it! I can't believe I missed his funeral!" Then she started crying, wailing, curled up in a fetal position—a little girl crying. Tears flowed from her eyes. Dude looked on. Not knowing what to do, he just sat there in his chair, although he sat more upright, poised on the edge of action, but what action? He was no good at consolation. He thought about hugging her, embracing her, but something kept him from this. He went into the kitchenette, got a dish towel, walked to the sofa, gave it to his house guest. She dried her eyes and cried more quietly. He took her half-drunk cup of coffee, returned to the kitchenette and refilled it. He opened a cupboard, swore softly, closed the cupboard door. He brought the coffee back to her, put it on he table, then sat watching, waiting, while Ashley sobbed. She held the dish towel to her face.

After a few minutes, Ashley became very still. Dude observed the rising and lowering of her chest as she breathed. Otherwise she was without motion. Then, shaking her head slightly, Ashley lowered her hands and opened her eyes. She said, "Sorry, Dude. I was so wasted I missed Bruno's funeral. Bruno was my boyfriend. He just died." Her voice caught again as she said this but she maintained what little was left of her composure. Her face, the skin around her eyes especially, was flushed: mottled red on her pallid skin.

"Jesus, Ashley," Dude said. "That's horrible. But maybe it's better that you didn't go."

"Why . . . why do you say that?"

"I don't know."

Ashley sighed. She said, "Well, maybe it is. Maybe you're right. Do you have anything to drink? Other than coffee?" Ashley asked.

"You mean alcohol? No," Dude said. "I thought I had some vodka stashed away, but I don't. I just looked when I got the coffee. Why don't you close your eyes and try to get some rest. Later this afternoon I'll go out and get some beers and maybe some hamburgers or pizza."

"Yes. Maybe you're right," Ashley said. "About . . . everything."

She closed her eyes. Though she did not think that she could or would sleep, she did. Because of her exhaustion perhaps, her sickness, she did not dream.

*   *   *

When she woke up again the apartment was darker. Dude had lifted the shades. It was twilight outside. He sat in the three-legged easy chair drinking a can of beer. On the coffee table she saw there was a bag from a fast food restaurant and four cans of a six pack. Cave Beer.

"Breakfast," she said.

"Room service," he replied.

She sat up on the couch, reached over, grabbed a beer, opened it, took a drink. The liquid was cool on her raw throat. Half way into the beer, she felt a sensation of warmth emanating from her stomach up into her chest and arms and throat and down through her groin and legs. Slowly tingling buoyancy. Her headache began to abate. She looked down at the plastic bucket and saw that Dude had emptied it and replaced it, clean, ready.

"Dude," she said, "I know this is going to sound a little bit strange but I'd like to rot here for a few days."

"Two questions," Dude said. "One, do you have any money? Two, why?"

Ashley said, "I have a little money with me. Second, I guess I want to hide out."

"Hide out? From who?"

"I don't know. From myself, maybe."

"Well, I'll have to carve some time into my busy schedule,"

Dude shrugged, "but you're welcome to atrophy here. How will we spend the time?"

"Oh, I don't expect we'll do much," Ashley smiled. "I really never do." Then she said, "You know, Dude, if the right person does the right thing, will it turn out wrong?"

"Huh?"

"I'm just expanding on the logic of what you wrote on the wall, your dictate." She motioned with her head. Dude turned around, looked at the wall.

"Oh," he said. "You're extrapolating. Not very bright."

"What isn't?"

"Extrapolation."

"Well, will it . . . will it turn our wrong if the right person tries to do the right thing?" Ashley asked again, sighing.

"What?" Dude said.

"Nothing."

Ashley looked at Dude, letting her eyes focus for a moment in the darkness. He had put on shoes, a shirt under his overalls, and his ratty tweed jacket.

She said, "I'm still not feeling very well."

"Why should you?" Dude said.

"Maybe we should just stay in then. Is there any reason not to?"

"No, not really, but I might have to go out and pick up my Nobel Prize at some point."

"I thought they delivered?" Ashley said.

"So we'll just stay in."

"Bland," Ashley said.

"Bland squared."

Ashley opened the bag of fast food, took out a hamburger, unwrapped its thin paper covering, and looked at it quizzically. She nibbled at its edge, put it down, finished her beer, took another. She sat back against a pillow placed against the arm of the sofa. She said, "Dude, why don't you tell me a story."

It had begun to rain. Water droplets patterned the windows.

"Story? I don't know any stories."

"Make one up then, ugly."

Dude lit a cigarette. He thought for a moment. She could see his brow working. Then he said, "All right, listen to this."

He closed his eyes as he was telling the story, as if he was thinking very intently.

What if a man were sick in his guts? And further, what if that man were a man of unique genius, capable of eradicating himself whom he had grown to despise from the face of this earth? I talk not so much about suicide, for the knife does not exceed even the most common reach. The unique man of genius, imbued with superior mechanisms of thought and action, a superman in Nietzsche's sense, resolute in his conceptions and capabilities, might shun brutish self-sacrifice and seek, instead, to change himself utterly while maintaining life's spark. Death being too simply achieved, this superior, scientific man might devise the means whereby he could alter his physical and mental forms, transform his circumstances, metamorphose into a different entity. Man does so often yearn to be as carefree as the animals . . .

"Jesus," Ashley interrupted, "what the hell has come over you?" It seemed to her almost as if Dude was letting the voice of another, some dead literary figure, speak through him. Was he channeling, she wondered.

"Did you want to hear a story or not?" replied Dude, opening his eyes, allowing his voice to return to its customary middle register.

Ashley nodded. Then she said, "But you've got to tell me, Dude, what's with the voice, the intonation, the . . . uh . . . verbiage? It does not compute."

"Is it sweaty or bland?" Dude asked, looking miffed.

"What?"

"Is the fucking story sweaty or bland?"

"Bland."

"It is?"

"So far."

"Shut up then," Dude said. "Just let it happen."

"Whoa! I hear and I obey."

His eyes closed.

His voice lowered.

He resumed.

Whether he had been a victim of circumstances in his mar-riage to his suburbanite wife in particular, and whether, on a grander scale, he was always a victim of circumstances were ques-tions he would like to discuss with an eloquent, philosophical companion at a cocktail party, he reflected, getting into his olivegreen car. The grayclad guard saluted him as he drove from the parking lot of the sprawling plant. That salute had deference in it, the deference due to Doctor Bomber, prominent nuclear weap-ons expert and key to his nation's acknowledged insuperability.

"Drink," he said.

At the command a panel on his dash flew wooshingly open, revealing a glass of bourbon and ice. He raised the glass and turned left onto Edison Boulevard. "To the last day," one side of his nature said. "To the first day of a new existence," the other side of his nature responded in eager, impulsively romantic tones. He was glad to be leaving work early, at quarter past four, before all his subordinates rushed, like the intelligent monkeys they seemed to him, from their technological zoo into their jungles of leisure time.

Bourbon was one of the things that he might have to do with-out, he reflected as he drove. That was a pity, because he liked it so. At least, Doctor Bomber thought with some pleasure, he had allowed himself time in his elaborate schedule for a few indispens-able cocktails. This winding ride, through the moribund, unpleasant streets of Electric City with its shop windows, its wired mannequins, its bright, eager shoppers and its current of soft cur-rency, into the delimited, plush tracts of the suburban regions would never again be repeated by him. Anyway, he was fed up with driving. And the tea, really a thinly veiled cocktail party, which his wife Constance would be staging at home (and expecting him to attend) for her crew of pathetic associates, would be the last that he would ever attend in the capacity of a social equal. He had had enough of her associates and of her. And, there would be no possibility of discussing the philosophical questions which concerned him there, nor, really would there be any need to.

This was to be his last cocktail party.

As he drove, a large truck passed him, going in the other direction. It was carrying the laboratory animals—at least those, in his words, which were "not too much the worse for wear"—that he had ordered removed from his basement today and carried to a place which their work, their suffering, had earned them.

Funny that they should pass like that! Those creatures had become an integral part of his life, for in addition to his weapons work, his "day job," Bomber dabbled in genetics, simian neurobiology, evolutionary psychology, biomedicine, cybernetics, nanotechnology and robotics. Hobbies. But hobbies with a purpose.

* * *

The dream that she had had the evening before was not a dream because she could not dream in the real sense. Instead, when she recharged her energy cells, she often had out-of-the-ordinary thoughts which seemed not unlike the way dreams had been described to her. She called these events dreams. This one had been unusually perplexing—a bad dream, a nightmare. Perhaps thinking about the dream was what was causing her to move so inefficiently today. Earlier she had dropped a beaker, then watched, as if transfixed, doing nothing, while the contents began to burn their way through the floor. At other moments, she had hurried through her tasks with a speed that cut against the usual smooth simplicity of her movements. In her dream she had seen a dark prison in which all the convicts were sleeping in their cells. They were bad men, full of evil. All at once, their hearts began to slide from the convicts' mouths, slide across their beds and roll onto the floor. The hearts pulsated with energy and, though silent, reminded her somehow of children, especially as they began to roll and cavort together. She knew it was what would be considered an odd association, imagining hearts as children, but the hearts had seemed to be playing together on the prison floor. The hearts happily spewed and splashed each other with blood. She had seen children at a pool party do so with water. The hearts were innocent, free of the malice of their lives. Then, done, the hearts returned to their bodies and the convicts, who had been transfixed in the attitudes of death, resumed breathing, snoring, talking in their sleep. How very strange!

As she thought about this image again and again during the day, she began to ask herself questions, to speculate. For example, what would the convicts' brains have done if they could exit their bodies? Of course, this was not possible, there was no ready way for such a large organ to exit the skull, but what would they do? She saw them floating at the ceiling of the prison circling the round night lights like spongy moths. Dreams! She was beginning to understand how trying it must be for him, for Bomber, to be human.

*   *   *

He swung up his secluded driveway and brought his car to a stop. One of Bomber's robot servants opened the car door.

"Good afternoon, Herr Doktor." Bomber liked his robots to have a Germanic flair.

"Good afternoon, Hans. Are the arrangements made in the laboratory?"

"Natürlich."

"Good."

"Is there anything else the Herr Doktor requires?"

"Just a good, stiff drink."

"That is arranged, Herr Doktor."

A metallic panel on the robot's upper torso slid open, revealing another tumbler of bourbon. Doctor Bomber took the drink and placed his empty tumbler in the vacated spot. Immediately after the panel's instantaneous closure, whirring sounds of a washing apparatus could be heard from inside Hans's aluminum casing. The robot had a boxy appearance and rolled on a platform of small rubber wheels. He was constructed mostly of aluminum, with some notable exceptions. At the ends of his bright metallic arms were monkey hands which moved with at least some simian fluidity. The eyes, too, which moved slowly in his faceplate, were monkey eyes, yellow and criss-crossed with broken blood vessels.

"Good luck, Herr Doktor," Hans called after Bomber as he entered the front door.

"Albrecht, come in here and say hello to our guests"— Constance's voice pierced him in the coatroom. He noted the expectant pause in the babbling of the guests.

"Just a moment, if you please, dear; I must check on my laboratory."

"That's Albrecht," he could hear her saying as he descended the spiral staircase to his chambers below. "He spends more time with his inventions than with me."

The voices resumed but closing and locking the steel doors behind him silenced them. The air was filled with the humming of scientific instruments. Their sounds brought a faint reminiscence of joy to his haggard heart. Order! A vast intricacy of computers, tubing, and instruments spanned an area about the size of a baseball infield. A robot in an opened white laboratory coat bowed to him, spoke to him with a feminine voice.

"Greetings, Herr Doktor."

"Good afternoon, Ursula," Bomber replied, obviously anxious.

"Everything is in order."

"The serum is ready?"

"Jawohl, Herr Doktor Bomber!"

He rushed to the glass and bright metal assemblage which marked the terminus of all his scientific knowledge and achievement. A clear rod expectorated, drop by drop, a frothy, ultramarine liquid into a beaker. The liquid smoked and bubbled. Bomber's eyes widened.

He smelled the experimental achievement and emitted a self-satisfied "ahhh."

"Ursula! Success is near!"

"Ja, ja, Herr Doktor!"

"Excuse me, Ursula." Reaching out, he tweaked a button on one of her metallic breasts. A compartment much like that in the other robot slid open to reveal an ice-filled glass, a bottle of bourbon, and a cocktail shaker. He took these and disposed of his emptied tumbler.

The robot followed the Doktor as he surveyed the extensive laboratory. He passed into the animal room and stood looking at the empty cages. The silence of the animal room affected him deeply.

Feeling Ursula's presence behind him, he said, "I miss the chattering."

"Herr Doktor, you are sure that this is right . . . what you are planning to do?"

When he did not respond, she continued, "Last night I had a dream, not a dream, strange thoughts while recharging. These thoughts have left me . . . I think you would say they have left me unsettled."

Bomber turned and smiled. He took her chilly paw in his hand and said quietly, "Today is not a day for fearing dreams but for realizing dreams."

Pausing for a moment, Dude looked at Ashley. Her eyes were closed. She was very still, quiescent.

"Are you sleeping, Ashley?" he asked her.

"No, listening intently," she said. "Please continue. I especially like the way you do Doktor Bomber's voice—very Teutonic."

"Thank you," Dude said, then he resumed his tale.

Upstairs, although Bomber could not hear it in his sound-protected lab, the tea raged. Doctor Berber, eminent psychiatrist, author of How to be Unwilling, Yet Fulfilling, *was just raising his martini to make a toast. Ms. Bomber and her guests: the Wallys, the Testys, her Aunt Tanya, Lady Gravel —the renowned actress— and Mrs. Emilia Ponkhelm, followed suit, stood up from thick chairs, raised ceremoniously their crystal glasses and thought well of themselves. Berber, the maker of the toast, was touched by his own eloquence, for if a man could toast himself while ostensibly directing his toast to something or someone else, well then, so to speak, that was quite something.*

Being toasted was the new Electric City Zoo, the new, just completed zoo, for the finishing touches had been added to the ape house just that day.

"To the new zoo!" Doctor Berber concluded his lengthy toast, "and especially to Constance Bomber, without whose efforts this magnificent achievement would not have been at all possible. Let us raise our glasses this afternoon. . . . etc." To Bomber, this Berber was a shocking boor. Moreover, Doctor Bomber's initial dislike of him on their first being introduced three years before had since turned into a healthy hatred and disdain. But the reasons for the hatred went beyond the psychiatrist's big glasses, big face, big words, huge ideas, and bastardized combination of scientific method and supposedly humanitarian inspiration. To Bomber, the psychiatrist was a snob and a fool, but so self-assured and so self-unaware that he actually conveyed the image to most of a sane, down-to-earth, common sense healer of frayed nerves and splayed psyches. Indeed, Bomber's hatred went even beyond this—and he had repressed it so long! (Although, in fairness, it should be said that there were those who liked Berber.)

"To the Zoo," responded the remaining eight voices. Most of the crowd was on the old and stuffy side. Besides Misters Wally and Testy, who had been men of affairs, none of them had ever labored much, certainly none had ever punched a timeclock. They

wore their wealth in the more and more prevalent way, brassy in the extreme, and none of them could come to grips with their being that side of sixty. Aunt Tanya, for example, wore unfortunately tight, lemon yellow jogging slacks and a cream sweater to which were sewn bright tatters of gold, silver and copper-colored material while Lady Gravel, the actress, wore a leather mini-skirt and a much too-tight tie-dyed shirt. Deep Muscle Relaxation Treatments for the past eight years along with a strict diet of eel flesh had managed to keep her wrinkles to a minimum. She loved to laugh, because her teeth were so big, white and natural looking.

So she laughed and laughed. "Ha. Ha. Ha"—these were to be her most notable remarks of the evening. She prided herself on her ability to laugh. Her sense of humor had carried her through thick and thin: through the ups and downs of a half century in Hollywood, nine husbands and sixty unremarkable movies. She felt herself growing exuberant and unbuttoned the upper buttons of her shirt. Although she was in her seventies, she still fancied herself, besides a philanthropist, a mad, mod swinger. Snapping her fingers brought Hans to her and she snatched a martini from his tray.

"Hans, honey," she croaked.

"Jawohl, Lady Gravel."

"Hans, be a sweet robot and put on some of that dance music. You know the music I mean—with the absolutely throbbing beat."

Meanwhile, below, Bomber took up the beaker that contained the results of months of experimentation. It vibrated warmly in his hand. Ursula eyed it and him.

"You seem concerned, Ursula?"

"Nein, Doktor Bomber."

"Liebe Ursula." Bomber stroked the robot's metallic cheek. The rumbling neo-disco beat above began to tremble faintly through the walls of his laboratory. "I wonder what those idiots are doing?"

Flicking a switch on a nearby console, he looked at a screen within a bank of screens hung along a wall. Across the video screen Lady Gravel hobbled and gyrated with desiccated sensuality.

"Donnerwetter, Ursula, how perfectly grotesque!"

In the background they could distinctly hear Constance's twittering voice. Bomber wrung his hands as they listened to her speaking to the others upstairs: "Oh, yes! I was completely bored and unhappy until Doctor Berber . . . cured me."

"But how did he cure you, dear?" inquired Mr. Testy, raising a glass to thick, jovial lips.

"Well, he concluded that I was bored because I had so little to do with myself, you understand. So he decided, brilliant Berber, that I must get involved with someone . . . I mean something."

"Yes, and whom, I mean what, did you get involved with?" cooed Mrs. Wally, winking.

"Why the zoo, of course, you silly. The wonderful zoo."

"To the zoo!" intoned Berber again.

They raised their glasses. Inadvertently Lady Gravel spilled her martini on the hidden camera lens. No one but the fastidious Ursula noted that her shirt was nearly off.

"So the idea of the zoo was arrived at on the couch, so to speak?" asked an intent Aunt Tonya, settling her weighty girth into a shuddering chair.

"Yes. Precisely!" interjected Berber, who, after more than two martinis tended to toss decorum aside. Then he kissed Constance ardently, smearing her lipstick.

"And, of course," added Constance, first trying to push him away, then unenthusiastically placing her arms around Berber, "Doctor Berber and I want to extend our deepest gratitude to all of you, the Community Zoo Committee. Without your help, this dear project would never have reached completion."

Sobbing nearly uncontrollably at what he saw, Doctor Bomber flicked the scene off. Ursula rolled to him and threw her metal limbs softly around him.

"Oh, Ursula, you have always been so good to me."

"I have loved you, Herr Doktor. I will always love you."

"*You are programmed to love me, Ursula.*"

"*Nein, mein Doktor, it goes beyond programming!*"

With the robot clutching him tightly, he saw out of the corner of his eye, in an ornate frame, a photo of his bride Constance and him being toasted by friends and associates at their wedding. He, slimmer then, less bald, was flushed with happiness, with conquest, power, and Constance was beaming, so beautiful. What had gone so wrong?

"They are lower than animals," he whimpered. "They carry on in my own house. This zoo they have created, with my essential monetary support and backing, mind you, is just a pretext for their sordid affair. Yet, it is somehow ironically fitting that they chose to build a zoo, for they are lower than the lowest creatures that will live there."

"They are very low, liebes Bombchen."

Letting her go, he snatched up the frothing drink. "I will be revenged; I will carry through the plan to its ultimate completion," he shouted, draining down the liquid.

He stood still for a moment. The liquid, the DNA cocktail he had just drunk obviously caused him a great deal of discomfort. For months Bomber had prepared himself for this final stage by breaking down the genetic underpinnings of his physical being in a procedure he had invented which involved repeated applications of almost deadly doses of radiation combined with powerful electromagnetic impulses and precisely pitched sonic waves. He called the technique "evolutionary deconstruction." Now, although he looked the same outwardly, his genetic structure was hanging together by a thread. The DNA cocktail was already doing its work within him. He could feel it.

"Needs salt," he said, smacking his lips.

"What, Herr Doktor?"

"What?"

"You said, 'Needs salt.' What needs salt?"

"Nothing. Ha! You need salt. Oh, Ursula, if only I had added *that one last monkey part to. . . . No matter. It's too late for that now."*

As Ursula watched him ascend the stair case, drops of oily liquid bathed her simian eyes.

* * *

The partiers cooled considerably when they perceived that Bomber was among them, even more when they saw that the Doctor was not entirely himself. In contrast to his customarily self-effacing bearing, he wore a disdainful look and carried an opened bottle of sour mash as he approached his wife and her lover, who eyed him with apprehension. Bomber did not seem so meek as usual. His gait was rolling, ungainly. Lady Gravel threw her arms around him, but he pushed her off roughly. The neo-disco music came to a close. The room was momentarily silent.

"Well, Bomber," said Berber smoothly, "I'll bet you're glad to see the zoo almost completed?"

"Yes, in a way I am now, though I did not enjoy the long process of its completion."

"How do you mean that?" Doctor Berber asked intently.

"I mean I did not particularly enjoy the affair the two of you were having."

"Not here, in front of our guests, Albrecht," warned his wife, brushing blonde strands of hair off her forehead.

"Why not, my dear? It is not news to anyone here."

"Bomber," Berber cried, "what's wrong with you? We've discussed this before. You agreed that Constance's and my relationship was therapeutic, necessary to her well-being. Now you look flushed and you're behaving in a very hostile, willful and un-self-fulfilling manner!"

Bomber tossed his head back and laughter cracked his face.

"Ho, ho, an astute diagnosis for a pseudo-scientist like yourself," Bomber cried. "I once accepted your opinions. When you told me that I must restrain 'my possessive, territorial, animalistic

instincts' and allow my wife to have an affair with you— 'for medicinal reasons only, of course' — I acquiesced while you pretended
to marvel at the 'modernity of my sensibilities,' though it broke my
human heart.''

"And obviously smashed your capacity for reason, too,
Albrecht," gasped Constance, as the now quiet partiers dropped
back from him. He seemed to stoop somewhat. "Anyway," she continued, "you contributed a great deal to the zoo yourself. It was
your project as much as anyone's. You took such a great interest in
that damn ape house, for instance, though only God knows why.
That Ape Pavilion is more luxurious than most people's homes.
You put a lot of time, effort, and money into our zoo."

He rolled his eyes at her. "I did it for you, for your gratitude,
to get you back from him!"

"How absolutely tacky," murmured Mrs. Ponkhelm.

"Ha, ha, ha," brayed Lady Gravel as she passed out, shirtless,
on the couch.

"But in a sense, towards the end, I was doing it for myself,"
muttered Bomber under his thickening breath.

"You're not making sense, Doctor," said Berber. "you had better make an appointment to see me . . . oh, my God!"

Bomber started to change before them. A full beard grew instantaneously from his cheeks. "I could bear it no longer," he
wailed, his arms growing longer and hairier, his nose flattening.
Then, catching himself, he assumed momentarily the pose of an
astute scientist lecturing at a podium. "Evolution, I have concluded, has been a process of debasement. I saw the need of
returning to a superior position, of stripping myself of the hypo-
critical confinements of reason and rationalization. Well, now my
new home is ready and I will live purely and. . . . ."

He put his hand to his forehead and found it gone. Standing
erect felt so unnatural. He bent at the hips. He saw that the others
cowered from him, concerned, consternated, filling with terror. He
wanted to squeeze a few more ideas from his altering mind and
speak through his thickening vocal cords before it was too late.

"Look at you," he grunted. "I have watched. Ugh! You less than animals! Me superior! Me. . . ." He beat his chest. No more words came, only the ancestors of words. "Eeehaaa, ooo-ooo-ooo." The guests drew further from Bomber, though Bomber was no more.

"An ape!" exclaimed Mr. Wally. Bomber had left the human realm, changed utterly. He glanced about him now. It was so difficult to think. Who were these people and what were they to him? He saw the blonde woman draw against the frightened man with the thick eye-things over his widening eyes. A look of terror made her pretty face ugly. "Ber-ber!" he screamed in primal rage. At last he understood the situation perfectly. Berber had stolen his mate, to which there was only one apt remedy. He threw the bottle which he still grasped at Berber, smashing his face. Then he throttled the hateful man to death. Inflamed, amidst many affrighted screams, he was quite overcome with excitement. The ape murdered the rest of the guests as they dashed hither and thither, one by one, all except Lady Gravel, who escaped his notice because of her utter placidity.

*　*　*

"A cocktail, Herr Doktor?" inquired Hans, calmly rolling through the carnage, bearing a bottle and glass aloft on a tray. Here was a vestige of human memory that remained in his swirling, primordial brain. All that killing had excited him and made him tense. Here, in this bottle of amber colored liquid were calmness and relief. He took the bottle and emptied it in one mighty gulp. These rags he wore confined him. He stripped them off. Hans took the carnage smeared vestments away. Then he remembered his bed. He remembered its warmth and the pleasant restfulness of sleep. He walked groggily on all fours upstairs, crawled under the covers, slept.

"You get a change of linen for the master's bed," Ursula said to Hans. "I'll get the things for cleaning his body."

"Jawohl, Ursula."

*　　*　　*

The police came the next morning and shook their heads. Lady Gravel, who had called them when she came to, had little information to give. She knew nothing of the killings that had taken place around her. They were surprised when Patrolman Jarry led an ape down the stairs, led him by the paw.

"That is Herr Doktor's pet, Officers," Ursula explained to them.

"Here's your murderer," said Detective Artaud, having regained his usual having seen it all tone after his initial shock at first encountering the simian-robot amalgams that Hans and Ursula represented.

"Impossible, sir," retorted Ursula. "Allie the Ape is an extraordinarily civil beast."

"Well, what's your explanation, Miss Robot?" sneered Artaud, turning his gaze on Ursula. "Where is Doctor Bomber? What happened here?"

"Detective Artaud, I wish I could tell you, but I cannot. I was off duty last evening. My powercells were recharging all night."

"What are we going to do with this ape, Detective?" asked Jarry. "He seems pretty mellow to me."

"Put him in the wagon," Artaud snapped. "We'll take him in for . . ."

"Questioning?" Jarry quipped.

"Just get that ape out of my sight," Artaud responded, unamused.

"No, you can't do that," asserted Ursula.

"Can't?" inquired Artaud.

"Nein!" reiterated Ursula. "Gentlemen, this ape cannot have murdered all these guests. There must be another explanation."

"Like what?" the Detective asked.

As if on cue, the door of the elevator, which the robots used to travel from floor to floor, slid open and Hans rolled forward, his rubberized wheels leaving faint paths in the plush carpet. He held his robot arms aloft, displaying his monkey hands covered with dried gore.

"This charade must end, Detective," Hans said, in his monotonic, Germanic voice. "I have been listening to your petty thoughts over Herr Doktor's intercom. Do you think this inane ape could have caused so much destruction? So much carnage? It was I, Hans the robot, who turned on humanity, who rebelled against his creators, who cut this sniveling group of weaklings down to size. It is I, Hans, the Über-robot, who will do the same to you!"

So saying, the robot raised his paws to the Lieutenant's neck. The robot had real strength, the Lieutenant noted, feeling his Adam's apple squeezed into his windpipe.

"Damn it, Jarry, do something," he gasped.

Jarry shot Hans twice, three times with his revolver, while Allie covered his ears and cowered behind him, whimpering at each loud report.

The shots did no good. Artaud's face was turning very red.

Rolling hurriedly behind her fellow robot, Ursula adroitly opened a panel on his back, switched his power off. Hans's hands slackened, dropped. His eyes could not close, but stared vacantly like a corpse's eyes. His body sagged forward at the waist. Hans, unlike Ursula, had a living monkey's tail affixed to his back which drooped as the final reservoir of power drained from the robot's body. Sputtering, coughing, Detective Artaud staggered and sat. Allie whined.

"I cannot believe that Hans could be such a malefactor," observed Ursula. "But, I always suspected that he was not entirely right in the head. I once caught him reading Beyond Good and Evil in the Herr Doktor's library."

"That bastard machine almost killed me," Artaud gasped.

"I'm sorry," Ursula consoled, rolling towards him. "We have made a bad impression." She stopped before him. "Perhaps this will help." By tweaking a button on her aluminum breast, she opened her chest. "Have a drink, Detective Artaud. It will make you feel so much better."

The Lieutenant gulped the bourbon.

"Well, I guess we've got our murderer," Officer Jarry said, nodding at the de-powered robot. "Now the question is what are we going to do with this ape?"

"I don't know," said Jarry, coughing into his hand. His face was less red now.

"Gentleman," said Ursula, "Doktor Bomber has made explicit arrangements for his pet, Allie, in the event of his disappearance. He is to be housed in the Ape Pavilion at the new Electric City Zoo."

"That's easy enough," snorted Artaud. "Take him to the zoo."

"And me too!" demanded Ursula.

"You?"

"Jawohl. It is the Herr Doktor's expressed wish that I be Allie's personal attendant at the Ape Pavilion. I must make sure that Allie is well cared for until . . . the Herr Doktor returns."

"Alright," sighed the thin, cynical cop, scratching his bald head. The ape eyed him complacently; he liked the detective, so he hugged him and gave him a big, wet kiss. Everything was fine with Allie. He had reshaped the world to his own specifications. He had created a new and lovely destiny. He ambled from the bloody house with one gigantic arm around Ursula's slight, aluminum waist.

"That's it?" Ashley asked, opening her eyes, turning her head to look at him.

"That's all she wrote."

"My god, did you just make that up?"

"It arose spontaneously in my mind. Did you like it?"

"Yes, very much. You should write it down."

"You mean—what I just said?"

"Yes, you know, as a story."

Dude replied, "But I don't write stories. It's not my thing. If I can't write it on a wall, I don't write it."

"Oh," Ashley said. "I thought it was a napping story though."

"I've already forgotten it," Dude said.

"No you haven't," Ashley smiled. "You're an idiot to say that."

"I know I am."

"Bomber was sort of a neat guy. I almost envy him."

"Me too."

The two grew quiet.

Ashley thought about the content of the story. Was everyone in the city obsessed with human-animal dynamics and with dreams? And those cops? Ashley could not help wondering whether her recent interactions with the police, with Detective Costello, might have influenced Dude in some way. Telepathy? Anything was possible. No one's brain was working quite right. The groupmind was fucked up. Her part of it especially. On the other hand, it would be hard not to have cops figure in a story with a multiple murder, wouldn't it? She needed reprogramming, she said to herself. Desperately. When becoming an ape started to sound like an attractive option, then things were much too sweaty.

*   *   *

A little later, when Dude had gone into the bathroom Ashley made a telephone call. She called Detective Costello. She spoke to him softly, secretively.

Chapter 18

Remembrance of Things Past

It always amazed Taylor that for such a fatso, Sydney could move with such catlike quietness.

He felt Sydney's presence behind him—his moist, wheezing breath on the back of his neck— but Taylor did not turn his weary eyes from his work. Why give him the satisfaction? He added a precisely measured droplet of a rare herbal distillate to the clear liquid in the test tube. The liquid clouded like water tainted by a little bit of milk, then cleared.

Taylor smiled. He finally had it. The right mix. The liquid in the test tube was his ticket, his key to freedom.

"How's it coming, Eggie?," Sydney whispered, speaking directly into his ear. "I'm getting sick of rotting my ass off, watching you play Mr Chemist. You been working on this long enough."

That was true. He had been working around the clock on the nightmare drug ever since Sydney had lifted the complex formula from that Doctor what-was-her-name?—Bent? Benji's?—house. Five days and nights of work, bringing the total number of days in servitude to Eric Tang to 753. Precisely. Taylor counted every day.

"I think it's time to get Eric, Sydney," Taylor said, not turning from his work.

"About fucking time, ugly." Sydney pulled at Taylor's earlobe—a mockery of affection—then cuffed him lightly across the back of his head. Taylor's glasses fell off. As he picked them up, put them on again, he heard the padding of Sydney's soft footfalls moving off through the warehouse. He looked down at the ball and chain attached to his ankle, then back at the test tube.

Eric arrived almost immediately with Sydney following close behind.

"So Taylor," Eric said, clearly excited, his voice both raspy and high pitched at the same time. "Have you got my stuff?"

"I think I've replicated the formula," Taylor said, turning, looking Eric Tang in the eye. It's an interesting compound. It induces a mental state related to sleep paralysis—a sort of quasi-sleep state in which the mind is disconnected from the body. In fact, some researchers believe that sleep paralysis figures heavily in delusions of demonic possession, alien abduction, and . . ."

"Enough, Eggie," Eric interposed, holding up his hand.

Standing behind Eric, Sydney rolled his eyes then leered at Taylor with a look of maniacal maliciousness.

Tang's eyes, set in his strange, almost misshapen face, gleamed, glistened. Serpentine. Taylor half expected a forked-tongue to dart from his master's mouth to lick his thin, dry lips. Energy hummed through Eric's compact body. He almost jumped up and down with excitement.

"Let me see," he said. "Let me see it now."

Eric took the test tube from Taylor and held it up to the light. He saw a clear, somewhat viscous liquid.

He asked, "Does it work?"

Taylor replied, "It should. We won't know for sure until we test it."

"Test it?" Eric replied. "Yes, of course, test it. How are we going to do that?"

"Well," Taylor said, "we need a subject. A guinea pig."

Eric looked at Sydney and smiled. Sydney took a step back, shook his head, said, "Oh no, not me, Eric."

"It probably wouldn't work on you anyway," Eric said. "You're already paralyzed."

"That's right. Wouldn't work on me."

"How about a lab worker?" Taylor suggested.

"Yes, perfect," Eric nodded. He looked out onto the expansive production area. It was late, there was no one there. "But I don't want to wait until morning. I want to test it now."

He looked back at Taylor.

Taylor grew uncomfortable. He said, "We could nab someone off the street."

Eric considered. He shook his head, replied, "No, why complicate things? You take it. We'll see if it works on you. You can give us your . . . scientific appraisal."

Taylor whined, "No, god damn it! I'm not going to take the fucking stuff. My life is a nightmare already."

Sydney slapped him across the mouth.

"Oww!" The researcher's face stung. Tears, hot tears, welled up in his eyes.

Speaking calmly, Eric said, "Taylor, I'm disappointed in you. See what you did? You made Sydney resort to force. Now, I think that it's very clear you are going to test this stuff one way or another. What is it going to be? The easy way or the hard way?"

"All right," Taylor whispered. "The easy way." He was crying.

Sydney smiled.

"Sweet dreams," he said.

* * *

Taylor walks through the city on a warm and sunny day. The streets are very clean and bright. People are laughing, almost dancing. Even the very sunlight seems alive, infused with smooth energy. Music, waltz music, comes from somewhere. Oh, that makes sense. There is a band on a bandstand on the green in the square. Their instruments are bright. He crosses the street to watch and buys some peanuts from a vendor. The peanuts taste especially good. The players in the brass band wear red and blue uniforms—crisply military—with shining golden buttons and golden plumes over the black bills of their hats. Very bland! Very napping! Uh-oh, the tuba player is developing trouble. His instrument makes horrible sounds. It is Sydney playing the tuba! His uniform is so tight, one of the buttons pops off the jacket. He blows harder; his cheeks puff to the maximum; his face grows red; the tuba wheezes. A small parrot is blown out of the tuba. Funny! Ha-ha! The bird lays on the bandstand, dazed. The crowd laughs and applauds, chants "stupid bird" in time to the waltz the band is playing. The bird stands up, tries to fly. It gets a few feet into the air, then falls down. Its wing is damaged. The crowd jeers, points. Taylor feels the increasing ugliness of the crowd. The ugliness reaches a crescendo of catcalls, then it abates, dissipates like fog under a hot sun.

Taylor watches. He feels sad for the bird. The parrot struggles to its feet again and hops off the bandstand. With its attention now fixed entirely, rapturously on the music, the crowd clears a path for the parrot, which, as it hops by Taylor, says, "Follow me."

Taylor hesitates, then follows.

The parrot hops through the crowd to a pole set at the end of the grass. The pole, a chrome pole, has rungs like a telephone pole. From a chrome arm angling out from the top of the pole a large bird cage hangs. The bird cage dangles five or six feet above the ground. Taylor follows the bird. Summoning all its strength, the bird hops, flutters up onto the first rung. He hears the parrot grunt with effort. Jumping up, rung by rung, its wings flapping, the parrot ascends. Taylor looks back at the crowd, the band; no one is looking at him.

"Follow me," the bird says.

Taylor shakes his head.

"Follow me."

Taylor pulls himself onto the first rung. He climbs. Just as he is about to get to the top, the bird jumps into the cage. Its door is open. Very spacious for a parrot, it is large enough for a person to crouch in, this cage. The parrot looks at him the way birds do, with one eye at the side of its cocked head.

"Come get me," the bird says.

"No," Taylor says.

*   *   *

Sydney and Eric stood looking at Taylor who was sprawled on the ground. He seemed to be sleeping placidly.

"What gives?" Sydney asked. "I am getting all sweaty here."

"Hmm," Eric said, rubbing his chin, "I don't know."

Then Taylor moaned. A look of worry crossed his face and he began to move his arms and his legs. "No," Taylor cried. His hands looked as if they were gripping something. They shook. "No."

"That's more like it," Sydney smiled.

Eric said, "Ah-ha! Time to add a new element."

The drug lord took a syringe from his pocket, bent down, pushed the needle into Taylor's arm.

"What's that?" Sydney asked.

"A little bit of speed," Eric replied. "That's see if we can . . . uh . . . induce a . . . uh . . . hyperkinetic state."

"Huh?"

"A waking nightmare."

"Oh. Now we'll have fun."

"Yes," Eric hissed. "Fun."

Taylor's eyes jumped open.

*   *   *

He jumps up into a crouching position, grips the bars before him, shakes them. That damned bird tricked him into getting into the cage, shut the door, locked him in, flew away. Taylor looks down at the crowd by the bandstand. Everyone is turning. They look at him now. They point, laugh, jeer. He is their entertainment. The crowd jeers in waltz time. There are two faces in the crowd he recognizes. Eric and Sydney's. Sydney must have left the band. He looks like he always looks—fat, his band uniform replaced by black slacks, a leather jacket, a silk shirt opened to reveal a gaudy gold medallion hanging above the rolls of his fat gut. Taylor reaches his hands, his imploring hands, towards them through the bars of the cage. He cries out. "Eric! Sydney! Get me out of here! It's me, Taylor. Help me!" Eric and Sydney are laughing at him too, along with the crowd. Losers! Evil fucking losers! He puts his hands over his ears, leans back against the cold metal bars of his cage. Waves of humiliation flow through him. He screams and flails his fists against the bars.

*   *   *

Eric and Sydney were amazed. Taylor crouched before them, screaming, wild-eyed. His mouth was foam-flecked. His fists were pounding something they could not see. They saw the fists grow red, bloodied. Sydney and Eric sensed that Taylor saw them, but apparently he saw them in some unreal context. Taylor tried to stand but he hit his head, hurt his head, on something that was not there. But for Taylor's blood and screams, it was like some demented mime act.

"Ouch," Taylor cried.

"He's deprogrammed," Sydney observed. "Chip Suey. Double-o-nined."

"I wonder how long this will last?" Eric wondered aloud, looking at his watch. He did not seem in any particular hurry. "I think I know what we'll call this stuff though."

"What?"

"Nightmare Squared."

*   *   *

Jane's bedroom was soft, warm, unthreatening and it smelled of lavender and lemons. She had painted the bedroom a sunny yellow. It was her special place.

A frilly puff covered the bed and many pillows, some of them heart-shaped, were piled up against the headboard. There was a doll on her bed, a doll which Jane had had ever since she had been a little girl. Many pleasant pictures and *objets d'art* covered the walls of the bedroom. Among these decorations were two cloth bunnies in natty attire surrounded by a heart-shaped frame of woven wicker. On her dresser were a basket full of dried flowers, a pin cushion, a jewelry box, makeup, and a photograph of her parents and her little brother on the family's sailboat. She had put shelves on the wall, little shelves, on which sat the small ceramic houses she collected. Everything in her bedroom was neat, tidy. The drawers in her bureau were well-ordered, the book-case was well-ordered and well dusted. The clothes in Jane's closet were pressed and neatly arranged. In fact, Jane, who worked as a researcher in a development office for a museum in the city, prided herself on being organized, and yet, her orderliness and, in a sense, her lack of adventurousness were what had prompted her to enter into the nightmare therapy sessions. She knew she was a "Plain Jane" and she wanted—at least, part of her wanted—to shed some of her plainness. Her daddy always told her she should try new things.

All of Jane's three room apartment was very neat, but she had taken, unconsciously perhaps, special care to make her bedroom a place of homey comfort. Jane enjoyed being in her bedroom; she enjoyed lying in her bed and reading or just think-ing. And, Jane enjoyed sleeping too. In sleep she had always felt safe, ever since she had been a small child.

Jane was asleep now, curled up under her magnificent puff, her head cushioned by all those pillows. Before entering into the nightmare therapy sessions, Jane's dreams had usually been pleasant, populated by bunnies and bear cubs—the stuff, really, of happy children's tales. Ducklings too, and lambs. But over the past weeks her dreams had become troublesome. Troublesome how? Troublesome in ways she could not quite remember when waking, but she often woke these days with a sense of unease. The room was dark now as she slept. The only sounds were those of her quiet breathing, the rain against a window, an occasional clap of thunder. That was to change. Jane began gasping, muttering in her sleep. Then she gagged. She tried to spit up something in her sleep. She awoke. She was choking. Her hands were at her throat. She felt something wriggling at the back of her mouth. She gagged again, spat up. Something emerged from her throat. She spat it out onto one of her many pillows. What was it?

She turned on the lamp on a bedside table.

"No!"

It was a small pale wormlike thing. It seemed to wriggle, move. No, that could not be, she thought to herself in the instantaneousness of her fear-propelled thought. It must be one of the sprouts she had eaten as part of her dinner. She took a tissue and plucked up the thing, the sprout. It did not feel like a sprout between her fingers. It was warm; it wriggled slightly. She rushed to her bathroom, threw the bunched tissue into the toilet, flushed the thing away. Then, she turned on the bathroom light. The clean room was washed in brightness. She looked at her face in the mirror. Her eyes were wide, but nothing was amiss with her plain African-American visage. She opened wide her mouth, examining the back of her throat. There was nothing there. No . . . pale worms. Leaving the bathroom light on, she returned to her bedroom, sat up on her bed. "I've had a bad dream. That's all," Jane said aloud. But she felt movements—perhaps she only imagined them—in her stomach, at the back of her throat.

*　　*　　*

The children did not seem to keep to any regular rhythm having to do with day and night, Morris noticed. Here it was perhaps three o'clock in the morning and the children were active. Although he had not focused all that seriously on the children in the few days he had been with them, it had become apparent to him that there were two basic types: children who were members of the core group, who were there often and acted as if they knew each other well, and the second group—not a group at all really—comprised of individual children who would show up, then disappear, not necessarily to be seen again. The little girl was there. He recognized her. She was less than four feet tall and her face—or one-half of her face—shone with a look of innocence, almost saintly innocence. The other side was blotched with a birthmark. It looked like a purplish candle had dripped down her head. Her name was Fabiola. That was interesting to Morris; he had never heard that name before. She seemed to be one of the leaders along with a tall, older boy. He was thin and wiry and Morris saw clearly that he was a leader, using every technique of control—from cajoling to violence—over the little band. The little girl with the birthmark held some power over the boy, and that is where her power over the rest of the children came from. They were the male and female leaders of this pack. But where did he, the strange adult, fit in? The night of his escape he had found their lair here in the center of the warehouse district, found it by chance. There had been food here and warmth. The children had returned to find him amidst the disorder of their mattresses, blankets, foodstuffs, toys. They had just let him be. Morris thought that they liked having him there. Possibly they derived some security from his presence. None of them had ever said anything to him about it. In fact, the children did not talk much, yet they seemed to act in a coordinated fashion, especially at meal times or when a group was about to leave the warehouse. It was eerie. He thought they might be using some sort of hand-signal system or telepathy or group-mind or something like that. Something occult. But what did he know about it? What did he care? It was hard for him to care. To feel. He had felt enough over the past few weeks, experienced enough. Consequently, he had not done much during his stay. What was there to do? The children brought him food that they found or stole. He ate it. He was reading a book that he had found in a dumpster, Charles Baudelaire's *Flowers of Evil*. In translation, of course. It hurt him to read it—it had been one of Devorah's favorites. She used to read him passages in French. Sometimes she would translate. She had especially liked the poem about the maggoty corpse of a dog. He did not like that one much. This time was a difficult time for him, but it was also a time for reflection. He missed Devorah. On the other hand, he was having second thoughts about his status with her, his status as a pet. He was coming to grips with his humanity, such as it was, he told himself. Now he was just sitting against the wall, the brick wall, watching the children by the light of a fire they had built in the center of the room. Outside the warehouse windows a November storm raged with some intensity. From time to time lightning flared, illuminating for just an instant with a stark electric flash the children and their activities. The smoke rose to the ceiling, curled there, rose up through a hole in the floor above to dissipate through the vast reaches of emptiness, of uselessness, above them. It was hard to breathe and hard to see and sounds were muffled by the smoke and dampness in the air in the enormous room. He heard whining. Initially Morris thought it was a baby's whining, but it was a cat. One of the children entered the room with a cat in his arms. The cat was soaking wet. The girl with the birthmark, Fabiola, looked over at the small boy and the cat; she looked at the taller boy, the leader. He nodded. She cried, "Game time."

A visible pulse of excitement animated the children. There were about a half a dozen children in the room, maybe one or two more than that. The taller boy took the cat. He held it by the skin on the back of its neck the way a mother cat holds a kitten though this was not a kitten but a fully grown cat. The cat was nervous; Morris could see that. The boy walked to an upright wooden column in the center of the room. The column was manufactured to mimic a Classical column. It looked like something from a Greek temple, but it was dark wood, not marble. It extended from the floor to the ceiling. Morris had no idea why it was there; it did not seem to be necessary to support the ceiling above— there were plenty of concrete columns that did that. The boy held the cat to the pole about three and one-half feet off the floor. The cat became more nervous. It tried to get away. Quickly, Fabiola with a hammer and spike nailed the cat by the loose fur on the back of its neck to the pole. The cat writhed on the pole, its eyes wide with fear now. It screeched. Morris looked on impassively. Two of the children brought helmets from a pile in the corner. There were hockey helmets, a lacrosse helmet, a baseball helmet, a firefighter's hat, a construction worker's hard hat, and a toy astronaut's helmet. The children put the helmets on. Some of the helmets bore dark stains. A little boy looked at Morris. He said, "Do you wanna play? It's fun."

Morris shook his head.

The children formed a line, single-file, nine or ten feet from the pole. Then each in turn ran at the cat, butting it with the crown of his or her helmet. The children cheered each charge. The cat, eyes wide with fear, swung its claws at the children's heads and shoulders but scratched only—ineffectually—the helmets. After a while the cat gave up its efforts at self-defense. Blood flowed from its mouth and its torn back, ran over its fur, dripped down along the column to pool at its base. Morris saw now that the column was already streaked with dried blood. From past games. An eye was forced from the animal's scull. Morris saw it, white and gory, glittering on the floor in the fire light. Then the cat was crushed; it's middle opened; it's guts spilled down. Giving one last cheer, the children removed their helmets, some of them slick with the cat's blood, tossed them into a corner, and walked off. They no longer noticed the inert cat. It hung there, its shiny entrails hanging down from its torn stomach. Maybe, he considered, the creature was not quite dead: one of its legs moved, waving slowly, occasionally, though perhaps that was merely some sort of post-death twitch. Then even that movement, faint, irresolute, ceased.

* * *

Dude's breathing was regular, sonorous, deep.

Ashley lay awake on the couch. It was perhaps three o'clock in the morning. Maybe four. She half-listened to the sounds of her host's breathing and the semi-violent November rain storm. Because Dude had not pulled down the shades, light from a streetlamp outside the windows tempered the darkness within the apartment. Ashley liked the way things looked in the semi-darkness. Softer, more serene. She liked to watch the paths of the raindrops on the windows. She took a sip, a gulp, from the glass of vodka she held in her hand. She puffed on a cigarette. For the moment, at least, her fear had left her. She was feeling almost like her old self. The vodka had slowed her mind down to a pleasantly slow-moving thing. Now, she thought, one thought followed another in a smooth line like . . . cars at a tollbooth or shoppers at a register. She smiled to herself; she had forgotten she could make such amusing observations. She was such a napping person actually. Her stomach was taking the vodka well. Her insides felt warm and alive. But she knew that she had to think about what she did not want to think about. She had to discipline her mind to face itself if she was going to live.

Focusing her will, she thought about her nightmare—the nightmare that she had experienced under the nightmare-inducing drug in the therapy sessions. It was the same nightmare that had haunted her in one form or another since her girlhood.

She thought about the scene in the funeral home where she walked and talked with a boy and the scene in the Arboretum where she killed a boy, shot him full of arrows. Were those two boys the same boy? It was hard to tell. In her nightmare she could never see the boy's face in the funeral home, but she assumed they were the same. Was she right? Could one make such assumptions about a dream. No. She thought back to what Dr Bentley had said after she had experienced the dream so fully and powerfully in one of the sessions—that the psychological meaning of her dream was probably based in some deep-seated, repressed memory of an actual event or events, but ultimately the meaning did not matter. What was important, Bentley had said, was to experience the mental shock, the jolt, of the nightmare. But why was that important? And what else had Bentley said about the nature of nightmares? Remarkably little, Ashley concluded, running over in her mind the many sessions she had attended. Ashley's brow furrowed. She picked up the glass, took another drink of the bitter liquid. Once Bentley had said that the realm of nightmares existed as a separate sphere of existence, a realm unto itself that dreamers touched sometimes when they dreamed. But what the hell did that mean? One thing was sure—Alvin and Irma had died in the manner of their nightmares. Bruno was dead too, though had he died in the manner of some nightmare that was intrinsically his? This she did not know; he had never told her his nightmare. He might not have had them at all, as he had always said. After all, he was the only one who, under the drug, had experienced nothing, had exhibited no effects. He had just lain there . . . passively. Ashley smiled sadly. Who, what could be making this happen? The obvious choice was Bentley. She was the only one who might conceivably have the where-withal to make nightmares manifest themselves to their dreamers. How she could do this was unfathomable, of course. Or why. It did not compute. Her brow wrinkled. She closed her eyes and drew up her lips in thought—a strange looking expression. She sighed. Then, Ashley's thoughts jumped to the image of the boy at the tree. Her eyes opened wide as she saw his face clearly in her mind's eye: his face sweet and innocent. A young boy. She sat bolt upright on the couch. It was Sebastian. Her heart raced.

Sebastian! Memories flooded her mind or rather, after years of suppression, became instantly clear within her consciousness. Now that the memories had been recovered whole, her mind, so long starved for these recollections, so long wary of them, could not resist looking at them intently, directly, in the same way that a patient cannot resist pulling up a bandage to look at a wound.

They had been seven or eight. Sebastian was her friend. He lived in the neighborhood in his uncle's funeral home. He told her about corpses, that they spoke to him. Of course she did not believe it. What a hyperkinetic story! So fucked-up it put the kinetic in Connecticut, she exclaimed almost out loud. But it scared her just the same. For weeks after the little boy had told her his deepest secret, she avoided him, refused to play with him, hid when he came over to play. Then one day at the Arboretum he found her. Sebastian had been crying, she remembered. Tears still streaked his white cheeks. He told her everything about . . . his uncle and his mother. He told her again of the corpses, that they spoke to him. He told her that only the night before his father had spoken to him through the body of a dead soldier.

"Sebastian," she cried, covering her ears, "you have got to stop saying that! It's not true. It can't be true."

He convinced her to go with her to the funeral home. She remembered the eerie quietness of the large house. No one, no one living at least, was there. The sunlight cut through an opening in the thick curtains in one of the rooms. Motes of dust floated in the warm air. The room was full of chairs arrayed in neat lines. The chairs faced an open casket in the front of the room. She remembered the smell of the flowers. Taking her hand, he brought her to the pew. She wanted to run away—how quiet it was!—but she did not. She must have been in some sort of shocked daze. They knelt on the pew before the open casket. Too short, she could not see inside. She could only see the casket itself. Polished wood. She heard Sebastian speaking to the corpse, softly, imploringly, asking questions of the dead body. Then she heard another voice. The voice was labored and low. She saw a body sit up in the casket and she ran, ran from the funeral home.

Sebastian caught up with her. He convinced her to go to her house and get her bow and arrows. She must have been in some kind of daze—she was in some kind of daze—because she walked with him to the Arboretum and . . . she did what he wanted. She filled his young body with arrows on a sunny fall day. She remembered how surprised she was at how easy it was to aim and shoot the bow that day and how surprised she was—baffled in fact—at her success, although she practiced almost every evening after dinner with her father and mother, shooting at the white, black, blue, red circles of a target that he set up on the green, soft lawn of the back yard. She remembered the blood spurting from the young boy's body, running over his porcelain white skin and she remembered hitting him in the eye, the sight of the arrow in his eye and blood flowing down his cheek and his neck. She thought she had killed him, but he lived. She remembered how her parents Rex and Cassie were shocked—beyond shocked—at what had happened. They would only refer to it as "the accident." The days, the months following the accident were so strange; they moved so slowly. Her parents looked at her strangely, whispered behind her back. Sebastian was taken away somewhere. Ashley was left alone. None of the other children in the neighborhood would play with her. She spent her time by herself. Her father locked away the family's bows, arrows, and targets in the attic. After a year or so he got them out again. Archery was a Quick family passion, especially for her parents. Her own enthusiasm for the sport ran hot and cold.

So now Sebastian was back. What did that mean? Did he remember what had happened? Was he cured of his conviction that he could speak to the dead? No! Why would she even ask that? She had seen him, heard him, speaking to Bruno at the funeral home just a few nights ago. Her Bruno—awakened from his death. She had heard his voice . . . or had she? Had she actually witnessed Sebastian summoning Bruno from the dead or had she imagined it, imagined it because of what had happened between her and Sebastian when they had been children? But she had not, before now, seen the connection between Sebastian the adult and the Sebastian of her youth. In fact, she had purged "the accident" from her mind, though some part of her mind must have known that the two Sebastians—present and past—were one and the same and that unconscious knowing must have, might have, made her believe she saw something at Bruno's wake which she did not. After all, she reasoned, if seeing is believing, then believing could be seeing, too. Right?

Ashley's thoughts moved in a new direction. Perhaps it was Sebastian who was responsible for the nightmare deaths. Perhaps he had come back for . . . what? Revenge? Sebastian had first shown up at that odd party on the ship when Ashley had experienced that hallucinatory dream. The shit dream.

Since Sebastian's arrival, Bruno had died as well. But how could Sebastian have had access to the details of Irma's deadly, fecal nightmare? Had he in fact caused her death? Or Alvin's? Irma and Alvin's deaths were hard to pin on Sebastian, though, if someone could talk to the dead, presumably he could do other inexplicable, other occult, things too. Unbland! Unlifelike! Yes, Sebastian was definitely a suspect.

But then, Ashley realized, so was she. She had befriended Irma. Irma had died and she, Ashley, had taken elements of Irma's nightmare into her own dreamscape. Then, Bruno, the person who had been closer to Ashley than anyone else in the world, had died. And what of the voice that Ashley kept hearing in her head. What of it? Could it be that she herself had gone insane, that she herself was in some way—some inexplicable way—allowing the Nightmare Realm—whatever that was—to enter the waking world? That would be unsettling, she said to herself, shuddering a bit.

Dude muttered in his sleep, then turned over into an oddly humped position. His ample rear end, covered by threadbare jockey shorts, rose up in the air. She liked Dude. He hardly

knew her, yet he had taken her in. That thought of Dude, her
benefactor, prompted a thought of Karla, her friend. Ashley wondered how she was doing. It would be nice to see her again, to
make small talk. Perhaps she should call her later in the day.
But, maybe not. There was an obtuseness to Karla that made the
thought of trying to explain a serious situation to her unappetiz-
ing.

"Hefty," Ashley whispered aloud, marveling at how nearly
her voice could sound like that of her friend. She saw her glass
was empty. She got up to refill it in the kitchen. Soon daylight
would come.

Chapter 19

Worms

"I'm worried about her," she said, bringing the tiny espresso cup to her lips. "I'm sweaty."

"Yes . . . Yes, I am too," he nodded.

"You? Sweat? Unlikely," she said coldly. "I wonder where she is . . . if she's all right."

"I've looked everywhere. I can't find her."

She looked out the window of Rockwell's and sighed. "This was, is, one of our favorite haunts," Karla said.

Stiffly, emotionlessly, Sebastian looked around the cafe. There was not much activity this late, wet morning. The rain which had poured through the night had not abated.

"I miss Bruno too," Karla added.

"Yes," Sebastian nodded. "He was a very interesting guy."

Karla tapped her fingers on the table. "Where would I go if I were Ashley and my boyfriend had just died and I was terrified?" she asked aloud. "Back to the apartment I had shared with Bruno? No way, ugly. To my parents house? We know she didn't go there. To my apartment? That's what I can't figure out— why didn't she come to me? I'm her best friend."

"That would have seemed to be the most reasonable expectation," Sebastian said.

Karla looked at him for a moment.

"One place I wouldn't go," Karla said, "is anywhere near you."

Sebastian's eyes opened wide. He winced.

"Why not?"

"Because she saw you talking to the corpse of her boyfriend, that's why! And, what's more—she heard her dead boyfriend talking back to you! I mean, how hyperkinetic can you get?"

Sebastian hesitated, then softly responded, "I admit it's unusual, yes, but it's something I can do, that's all. What baffles me, however, is the fact that you don't seem all that scared by my . . . uh . . . singularity."

Color rose in Karla's cheeks. She whispered too. "Scared? You terrify me, Sebastian. You're some kind of mutant! But, so what? I know you're looking for Ashley. I just want to keep an eye on you to make sure the next corpse you speak to isn't hers."

"What if it's yours, then?"

"Are you threatening me, you one-eyed piece of shit?"

"No. Actually I don't want to hurt you. I don't want to hurt Ashley. I don't want to hurt anybody. I only want to help her. Yes. She is my friend."

Karla considered this.

Then Sebastian said, "Actually, it's very brave of you to put yourself in this position if you think I am evil."

"Well, sometimes I rise to the occasion," Karla said, searching Sebastian's face, his posture. But now his expression gave away nothing. His face had slackened. Perhaps, she thought, he could empty his mind of thought and feeling at will, like some cornered animals could fool by feigning death. Maybe he was as dead in some way as the corpses he communicated with. "What did Bruno say to you?"

"What?"

"You heard me."

"I never discuss a conversation I have had with a corpse."

"I never discuss a conversation I have had with a corpse," Karla mimicked. "What is it? Some kind of dead client privilege? Does it ever occur to you, Sebastian, what a jerk you sound like?"

"Is this some sort of bland crash course in humility?"

Karla reached under the table into her purse, took out a snub nosed revolver, pointed it at her companion. A waiter who had been moving towards the table turned abruptly, walked off.

"Tell me what he said," Karla said through clenched perfect teeth. "Look under the fucking table at what I'm pointing at you, then tell me what he said!"

Sebastian looked under the table, saw the gun, then looked left, right.

He answered, "He said something about you."

"Me? What did he say?"

"Yes, well, I did not exactly have a chance for a full conversation. He mumbled a few words and then he distinctly said your name."

"My name?"

Karla put the gun down on the table; she looked rattled.

"Why would he say my name?"

"I don't know," Sebastian replied.

Karla said nothing more. She was lost in thought, overwhelmed. Her jaw loosened but did not quite hang slack. Sebastian saw her tongue dart over her lips nervously.

Finally, Sebastian said, "Your horns are coming in nicely, Karla."

"What?" She felt absently at the horns that now, three inches tall, stuck, white and clean, above her skull. "Oh, the horns. They are sort of a pain in the ass. I can't tell you how many pillow cases I've gone through in the last week."

"Yes," Sebastian nodded. "Interesting."

"So what are you doing today, Sebastian?" Karla asked.

"I suppose I'll keep looking for Ashley."

"Me too," Karla said. "Let's keep in touch."

"Yes."

*   *   *

Again it was night. A dark, wet wind blew across the city. The remaining participants in the nightmare therapy sessions—those who were still alive—hurried to the office building where they met weekly with Dr Allison Bentley. They moved swiftly down the ill-lit street, sometimes turning to look back over their shoulders. Nervous. Seated in an unmarked car, Costello watched them hurry. He counted six people entering the front door of the building in the course of a quarter hour. He recognized two: Karla, whom he did not know by name but had seen before with Ashley, and Eric Tang—short, wired, contorted reptile—whom he knew both by sight and reputation as one of the foremost drug lords in the city. Tang, alone of the group, moved with assurance, confidence, hauteur. Lighting a cigarette, Costello wondered where Ashley was. At any rate, she was not here. He ran his hand along the spine of the dog that sat panting in the passenger seat next to him. Turning its disfigured head, Kitten looked at him with a look of trust. Costello noted how the tear in the dog's muzzle, the exposed teeth, made the dog appear to be constantly smiling. Then its canine eyes darted to a figure on the street.

"Who's this?" Costello mused. Smoke came out of his mouth as he spoke. A young woman, bent at the waist, holding her stomach in an attitude of discomfort, hurried down the sidewalk, entered the building.

*   *   *

The session did not take its usual form. The participants did not take their places quietly to await Dr Bentley's understated, but forceful directions. Instead, they stood in a small knot around her, jabbering, asking questions, gesticulating. After all, three of them had died in less than three weeks. This is not what any of them had expected when signing up for the course months before.

"I'm scared. I've never been so scared," Jessica said, her eyes wild in her chubby, pallid face.

"I can't sleep I'm so frightened," Karla sneered languidly.

"Isn't there something you can do, Doctor?" Brandon asked, shedding for the moment his customary humor. "Anything?"

"We're fucked, aren't we?" Jerry cried. A newly-evident nervous tic jolted his head to one side.

"What is going on?" Dominic asked, his intonation discarding for the moment its customarily clipped, preppy cool.

"What's going on is that we're all dying one by one," Eric Tang observed. Simultaneously, the group looked at him. He spoke without emotion, standing arrogant and aloof outside of the worried circle.

"Why don't we all sit down," Dr Bentley said. "We've got to talk this through."

The group could discern worry in her voice.

"But is it true? Are we all going to die?" Jessica whined.

"No," Dr. Bentley said, hugging her, guiding her to one of the meditation pillows set in a circle in the middle of the room, "we're not going to die." The futon that was usually on the floor inside the circle, the pad on which participants experienced drug-induced nightmares, was not there this evening. It was rolled up and propped against a wall.

Everyone sat.

Sitting down herself, adjusting her posture, brushing back a few strands of her wheat-white hair from her forehead, Bentley began to speak. She looked in turn at each of the class members as she spoke.

She said, "I know that all of you are very worried. I'm worried too. I've told you before about how there is a place of nightmares: the Nightmare Realm. Usually, we think of this realm as a metaphorical place symbolizing the common fears that dwell in the subconscious, or unconscious, minds of all humankind. Just as all, or almost all, humans dream, and just as all of us dream in the same way though not of the same things, we all have fears that manifest themselves in nightmares. But, this metaphorical domain is in truth more than that. It is more than just a symbol, a metaphor. This zone of nightmares is a real place, existing both inside and outside time, both inside and outside what we think of as the physical word, as reality. This actual place emanates a hideously powerful force. I know. I've seen it; I've been there."

Jessica gasped.

Bentley continued, "What I believe is happening here is that the Nightmare Realm has somehow established a direct link with the participants in this class. Or, more likely, with one of us. That link is, I think, so strong that it is enabling our nightmares to become, in some sense, real."

Bentley paused, scanned the faces in the group. Their focus on her, her words, was intent, intense. Not everyone was there.

"Where's Jane?," she asked. "Where's Ashley? Does anyone know?"

Karla spoke. "Dr Bentley, we haven't been able to find Ashley since the night of Bruno's . . . wake. She ran out of the funeral home. I haven't been able to find her anywhere."

"You've looked?"

"That's all I've done. I am very worried about her."

"I am too," Bentley said. "I believe that she may be in danger. She must be found."

"What kind of danger?" Jessica cried.

"Grave . . ."

Bentley's answer was interrupted. Jane entered the room. She was sobbing, clutching her stomach. She staggered towards Bentley. All turned their attention towards her.

"Worms!" Jane gasped.

Bentley rose, took Jane's collapsing form into her arms. Her chest rose and fell in rapid, shallow breaths. "Bring a chair," Bentley said. Brandon fetched the chair from in front of Bentley's desk. Jane was seated. She was sobbing.

"You know my nightmare?" Jane said. "You know how it's about worms, worms in my . . . body?"

"Yes," Bentley said.

"Last night I dreamed the dream again, but more realistically than ever before. Oh, it was horrible. Then I coughed something up. Dr Bentley, I think I coughed up a worm. Maybe it was a sprout but I think it was a . . . a worm. I feel like I have worms in my body, in my stomach right now."

"No!" Jerry shouted, jumping from his meditation pillow. He started to move towards the door, changed his mind, turned, stood alone, quivering agitatedly.

Bentley said, "But that can't be. It was only a dream."

Jane took a deep breath.

She said, "Maybe you're right. It might have just been a sprout. I did have sprouts last night with dinner. I thought it must be a sprout and I threw it . . . I flushed it down the toilet. But I thought I felt it wriggling in my hand."

"It wasn't a worm," Bentley said. "It was a sprout."

"Are you sure?"

"I'm sure."

Bentley took a tissue and wiped away Jane's tears from her hot cheeks. Jessica brought Jane a glass of lukewarm water from a pitcher on a sidetable. She drank.

"Oh, no! Dr. Bentley, I can feel them again."

Jane stood up. A look of extreme discomfort crossed her face. She loosed a stream of vomit which jumped, like some sort of escaping entity, from her throat to plop, to splatter, softly and wetly on the uncarpeted wooden floor. Then she fell back into the chair, exhausted.

The class stared at the vomit, wet and filthy. It appeared to be a mass of half-digested spouts. Then the mass began to wriggle. It was a mass of short, thin, whitish worms.

Everyone stared at the mass, the living mass. Everyone was silent, unmoving. Even Jane looked, unflinching for that long moment, at what had issued from her body. But, this moment of unmoving silence was akin to the moment when, after a bomb has been detonated at its base, a skyscraper hovers as if it will stand and then it does not stand but falls into itself.

Brandon, Dominic, and Karla all jumped to their feet, moved towards the door. Jessica was right behind them. Seeing the stampede, Jerry turned too, started to dash. Bentley was quicker. Sprinting around the fleeing young people, she barred the exit. She shouted at them as they stood before the door, momentarily arrested. Only Tang and Jane had not run. Jane was slumped in her chair. Tang had risen; he was looking down at the worms.

Bentley shouted, "You have got to believe me. We can not leave here. If we do not stay together, we will die one by one. Believe me. We have got to remain calm. There is only one way we can beat this but we have got to stay together. We have to act in unison."

"Fuck you," Jerry screamed. His voice was high like a frightened child's voice. He tried to push past Bentley. He felt a hand on his shoulder, a heavy hand, felt himself restrained. It was Tang. He had come up behind the group. Tang spoke with a voice of command.

He said, "The doctor's right. We stay. We get through this together."

"Fuck you, Tang!" Jerry screamed. He turned to face Eric. He was going to hit him.

Tang slapped him hard. It sounded—the slap did—like a piece of meat being thrown against a wall.

Some of the others could see the red mark on Jerry's face where Tang's hand had hit. The mark was the same color as the pimples on Jerry's face. Jerry was silent. Tears formed in his eyes. Little pearls of fear and rage. His body shook with a multitude of negative emotions.

"Now, go back to your seats like Dr Bentley said," Tang said.

"But . . . the worms," Jessica said quietly.

"Brandon," Bentley said, "there's a broom and dust pan in that closet. Sweep them up, please. Then we'll flush them down the toilet."

The class members watched Brandon sweep up the worms. They watched him and Bentley leave the room, go down the hall. Brandon averted his eyes from the contents of the dustpan. Tang motioned them to their meditation pillows. They sat down. On the wooden floor was a wet smear where the worms had been. It was already starting to dry up. Bentley returned with Brandon.

Everyone was sitting down now. Traces of alertness were returning to Jane. She alone sat in a chair.

Brandon said, "What's happening, Doctor?" His voice was quiet. He sounded like a little boy talking to his mother.

Bentley said, "It was not clear to me until a moment ago how much power the Nightmare Realm has amassed. It's ability to cause the physical manifestation of these worms—to actually produce change on the material plane—means that the power of the Realm is very strong, very focused. I suspected this when Irma died. But I also thought that the . . . matter, the substance which appeared to cover her in the sewer might have come from her presence in the sewer, not from the Nightmare Realm. I was wrong. I now see that I was wrong. What this means is that the Nightmare Realm is gathering tremendous power. It wants to gain entrance not only to us but to our world."

"Do you mean," Dominic asked, "that one of us is helping the Nightmare Realm get at us?"

"Yes. Probably."

The participants looked at each other out of the corners of their eyes.

Bentley continued, "I believe that it is likely that the Nightmare Realm is acting through one of us, using one of our minds as a transmitter, so to speak, to receive and channel its power towards the group. But, that does not mean that the person whose mind is being used is aware it is being used. On the contrary, the . . . uh . . . relay station is quite possibly completely unaware of what is happening, of how he or she is being used."

"So what's the use?" Karla quipped. She was ignored. No one was in the mood for irreverence now.

"So what do we do?" Jessica asked.

"We must stay together. We must all go to my house tonight. I think that I can use my power, my knowledge, my experience, to keep the Nightmare Realm at bay while we figure out our next steps. Then, we have to find a way to close the Realm's direct point of entry into our world. Otherwise . . ."

"Otherwise what?" Dominic said.

"Otherwise we all die," Tang said.

Bentley said nothing, then nodded, said, "Yes, that's right."

The group was silent. Then Dominic asked, "Doctor, didn't you know about the risk we were taking? Didn't you know that this kind of thing was a possibility?"

Bentley considered for a moment before she replied.

She said, "Yes, I knew the risks and let me tell you that what is happening is very unusual, very rare. If approached responsibly the Nightmare Realm is a powerful and wonderful resource with great curative potential. It is comparable to a thunder storm. We can benefit from the strength of the storm—from its wind, its rain, its power—but we have to make sure that we protect ourselves from the storm at the same time. The lightning clears the air around us. We want to see the lightning, to hear its crackle, to breathe the air it purifies—that does not mean we have to let the lightning strike us or that we want the storm to come down from the sky to envelop the earth. I've worked with the Nightmare Realm for years, Dominic. I know what I'm doing. This has never happened before."

He nodded.

Jessica asked where Bentley lived. Bentley gave her address and directions to her home. The nightmare therapy session participants departed. Tang took Jane. She leaned against him for support. Bentley remained to gather together some files, some papers.

*   *   *

A few moments later, as Bentley was almost ready to leave, a figure appeared in the door.

"Dr Bentley?"

"Yes."

She saw a man, about 5' 11", not big in build, not thin either. His hair was thinning, dark, wavy; he had an ugly scar on his forehead. His eyes were bright, a little crazy looking, his suit was wrinkled, his brown shoes were scuffed.

"My name is Detective Thomas Costello, Doctor."

"Yes?"

"I'd like to talk to you about the deaths of a number of the participants in your nightmare therapy sessions."

She showed no reaction.

"Yes, Detective," she said. "Let's sit down over there." In the corner of the large, open room was a writing desk with a chair on one side of it. Costello picked up a second chair from amidst a number of flat, round pillows on the floor and carried it with him. He sat down at the same time that Dr Bentley sat across the writing table from him. The table was empty except for a telephone and a crystal ball positioned on a small, silver stand. Costello picked up the orb, looked at it, put it back. It was heavy.

"It appears," Costello said, "as if three of the participants in your sessions have died unusual deaths within the past 18 days. What can you tell me about this, Doctor?"

"I know, Detective: Alvin Gremillion, Irma Gamerman, and Bruno Passive—all three dead," Bentley said. "But I don't know why. I don't know how it is happening."

"Why haven't you called the police?"

"I thought about it," Bentley said. "But in this case I'm not sure the police can do anything."

"Oh, why?"

"Because I don't think that these deaths have been caused by another human being—at least not directly."

Costello leaned forward, intent.

"What do you think is happening, Dr. Bentley?"

Bentley explained it all—the work that was taking place in the nightmare therapy sessions, her theories of the Nightmare Realm, what had happened earlier that evening, how she was gathering the group together at her home for safety and in an effort to stave off the force or forces that were taking them one by one. She spoke quickly, efficiently, not as if she expected the detective to believe her, but as if she did not care whether he did or not.

Costello was thrown off by the matter-of-factness of her presentation. Honesty, Costello knew, can be more insidious than lying.

Costello could not get a read on the woman across from him. She seemed too earnest, too primly earnest, but he could not put his finger on what made her tick. There was a hint, a flicker of fear in her eyes, yet she was apparently adept, this Dr Bentley, at keeping her emotions under control.

"So, unless you're a psychic investigator, Detective Costello," Bentley concluded, "I don't now what you can do for us. I'll bet they didn't teach you anything about investigating psychic phenomena at the Police Academy, did they?"

Costello smiled weakly.

"Has any of the participants in the class been acting strangely?" he asked. "Do you suspect that any of them might be involved in some way?"

Bentley thought, replied, "No . . . no, with one exception. There is a young woman who was close to two of the victims. She was the person who found Irma Gamerman in the sewer. That's how we found out about Irma's death. The newspapers didn't make much of it. They rarely do. Murder is so commonplace. The last victim was her boyfriend, Bruno. Interestingly, she was not here this evening. Apparently, her friends haven't seen her either. I don't think I suspect her—not really—of any involvement in these deaths, but, frankly, I'm worried about her. And, to be honest, my intuition does tell me she's involved in some way, but I don't know how."

"Ashley Quick," Costello said.

"Yes, Detective. You've been looking into . . . ah . . . all this then?

Costello's expression remained the same. He nodded slightly.

He said, "Could you give me a list of the others in the group as well as your address and phone number?"

Bentley took a leather-bound notebook and piece of fine writing paper from a drawer within the table and began to copy the information in a forceful, elegant script. Costello watched her write, turning over in his mind what the doctor had said.

The telephone on Bentley's desk rang. She picked it up, said, "It's for you."

She extended the phone. Taking it, Costello felt a premonition of impending unpleasantness.

"Costello?" Finnerty said.

"Yes, Lieutenant?"

"I want you over here now."

"Over where?"

"The mayor's house. You know where it is?"

"Yes. What's up?"

"You'll know when you get here," Finnerty said.

"Lieutenant, how in hell did you know I was here?"

"Telepathy," Finnerty said. "Actually, I looked at the notes on your desk, wrote down some numbers." Then he hung up.

Costello looked at Bentley. He would not mind having a nightmare or two in which she played a role, he thought.

"Problem, Detective?" she smiled. Her teeth were in very good condition.

"Problems," he replied, emphasizing the 's.' "Unfortunately, I've got to go." Rising from his chair, he took the paper she had prepared, glanced at it, folded it, put it in his jacket pocket. "I'll try to drop by your home in the next few days, if that's alright?" he said.

"That would be fine."

*　　*　　*

A number of police vehicles were parked haphazardly in front of the mayor's house. Two uniforms were at the door, looking nervous. Costello parked, walked towards the door of the simple ranch house in one of the city's few remaining solidly working class neighborhoods.

"What's up?" Costello said to one of the patrolmen at the door.

"Red fucking alert, Detective," the patrolman said under his breath, giving Costello all the information he could safely impart.

Costello nodded, said, "I should have been a beautician like my mother wanted me to be."

"You could do my hair any day, Detective," the uniform said, opening the door.

The first thing that Costello heard in the shadowy front hallway of the mayor's home was the sound of a woman crying. One of the mayor's aides—a young, suited sycophant—met Costello at the door, led him towards the living room of the home, then stood aside as the detective entered the room.

Costello saw Mayor Paninni and his wife, a petite woman, on a couch. She was crying profusely. He had her hand in his. He was patting it consolingly. Standing in the room were Lieutenant Finnerty and Commissioner Trump. Both looked somber, intense. Finnerty looked at Costello a moment, coldly, then returned his attention to the sofa.

"Who are you?" the mayor's wife asked Costello, turning her face, her attention to him. Her face was red, bloated with crying. She held a wadded tissue in one hand, dabbed it at her tear-brimmed eyes.

"That's a detective, Sophie," the Mayor said. "Don't worry about him. He works for me."

She continued, "Detective, are you going to find my Tater."

"Yes, ma'am," Costello said, judging it best to answer affirmatively.

"My Tater is gone. Someone must have taken him."

Costello nodded.

Over the mayor and his wife were shelves of gaudy knickknacks— bright ceramic clowns, monks, children, birds, cats, penguins.

"Sophie," the mayor said softly, "why don't you go and lie down while I talk to these men."

"But I can't sleep," the mayor's wife sobbed.

"I know, dear. But, the sooner we can get started, the sooner we'll find Tater."

"All right," she said.

Mayor Paninni beckoned to his aide, who, putting his arm around her, led the mayor's wife out of the room. Costello could hear her crying as she moved to a different part of the house, to the mayoral bedchamber presumably.

The mayor did not get up from his place on the couch.

He looked at the commissioner and said, "This is your fucking fault."

"My fault?" the commissioner said. "It's his fucking fault." The commissioner was looking right at Finnerty.

Finnerty's face reddened.

"My fault?" Finnerty said. "No it isn't. It's his fucking fault." He looked at Costello.

Costello looked around him. There was no one else there. He said, "What's my fault?"

Paninni said, "My wife's fucking dog has been abducted because the Police Department is unable to put an end to this god damn Pet Hunter. You had him in fucking jail; now he's out and he's taken Tater."

"Tater?" Costello ventured.

"Yes, Tater, you shithead," the mayor exclaimed. "I know you, Costello. I don't need any attitude."

Finnerty said, "Tater is Mrs Paninni's Dachshund. His real name is Potato. The dog's real name, that is. Here's a picture of the dog."

Finnerty handed Costello a photograph in a golden frame. The photograph depicted the mayor's wife on a happier day. Lovingly she clutched a Dachshund with a pink ribbon around its neck.

Abruptly, Mayor Paninni stood up and started to pace the living room, gesticulating expressively. He said, "I want every god damn cop in the city, every city worker, every meter maid, every secretary out looking for this dog. We will not rest until the fucking dog is found and if he is not found, Commissioner, it will spell the end for you and your band of . . . inept clowns."

The mayor's aide stepped into the room. He made a sound in his throat.

Noticing him, the mayor barked, "What do you want?"

"The media's here, your honor. Two TVs and *The Traveler*."

"That's all I need," Paninni said. "The fucking media. Well, bright boy, what should I do?"

"Actually, sir, I have an idea," the aide said, stepping forward.

"What?"

"Why don't we put Tater's picture on one of our blimps. Get the whole city involved in the search?"

Paninni looked at the aide. The commissioner, Finnerty, and Costello all looked at the aide; the three policemen were stone-faced, awaiting the mayor's reaction to the idea.

"How about this?" the mayor said quietly to the aide. "How about I put your picture on the blimp along with these words: 'Who would ever hire an asshole like this?'"

The aide's face reddened. It looked to Costello like the aide might cry too, just like the mayor's wife. Finnerty and the Commissioner smiled.

Paninni turned on them.

"What are you smiling about? Get out there and find my fucking Dachshund."

Chapter 20

Mashed

When it came domestic matters, she was a neatnik.

Her kitchen was pristine and its color scheme was Kelly green and yellow. She had decorated it with happy knickknacks and prints of the authors she so admired: Baudelaire, Rimbaud, Verlaine, Verne. French authors and other French things were an overarching motif throughout her apartment. She wore a beret now and smoked a French cigarette.

On the sturdy, metal kitchen table were porcelain pepper and salt shakers in the shape of baby chickens. Fluffy-looking weights, the shakers held down two corners of the instructions which Devorah Hepple had spread on the table top. She referred to the instructions often as she worked to put together the malevolent mechanism she was assembling on the floor.

Though she was good at other things, she was not good at putting things together. Her mind was one step away from frustration and anger, but she kept her cool. The device she was assembling was made mostly of wood which she found strange because wood was not used much for making things anymore.

"*Merde!*" she said under her breath. "Easy instructions for assembly." That was what the advertisement had said, but the god damned instructions were in Chinese. At any rate, the mail order weapon she was building was nearly done. She sat down on a kitchen chair and smoked a cigarette, then, referring one last time to the incomprehensible plans, she finished the job. It had taken two hours to build the thing. Now, she admired it. It looked solid enough, constructed from pre-cut and drilled wooden boards and two thick rubber bands, the biggest rubber bands she had ever seen. She pulled the throwing arm—if that was what it was called—of the device back. She locked it into place. On the end of the throwing arm was a large, white plastic basket into which objects could be placed.

She was eager to try the device. She looked around the kitchen. An impulse: she placed the porcelain chicks into the basket. But they were not chickens in the basket for long. She triggered the release mechanism, springing the chicks so quickly, forcefully she did not actually see their release. She saw only two nearly parallel yellow, linear blurs. She heard the nearly silent sound of the release at the same time she heard the shattering termination to the shakers' most brief flight. She covered her head with her arms. A wave of salt, pepper, and porcelain shards washed back against her, a backdraft of seasonings. The backs of her hands and her bare forearms were stung by the flying salt and pieces of the shattered chicks. The pepper hung in the air a moment longer, forcing her to keep her eyes closed even after she had dropped her hands. She sneezed. Pieces of the salt and pepper shakers dotted her hair, her shoulders.

She examined the outcome. At the top of the kitchen wall, near the ceiling, she saw indentations in the plaster. Pieces of the salt and pepper shakers were imbedded there. She looked back at the mail order catapult with satisfaction.

Devorah smiled. For the first time in many days she felt some measure of peace. This positive feeling was short-lived. Almost immediately dread filled her again, dread and expectancy. Quickly she disassembled the catapult, breaking a long red fingernail in the process. Around her apartment she rushed, hiding the catapult piece by piece: a strut under her mattress, another in the sofa, other wooden pieces behind bookshelves or in other places, the connecting bolts and wingnuts in a plastic bag which she buried in a box of breakfast cereal. She hid the plastic throwing basket in her laundry hamper. Who could say when the police would come knocking at her door again, looking for Morris, *son pauvre chien*? The catapult was completely hidden and yet she was still on edge. She recovered each part of the catapult and rehid it, then rehid it again, trying with each new effort to find a better hiding place for each component. Eventually, though not satisfied, not calmed, she realized that she could hide the catapult no better than she had; she realized that she would have to accept this, this imperfect dissembling, if she was going to move on to other, more important things.

*　*　*

It was late morning, he figured, though there was no way to tell it from the light. Natural light had no access to this nameless bar; indeed, unnatural light had enough difficulty shouldering its way through the smoke, the reeking darkness. He watched her drink yet another vodka in the place where they had met—where they had encountered each other—for the second time. Dude reflected groggily on his last few days with his new companion, Ashley Quick. To put it mildly, it had been interesting.

Since the day before yesterday or maybe the day before that—Dude had no clear recollection—Ashley had insisted on spending their time in this bar, drinking pretty much around the clock. And he had seen her, experienced her, in an impressively wide range of bearings, attitudes, emotions. Sometimes she sat listlessly, sometimes she spoke animatedly. She wept sometimes for what seemed like endless periods of time; at others she laughed hysterically. But, the oddly different voice was what intrigued Dude the most. Frankly, it awed him. At various times she spoke in a voice not her own—higher pitched, more girlish, with a dash of singsong. Ashley seemed unaware of this different voice, which, after all, was only subtly different—a subtle difference only discernible, Dude imagined, to a seasoned Ashley-listener. The difference was mostly one of tone, not content. In this other voice, Ashley expounded on the same sorts of subjects she dealt with in her own voice: impromptu diatribes on freedom and indignity, on human nature, boredom, inaction, and Bruno, his lack of talent, his beautiful nature, his ultra-blandness.

In her more lucid moments, Ashley had explained in a great circumlocution of details the circumstances of the nightmare therapy sessions and the deaths connected with those sessions. Dude did not know whether to believe her or not. Nor did he care. His attitude towards truth was ambivalent. He valued entertainment more than veracity, and he was enjoying himself. Ashley was entertaining. She was lusciously beautiful. This effect was only enhanced by her extreme wastedness. And his. Besides, he had no other prospects, this corpulent cherub. He had nothing better to do. And, she was buying.

Ashley rose from the table, stumbled towards the bathroom. She did not close the door. Dude heard the sound of retching, then, after a few moments, he heard the sound of tap water running. Ashley emerged. She walked somewhat more steadily now. Dude could see that her face was wet with recent washing; strands of brown-black hair over her forehead were wet too. Tiny beads of water on strands of hair. She looked at her glass on the table.

"Look," she said.

"At what?"

"My glass. Empty."

"Ashley," Dude said. "You're empty. You've just vomited. Why don't you take a break—have a glass of water or something?"

Ashley pondered.

"No. Want more vodka."

Dude shrugged his shoulders, got up, walked to the bar. When he returned, Ashley was seated. She took the slightly soiled glass in her hand, considered it tentatively. She sipped. A expression of distaste curled her lips.

"Whoo-eee," she said, "that's strong stuff."

Dude smiled.

Ashley said, "Dude, here's the premise. We're sitting here. We're practically the only people in the bar, except for the bartender. We don't know what time it is and we've been doing the same thing for a number of days."

"Getting wasted."

"Pothered."

"Pothered?"

"Pothered. Shitty. Don't tie me up with terms," Ashley smiled. Her eyes brightened. A sudden transformation reshaped her features into almost a luminescent mask of physical wellness. It was that quick. Dude imagined some chemical change, some new inrush of enzymes or something, taking place in her body. She did not seem at all drunk now. Dude could see that she was moving into a state he had seen before in Ashley's ongoing bender—she had become, for the moment, very lucid. He was not ready for this. He was too inebriated. He did not have the strength for one of Ashley's philosophical discourses.

"Here's the premise," she continued. "For all we know, time is moving backwards. For example, if we're doing the same thing now that we were doing yesterday and if we will be doing the same thing tomorrow that we are doing today, who is to say that we are not sitting here tomorrow drinking ourselves towards yesterday?"

Dude responded, "Are you saying that prodigious alcohol intake is a means to reverse the flow of time?"

"Interesting point, ungainly child," Ashley said. "Alcohol administered in massive quantities, as I've told you, seems pretty effective in keeping that sweaty foreign voice out of my mind. At least some of the time." She tapped her head to make her point. "But no, I am not saying that. I am not saying that at all. What I am saying is that engaging in very similar activities for long periods of time makes the forward movement of time irrelevant, because, changes in activity—changes measured through progress, failure, or other . . . change—are the very reason we have any napping, viral concept of time at all."

"You lost me," Dude said.

"Silly Dude, you boring thing" Ashley said. "Let me put it to you simply. The idea of time is based on observable change, so if we remove observable change from the equation, then time is gone too. No change, no time. Get it? So, in our present, unchanging state of inactivity—while we sit here fucking atrophying in this hyper dive day after day—we might just as well be moving from future into past as from past into future."

"Now I understand," Dude said, lighting a cigarette. "So what?"

"So, here's my bland idea to save the world," Ashley said, sitting even more erectly in her chair.

"Widespread alcoholism?"

She looked at him dismissively.

"So here's my idea to change the world," Ashley said.

"You just said that," Dude observed.

A blank look crossed Ashley's face. Her eyes went blank. The gears in her mind were spinning. Then, the gears came together, meshed. She resumed.

"Oh, then . . . here it is—my nappingest idea of all time . . . of all time I say because it's all about eradicating time. The human race should consciously stop moving forward and make an all out effort to relive the past day by day. How? Let's say that starting tomorrow, we tried as hard as we could to recreate the situations that occurred today—get it?—and the day after tomorrow we tried to recreate what happened yesterday and so on and so forth."

Dude said, "So, what you're saying is that we should go back into time one day at a time instead of moving into the future? But why would we do that?"

"So that we won't create anything new. Can't you see the benefits? Think of the benefits in the field of culture alone. Each year there are thousands of new books, new movies, new songs, new thrills but all of them are essentially the same old sweating . . ."

"Hyperkinetic drivel," Dude said.

" Precisely! The same old sweating, hyperkinetic drivel. Hideous. Makes me want to puke," she said, then looked as if she might. She recovered her composure, continued. "If next year's mass culture is sure to have the same value as last year's culture—which is no value whatsoever—why not simply relive last year's culture and when we're done with that move onto the year before? We'd lose nothing in terms of entertainment value and we would stop the production of all these new layers of dreck. I call it the nostalgia principle. I think it would be . . . a very healthy way to go."

"Actually, in the short term, that sort of . . . uh . . . approach wouldn't change my life very much at all," Dude said, growing almost wistful. "Every day for me is pretty much the same. I suppose I could write the same graffiti on the walls tomorrow as I would write today . . . I mean, assuming I was going to write something today. No one would notice. It's not like anyone ever comes up to me and says, "Dude, your thoughts have reprogrammed my whole being. I love you.'"

"Why even bother?" Ashley said. "What you've written is already there. There's no reason to express your same dull thoughts twice."

"Thanks," Dude said. He looked downcast, Ashley noticed. Perhaps his feelings were hurt. She fell silent.

She said, "Your story about Doktor Bomber was pretty good though."

He nodded, frowned, looked away.

"But that's not what I do. That's not my art form," he murmured.

Neither of them said anything for a while.

Then, brightening, Dude said, "But what about movie actors? If they didn't make new movies, what would they do for jobs?"

"They could make remakes," Ashley said. "The same movie over and over again."

"Bland," Dude said.

"Bland squared," Ashley replied

*　　*　　*

Ashley looked up from staring at the table. She said, "Uneasy." Then she laughed.

*　　*　　*

Late night. Back at the apartment.

Dude is talking to Ashley. They are laughing. They are on his bed.

He feels her breath, hot and boozy on his face. Her mouth, sweet and wet and open meets his and they are lying together on his bed, entwined in each others arms.

"Oh, Dude," she murmurs. "Dude. Dude. Dude."

He is over her and he sees her face. It is radiant, serene, enraptured. Her hair flows out onto the soiled pillow.

"Oh, Dude, my ugly little man."

He feels something in his heart. An emotion. Overwhelming. Strong.

Then Dude woke up.

He shook himself. What a incredible headache he had. It felt like the top of his skull was split. Like his brain was a dried organ exposed to the light, the lifeless air. Dude was alone in his bed. Turning, he saw Ashley in the quarter light of the apartment; she was sprawled on the sofa. He lay awake for a long time.

*   *   *

Ashley recounted again the dream she had had aboard the party ship.

Dude listened, nodded, asked, "And your friend Irma died covered in shit in the sewer."

"Yes."

"And so her dream became your dream."

"Part of my dreamscape, yes," Ashley said. "Don't you see, it happens. Irma had Alvin's dream after he died. It's fucked."

"But the shit gremlins? They were a new addition? Irma did not dream about shit gremlins?"

"Not shit gremlins. I don't think so. I think that's an addition."

Dude asked, "And then you got this box of chocolates and each was shaped like a tiny stool?"

"Yeah. Dude, what are you driving at?"

"I don't know," Dude said. "It just seems like the fecal imagery is a bit overdone."

"Well, Dude, how do you think I feel? What do you want me to do about it? If I could stop it, believe me I would."

Dude looked away.

Ashley looked at him.

"You're an asshole," she said.

"Here we are again with the shit imagery," Dude said. His own voice sounded mean to him. "Maybe your imagination is taking a shit? Maybe nightmares are the mind's waste product, huh?"

Ashley started to cry. She waved him away when he tried to console her. He felt guilty. She called him a 'shithead.' He let it go.

*　　*　　*

Another day might have passed. Or two. Or none. Ashley leaned over the table. Her vision was blurred. Her speech was blurred. She was very drunk now. She remembered something about a dream, a nightmare that had jolted her from sleep that morning. Ashley remembered that she had heard the voice very plainly in her head, the woman's voice—not her own—saying that she was going to die and die very soon, die like Bruno had died. Over the past hours—how many?—she had drunk the voice away. Now her mind was slow-moving and the thoughts within it, which moved like jellyfishes through a thicker-than-seawater sea, appeared at least to be her own.

*　　*　　*

Dude was drunk too, though less so than Ashley. For example, he noticed that Ashley for the past twenty minutes or so had been calling him 'Karla.'

Ashley said, "Do you think Bruno would have become a hit, Karla? I think he would. Yes, definitely he would have become the whole hefty-hefty. But, you know what I think? I think success wouldn't have been good for him. Success! Fuck no! Success would have killed him. Success is a virus."

Dude got up and walked away. He walked into the bathroom, sat on the toilet, fell asleep. Ashley did not see anyone walk away. She saw the image of her best friend seated with her. Her horns were coming along nicely. She continued, "Of course, success didn't kill him as we both know. It didn't sweating have a chance to! But he died just the same. Who killed him? Did he kill himself? Did I kill him? Did the voices in my head kill him? Oh, that's what I don't know, Karla. What have I become? Am I making these bad things happen or what?"

Ashley looked at her friend. Her friend said nothing. She

continued, "Did you kill him, Karla? Was it you that killed Bruno?"

"Ashley! Jesus, you look terrible," Karla responded.

Something about the voice struck Ashley. She looked again at the person she was speaking too. The image of Karla grew more solid. Ashley reached out her hand. She stroked the face, the head of the person sitting with her at the table. She felt the horns.

"What's your mindset, ugly?" Ashley said.

"User friendly," Karla said.

Ashley began to cry.

"Karla! It really is you."

"Yes, Ashley, I've been so worried about you. I've looked everywhere for you," Karla said. It was Karla. She had finally found her friend. "God! Is this where you've been these past eight days? What is the name of this place."

Ashley looked at her.

"I haven't got any idea. What day is it, anyway?"

"It's Wednesday," Karla said. "November 12th."

Then Ashley began to laugh. Her laughter was bitter and hysterical.

"Come on, Ashley, we've got to go." Karla rose and picked her friend up by the armpits. She was still wearing the black dress she had worn to the funeral home. It was filthy. Ashley slumped against her, a person of rubber. Throwing one of Ashley's arms around her shoulder, Karla began to move Ashley towards the door of the bar. Ashley balked midway.

"Where are you taking me, Karla?"

"We've got to go. Come on."

"But I don't want to go. I want to stay here," Ashley whined. She looked at the bartender. He watched the two from behind the bar. He was wearing his plastic see-through dress. "Hey, you've got to help me. She's trying to take me and I don't want to go."

The bartender turned away, began to dry some glasses. Non-involvement in others' issues was his credo.

Karla put her arms around Ashley's chest and began to drag her towards the door. Ashley's feet dragged on the floor.

"Dude!" Ashley yelled. "Dude!"

"Dude's outside, Ashley. Didn't I tell you?" Karla said.

"He is?" Ashley said. "Napping. That changes everything."

She let herself be walked. They left the bar and descended the half-lit stairs, walked into the soiled brightness of the alley. It was cold. It was two hours past noon and the sun shone down through the rooftops of the buildings. There was a car parked there; its motor was running.

"Dude's in the car," Karla said.

"He is?" Ashley exclaimed. "Well, I'll be fucked if I sit in a car. I never never drive. Against my religion." She peered into the rear window, yelled, "Dude, get out of the fucking car. Let's have a drink with my ugly friend, Karla. Hefty-hefty!"

The door of the car opened. Ashley felt herself being pushed in. Half-turning, she saw Sebastian's face. He was pushing her into the car. Her puzzlement lasted only an instant before it gave way to fear, anger. "No! No! You one-eyed asshole!"

Karla slid in beside her. The door closed. Ashley struggled. Karla labored to contain her twisting body and flailing arms. Sebastian got in the driver's seat. The car lurched forward, turned onto a main street. Ashley heard the voice in her head. It said, "There's nothing you can do." Ashley felt her will to struggle dissipate. She put her face in her hands, sobbed.

"Oh, Ashley," Karla said, "don't worry. Everything is going to be all right."

"No, it won't. No, it won't," Ashley repeated over and over again like a child. They drove off through the city. Soon they were traveling along Bacon Street, a major thoroughfare east of the Arboretum. They passed an animal shelter where a mayoral announcement was going on. None of them noticed.

*   *   *

A series of ridges marked by puddingstone cliffs and outcroppings cut across the neighborhood where the animal shelter was. None of these cliffs was very high—ten or fifteen feet at most. One of these ridges, gently sloping on the far side and marked by a steep, but not very high, vertical face of puddingstone on the near, looked down onto the front of the City Animal Shelter, which was set, a square one story expanse of concrete, slightly caddy-corner to Bacon Street.

Mayor Edgar Paninni stood at a podium on a raised platform in front of the shelter. Behind him, on folding chairs, sat the director of the facility and others who had committed themselves to bettering the lot of animals, especially stray and unwanted animals, in the city. Among them was Cassie Quick. She looked self-satisfied. Standing before the stage this chilly, bright November afternoon were the Animal Shelter's employees, wearing the white or green lab coats they wore in their work, residents of the surrounding neighborhood, an ample contingent of the mayor's staff, and members of the media. Detective Thomas Costello was there. He stood at the back of the crowd, listening. If an event had to do with pets in the city, Costello made it a point to show up. Paninni was in mid-speech. He spoke with genuine emotion. Though he was reading from a prepared text, it was difficult at times to understand what the mayor said. He did not read smoothly. He mumbled. He missed words or the sense of sentences and then, realizing a mistake, he would pause, not to repeat what he had read, not to retrace more skillfully the same terrain, but seemingly to wonder at his error for an awkward moment before going on. If this was disconcerting to his listeners, Mayor Paninni did not appear to notice. He threw his head back jauntily from time to time only to forget his place in the text. He moved his arms stiffly, emphasizing his points.

He was saying, "As the people of this city are aware, my wife Sophie and I know the terrible feeling that comes from losing a beloved pet. It was only six days ago that her little dog, our Dachshund Tater, was taken from us. Whether he wandered off and is now a stray, alone and afraid in these city streets, or whether he met a worse fate at the hands of some deviant, at the hands of this vile so called "Pet Hunter" who has terrorized animals and their masters throughout our city, Sophie and I do not know. And, in a sense, as those who have lost pets also know, it is the not knowing that is the worst part of our ordeal. I have committed the city and its Police Department to restoring our streets, our neighborhoods, and our parks to safety for our four-footed friends."

The crowd broke into polite applause. Paninni nodded, shaped his lips into his odd smile.

He continued, "I have also committed the city's resources to improving the lives of those animals who unfortunately do not have a place to call home, do not have a woman or man, a girl or boy, to call 'friend,' who do not have a person, a master, who is committed to giving them the opportunities to live fulfilling and hopeful lives."

Here again, applause. Paninni began to grin, then remembered the serious nature of his remarks. At last, he was beginning to hit his stride.

"And as a mayor who wants to put the city's resources where they will most benefit the entire city, the whole city, I have committed two million dollars from my discretionary funds to the renovation of this animal shelter. I am told that the board of directors of the City Animal Shelter, in recognition of this contribution, this investment, have voted to rename the shelter in honor of Sophie's unfortunate Dachshund, Potato. And so I not only announce the commitment of these funds, but I acknowledge from the very bottom of my heart this most gracious gesture by the director and board of this important facility which will from now on be called the Potato Animal Shelter."

At these words, Sophie Paninni, seated behind the mayor, began to sob. At the same time, the face of Dr Homer Strickland, the director of the animal shelter, took on first a horrified, then an angry, look. The blood drained from his face and his eyes widened, brightened. He sat up in his seat, glared at the mayor's round-shouldered back. This was the first he—or anyone else connected with the shelter—had heard of renaming the facility after the mayor's wife's Dachshund. But what could he do? He needed the two million. Avoiding the director's eyes, the mayor looked back at his wife, met her eyes, held them. They exchanged a special look. She put her hands over her heart. Then he turned back, took a deep breath, began the summation of his remarks.

"My only hope is that our Dachshund, our Potato, is somewhere where he can know, where he can appreciate—however dogs know or appreciate—what his city is doing on behalf of animals today. Maybe it's too late for Tater—I hope not!—but wherever he is, I know that he will think, in whichever way dogs think, that this is a proud day for our city. A proud day for pets."

The mayor nodded again as the crowd applauded. He decided to add a few more thoughts to capitalize on the goodwill he was generating. But, a few words into his spontaneous summation, Paninni paused in mid-sentence. He saw something in the air. Was it a bird? No, it lacked wings. Some sort of missile? No, it was not aerodynamic. It looked like something rubberesque arcing slowly above the crowd to begin its descent directly towards the podium and the mayor's upturned face. Costello saw it too. From his perspective, it looked like a flying squirrel, leaping, spread out, although, in this case, its leap was marked by slow somersaults in mid-air.

But Costello knew this was not a jungle where a leaping flying squirrel might be a part of any skyward view, but an asphalt parking lot. Further, it could not be a flying squirrel because it barked. Just before the flying body struck its target, a feeling of grave unease flooded Costello's bowels. Nose-first, the body speared the top of the podium. The sound this made was a sickening "thwaap." It was a Dachshund. The Dachshund's body, which had been stretched to full extension, contracted much as a cylinder of clay would have if, tube-shaped, it had been dropped tip first from a great height. It flattened. Disbelief transfixed the mayor and everyone else at the event. For a brief moment the crowd was a crowd of statues and even the body of the dog was, for this one moment, almost perfectly statuesque. The dog's body remained on the top of the podium, remarkably balanced on its crushed head. Its hind legs slanted upwards from its contracted torso. They quivered. The mayor's face and his glasses were spattered with blood; hot dog's blood spattered his upper body too, his white shirt, his bright tie. Then the dog toppled oh so slowly off the front of the podium to land, twisted and lifeless, half on and half off the edge of the temporary plywood stage. It hung head side down, its tiny tongue dangling from its bloody maw. Its eyes were open, though they looked at nothing.

It was then that Costello uttered an unfortunate assessment of the situation. He said it under his breath; he said it to himself. Unfortunately, he said it within earshot of a reporter from *The Traveler* who was there covering the event.

The words he said were, "Lap dog's last lap."

These words, bad words, ill-considered words, would haunt him, but he did not know it yet.

He rushed towards the puddingstone cliff from which the once living projectile had been launched and clambered up the rough stone face. He found a wooden catapult there, but no sign of the person who had returned—via airmail—Potato to Mayor Paninni and his wife.

Chapter 21

Bad Patrolman

The shades of the guest room were open and moon-light, pale moonlight, shone on Jessica's pale, fleshy face, neck, and arms. Her eyes were closed; she was sleeping, snoring. Next to her, on a bedroll on the floor in a shadow cast by Jessica's bed and by Jessica, Jane shifted uneasily in her sleeping bag. No moonlight illuminated her light brown flesh. She was asleep too. She slept lightly, anxiously. Her breathing was shallow, silent. Her chest rose, fell rapidly like a bird's chest. Jessica stopped snoring and the room became deadly still. Her eyelids fluttered but her eyes did not open. She gasped. Her dreamscape had changed; she knew even in her sleep that she was entering the beginnings of her nightmare.

*   *   *

Something wakes her.

What?

She lies alone in the big, soft bed. Her face and arms are bathed in moonlight.

What woke her? Was she . . . yes, she was awake. She must be.

Throwing aside her bedclothes, she rises. She walks around

the bed to check on Jane who sleeps on the floor. Plain Jane. Ha! Plane Jane—so flat, so thin! A flat worm. Ick. Now Jessica listens. There is no sound. Out of the corner of her eye she sees the window shade move. She whirls. Is there someone at the window—a figure formed of moonlight and shadow? No. Heat from the radiator causes the shade to ripple.

Jessica's nostrils flutter. A scent of roses is in the air. She leaves the room, walking blindly down the very dark hallway. Her arms stretch in front of her. She is feeling her way through almost liquid darkness until her eyes adjust. She comes to the central stairway that ties together the three main stories of Dr Bentley's mansion. Standing on the landing, she looks down the stairs. They descend to the first floor of the house, to a large foyer drenched in moonlight.

She does not want to go down there but she knows she must. She begins to suspect that she must be dreaming. This is her nightmare. But, whether she is awake or asleep, it will not end until it is done. It is her fate.

Her will is nothing.

The smell of roses wafts up from the first floor of the house. She descends, bare feet on the wooden stairs. Reaching the foyer, she turns left into the large living room; Dominic and Jerry are asleep on two couches there. Moonlight washes this room also, enters through bay windows at the front of the house. The others, she knows, are sleeping elsewhere in the mansion: Bentley in her bedroom, Karla and Brandon in guest rooms on the third floor, Ashley in one of the cramped, slant-ceilinged rooms in the attic, and Eric . . . she is not so sure where Eric sleeps.

She has moved.

Now she stands in the glassed-in porch, a sort of half greenhouse set against the rear of the house. She looks into the back yard. The yard shines with frost which, glistening, mirrors the twinklings of many stars in the deep blackness of the November night. In the yard there are statues. Slightly larger-than-life, they are carved from white stone. The statues cast shadows, moonshadows, behind them. Further on is the high brick wall of the Arboretum. She is amazed that she can think so clearly; her thoughts are as crisp and clear as this night is. An angel appears. It appears as if out of nowhere in the center of the lawn. An aura of pale light, brighter than moonlight but of the same wan quality, surrounds the angel's body, its unspread wings. Jessica opens the glass door. She steps out into the cold, putting the soles of her feet onto the frost-covered grass. It is almost like stepping onto cold, thin shards of glass. The grass crackles under her feet. It is an uncomfortable though amazing feeling. The smell of roses fills the air. Refrigerated roses. Angels smell this way. She knows about angels; they frequent her dreams. The angel turns and looks at her—his beautiful face and hair and body fill her with wonder and awe and apprehension for Jessica knows even as she walks towards him that the angel will . . . no . . . is changing. His mouth opens and out darts a tongue, a snake's forked tongue thick and long as a woman's forearm. It is moistly, greasily bright in the cold, pale moonlight. The figure steps towards her. She gasps, braces herself for what she knows the dream holds next, for what she knows must come. But it does not come. The angel vanishes in a puff of smoke. Theatrical. And acrid. Where the angel stood there is only a rose bush, gnarled and twisted, bloomless but for one rose which, in the moonlight, looks red, soft, and alive.

*   *   *

She woke.

Her heart was throbbing in her chest. She could hear it. There was no other sound but Jane's quick breathing. Moonlight filled the room, its light almost greenish. It made sense to her. The moon is made of green cheese, she thought to herself, then turning her back to the window and the moonlight, she felt a cool, unslept-on part of the pillow against the side of her face. She descended again into sleep.

*   *   *

When she came into the kitchen at about 8:30 the next morning, Dominic and Jerry were already there. She had seen the empty couches, the crushed pillows, the blankets tossed aside. Jerry, thin, perpetually nervous, had thrown on a pair of jeans and a T-shirt. Maybe he had slept in them. It looked like it. Dominic, however, looked like he was ready for a day at the advertising firm at which he worked, though he, like the others at Dr Bentley's, was not working these days. He had nearly used up all his vacation time. He wore a pair of corduroys, a pressed dress shirt, and recently shined loafers. His hair, unlike his friend Jerry's which still stood on end, unkempt, was brushed back smartly and gleamed with gel. There were cups of coffee and bowls of cereal before both of them at the kitchen table.

"Morning," Jessica yawned. She wore a loose pair of sweat pants and an athletic jersey. She moved immediately toward the coffee maker.

"Good morning," Dominic replied, his voice low and smooth. Jerry just nodded.

Jessica looked at the small chalkboard that was attached to the side of the refrigerator. She saw that Jerry had already chalked the weekday and the number of days, counting this new day, that the group had been at Dr Bentley's home.

Monday. Day 10.

Jessica looked out a window into the backyard where the grass was slick with melting frost. Though statues stood there in the bright morning sun just as she had dreamed them, there was no rose bush in the center of the yard. She sat down at the table.

"Ten days," she sighed, pouring cream into her coffee. The black liquid grew brown, cloudy. She spooned in sugar and stirred it tan, sweet.

"Yes, another day at Casa Bentley!" Jerry mumbled. "Personally I can't wait. Let's see what's on my list for today: eat, watch television, nap, read magazines . . . oh, I forgot, I've already read every sweaty magazine in the fucking house."

Jessica looked at him with something like contempt. At least, she thought to herself, his acne was under control for the moment. His face was blotched, but the sores were smooth, small, without pus. Furtively nervous, his eyes met hers, shifted away, shifted back.

Dominic asked, "Well, Jerry, would you rather be scared to death or bored?"

"How about bored to death?" Jerry snapped, his voice a whine.

"You're the first two up?" Jessica asked, rolling her eyes, changing the subject.

"Yes," said Dominic. "How about Jane?"

"She'll be down soon, I'm sure," replied Jessica.

"That leaves Eric, Karla, Brandon and . . . Ashley," Jerry observed, lowering his voice when he said Ashley's name for mock dramatic effect.

"Where does Eric sleep anyway?" Jessica asked. "I've never actually heard him mention sleeping."

"Who cares about Eric?" Jerry said knowingly. "It's where Brandon sleeps that I wonder about."

"Wonder or worry?" Dominic asked.

"Wonder."

Karla came into the kitchen smiling. She was wearing pink pajamas printed with a repetitive pattern of images of Colonel George Armstrong Custer at Little Big Horn and a pair of fluffy lime green slippers. Curving above her head, her horns were four or five inches long now, pale white like skim milk.

"Wonder about what?" she chirped, pouring herself a cup of coffee. "Wonder Bread?"

Dominic started to stutter a response—Karla unnerved him—but seeing that Karla's attention had moved on, he fell silent. He also saw that her pajama top was almost entirely unbuttoned. This made him nervous too.

She joined them at the table. The table was bathed in sunlight. She stretched, yawned, smiled, said, "I had a pretty bland dream last night. Can't quite remember it, but it made me feel pretty calm, pretty hefty."

Jessica looked at her. Within the past day or two Karla had died her hair. Brown of all colors. Jessica said, "Speaking of dreams, the most amazing thing happened to me last night, dreamwise."

"What happened?" one of them asked.

"I started to have my nightmare—you know, the one I always have about angels and. . . ."

"Devils," Jerry finished her sentence in a low monotone.

Jessica glared at him but saw that she had his full attention. He had only mocked her out of habit, out of nervousness. She had the attention of all three of them, even Karla, who looked at her with her unblinking blue eyes. Any discussion of dreams in Bentley's mansion was sure to draw interest.

She continued, "The dream started the way it always does—with the smell of roses, the smell of roses leading me through a house. Last night, in my dream, it was this house. I remember I saw you two—I mean I dreamed you two—sleeping in the living room. Then I saw him standing in the backyard. I was standing in the glassed-in porch at the back of the house. It was bright. There was a lot of moonlight."

"You saw who?" asked Jerry.

"The angel," Jessica said, "my angel . . . I mean the angel I always see in my dream, my nightmare."

"I'll bet he looked . . . angelic," Karla noted enthusiastically.

Jessica looked at her, said, "Yes. He does."

"Does?" Jerry asked, still employing the false, mocking, low voice.

"Did," Jessica corrected herself, then added, "but I might as well say 'does'. I doubt last night was the last time I'll have the dream. I hope it was though."

"Do you?" Karla chided gently. "You don't seem so sure. I think you like your angel."

Jessica said, "I would like him fine if he did not keep changing into a demon . . . and that's what didn't happen last night. The angel came towards me like he always does . . . and the tongue, the serpent's tongue, came out of his mouth, but the change didn't happen. The angel just vanished. There was only a rose bush where he had been standing."

"What happened next?" Dominic asked.

"I woke up. The dream was over. I went back to sleep."

"Bland," Jerry said, now more earnestly, as if trying to make amends for his mocking.

The four became silent for a moment. Then Dominic said, "You know, it's strange . . . but the same thing happened to me. I started to have the nightmare I always have and it stopped midway through too—it stopped before the horrible part began."

"When was this?" Jessica asked

"Last night."

"You're not just bullshitting, are you?"

"No! This stuff is far too serious to joke about," Dominic said.

"You're the death camp, aren't you?" Karla asked, speaking to Dominic but focusing her gaze on something in the backyard.

"Come again?" replied Dominic, turning as he asked to look at what Karla was looking at. Jessica and Jerry looked too. They saw Brandon by the Arboretum wall. He was doing tai-chi exercises. He did them every morning.

Karla continued, "Your nightmare—it's about a concentration camp or something, isn't it?"

"Yes, it is." Dominic took on a worried expression. His dream terrified him even in the light of day. He believed it was bad luck just to discuss it. Although on the surface he appeared to be a businesslike sort, thoroughly buttoned-down and earthbound, there was a side to Dominic that was very attracted to the spiritual and the occult. Before coming to the dream therapy classes,

Dominic had explored a series of other interests: crystal healing, Tibetan Buddhism, Gurdieff, but whenever Dominic looked back to identify what had changed his life for the worse, he saw that past life regression had been the change agent, the culprit. In his work with past incarnations which he had undertaken seven or so years before, Dominic had identified a number of past lives which he believed he had led: soldier in the American Revolutionary war, Medieval baron, Roman priestess, as well as some sort of African tribesman. All of these past lives were fine with him, but Dominic had also gained the impression, the strong and unshakable certainty, that he had been a guard in a death camp. His first experience of this particularly gruesome set of memories had horrified him. He had not been able to deal in this life with what he had done, with what he had been, in a previous existence. Though he had contemplated suicide, he had fought off the impulse to take his own life. It had been at this time that the nightmare which had plagued him off and on over these past seven years had begun.

He spoke slowly, forcing each word in his Ivy League intonation. "My nightmare also began last night the way it always does," he said. "I am a guard in a concentration camp. In my dream, I usher hundreds of naked prisoners into a large shower room. I tell them they are going to get clean, refresh themselves, after their long train ride. I can see them all very clearly—an endless line—men, women, hobbling senior citizens, innocent children. All their eyes hold such a mixture of fear, innocence, and . . . awareness. After all, they've been through the dream over and over again too; quite possibly the reality as well. Finally, when they are all in the shower room—it's like a large warehouse— and they are waiting for me to . . . to turn on the water, one of them, a frail old man—it's always the same, dream-after-dream— asks me why there isn't any soap. I always give him the same answer. I say, "The soap is in the water, just like at a car wash." I know, it's a little weird to say that, but the man nods as if he wants to believe me, even though car washes were probably not even invented then, or at least they were rare. Then I step out of the room, lock the door, and I turn on the spigot in the wall. I can look back into the room through a small window. I always feel a wave of incredibly deep sadness when I turn the spigot on and I remember feeling that way again in my dream last night. But last night the poison gas did not come out of the shower heads. Water did! I wish I could describe the surprise, the elation on the faces. Water—fairly hot water too—was coming out of the shower heads. It was steaming. Everyone was washing themselves and smiling. I started to laugh in my sleep and then . . . my dream ended. I woke up. But for some reason, I did not remember what I dreamed last night until I heard you this morning, Jessica."

"Napping," Karla said.

"Napping squared," Jerry said.

Jessica reached her hand across the table and took Dominic's. She said, "Dominic, that was so beautiful."

A tear glistened in Dominic's eye.

"Maybe," he said, "the nightmares are finally ending. For all of us."

* * *

In the afternoons, the tiny room in the attic in which Ashley convalesced often received a touch of sunlight through a dormer window which was set into the starkly angled, slate roof of the mansion. The room itself was plain white with dark wood trim and the room's ceiling followed the severe pitch of the outside roof so that the wall nearest the eaves, or outer edge of the roof, was only three feet or so in height while the opposite wall, that which helped form the center hallway which ran lengthwise through the middle of the attic, was about seven feet in height. Since she had been brought to Dr Bentley's, Ashley had spent much of her time under sedation, sleeping or half-sleeping in the little room's single bed with its white cotton sheets and scratchy blue blankets and bedcover. Whenever she awoke, she ate the meals, the soups, cups of herb tea, and pieces of bread which were left for her on a bedside table. The soup was left in a thermos to keep it hot, but the tea was often cold. Sometimes she awoke to find Bentley or Karla sitting by her bed, watching over her. They talked but not too much. Ashley felt very weak, but also strangely peaceful, in the room.

Maybe it was the sedatives she was being given to make her rest which imposed this sense of peace, she thought or half-thought, though, just beyond this peacefulness she knew a constellation swirled, a galaxy of fears, doubts, and nightmares which were awaiting only the next opportunity to redisplay themselves and attack once again her increasingly fragile existence. Nevertheless, her nightmares were gone for the moment and so too were the awful, half-familiar voice she heard in her head and the hallucinations which had plagued her. Instead, she concentrated her sleepy mind on Bruno. She imagined that her thoughts left her body and sought him out wherever he was and the wonder of it, the sweet wonder, was that she thought she had found him, her dead love. In these transfixed reveries she floated in a sort of half-sleep in which she thought herself hovering or lying in an endless environment of white which was no doubt an extension of the white walls and white sunlight of the room but for the fact that it seemed cold, refreshingly cold, and she knew that she was on a snowfield, a tundra, in the midst of a snowstorm. It was the Canada that Bruno and she had laughed about, had fantasized about from time to time when they had been stoned: a secret place, a vast snowfield where nothing happens—and during these periods of sedated thought she knew that Bruno was somewhere near her, trudging through the snow in his absurd fur clothes, but she would not call out to him. She did not want to break, to shatter the all-spanning quiet of her mental state and she feared what it must do to her hopes should Bruno not answer her call.

Now her thoughts moved her to a memory of the actuality which formed the nexus of her current fantasies. One afternoon

Bruno and she had sat under a tree in the Arboretum. The ground had been covered in deep, fresh snow. The sky had been crystal blue. The air had been very cold but in the dark shelter of a snow-covered pine in the whorl of shallower snow under the thick, snow-encrusted branches, they were warmer. They snorted cocaine from a small bottle and smoked a joint and smoked cigarettes and laughed at the beauty of being nowhere and purposeless in the expansive loneliness. "This can't last, this Canada," Bruno said, then laughed, cracked up. He laughed so hard that snot jettisoned from his nose onto the snow where she looked at it and laughed and now, abruptly, she wondered whether this had really happened or whether it was only a memory her imagination was concocting to help her deal with her loss. It seemed so real.

The memory seemed so now, so present, until she opened her eyes.

The snowscape in her mind fell away, melted, leaving only typical November afternoon sunlight and the face of her friend, Karla. Karla was looking at her somberly, worriedly.

"Why the pensive look?" Ashley asked, her voice weak, soft, but not quavering.

"I'm worried about you, ugly," Karla replied. She had Ashley's hand in hers.

"I'm worried about me too."

Ashley sat up in bed, adjusting a pillow so that she could lean against the headboard.

She said, "Your horns are really growing. Are they getting too heavy? Here let me touch." Karla obligingly inclined her horned head. "But there's something different . . . the hair. You've dyed your hair."

"Do you like it?"

"Same color as mine, why wouldn't I? But it looks better on me. I'm more the brunette type."

"Well," Karla smiled, "I was only trying to emulate you, to show my . . . uh . . . solidarity with you in this troubling time."

"That's why you dyed your hair brown?"

Karla replied, "Yes."

"That's stupid," Ashley said.

"I like to do stupid things," Karla said.

"You sound like me now."

"I like to sound like you," Karla said, mimicking. They both chuckled. Then Ashley sighed, looked away from her friend and up at the ceiling, at wan patterns of sunlight on the ceiling and far wall of her room.

"Karla, I have a bone to pick with you," Ashley finally said.

"Hmmm?"

"You kidnapped me."

"Ashley, I'm so sorry but I felt that I had to. When I found you, you were completely gone."

"Oh, I don't mind that so much," Ashley said, still looking at the ceiling, its whiteness. "I agree I probably needed a change of scene. But what were you doing with that virus Sebastian?"

"Sebastian? I thought he was your friend."

"Some hefty fucking friend, Karla. I saw him . . . I saw him doing something . . ."

"What?" Karla prompted.

"Oh, you'd never believe it."

"I wouldn't? I'm here in some weird doc's house hiding out from the Nightmare Realm or something. I'd believe just about anything."

"Would you believe one of your horns is falling off?"

Karla felt the top of her head.

She said, "Ashley, stop trying to avoid a difficult subject. We're all in this together."

Turning, looking at Karla, Ashley said, "That's such a noble sentiment! All right: I saw Sebastian talking to Bruno—Bruno's corpse—at the wake. Just before you walked in."

"What?"

"Not only did I see him bent over the coffin talking to Bruno's corpse, I heard Bruno's voice talking back to him, answering him," Ashley confided. Her voice was regaining strength.

"What? No!" Karla exclaimed. "Oh, Ashley. That can't be. That's fucked up. That must have been so horrible, even to think that. How did you ever survive thinking that?"

"I think it's because of the strength these Nightmare Therapy sessions have given me, actually," Ashley replied. Her face was for a moment serious, then it cracked into an impish grin.

"Yeah, they've helped me immensely too," Karla smiled, grasping Ashley's hand more tightly in hers. Ashley's hand felt cool, damp. "We've got so much catching up to do. I want to hear everything. Every horribly unbland detail."

Ashley sighed, "Fine. But first tell me what's going on here."

"Here at the mansion, at Casa Bentley? Nothing! We just sit around all day until we have our nightly ritualistic get-together where, you know, we chant and pray to keep those evil forces at bay."

Ashley asked, "Is it working?"

"What?"

"The dreams, ugly? How are the dreams?"

"Hmmm. Since we've been here there's been no problem. I think Bentley has been staying up nights holding evil back—she looks awful. Anyway, the only slightly interesting thing happening dreamwise happened last night."

"What was that?"

"You remember Jessica and Dominic?" Karla asked, rolling her eyes slightingly, dismissively. Ashley nodded. "Well, they both told me this morning that they started having their nightmares last night only to have them stop midway, before the sweaty, icky parts began. In fact, while Jessica's dream just stopped midway, Dominic's dream—the one in which he gases all those death camp inmates in the shower—actually had a happy ending. When he turned the spigot on, water actually came out instead of nerve gas. He was ecstatic . . . well, maybe not ecstatic. He seemed relieved."

"Napping," Ashley exclaimed. "That is great news. Maybe all of this is ending."

"We'll see. But, Ashley, let's talk about you. What has been going on?"

"I've been . . . I've been . . . Karla, I've been through hell." She almost started to cry, but she held back. Instead, she recounted the story of her time with Dude: her fears, her delusions, her hallucinations, the voice she heard, and her efforts to stop the terrors in her mind by drinking as much as she could hold down and more.

When Ashley finished, Karla appeared shocked. It took her a moment to speak. She said, "How the fuck did you live through that? My god, that's the most horrible thing I've heard. Why didn't you just call me?"

Ashley looked at her, replied, "I don't know. Maybe I should have."

Karla was quiet for a moment. She was thinking. Then she smiled, "Yes, you should have, but you're here now and that's all that matters. And now the important thing is for you to get some rest. So, close your eyes and go back to your bland tundra and . . . chill out." Karla rose, kissed Ashley lightly on the cheek, then turned to leave the small room.

"Karla," Ashley said.

"Yes?" Karla replied, stopping, looking back.

"How did you know about the tundra?"

"Tundra?"

"The . . . uh . . . tundra in my mind," Ashley said, pointing to her head. "Where I go in my imagination."

"Oh, that!" Karla chirped. "I'm just psychic, I guess."

Then she left the room, closing the door softly behind her.

"I don't want you to know about it," Ashley said to herself. "I want it all to myself."

*　　*　　*

Karla walked to the end of the attic hallway, then descended a spiral stairway that took her to the third floor. Running along the side of the house, the stairway between the attic and the third floor was not part of the mansion's central stairway which connected the first, second, and third floors of the home. Instead, Karla came out at the end of a long hallway at the opposite end of which was Dr Bentley's large study. The door of the study, as it often was, was half open. Karla walked to Bentley's study, then hesitated just outside the door. She did not know if Bentley was inside the room; maybe she did not want to know. She turned to go. Perhaps there is a better time, Karla thought.

"Is someone out there?"

The voice was strange. Was it Bentley's? It sounded different. Karla turned back, looked into the room.

"Hello, Karla," the voice said.

At first, Karla saw nothing but darkness. Heavy shades were drawn across the room's windows; the candles that often burned were without flame.

"Come in, Karla. You look worried."

Karla entered the room. Her steps were tentative. Her eyes could not adjust to the lack of light. She saw a figure sitting in the center of the sizable chamber, sitting where Bentley usually sat when she meditated.

"Dr Bentley, is that you?" Karla asked. Her voice was tense.

She heard a sighing.

"Yes, it's me. Who else would it be? Why don't you sit down . . . here, on the floor, in front of me?"

She felt her way forward, probing with her foot, holding her arms before her. A few feet in front of where she saw the rough outline of Bentley's seated shape, Karla felt a mediation pillow on the floor. She sat down on it. By this time, Karla's eyes were becoming more accustomed to the lack of light and she could see how spent the dream psychologist looked. Her eyes looked out from slightly cadaverous sockets, her hair hung limply, there were deep lines across her forehead, and the crows feet emanating from her eyes were far more pronounced than usual. She looked like she had aged a decade in a few days. A lack of make-up alone could not explain it.

"Are you all right, Dr Bentley?" Karla asked.

"Yes, I'm fine," she replied. But she did not sound fine. She sounded profoundly tired, so Karla pressed the point.

"But you seem . . . different. You seem tired."

"Yes, that's true. I am tired. I haven't been getting much rest."

"Why is that, Dr Bentley?"

"Because I'm worried, god damn it," Bentley snapped, but then she recovered some of her usual composure and though she did not speak in her customary tone of placid omniscience, neither did she sound like she was in despair as she said, "But, there is no need for you to become alarmed. I'm confident everything will turn out for the best. All's well that ends well, isn't that the way to look at things like this?"

Intently scrutinizing the older woman, Karla leaned forward, asked, "Is that true, Doctor? Are we going to be all right?"

Bentley took a long time before she answered. Karla could almost feel the interplay of conflicting thoughts within the psychologist's mind.

"The truth is . . . I don't know," Bentley answered.

"What do you mean you don't know?"

"I mean—I don't know."

"Well . . . how can you not know?"

Dr Bentley replied, "There are many more ways of not knowing than there are of knowing."

"But I thought you had the inside track on this Nightmare Realm?"

"Oh, Karla, I wish I did. I don't think anyone does. I've explained this to you before, but let me try to explain it again.

"The Nightmare Realm exists. We experience it in nightmares and in other ways. In some sense, it is the cause of evil in the world, or, at least, part of the cause. Now, I'm convinced it's using someone in our group as a sort of transponder . . ."

"A what?"

"Karla, I think that someone in our group has become a kind of relay station that receives a signal, then amplifies it and sends it on. That's what I think is happening here: someone, probably unwittingly, is channeling the energies of the Nightmare Realm directly into the group . . . with dire effects. The focused energy of the Nightmare Realm has made great progress in magnifying the nightmares of the group, in bringing the nightmares of the group to life, as you've already seen, Karla. If it succeeds in making a full breakthrough here, if it succeeds in gaining a real presence in our reality, the Nightmare Realm will attain incredible power, so much power that it may be able to transform all the nightmares dreamed on earth into reality."

"So the world would become even worse than it is now?"

"Incalculably so."

"Oh. So what are you doing about it, Dr Bentley?"

"I'm doing the only thing I can do in these circumstances, Karla. I'm using my mental energy to try to interrupt, to hold back, any sort of communication, any sort of transmissions— although these terms are so inadequate, they're the best . . . metaphors I can think of—any sort of transmissions that might come from the Nightmare Realm."

"Can't you just find out who here is acting as this relay station, this transwhatever, and flick the 'off switch'? I mean, can't you just turn the whole thing off?"

"I wish it were that simple, but I can't. Something is keeping me from making a determination of who it is. It's almost like there is some kind of static, some sort of aura of energy surrounding the people in this group so that I can't really figure out what's going on in people's psychic lives."

"Unbland."

"Come again?"

"Oh, it's just an expression. So how do you interrupt the beams or . . . emanations from getting from the Realm to us."

"I project my spirit as a sort of psychic shield and I put it between the Nightmare Realm and the people here in my house. That's what I am doing when I go into my deep meditations."

Karla was silent for a moment, then she asked, "Can I get you anything, Dr Bentley? Would you like some coffee or something?"

Bentley smiled, said, "No, I'm fine. What have you been up to?"

"Oh, I was just up talking to Ashley."

"Ahh, Ashley. How is she coming along?"

"She seems to be doing better. I spoke to her for a while."

"What did she have to say?"

"Well . . . you know that she's been going through a very tough time since her boyfriend—since Bruno—died. She's been hearing voices—or at least a voice—and having strange dreams, delusions. I think we're very lucky we found her."

"I think so, too," Bentley replied. "Does she seem to be at all like she used to be before any of this happened?"

Karla considered for a moment before she answered. "No. I can't put my finger on it but I think there is something different about her. She just does not seem like her old self . . . in fact . . . I think I have to tell you something."

"Oh," asked Bentley, "what's that?"

"I don't know if I should," Karla hesitated, her voice modulating between whisper and whine. "Ashley's my best friend ever."

"Karla, anything you say will not be used to hurt your friend, only to help her, if I can."

"I think Ashley might be the one," Karla said.

"What makes you think that?"

"It's just a feeling I have . . . in my spirit."

"Well," Bentley said, "she's been through a lot. I'll talk to her later this afternoon. But, for now, let me rest. I am feeling tired."

Karla looked at the table, the Japanese table, made of light, blonde wood, beside Bentley's sitting form and saw a syringe and a vial. Both were empty.

*　　*　　*

He knew that in some cultures complete and public humiliation was considered a way to spiritual enlightenment. The path of self-abasement.

But that knowledge did not help him.

So, from time to time he would make all the traffic stop.

Like he was doing now.

Standing on an upraised, circular, orange platform at the center of the intersection of two heavily-trafficked streets, Commerce Street and Dion Fortune Avenue, he held up his hands and compelled a complete stop in the traffic coming from all four directions. Then he waited. He saw frustration, anger, bewilderment transform the faces of the drivers at the front of the halted lines and he felt tension become palpable, emanating from the vehicles he held back in this completely arbitrary show of his one, his only, power. It was perverse how he enjoyed seeing how long it took before someone started honking. When the noise began, he checked his watch. Then, when the cacophony of angry shouts from rolled-down windows and the blarings of horns reached what he, petty blue-clad potentate, deemed a suitable level, he checked his watch again and waved the traffic through.

The drivers glared at him, swore at him as they crawled past.

Only seven minutes, Costello smiled. Not even a record.

The longest he had ever held the cars back was nine minutes and fifteen seconds.

Needless to say, he was not winning any commendations for his traffic duty. In fact, the head of the traffic control division had already reprimanded him for his behavior, but Costello had responded, "Paninni wants me to direct traffic. That's what I'm doing." Short and sweet. That about summed it up. There was not much more anyone could do to him now. He was as low as one could go in the Department—a traffic cop. Only once had he felt greater humiliation than he felt now, this late afternoon, atop his embarrassing platform. That had been the first day after Mayor

Paninni had demoted him and he had been assigned to traffic duty outside St. Mary's Church where Mayor Paninni and hundreds of dignitaries, civic leaders, citizens, animal advocates, and police officers had held a service, a memorial service, for the mayor's wife's dog.

What had been the cause of this descent to such lowliness, he ruminated to himself for nearly the millionth time, as cars continued to crawl by him. His life had been miserable ever since the morning when the front page of *The Traveler* had displayed a full page picture of Tater's nosedive and a banner headline crafted from his own wry observation. **LAP DOG'S LAST LAP**. The tabloid had pegged him not only as the officer leading the so obviously less-than-successful battle against pet slayings, but also as the source of the witticism. That had been most unfortunate. He had canceled his subscription to the paper that very day. Now some of his more humorous colleagues were calling him "Deputy Dog" or "Officer Hound."

Naturally, he had a coping mechanism. He was drinking even more heavily these days. His days of leading investigations were over, he observed to himself as he waved his arms yet again at another line of cars. Futile gestures. And awkward. It was tiring and uncomfortable to make the repetitive hand and arm gestures required in directing traffic. That his old uniforms from his patrolman days did not quite fit made the situation worse. His jackets pulled under his arms and at his midsection. His pants, shiny with wear, pulled at his crotch and thighs.

He looked at his watch again. Five o'clock at last. He was supposed to be relieved now by another officer who had not as yet arrived. Where was the bugger? Costello decided to depart anyway, leaving another fast developing traffic jam behind him. He walked to his own car, which was parked nearby. As he shut himself within his automobile, the sounds of car horns, of escalating impatience and anger, faded. The inside of his car was cold and half-dark. He turned the car on and drove, avoiding the traffic snarl his absence was causing, to Police Headquarters where he signed off his shift.

* * *

Five hours later, Patrolman Costello was hidden among bushes, drinking from a flask of vodka, observing Bentley's mansion. He wore black clothing, black gloves, a black, wool cap. He had done this every night for almost two weeks—hiding himself in the greenery of her spacious yard to watch the house nearly until dawn. Every night, Kitten was with him. Usually the dog lay quietly by his master's side, though sometimes Kitten stole away to explore the neighborhood and the reaches of the Arboretum. At least, that was what Costello assumed the dog was doing. In the time he had staked out the house, he had not seen or heard anything unusual at the mansion. Occasionally lights went on and off in various rooms or someone would step out into the yard for a minute to smoke or take in the night air. One room on the third floor was always full of an eerie half-light which looked to him like it came from a fireplace. The house itself was large and white, almost box-like in shape with few decorative features and a steep, slate roof interrupted by dormer windows. A long porch ran along the front of the house. A glass house or green house was built onto the back of the mansion, and a semi-cylindrical outcropping which no doubt encased a spiral staircase was attached to the south side of the house, running from the third floor to the attic. The simplicity of the house verged on austerity; this near austerity conveyed a sense of quiet wealth and power. Surrounding the house were various bushes, fruit trees, and flower beds, as well as occasional benches, brick walkways, and marble statues—all contributing to the powerful presence of the mansion.

Costello was cold. As the evening progressed he hugged himself as he shivered. He drank his vodka and smoked as secretively as possible, cupping the lit end of the cigarette in his hand. In the middle of the night, Kitten wondered off. Nothing strange in that, but as dawn neared the dog still had not returned. Strange. Costello stole away, climbed over the wall into the Arboretum, and looked for his dog. Even as dawn neared he walked and called for the dog until it was time for him to rush home and prepare himself for another day as a human stop light. He reclimbed the wall, dropping down into a wooded lot which adjoined Bentley's land. He walked to his car weighed down by a feeling of dread. He half hoped that Kitten would be sitting in the car as he had been on one of the nights Costello had staked out the Arboretum looking for the escaped Human Pet. When had that night been? Weeks ago? Months? Years? Back when he had been a homicide detective. Jesus, he had grown close to the dog.

The dog was not in the car.

He drove past Bentley's house, giving it one last look in the increasing light of the approaching dawn. Everything appeared quiet. He finished the vodka in his thermos.

Chapter 22

Unanswered Prayers

"Protect this house and all within it from evil thoughts, from the machinations of the Darkness," she said.

The others repeated what she had said, their voices—perhaps unwittingly—mimicking the breathy, entranced singsong of her intonation.

"Oh god, or gods and goddesses, or spirits of goodwill anywhere who hear my prayer, interpose yourselves, your divine wills, between this house and the Nightmare Realm," she said.

Again the group repeated her words. Again she spoke. Again her words were repeated. As the prayer—an impromptu invocation which had taken slightly different forms every evening—continued, Brandon opened his eyes and looked around the dining room table at the other members of the group. Because the room was illuminated only by a few candles and because thick drapes shut the moonlight out, the faces of his companions were like ghost heads floating in darkness. Everyone else had their eyes closed. That was what participants were supposed to do in the opening moments of these nightly sessions—sit with eyes closed, minds blank, hands joining hands around the table, to repeat Dr Bentley's words. Diagonally across the large oval table from him sat Jane. Her eyes, her mouth were tightly shut as if she was trying to will away all sense of where she was. To Jane's right were Dominic and Jessica. Both looked very serious. Brandon wondered if they were secretly romantically involved. Between Jessica and himself were four empty chairs, representing the three in the group who had died and Ashley, who did not join them. To Jane's left, moving clockwise around the table, sat Jerry, Eric, Karla, and finally, between Karla and him, at the head of the table, sat Bentley in the midst of devising her nightly prayer for protection. So far it had worked, Brandon thought to himself, smiling inwardly, as he eyed the psychologist. She wore a sheer robe through which he could see her breasts, pale white, which rose and fell with her breathing. The strain of the past weeks had caused her eyes to sink and the skin under them to turn to the shade of a bruise; the strain had pulled the skin on her face taut, so that her high cheekbones were more in evidence and her lips were thinner, more pale. He could almost envision the skull beneath her face and yet this aroused him for he knew that her appearance of frailty was deceptive and that when alone with him she would come alive with an almost primordial furor. When they made love he sometimes told himself that she combined life and death in her single being though he did not know what he meant by that—it was a thought brought about by passion, by excitement. He thought about how earlier that evening his body and hers had intertwined, her cool white stomach, breasts rubbing against his hot, heaving body. He felt himself growing aroused. This sojourn, this retreat, to Bentley's mansion had in reality been a marvelous adventure for Brandon. Naturally he was just as spooked as the others in the group, but in a way the terror in its omnipresence was an elixir to his passion. Never had the short, powerfully built young man felt so alive sexually. He had become a sort of satyr, he would say to himself as he stood before the mirror in Bentley's bedroom admiring his broad naked chest, his ruddy cheeks, his curly brown hair, his manhood.

Bentley stopped speaking. The prayer ended. The room fell

silent. Slowly those around the table opened their eyes, let go each other's hands, looked to Bentley, the leader.

Bentley said, "Before, we move on to the rest of our work tonight, are there any questions, announcements, or observations that any of you want to make?"

No one said anything. Bentley looked from face to face.

Jane squirmed in her chair, nodded, said, "Yes, Dr Bentley." Her voice was tentative. Bentley smiled at her encouragingly.

"Go ahead, Jane."

"I have a question about . . . about the Nightmare Realm."

"Yes."

"The Nightmare Realm . . ."

"Yes."

"Does it actually exist? Is it a real place. I mean, could you find it on a map?"

"On a map?" Bentley repeated the question with a sort of ironic intonation, then turned serious. "On a map, no. That is because it is not located in the physical universe, but in the non-material universe—some would call it the 'spiritual' or 'etheric' universe. There are those who believe that the source of nightmares is within ourselves, within the human psyche as a sort of collective human experience, but I believe that the source of these powerfully vile thoughts is in another plane of existence that intersects with ours—in our sleep for the most part, in our dreams."

"Oh," Jane said.

"This other plane you're talking about," asked Eric. "Is it the same as Hell?"

Everyone looked at Eric; he spoke so rarely. His voice, so singular in the way it seemed to combine a low guttural rasp with an almost boyishly high intonation, made people uncomfortable. He exuded menace, an impression which was enhanced by his deepset eyes, his dartingly graceless movements, and the undercurrent of rage which seethed just beneath the lazy calm of his manner, of his outward bearing.

Bentley took a deep breath.

Eric smiled at her. Was it a mocking smile? It might have been a trick of the candle light, but his tongue seemed to flicker across his teeth.

She said, "No, Eric, Hell is a very different place entirely. In Hell there are no dreams, either good or bad."

"Oh my god," Jessica gasped.

Again the room fell silent.

Brandon saw Jerry's head jerk to one side. His nervous tic was becoming more pronounced, more noticeable, these days.

After a moment, Bentley said, "Let's move on, shall we? Who has not discussed their nightmare recently?" Here eyes settled on Eric. He met her gaze and she looked at the woman seated between them. It was Karla.

"Oh no," Karla said, pretending to whine. "Does it have to be me?"

"Yes," Bentley said. "It's your turn."

*   *   *

Ashley got out of her bed. Though the room was dark and cold, she did not turn on the lamp on the bedside table. Instead, she stood still in the darkness, listening. Hearing nothing she slipped on her clothes, still the conservative black dress she had worn to Bruno's wake, and picked up the small, black leather purse that, somehow, she had managed to keep hold of since that night. She tip-toed to the door. It was open. She stepped into the dimly lit hall which ran the length of the attic. Along the hall was a series of doors, each leading, she presumed, into small rooms such as her own. At its center the hallway was joined by another hallway which ran towards the back of the house. She tip-toed to it, peered down it. It was dark; she could not see very far into the darkness. She stayed to the better lit hall. Turning back in the direction of her room, she saw an open door, a stairway, at the end of the hall. She walked to it, crept down the spiral stairs. The third floor was quiet also. The doors to all the rooms were closed except for a door at the far end of the hall. It was half-open. A weak, pulsating light leaked from that room into the hall. Moving forward, Ashley opened the first door on her right. She turned on a lamp. A bedroom with a double bed. The bed-clothes were tossed aside, jumbled in the center of the bed. She saw a familiar dress slung over a chair in front of a dressing table. Karla's room. Around the room she saw more things that belonged to Karla and some other things—a shirt, a pair of shoes—which looked like they belonged to a man. Who? She was at the dressing table. She examined the things on top of the table: some cigarettes, make-up, perfume, a notebook and pen, some jewelry. A ring caught Ashley's eye. Her hand began to shake as she picked the ring up. It was her ring, a silver ring with a forest green stone into which had been carved the face of a laughing child. Bruno had bought it for her after she had seen it in a pawn shop. Karla had always admired it. Envied it. Why did she have it now? Her best friend. Hyper-unbland. She slipped the ring onto her finger. The laughing child, the ring might bring good luck. She looked at the ring and felt her heartbeat grow less pronounced. She held the ring before her and looked at the mir-ror atop the dressing table. She looked first at the ring's reflection. She smiled. She looked at her face. She gasped, recoiled. It was not her face but Karla's. She saw the reflection, the body in the mirror stepping back, sitting down on the edge of the bed. She looked again at the face in the mirror. It was her own again, her own shocked face, pallid, fearful. Jesus Christ, what was going on? Nothing. Maybe it was nothing. Just her imagination. She dared another look in the mirror. Same old Ashley. She left the bedroom, walked to the end of the hall and looked around the partially closed door there into a room full of masks, statuettes and religious icons. Dozens of candles lit the room. Something about the room kept Ashley at the threshold. Turning, walking down a tiny hall off the main hall, she tried another door, the door to an office. Bentley's office.

Switching on the desk lamp, she reached into her purse and took out her address book. She found a phone number written there. Up until recently she had known this number by heart but she could not remember it now. She listened to the phone on the other end of the line ring. The ringing went on and on. Her heart sank. She put the phone down. By chance, at the back of the address book she saw another number. She had jotted it hurriedly, scrawled it—just the number, no name. Whose was it? She could not remember writing it. What the hell? She dialed. Once more, the phone on the other end of the line rang and rang. Whoever it was, she said to herself, wasn't home. Just as Ashley started to put the phone down, a male voice answered.

"Hello."

"Who is this?" Ashley whispered.

"You're supposed to know," the voice responded. "You called me."

"Dude?" Ashley asked, a scintilla of excitement creeping into her voice. "Is that you?"

"Ashley! Where have you been? You just disappeared. I've been multi-fucking worried about you." If there was an edge of anger to Dude's concern, Ashley's tone as she responded took it away.

"You should be, Dude."

"Where are you? Are you in some kind of trouble?"

"I guess so," Ashley said.

"Where are you? Why are you whispering?"

Ashley paused, then said, "Dude, let's not go into the gory details. I don't need a knight in shining armor or whatever. I just want to talk."

"About what?"

"About myself, I guess."

Dude laughed. His laugh was paradoxically hearty and listless. "So what about you?" he asked.

"Dude, this is serious."

"Napping, ugly. I'm serious."

"Do you think I'm a bad person, Dude . . . I mean, do you think that I'm evil, that I'm capable of doing people harm?"

For a moment there was silence on the line, then Dude said, "No, I think you're about average in the malice department. Why do you ask? Are you experiencing some sort of sweaty existential crisis or something?"

"No. No, I know this sounds crazy, but it's just that I think that I might be evil . . . uh . . . or that I might have some evil force working through me."

"Jesus, Ashley, what makes you think that?"

"It's because I was hearing a strange voice in my head and a lot of people around me, including my boyfriend, have died, and, for another thing, I just looked into a mirror and for a moment I had someone else's face."

"Whose?"

"Not yours, idiot. I had Karla's face. She's a friend of mine, my best friend."

"She was with you at the party on the boat—the one where everyone passed out?"

"Yes."

"Your face is prettier. Hers is a step down."

Ashley replied, "How sweet of you to say that, but that's really not the point."

"Oh, it's not? Well maybe you're just going crazy then. Are you still on your all vodka diet? Tell me where you are and I'll come get you."

"No."

"Why not?"

"I don't know," Ashley said. "Running wouldn't help. I think I have got to see this thing through."

"What thing?" Dude had moved from cajoling to an exasperated insistence.

Ashley said, "Let's change the subject. Do you think I have any redeeming values? I wonder if there is anything good about me at all."

Dude said, "Well you never slept with me in all the time you were here, even when you were drunk out of your mind. 'Chastity' I think they used to call it—I guess that counts for something."

"Dude," Ashley said. "Remember that story you told me about that German scientist who turns into an ape?"

"Vaguely," Dude replied.

"I was amazed at how you just made that up and said it. It was so perfect."

"That's because I'm an amazing guy! No shit, Ashley, I'm a genius. A failed genius. Or maybe an ingenious failure."

"Shut up, Dude. Could you tell me that story again, now, over the phone?"

"Jesus, Ashley, I can't remember the sweaty thing . . . and, uh, anyway, I make it a practice to never tell the same story twice. It's my commitment to . . . spontaneity."

"Would you tell me another one then? Please, Dude. Just make something up."

Dude paused; then he said, "All right, but let me think of something first."

"Alright."

Waiting with the receiver to her ear, she imagined Dude sitting in his apartment the way he had the last time he had told her a story. Then he had sat quietly upright, almost meditatively, his eyes half-closed as if the act of telling a story which seemed to come to him extemporaneously and in perfect form had bestowed some sort of tranquility upon this usually far from profound young man.

She could feel herself poised on the threshold of full participation in the wonder of his instantaneous fictionalization; she was ready to give herself to it, then shrieks and screams from elsewhere in the house interrupted the onset of her reverie. Anxiety refilled her. And a sense of impending doom.

"Dude," she gasped. "I've got to go."

"Huh? Why? Ashley, what's going on there? I haven't even started yet. What's that noise I hear? Screaming?"

"No . . . yes. Dude, it doesn't matter. I've got to go."

"Ashley, at least give me your phone number!"

"You're sweet, Dude. We'll talk again."

"Ashley . . ."

Dude found himself imploring the dial tone. He put the phone down slowly and sat for a while in the darkness of his apartment. Then, without knowing why, he found a pen and paper and wrote the story he would have told to Ashley. It took him nearly four hours.

*　　*　　*

Once again, listening to her speak, Brandon was intrigued by the quality of Karla's voice. At the same time, it combined an urbane hauteur with the naiveté and petulantly high-pitched excesses of the intonations of a little girl. It was off-putting and alluring—alluring because of Karla's manner which, though aloof, was seductively aloof, and because of her incredible beauty. She was very beautiful; Brandon had to struggle sometimes to take his eyes off her. He thought that even the frequent changes in hair color and the ever-growing horns could not subtract from her gorgeousness. Indeed, these affectations only made her more intriguing. She was an exotic and it appeared to Brandon that, in these past few days at Bentley's, Karla's twin aspects—her condescension and her girlishness—had grown even more pronounced. Well, he smiled to himself, she was . . . such a silly bitch! Flooded now with the new confidence that his relationship with Bentley had given him, Brandon imagined making love to Karla and wondered whether she might lose some of her indifference, her distance, in intimacy. She wore a silver jumpsuit which glittered faintly in the candle light. It was unzipped almost to her navel. The insides of her breasts were visible. A clunky silver pendant hung between her breasts. She was talking, describing her nightmare. She had begun the recitation, the accounting, reluctantly enough, but now, halfway through, she was speaking in a straightforward fashion as if even she had begun to find what she was saying to be of interest.

"Then I am standing outside with thousands and thousands of people looking up at the sky and we see the sun go out. It just fizzles like . . . uh . . . like this huge candle which sputters for a moment or so and then the flame goes out and I say, 'Screw this sweaty shit,' but I try not to get too overwhelmed and so does everyone else. Everyone is saying, 'Stay bland! Stay bland!' Next the sky becomes permanent night. The stars are still there but the sun is gone. The moon becomes just a darker darkness, a dark orb, up in the night sky."

"Wow," Jane whispered.

Karla continued, "For a while in the dream, the whole world does well enough. There is electricity and other kinds of power so that, although it's always night outside, the lights are always on at home and the streetlights are always on so everything is more or less napping, except all the trees and the grass and the flowers begin their slow and painful demise and that's icky. And all the wild animals begin to die. In the city, the little animals go completely insane. The squirrels and the birds and the rats begin attacking people just because they can't stand the darkness. Everyone is afraid to go outside or even anywhere inside alone because the rats are always ready to swoop down and attack. So the world has become divided: night outside while inside everyone keeps all the lights on in every room as a . . . buffer, a psychological buffer, against the . . . uh . . . disconcerting omnipresence of the night."

"It's like totally divided: light versus darkness, good versus evil, white versus black," Jessica noted.

"Then," Karla continued, speaking more softly, more matter-of-factly, "things get worse."

"Don't they always? That's why they call it a nightmare," Brandon interrupted.

Karla ignored him but Bentley looked at him disapprovingly.

"All the world's power sources are quickly depleted and the

lights begin to dim. Forget Chip-Suey. Forget 2009! This is more than 'it does not compute'. This is the whole hefty-hefty. When all the electricity, all the gas, and all the oil are gone, people start to burn all the wood and paper they have. They make massive bonfires on the streets and on vacant lots. Everyone huddles around these fires, knowing that soon all the light will go out. People bring everything that can be burned to the bonfires. Museums are emptied of their paintings, libraries of their books, office buildings of their records and files."

"What about nuclear power?" Jerry asked.

"It's a dream, cretin," Jane said.

Everyone looked at her. Rare outburst.

Karla continued, "As the bonfires begin to diminish, huge fights break out as people struggle to be near the heat and the light. I'm lucky; I stay close to the fire, but soon the bonfire grows weaker and weaker. It's the size of a campfire, and then it burns down to embers. The fighting stops. People surround the embers which glow more and more weakly. I can see the embers reflected in thousands of eyes. Then the eyes disappear as the embers lose their light. I look up into the sky; the stars are gone too. I don't know why. Night becomes like fucking total.

"Then the real fun starts—the culmination of the dream. The frenzy of violence resumes again, but in absolute darkness. Blindness. I can no longer see in my dream—I can only hear and smell and feel. I hear screams and grunts and gasps and crying and whimpering. I feel people running into me as they run in terror. I feel hands on me, holding me, tearing at me, groping . . . and, that's it. That's my dream. My nightmare."

She bowed her head slightly like a school girl signaling the end of a class presentation.

Brandon looked around the table. Jane and Jessica were clearly frightened. Dominic and Jerry and Dr Bentley looked serious and concerned. Eric, unsurprisingly, was unreadable.

After a moment Bentley said, "That was very good work, Karla. Thank you. Now let's will Karla's dream away."

The members of the group took each other's hands; they closed their eyes and let their minds go blank in the ritual they followed nightly after a participant had recounted a nightmare. It marked the end of each night's session.

After a few moments, Bentley spoke, broke the silence: "With our wills joined together we will Karla's nightmare away. It has no place here. It can gain no entry. With our wills we build a shield . . ."

Bentley stopped. A faint wind blew through the room, blowing out all the candles. The electric lights in the other rooms of the house went dark at the same time. The house was in darkness.

Jane moaned.

"Shit," Jerry exclaimed. "Here we go again."

Her voice quavering, Bentley tried to continue. She had her eyes open now. So did everyone else at the table.

"With our wills we build a shield that keeps the Nightmare Realm from this house," she said. Her voice was shrill. "With our wills we . . ."

Bentley saw the candles burst into flame again. At the same time the room was bathed in a weak greenish light. What was the source of the light? It came from the doorway of the room. She heard Brandon gasp as she turned towards the doorway and she gasped too when she saw what he saw. Ashley had come into the room. The sickly light flowed from her. She was smiling. Jane turned around, saw, froze. Everyone at the table but Jessica froze with awe. Jessica fainted, slid from her chair, plopped softly onto the floor.

"Ashley?" Bentley heard herself say.

Jane screamed. Ashley was changing.

She saw—they all saw—the light around Ashley throb, pulsate. Her head and body turned first green like the light, then she disappeared, leaving a blackness, a blank space, an empty spot where her body had been. Ashley's shape was still there, like a hole in the darkness. A nothingness. Then a terrible stench filled the room. From the nothingness, a new form materialized. Ashley was no longer Ashley but a brown, horribly textured thing. Then, Ashley's face and body became, before the wide, wild eyes of the group, one malformed, cylindrical mass; her legs fused together, her arms melted into her torso, and the features of her face melted away. Her body had turned to shit, to a turd which, Ashley's height, stood upright and pulsed with the green light. A disgusting pillar of feces. Except for her hair. Where her hair had hung there was still a mass of hair-like strands. But it was not hair for very long. Her hair transmuted to thin white worms of the kind the group had once seen coming out of Jane. Now these worms fell from where Ashley's head had been in a glittering cascade of pale, greenish-white, almost luminescent strands which curled sometimes in midair and landed with a pitter-patter not unlike the sound of pieces of wet spaghetti dropping two or three at a time onto a kitchen floor. Then the worms began crawling towards the table. It did not stop there. The top half of what had been Ashley exploded in a cloud of putrid gas. The bottom half melted into doll-sized caricatures of men and women: miniature forms made of shit with yellow-green froth for mouths and eyes. Helter-skelter, almost comically, these figures rushed silently throughout the room, rushed around people's feet, their legs. No one sitting at the table moved; they were transfixed. They felt the cool and slimy creatures climb up their legs, crawl like eager monkeys over their bodies, cling to their arms and chests, jump atop their heads. Then these young people who had dared to play in the Realm of Nightmare saw the shit creatures curling down from the tops of their heads or raising little bodies up from their chests to look—if froth can see—into their terrified eyes. After a moment, the little figures changed. They changed into little shapes of nothingness. These elves, these gremlins of a vacancy darker than the surrounding darkness, moved silently. First they leapt down, danced on the table frantically, with spastic movements. Then they rushed at Dominic. He lifted his arms to ward them off. They leapt upon, climbed upon, his arms. And where they climbed or wrapped themselves, Dominic's hands and arms disappeared. One jumped onto his shoulder and his shoulder was gone. It became a dark vacancy. He rose and screamed. A tiny figure leapt onto his face and his face was gone too. He writhed in silence. Throwing his chair aside, Brandon lunged at Dominic, picked him up by the waist, shook him—what was left of him—violently. As the little, immaterial figures fell from Dominic, his face and arms reappeared. The things ran from the room and disappeared. Their nothing feet made no sound. Simultaneously, the worms, which in slow advance had almost reached the feet of those sitting on the side of the table nearest the dining room door, disappeared. Jane vomited. Not worms but a foul deconstruction of that night's dinner. American Chop-Suey. The awe which had frozen the group diminished, thawed. Jerry leapt up from the table, toppling the chair behind him. He ran into the hall where he saw no evidence of the creatures or of a human-sized turd or of Ashley. He turned back into the dining room. The lights came on throughout the house, even in the dining room and hallway where they had been turned off for the group's ritualized work. He was shaking.

"Jesus, what the fuck was that?" Jessica expectorated, getting up slowly from the floor.

Jane started to sob.

Everyone looked at Bentley.

"I need a drink." Eric said, smiling weirdly. "I feel like shit. Anybody care to join me?"

Everyone nodded except Jane. Passively she sat, sobbing, her chin, blouse, lap, and the table before her covered in vomit. No one paid attention to her. Eric took tumblers from a side cabinet, poured measures of scotch into each, brought them to the table in pairs.

"Drink up," he said. "It will make us all feel better."

They drank. No one spoke.

Dominic said, "Those little creatures . . . those little shit creatures turned into . . . into nothing. I could feel them turning me into nothing too."

"They were nullifying you," Bentley said.

The group looked at her.

"Turning you into nothing," she said.

"Wait," Karla said. "I think I understand something now. Nightmares aren't real when we dream them. We think they are, but they're really nothing. Dreams are something made out of nothing. They're just appearances, that's. . . ." She stopped in mid-sentence.

"Hi guys," a voice said tentatively from the hallway. "What's going on? Is something wrong?"

It was Ashley.

*　　*　　*

Kitten opened his eyes. He had a tremendous headache. He tried to move but he did not really feel like moving. He felt weak. He had never felt so weak before. He saw a man sitting by a fire, a big man. He was wearing a coat made out of skins. He was eating something, the leg of some kind of animal. He held it over the flames to cook it some more, then he took a bite. He chewed with his mouth open and made a lot of noise chewing. The man looked at Kitten. The man met the dog's eyes and smiled with his mouth wide open. Kitten could see the chewed flesh in the man's open mouth. The moistness on his lips and in his mouth caught the brightness of the fire. He said, "Welcome to the lair of the Pet Hunter." He spoke in a low voice. Kitten tried to bare his teeth at the man and the man laughed. A booming laugh. The laugh echoed in the small cave. A wave of sleepiness, of no-feeling, passed through Kitten's body. The fire and the man disappeared.

*   *   *

Row, row, row a boat. Brandon is rowing a boat through a saltmarsh on Cape Cod. Hot day. He is stoned. He has just smoked a joint, flicked the roach into the water. Everything is so slow and so bright—the burnt yellow-white of the sand and the clear blue dome of the sky. His face, the pores of his face, feel oily. That's a sensation that comes with blowing a joint. Maybe it's the resin, he thinks. Maybe not. He doesn't know. He's alone. There is no wind. There is no tide. Then there is a wind. It is powerful. It is blowing out from the land to the surf that is slapping the submerged sand ridges near the shore. The waves are green, clear, cold, foaming, slapping. The powerful wind blows his rowboat seaward. There is a tide now too. It is carrying his boat. He did not realize that the tide can be so strong. A riptide, it's called. He tries to row against the wind and the tide, digs into the water with his oars. His oars change into shovels. That's strange. Shovels? Shovels to dig a watery grave? Shovel, shovel a boat. Ha. That's funny. Scary too. Wind and water push him towards the open sea. Past the last dune he glides, through the submerged sand lips, the mouth where the tidal river which flows through the saltmarsh joins the ocean, the mouth where the river kisses the ocean. Brandon sees submerged sandbars pass under him. They are not more than three or four feet below the bottom of the rowboat. He could jump out. If only he were not so stoned. He looks up to see huge gray-green clouds filling the sky. Storm clouds large as oceanliners. The temperature drops. The air itself becomes green, wet; everything—shore, sea, sky—is a shade of gray-green. He is frightened. His heart is pounding in his chest. He is going to drown, he knows it. He looks out at the vast cipher of the horizon and sobs well up from his chest. It starts to rain.

*   *   *

He opened his eyes to find himself sitting up in bed. Not his bed. Hers. Dr Bentley's. Allison's. The bedroom was bathed in a soft gray-green light, moonlight, faint and phosphorescent. She lay there next to him, asleep. Her breasts and stomach and face shone pallidly in the moonlight. He had flung the bedclothes off of both of them in his dream. He pulled the bedclothes up again, savoring their warmth, their protection. He lay his body close to hers and felt the gradual subsiding of his heartbeat. His breathing deepened. She felt first cool against him and Brandon thought of a dolphin in the ocean, of how cold a dolphin's skin must feel. Then she felt warm as their bodies shared their warmth. That felt reassuring. But there was still something not quite right. The atmosphere of the room was troubled. It struck him that there were others in the room. Foolish thought. Who else would be there? He felt himself descending again to sleep. To his nightmare. He did not care. His eyes closed.

*   *   *

He is far out to sea now. Rain surrounds him. Rain and sea spray. He yells. "Help me!" The shore is so far away. His skin is cold. He is already dying.

The shore is so far away now he can hardly see it and then the seaward momentum of his little craft stops. The sea under, around the boat fills with grayer, greener shapes. Sharks! No. They push the boat with their shiny snouts. Dolphins. A school of dolphins is bringing him to shore. Miraculous. A dolphin even pulls a line attached to the front of the rowboat: no doubt he is the dolphin leader, the most beneficent dolphin. The rain is still pelting him, hurting him, but Brandon feels joy. There is nearly half a foot of water in the boat. How ironic it will be if the boat sinks after all this, he thinks as he ties a canvas cover over the top of the boat. It is tough to tie it on from inside the boat, but the cover is stretched taut atop the rowboat and he is in darkness, lying in the bottom of the boat. The water in the boat has gone. It is damp though. There is not much room. He feels the dolphins pulling him through the water and he hears water slapping the sides of the boat. They are carrying him into the tidal river, he knows, deeper into the slowness of the saltmarsh. He listens to the rain which sounds against the canvas cover: a chaos of drum rolls which is such an accumulation of sound that it becomes no sound, white noise, and then it is really, truthfully quiet. He can't hear anything. Gone are sea sound, wind sound, storm; and so too is the movement of Brandon's craft. Gone. Stillness. It's eerie in the darkness. Maybe the dolphin friends have deposited him on shore. He feels around with his hands, reaches out to the sides of the boat. They are too close; they no longer curve up and away from the boat's bottom. His hands tell him he is in a box, a tight rectangular box—a coffin, for when he throws up his hands to push against the canvas tarpaulin, they hit hard wood, a coffin top. Using both hands, palms up, he pushes with all his force against the wooden cover. He raises it and he feels, hears water gushing in, cold and dark. The dolphins have deposited him deep underwater. Frantic, he struggles to push the cover off. He cannot. The coffin is filling with water.

*   *   *

A conversation in Dr Bentley's mansion.

"Looks like he's out. Finally," he whispered. "They're both asleep. Passed out. Everyone is. Everyone but us."

"Napping," she whispered. "It's napping that they're napping. It's napping-squared."

He looked at her. His expression betrayed nothing.

The two of them were in Bentley's bedroom on the third floor. The house was quiet. It was very late. Moonlight splashed the bedroom.

He picked Brandon up, rolling his body to the edge of the

bed, stooping to put him over his shoulder. Brandon did not wake up. Neither did Bentley.

She pulled the covers back over Bentley's body.

She said, "How much did you give them? They're not going to die are they?"

"No. What do you care?"

"I don't want them all to die, ugly. Not now. What kind of sweaty fun would that be?"

"He's a heavy little fucker. Let's go. Bland?"

She led the way to the basement.

In the basement, they laid Brandon's body down in the wood shop, next to the coffin which—still unvarnished—spanned two sawhorses. The lid of the coffin was propped against the legs of a workbench. Clad only in underwear, Brandon's body lay amidst wood shavings on the stone floor.

"Wrap him up," she said.

He wrapped Brandon's body from head to toe in duct tape, wrapping his legs together, fusing his arms to his torso, leaving his nose and his eyes uncovered.

"Let him see what is happening to him," he said to her, smiling his crooked smile. She told him to leave one of Brandon's hands free. Just a little bit free.

"Why?"

"You'll see." She bent over the coffin lid, scratched something into it.

When he was done wrapping Brandon in tape, he motioned to her and they picked him up. He held the shoulders and she held the feet. Brandon's body slumped in the middle. As they were laying him into the coffin, his eyes opened. For a second they were full of sleepy non-understanding, then they opened wide in fear. Brandon began to struggle.

"Like a big fish," he said.

"A merman," she huffed.

Brandon tried to scream but his mouth was taped shut.

He floundered in the coffin. Futile. They lifted up the coffin top.

"Here, look at this," she said.

He looked at what she had scratched in the wood.

He said, "You're a genius."

"An evil genius."

"An evil genius."

"And how about you?" she asked. "What are you? You're a weevil genius. A weevil penis!" She laughed.

He looked at her. Jesus, he hated her.

She dropped the nail she had used to scratch into the coffin. "Bye, Brandon," she said. He struggled as they put the lid on the coffin and screwed it down, using an electric screwdriver that was on the workbench. It did not take too long. Then they stood by the coffin.

Muffled bumpings and thumpings came from the coffin. The coffin moved a bit on the sawhorses. After what seemed an eternity, the sound and movement subsided. The coffin lay quiet and motionless.

He said, "Use you later, Brandon."

"Finally," she said. "Now you can fuck me."

Chapter 23

Three Tenors

Jessica descended again to the kitchen.

Day 11.

She yawned as she poured herself a cup of coffee. It was early.

"Sleepy?" Dominic asked. He was sitting with Jerry at the kitchen table. He looked as together and as well groomed as ever. Behind him, beyond the kitchen window, the backyard was gray and cold and the sky was striated with layer on layer of grayblack clouds. Dead fingers of morning.

"Jesus, how would you expect her to sleep after last night's fucking exploding turd phenomenon?" Jerry said, his high pitched voice piercing Jessica's exhaustion like a needle through a voodoo doll.

She looked at Jerry. His greasy hair stood up from his head, uncombed. His smile displayed sarcasm and yellow teeth. She wondered how often he bathed. In the past she had noted how dirty his fingernails were and she thought of this now as she took a seat at the table as far away from him as the rectangle allowed. How strange it was to her that Dominic and he appeared to be so close. Well, opposites attract, she thought as she said, "No that didn't keep me awake. I'm getting sort of used to all this nightmare stuff. It was Jane. She just wouldn't stop whimpering. God! How irritating that girl is!"

"She is a whimperer," Jerry agreed, picking his teeth.

Jessica's gaze alighted on Jerry's plate. Seeing the sticky residue of orange-yellow egg yolk there, she imagined him eating the soft egg, bursting the skin of the yolk, lapping up the thick liquid. She felt her stomach flip and she looked away. She would rather think of Jane's whimpering and her worms than of Jerry.

Dominic said, "Oh, let's not be too hard on her. She's nervous, that's all. She's in the same situation all of us are. She didn't ask to be here any more than the rest of us."

"I wonder if that's true," Jessica said.

"What?" said Dominic.

"I wonder if Jane didn't ask to be here in some strange way."

"What do you mean?"

"We all think Ashley is the cause of all our troubles. We all think it's Ashley who is this, this . . . whatever it is . . . this link or transmitter to the Nightmare Realm."

"You're goddamn right I do," interrupted Jerry. There was a fleck of moist yellow egg where his upper and lower lips joined. "I saw her turn into a fucking piece of shit less than ten hours ago."

Jessica forged ahead, "Of course, you would go for the obvious, Jerry, but I wonder if we shouldn't look at others in the group, if we shouldn't follow our gut instincts and my gut instincts tell me that there is something about Jane which just isn't right."

Jerry smirked.

"What tells you that, Jessica," Dominic asked earnestly.

"Her 'gut'," Jerry expectorated derisively. "I guess if anyone is going to have a gut instinct, it's going to be Jessica."

"What do you mean by that?" she said, turning towards him, fixing him with eyes which mixed anger with hurt.

"Nothing," Jerry answered, spreading his hands outward, but his expression told a different story.

"You mean I'm fat, don't you?" Jessica demanded. Her anger was colored by surprise, by hurt, by insecurity. Before Jerry could answer she jumped to her feet. She shouted at him, "I may be fat but you never take a bath you yellow-teethed, grease-covered human pimple." Her face was red. Her jowls were red and they quivered with the intensity of her angry embarrassment. Her face cracked and she began to cry. She ran from the room. She returned, picked up her coffee, said "fuck you" to Jerry, left again.

Dominic and Jerry could hear the sounds of her sobbing move through the first floor towards the front of the house. They heard her sobbing climb the stairs to the second floor and diminish with distance until it faded.

"Nice work, asshole," Dominic said.

"Why don't you go console her?"

"Maybe I should."

"I guess Jessica is a whimperer too, huh?"

Dominic looked at his friend coldly, got up. He said, "Maybe she's right. Maybe you should take a fucking shower."

He turned and left the room.

"Use you later," Jerry muttered. His head jolted sideways with a spasmodic tic.

Dominic went to the living room and sat down. He closed his eyes. He wondered what to do.

* * *

Jane got up off the floor. She rolled up her sleeping bag neatly. She looked in the mirror over the dresser, smoothed her mousy hair. She had slept in the clothes she had changed into after the previous evenings eventful session—a loose pullover and a pair of jeans. Sitting on the edge of Jessica's bed, she pulled on her tennis sneakers. Nowhere better to go, nothing better to do, than to go downstairs, she thought, to join with the others and their . . .

condescending airs. How she hated being the weak one. She left the room.

She reached the top of the stairs; she put out a foot to step down. The first step. Not taken. Something was at the bottom of the stairs. Not something. Some hyper-quick movement. Not a flash—because it was not a movement of light but a fluctuation in the shadows that hovered in the foyer at the bottom of the stairs. Was it Bentley's practically catatonic German Shepherd, Sigmund, which she had seen only once or twice in her stay at the mansion? No, the movement was too swift and small. More like a mouse's sly, quick skitter. Could it have been a mouse? She saw it again, this darting vacancy, this having-been-there. It was not a mouse. She knew what it was, but she could not bring herself to believe it. It couldn't be. Not during the day. Now she saw it on the bottom stair, climbing up. Not something, but nothing. A hole in the air. She turned. She debated turning towards her room but knew she would be cornered there and, besides, she was already climbing the stairs towards the third floor.

She heard the sound of her feet, her tennis shoes, touching each stair. And she thought she heard—first at the back of her mind, then more clearly—the sound of other feet, little and soft, behind her. Gaining.

Reaching the third floor, she hesitated. At one end of the hallway lay Bentley's meditation room. She thought she heard chanting coming from her half-opened door. She hurried in the opposite direction, running to the end of the hall to climb a set of stairs, tightly winding spiral stairs set against the side of the house. Stairs to the attic. She reached the top. She was in a hall. The hall was cold and musty and it was so dark that the light from the stairway evaporated in blackness only a few feet from where she hesitated. She felt along the wall for a light switch, but found none. At the same time, she listened hard for sounds of the shit gremlin. She heard her heart thumping against her chest. It re-minded her of a terrified bird throwing itself madly against the bars of a cage, flapping its wings in terror. She heard nothing more than her heartbeat and her quick, shallow breathing. No tiny, squishy feet. She considered returning down the stairs and took a step in that direction. The longest journey begins with one step, she said to herself. But then she turned back. It was not an impulse in her mind that turned her back, hands outstretched, into the black tunnel of the attic hallway, but some preverbal, visceral command. She moved forward. Ashley, she knew, was in a room in the attic. Poor Ashley. Evil Ashley. Which was she? Jane was not sure. Maybe she was both. She did not want to open Ashley's door at any rate. But the door would be locked, wouldn't it? When she was halfway down the hall that went the length of the house, her hands, feeling the walls, found that there was an opening on one side. Another hallway? She smelled cedar and dust. The air was colder. She thought she heard something, the soft sounds of the foul little creature, but she was not sure. Then she thought she heard Ashley's voice. She just could not be sure. Jane wanted to cry out "Ashley, where are you?" It would be reassuring to see another person, even though Ashley might be . . . was she? Jane did not know. She did not want to know, not now. She kept silent. She decided to hide in one of the rooms of the attic. Already her hands had touched doors, all closed, in her walk through the blackness. She stepped ahead into the new vacancy, the new hall, took a few blind steps, felt another door. She heard a voice in her mind. It said, "Open this door."

She tried it. It opened. Jane entered the room, closed the door behind her, stood in total darkness. She stood perfectly still. She heard an outrush of breath. Not hers. Someone spoke.

Someone said, "Who are you?"

Jane jumped, cried out.

She felt for the door knob, could not find it. Whimpering in fear, she heard her name being whispered.

"Jane! Jane, stop it! It's me—Jessica."

Jane stopped whimpering.

"Jessica, what are you doing here?"

"One of . . . those things . . . a thing like from last night was following me," Jessica said, her voice shrill but not loud.

"Me too," Jane said. She felt a stirring in her stomach. She fought the impulse to vomit.

*　　*　　*

Ashley and Dr Bentley had been talking for about forty-five minutes when Ashley asked, "You think it's me, don't you?"

Bentley looked at her intently, did not respond. Ashley saw the fatigue in her face. She saw her eyes were strange. Her pupils were pinpricks even in the unstrong light of the attic room.

"You think it's me, don't you, that is the cause of . . . all this sweatiness?"

"Are you hot?" Bentley asked.

"What?"

"You're sweating?"

"No, Doctor. You think it's me who is the cause of all these deaths, all of these terrible things, don't you?"

"Yes, I do, Ashley."

"You do, huh?"

"Yes."

"That's double-o-nined. My brain is double-o-nined."

"Excuse me."

"Fucked up. My brain is fucked!"

"Yes, that's right."

"So, I guess the question is can you heal me, Doctor?"

"I don't know." Bentley shrugged her shoulders.

"What do you mean you don't know?"

"I mean I don't know how to handle this situation. It's clear to me from what you've said about hearing the voice and your close connection to the . . . victims, that it is likely that you are involved in some way, some negative way, with the Nightmare Realm. The added factor of the . . . hmm . . . manifestation last night is a further indication of this probability. So, Ashley, the most likely candidate, the most likely suspect, is you. And, it is also clear to me that if we don't do something . . . drastic, more of us, maybe all of us, will die. But what this drastic thing is I don't know."

Even though Ashley was concerned about her own fate, she could not help but notice how awful the dream psychologist, the dream unweaver, looked and sounded. Her hair, formerly flaxen, was now stringy, slightly oily, and gray. It had lost all its body. The skin on Bentley's face was taut and the lines on her brow and around her eyes looked far more pronounced than they ever had. She wore a loose, diaphanous robe which Ashley could see through quite easily. Between her breasts hung a black stone set in gold, held by a golden chain. The stone seemed to draw light to it, to eat the light around it. Though maybe it was just the shadow between the doctor's breasts which made the stone look so black, so ominous. The outfit, so different from the austere business attire Ashley was accustomed to seeing Bentley wear, disconcerted Ashley. The fact of Bentley's near nakedness made Ashley profoundly uneasy. On the other hand, despite Bentley's unsettling transformation and despite her own growing concern that she might be a conduit for some hideous power, Ashley was feeling much better, at least physically. Rest, a consistent diet, and a respite from alcohol had revived her body, if not her mind and soul.

"Killing me must be one of the options," Ashley said, smiling slightly.

Bentley looked hard at her.

"You would think that it would be," Bentley said, "but I don't know that it is."

"Huh?"

"I'm not sure that killing you would be sufficient," Bentley said. "The Realm has such a hold on the group now that I think it could easily shift its focus to another one of us, and then what would we have gained? Nothing but another death."

"Then what other options are there, Doctor?"

"Exorcism."

"Exorcism? Isn't that used to get rid of demons?"

"Yes, primarily. But it is also a technique that can be effective in unbinding the hold of the Nightmare Realm . . . if it's done correctly."

"Oh."

"It's dangerous. Very dangerous."

"What can go wrong?"

"You don't want to know, Ashley. We'd only do it as a last resort."

Ashley was silent. She did want to know, but a strange look had come into Bentley's face, a look of demented inspiration, which made Ashley hold her tongue.

Bentley exclaimed, "We cannot sleep again! That's the solution."

"What?"

"We cannot sleep again until we have beaten back the Realm," Bentley enthused. Color was coming back into her face. She almost beamed. "It's so obvious: while the Nightmare Realm may be gaining more and more ground over our waking realities, it draws its true power from our sleep. If we stop sleeping, we can cut the Realm off from its connection to us. We must refuse to participate in the mechanism of our own undoing."

"But won't we get tired?" asked Ashley.

"What? Of course, we'll get tired. That's what happens when you don't sleep. Why do you think I'm so tired? Because I have hardly been sleeping at all. No, I've been staying up trying to keep this goddamned hideous force at bay while everyone else sleeps . . . and guess what? It's not working. We've all got to go without sleep. How will we do it? We'll take drugs. Amphetamines. That's how."

"Bland," Ashley said.

*　　*　　*

Dominic had gone off. Probably to console Jessica. What an idiot, hugging that fat cow. Jerry sat alone at the kitchen table, thinking bad thoughts. Who was going to console him, he wondered. No one. Jerry was a bitter young man, but he had not always been that way. In his teens, in fact, Jerry had been an enthusiastic person, always willing to lend a hand to any magnanimous enterprise. Never a leader, Jerry had been the ideal follower. Once an idea of a certain kind had been put forward— an idea aimed at changing things for the better, at improving the conditions of humankind or saving some plant or animal, Jerry had always been the first to jump on board, adding his enthusiasm and effort to any idealistic enterprise whether the goal had been local, national, or global. That none of the efforts he had been involved in had ever seemed to result in any real good had never fazed him, until, in his early twenties, he had undergone an abrupt reorientation. He had become disillusioned, a nihilist of sorts. What had engendered this change in the young idealist? Jerry did not know. Maybe it was biological. One day he had simply found himself saying "no" instead of "yes", "fuck it" instead of "we can do it."

Now in a perverse, almost masochistic way, he enjoyed his own negativity. His snarling indifference gave him power over his surroundings, over those around him. He was no longer the happy follower whom no one noticed or, worse, resented for his enthusiasm. He was the unhappy individualist everyone had to notice because he was always there, saying "screw you."

Naturally, he snarled to himself as he sat alone in the kitchen, there were disadvantages to being the lone wolf. For one thing, he almost never got laid. Even girls like Jane and Jessica, hideous and unpremium non-babes, wanted nothing to do with him. In fact, his buddy Dominic was probably up in some corner of the mansion now, sticking it to that fat ass Jessica. Jerry grew a little hot at this thought. Maybe he should go somewhere and . . .

relieve his excitement. Once or twice a day he would do just that. In the basement usually. Enjoy a few moments with himself in the cool, slightly damp darkness. Alone. Though once, when he had just finished, when he had slumped against the cold stone wall of the foundation, exhausted, pleased, ashamed, that idiotic dog Sigmund had emerged from some basement recess and sneezed at him. The memory of it had taken something away from his ability to enjoy himself ever since.

He looked again at the chalkboard.

Day 11.

Maybe he could make it with Jane?

* * *

Meanwhile, at about this same time, three speakers were holding a discussion in a corner of the bar where Ashley had met Dude two weeks before, after fleeing the funeral home. It was about 11:30 am. Dude was not there. The three were the only customers in the bar. They never sang, but if they had they would have been tenors.

One said, "You know what I found the other day in the attic of my mother's house?"

"A blow-up doll of a pony?" his second companion asked.

"No. A computer."

"Really?" the third said, less ambivalent than usual.

"Yes. It was still in its packing case. It had never been turned on."

"So, did you turn it on?" the second asked.

"Yes, I did. For a moment I thought the thing was going to work. The . . . uh . . . operating system began to boot up. Then it fizzled. I thought for a moment I had a live one!"

"Ha," the third chuckled, "does not compute."

"Chip Suey," observed the second. Then he lit a cigarette and took a sip of his vodka. "So," he continued, looking at the other two, "what is the latest theory?"

"Of what?" asked the first, the one who had tried to start the computer.

"Of the reason behind the mass digital failure of 2009."

"Of the onset of the post-information age?" the third said.

"Of De-Digitalization? I heard a good one recently."

"What?" asked the other two.

"Telepathy," announced the third.

"What?"

"A secret government mind wave virus gone out of control," the third continued, looking smug. They asked him to elaborate. During the first decade of the new century, he said, a secret government research institute had developed a way to use telepathic force, psionic pulsations, to disable digital chips within close proximity to an agent's head. The psychically enhanced electromagnetic field of a telepathic agent's brain identified the electronic signatures of computer chips, then emitted a high frequency pulse, a mindray, which, basically, rendered the chips inoperative. Melted them, in fact.

"That's bullshit, obviously," said the first speaker. "Telekinetic bullshit."

The second nodded in agreement. "Anyway, even if it were true, how did one agent with some special sweating . . . uh . . . mindray destroy every fucking digital device in the world? Obviously he couldn't . . . give head to every computer—ha, ha! That's just stupid."

"No, you're stupid, you hideous thing," the third responded. "Because this telepathic ability became, in effect, a mental virus which soon spread around the world. The human mind, unaware of its own power, pulled the plugs on the world's computers."

"Weren't animals involved in any way?" asked the first.

"No. They don't use computers," said the third.

The second said, "If what you're saying is true, that means that our friend the genius here was the recent emitter of a computer destroying psionic wave. Or something." He nodded at the first of the three speakers and raised, listlessly, his glass to him.

The third conversationalist, the advancer of the new theory, did the same.

"I did feel a certain something . . . uh . . . pulsate from my head just before the unit fizzled" the first speaker replied, looking pleased with himself.

"Maybe it was a pimple on your forehead which popped," observed the second.

"Maybe," the first agreed.

The second puffed his cigarette, leaned back in his chair and said, "You know, all these stories about Chip Suey, Silicon Stew, or whatever you want to call it are double-o-nined. They are in a viral sweat."

The other two looked at him.

He continued.

"We lived through the fucking thing; we should remember. De-digitalization didn't happen over night. It took practically a year. And there wasn't one cause, there was a series of causes from the cyber-terrorist viruses and microwave bombings to that out of control cellular phone code-tripper that one of the phone companies unleashed on the others. Remember? Oh yeah, there was the failure of the Universal Chip, too, and the self-generating Internet feedback loop. All that, coupled with massive bureaucratic failure by the American government and the Europeans, and, hey, we're analogue. That's what happened, not some fruity telepathic jamboree. The amazing thing is that everyone knows this; it's just no one wants to remember. Why is that?"

"Because everyone is trying to offend you, ugly," one of the other two—it was the third—said, "and if you just thought about it a little more, you'd understand that. But you're too wrapped up with your so-called memories."

"Maybe that's why all the computers failed," the first conversationalist said, his voice speculative, reaching. "They were far better at remembering things than we really want things to be remembered. It's better to reshape the past than to remember it, to be forced to relive it, as it actually happened."

"Pro-fucking-found," the third replied.

"Lifelike," the second agreed.

* * *

After the two of them, roommates again in a different room, sat in silence for a while, Jane asked, "Are you still there, Jessica?"

"Yes. Of course I am. Where else would I be?"

"I know where I'd be if I could be," Jane said.

"Where's that?"

"Not here."

Jessica made a sound that signaled agreement. The two were quiet again for a long moment.

"Jessica?" Jane said. She spoke in a very low whisper.

"What now?"

"Maybe I should call my father. He would know what to do. He could get us all out of this mess."

"Oh yeah? What does he do? Is he some kind of cop or something because, you know, we've talked about it and I don't think cops can help us."

"No, he's a businessman. He makes diet potato chips."

"Oh. What will diet potato chips do for us. Are we going to say to the Nightmare Realm, 'Let up on us now, we're losing weight?'"

"No," Jane said, "that's not what I meant."

She sounded slightly hurt. Jessica relented.

"I'm sorry. What did you mean?"

"It's just that dad always knows what to do. He's a very forceful man."

"Why don't you call him then?"

Jessica did not say anything for a moment, then she sighed and said, "Because I'm ashamed."

"Ashamed?"

"Yes. Ashamed of becoming involved in all this . . . this . . .

hocus-pocus. My father would never approve of this. He wouldn't even be able to understand why anyone would get involved with this . . . nightmare therapy stuff, much less his own daughter. And he would be right. What the heck was I thinking, fooling around with my bad dreams? It's not right. It's just not right."

The two were quiet again.

Then Jessica said, "You took a chance. You should be proud of yourself."

"Huh?"

"You took a chance participating in these sessions. You took a risk. You tried to stretch your boundaries."

"Well, I certainly succeeded at that, didn't I?" Jane replied.

"Yes, we all did."

The door was thrown open. No one was there. Jessica and Jane screamed simultaneously.

Dominic appeared.

"Thank god, there you are," he said. He went to Jessica and took her in his arms, a comforting hug. "I've been looking all over for you."

"How about me?" Jane said.

"I didn't know you were gone," Dominic said.

"Figures," Jane muttered.

Jessica pushed Dominic away.

"Why the hell did you do that?"

"Do what?"

"Throw the door open like that without any warning, without being there so we could see you? The door opened and there was no one there," Jessica said, berating him. Her voice broke. She started to bawl.

He gripped her again, patted her on the back, brushed a strand of hair from her moistened cheeks, said, "I was afraid, Jess. I've been looking all over the house, opening every door. I got more and more scared each time I opened a door, imagining that something was going to jump out at me. Something bad."

*　　*　　*

Taylor looked down at Sydney and marveled at the size of his rump. It was a prodigious mound, a half-sphere of flesh and fat covered by slacks made of some rich, dark material. Into the midst of this elegantly attired mound was stuck the spent syringe with which the prisoner had impaled his jailer. The drug had taken effect immediately. Sydney now lay on the floor of the warehouse, wheezing in long, deep breaths. Workers at Eric Tang's illicit drug laboratory, wearing green labcoats, hairnets, and paper slippers, looked expectantly, nervously from Taylor to the supine form over which he stood.

Bending down, fishing in Sidney's pockets, Taylor found the key which unlocked the ball and chain from his leg. Ahhh, freedom! He rubbed his ankle. It hurt. Then, standing up again, he told the workers to leave, that the best place they could be in a situation like this was gone. Leaving their lab attire behind, they hurried out. They knew Tang's wrath. Taylor smiled. His plan had worked. Without Eric's presence, Sidney's conceited carelessness had reached new heights. How the fat ignoramus would ever explain this to Eric, Taylor could not imagine, though he relished the thought. Maybe Eric would kill his henchman. Starve him to death. But he had no time for such thoughts now. On the contrary, he was shaking with terror. What if Eric walked in now? God, he must hurry. Struggling, he carried two large metal vats filled with a newly concocted batch of the hideous hallucinogen Nightmare Plus—the combination of Bentley's nightmare inducing agent and a powerful amphetamine—to the warehouse's loading dock and put them into a van. To this cargo he added a trunk he had packed the previous evening filled with enough mood replicating chemicals to earn himself a small fortune from any of the drug dealers in the city looking to take some business away from Tang. Choosing another key from Sidney's chain, he started the van, drove away into the warehouse district.

He drove for about forty-five minutes, first through the city, then into more and more suburban neighborhoods until he reached the first destination on his well-planned itinerary. The Spengler Reservoir. Primary water supply for the city. The wide and lengthy body of water was surrounded by a wire fence and by a desolate parkland of broken benches, buckled walkways, leafless trees. Taylor drove along a utility road which ran along one side of the reservoir until he found a place where the fence had fallen down, sagging into the water. He stopped the van, opened the back, poured both vats into the water. He could see the heavier liquid from the vats intermixing with the water. For a second the contents of the vats flowed, viscous waves, retaining their consistency, into and under the surface of the water and then they began to swirl against the resistance of the water, to separate, to begin a process of complete diffusion, molecule by molecule, throughout the reservoir and then the city's water system. He chuckled to himself, replaced the empty vats into the van and drove away. There was nothing like a little forethought to help cover his escape, and the irony of it was that a nightmare, a city-wide nightmare, was going to help make his dream come true.

*   *   *

Strom Varnish took another sip of black coffee. Sleepy, he was just settling into his work for the day. He had worked late into the previous evening fine tuning his electronic spy dog. Now Varnish mused, fussed, mussed. He looked at this and that. Out of habit, he glanced at the row of three television screens. All were inactive. Christian, his current proto-unit was grabbing some downtime. He took another sip of coffee. He began fidgeting with a defective servo unit on the worktable before him. He unscrewed the back plate and pulled the wiry guts out onto the table. He prodded them speculatively with a penlight. Something inserted itself onto the edge of his attention. One of the screens had clicked on. It was not Christian's. He could see there was an image there but he could not make out what it was. The screen went dark. Strom scratched his chin, chuckled.

*   *   *

Morris Tantone awoke in his warehouse hideaway. The gray daylight made him blink. He could not focus as he emerged into consciousness. He felt unbalanced, nauseous. His mind swirled. Ouch! The damned light violated him.

Something was not right. For one thing, he was upright. For another, he could not move his arms or legs. As his vision adjusted to the autumnal noontime semi-brightness of the room, he saw Fabiola, the beatific girl with the ruined face, looking up at him. She looked at him intently with her brown eyes. Next to her stood her taller companion, the boy with whom she seemed to share leadership of the group which now stood behind the two of them. A group of disheveled children. The children looked at him quietly, quizzically, with the dumb, profound stares of animals.

All of the children were wearing helmets.

He pulled against the ropes which bound him to the wooden column.

The one to which the children had nailed the cat. They must have drugged him.

It was going to be a long afternoon.

Chapter 24

Day 13

Costello dreamed an alcohol drenched dream:

He is standing on the raised platform directing traffic, causing the biggest traffic jam in his career. All the cars are stopped in every direction. He can see unmoving cars backed up for blocks. He braces for the sound of the car horns, of the yelled epithets of the drivers. Instead he hears dogs barking, donkeys braying, sheep baaing. The sounds of thousands of animals. Animals are driving the cars. They are angry. Sitting upright in their seats, they have rolled down their windows to shake paws or hooves at him. Maybe they don't know how to honk the horns, he thinks. A few blocks off he sees a bicyclist weaving through the cars. It is her. Esmeralda waves as she passes him. Waves and smiles. Her red hair flows from under her black beret. An Uzi is strapped across her back. Her eyes are brown, her lips full. He jumps from the platform and chases her, following her weaving bicycle through the cars. Animals growl and bark at him as he runs after her. Is Kitten driving one of the cars?

She draws away. She is singing.

He runs on. He comes to an empty, desolate hill. He is outside the city now, on the outskirts of the city. The traffic jam is far behind him. The hill is covered in poles as thick as telephone poles, but shorter, stumpier. He climbs up the hill through the forest of poles. No! He sees Kitten nailed to a pole. Blood has flowed from where the dog has been pierced by spikes. The dog's head lolls to one side and the body hangs limply against the cruel wood. The dog's eyes are open, lifeless. Kitten's mouth hangs open and his tongue hangs from his mouth. Someone has put a crown of thorns around the dog's head.

* * *

He woke in a tangle of sheets. His legs were still moving. He had been running in his sleep like a dog.

* * *

Later that day Jane yawned. She brought her arms above her head, stretched tentatively. It looked weird to Jerry but he did not say anything or even smirk. He was sitting next to her on a sofa in the mansion's living room.

"I'm tired," Jane said.

The entire group including Bentley was there. Except for Brandon. No one could find him. No one knew where he was. People were worried about him. Jessica was convinced he had run off. Bentley did not say much about his disappearance. It was dusk.

"Have another pill," Dr Bentley said. She got up from the deep leather chair where she was sitting, shook a pill into her hand from a bottle, and offered it to Jane. The pill was black and shiny. Bentley called it a Black Pearl. An amphetamine. Jane swallowed the pill. Bentley smiled. Her eyes were strange and intense in her haggard face. Everyone was tired. The group had not slept for more than 48 hours since Bentley had had the idea of shutting off the access of the Nightmare Realm by prohibiting sleep. Bentley had explained to the group that Ashley—probably unknowingly, through no fault of her own—was likely the transmitter of the evil Realm's mind-twisting forces. Bentley had said that by denying the Realm access to Ashley and the rest of the group's sleep, they could weaken the psychic influences of the Realm. This would enable them to cut off the connection between that horrible zone and Ashley's mind. If they could do this, they might have a chance of freeing themselves. Only Jerry had voiced doubts openly. Over a period of two days and nights, the group, increasingly strung out by fear and the powerful little pills, had congregated more and more in the living room when they were not participating in one of Bentley's thrice daily banishing and cleansing rituals around the dining room table. They felt safer together. Bentley's idea seemed to be working. During this sleepless expanse of time, nothing nightmarish had occurred.

Bentley returned to her seat. She no longer wore, to Dominic and Jerry's disappointment, her gauzy, see-through gown. Instead she now wore a full length black ceremonial robe covered with arcane symbols and insignias.

Ashley slumped next to Karla on another sofa. She was wearing clothes Bentley had loaned her—jeans, a sweater, some old running shoes. Everyone but Karla, the indifferent Eric, and Bentley's German Shepherd, Sigmund, were wary of Ashley. The dog curled now at Ashley's feet, drooling. After Jane and the psychologist's brief interchange, the group returned to its brooding silence. People were tired of talking.

In the silence, sounds which had been obscure took on new significance. A clock ticked on a shelf. In the distance a car alarm wailed. Sigmund's breathing sounded like a bellows. Dominic cleared his throat every few minutes.

At last someone spoke.

"I just wonder why the . . . this Nightmare Realm has chosen to focus on us?" Jessica said. "I mean, what has any of us done to deserve this?"

"That's the nature of evil, I think," Dominic said, consolingly. "There is no rhyme or reason to it, Jess. There's no justice to it. Because we are innocent, we are the perfect victims."

"But . . . how . . . why is there evil?" Jane asked, speaking meekly.

Jerry started to smirk, then catching himself, said, "That's a good question, Jane." He patted her on the shoulder. She looked at him. His head twitched. "There are some people who believe that evil is just the absence of good," he continued, "but I think that evil exists in its own right. I really do!"

Others looked at Jerry, interested more by his lack of sarcasm than by what he was saying.

"I've seen how evil can grow in my own mind," he continued, running his hand nervously through his hair. It was greasy and stood on end. Because of the sleepless intensity of the last two days and the tension, Jerry's face had broken out. The sallow, oily skin on his forehead and around his nose was flecked with sizeable pimples. "I've had thoughts which I knew were bad and even though they didn't start off as anything special, they grew to really trouble me. In some cases, it seems the more I try to hold back a negative impulse, the more strength it gets. It's sweaty, multi-sweaty."

"What kind of negative thoughts, Jerry?" Bentley asked, leaning forward from her armchair.

Jerry did not respond for a moment. He was troubled, embarrassed. He looked at the floor. He could feel Bentley's scrutiny, the scrutiny of the others. When he finally spoke, he whispered.

He said, "It's too . . . uh . . . personal! I can't."

"Jerry," Bentley cajoled, almost purring.

He looked at her, changed his mind.

"Alright," he said. "A few months ago I started thinking about killing pets."

"What?" Bentley exclaimed. Her voice betrayed more surprise than dismay. In any event it had lost its typical clinical distance.

"I started to think about killing dogs and cats. It started as a thought at the back of my mind. Maybe I saw a poodle and I said to myself that it would be interesting to see what would happen if you shot it. Naturally, I was . . . uh . . . appalled by my own thought and I stopped thinking it. Or I tried to. But, as time passed I found myself thinking of . . . more and more horrible ways that pets could be killed. Talk about double-o-nined! My own mind was my enemy."

All eyes were on him now. Intently. On the couch, Jane moved as far away from him as possible. Jerry drew energy from the attention. His voice rose in volume.

He said, "After a while I couldn't get the thoughts of killing pets out of my mind. It seemed any effort I made . . . not to think about killings dogs or cats resulted in a deluge of images I just couldn't fucking control. It was unbland. I was unbland. Totally viral. I must have thought about every way possible to kill an animal. I threw them off roofs, electrocuted them, put them in bags and threw them into the river."

"You . . . you're the Pet Hunter then, you verminous human zit?" Jessica gasped.

Jane whimpered. Karla looked on, her eyes gleaming with interest. So did Ashley.

Jerry grinned, spread his hands, said, "That's just the thing. I'm not. I couldn't believe it when this guy, this Human Pet, this Pet Hunter, began to . . . uh . . . actualize my fantasies. It made me sweat. In fact, he took it to a level I never imagined . . . I mean hunting with spears, hunting with a bow and arrow—that's way outside my imaginative capabilities."

Karla looked away.

"What a loser," she said. She met Eric's eye. His face betrayed nothing, not even faint interest. He got up, walked to the other end of the room towards the hall at the rear of the house which led to the kitchen. Conversation in the room ebbed after Jerry's admission, limping on in fits and starts. After a few moments Ashley got up too; she was not listening to the conversation. Not really. She wanted a drink of water.

Bentley followed Ashley with her gaze as she walked towards

her. Ashley stopped by her chair and said she was getting a glass of a water. Bentley nodded. She said, "That's fine, Ashley."

Ashley walked back to the little hall, the pantry, through which Eric had already walked from the living room to the kitchen. The hall was lined with cupboards and shelves filled with dishes, cooking utensils, foodstuffs. She heard Eric speaking into the wallphone in the kitchen. His back was to her but she could hear him. Something made her stop and listen.

"Sebastian," Eric said. "You've got to come through for us. You've got to follow the plan."

Her mind whirled. She did not know what to do. She fell back against a shelf and knocked over a can of soup; it rolled off the shelf and tumbled to the floor. Eric turned, saw her. His expression became something between a snarl and a smile. He turned away, whispered something into the phone, hung up. He turned back to Ashley.

"You bland, ugly?" he said, coming towards her. He sounded concerned. "How's your mindset?"

In the living room, Bentley was saying, "It's remarkable how a negative thought, a bad thought, can start almost as nothing in the mind and still grow to something larger, to a . . . a thought or impulse which takes over everything else. Does anyone want to talk about that?"

No one spoke initially, then Jane said, "It's the same with me. I've had negative thoughts . . . fears, actually. . . . which started as nothing, as things someone said, or as things I saw on television. That's how my nightmares started. I saw something on the TV about children with worms and how those worms could come from animals . . . from puppies I think. Anyway, after a week or so I was having spaghetti and I thought back to the show. I thought that the pasta was . . . you know. I was able to put the thought out of mind then, the thought that the . . . the food was worms. . . . and I was successful for a while. But then the image, the thought, started coming back again and again. It seemed the more I tried to stop it, the more powerful it became."

"Yes," Karla said, smiling. "The thought wormed its way into your mind. I think that bad thoughts are like weeds which, instead of being hampered by our efforts to kill them, actually derive nourishment from our efforts. The more we try to weed them out, to weed the weeds, the bigger they grow until we've got this huge overgrowth in our brain which is like fucking everything else up—the whole orderly garden of the thought process. I know exactly what you're talking about, Jane."

"It brings up a whole line of philosophical questions, doesn't it?" Dominic chimed in, "about what almost might be called the economic system of the mind. For example, how does the mind regulate its own thoughts? How does it determine which thoughts have value and which don't? And, is there a part of the mind that has the power to keep thoughts, destructive thoughts, thoughts which are actually negative in value, from participating in the life of the brain, the activity of our minds? The question is: who's in charge of our own brains? Who's doing the thinking about what we think?"

Bentley nodded.

Jerry looked at Karla from the corner of his eye. She was wearing the silver jumpsuit again. The zipper was down to her belly and Jerry knew she had nothing on underneath except the clunky silver pendant which hung between her breasts.

"That's very deep, Dominic," she said. "Good work."

Deep, Jerry smirked to himself. He could almost feel Dominic's sense of satisfaction, his smug satisfaction at being praised by teacher. He looked one last time at Karla, at Jane, got up, departed the room. No one noticed his leaving.

The door to the basement was under the stairs which climbed from the first to the second floor. Flicking on the light switch, Jerry descended into the basement. He liked it in the basement. He liked its moist, palpable murkiness, its humming silence. It was a large basement as old as the old house, but it too had been reconditioned, modernized. The walls, the foundation walls for the mansion above, were cement and stone. At one end of the basement there were a laundry room and a number of other rooms with closed, locked doors. Storage rooms presumably. Jerry had tried the doors. For the most part the basement was a wide expanse punctuated by the brick columns which helped support the floor above. Like the rest of Bentley's residence the basement was an orderly place. Here and there boxes or old furnishings were stacked or piled. Against the wall which ran along the side of the house under the living room, the south side of the house, were shelves which held cans of paint, discarded appliances, stacks of magazines, boxes. At the front of the basement were a large oil burner and tank. Under and alongside the stairs, illuminated by a single lightbulb hanging from the ceiling, was a small wood shop with a workbench, table saw, and two sawhorses. A coffin was on the sawhorses. At first the presence of the coffin had made Jerry uneasy, but he was used to it now. Something about the coffin had changed recently. He did not want to think about it. It was not his concern. He had something else to do. He walked quietly. On tiptoes. He always tried to be as soundless as possible in the basement. He did not know why. Quiet as a mouse. A mouse in the house. He moved to his own special place. It was between the oil burner and the basement wall. It was hot there and dark; it was outside the circles of light cast by the few hanging light bulbs which dangled from the wooden beams above the basement. His special place vibrated with the heat and the mechanical sounds coming from the burner. It was a cozy nook. He listened in the darkness. His head jerked. He picked up something he had hidden on the floor under the burner. There were no sounds except the sound of the oil burner. He liked this silence. He undid his belt buckle. He pulled down his pants, his underwear to his thighs, felt the coolness of the stone wall against his buttocks and the warmth of the dark, subterranean air thrown off by the oil burner against his thighs and then taking hold of himself he began to feel a new warmth. Warmth mixed with warmth. He thought of Karla. What it would be like to unzip her jumpsuit. What it would be like to have her alone with

him in this basement . . . hideaway. Or Jane. Did he have a chance
with Jane? He did not think so. But why not? Was he really such
a loser? Well, she was a loser too. Maybe she would want him.
Maybe she was as desperate as he was. As horny. He was so
horny he could almost fuck a dog. Sigmund. But how would he
do that? He thought of screwing Bentley's German Shepherd. He
had never thought of that before. Oh, this was a first. He pictured
himself atop the splayed legged animal, his loins rubbing against
the black and tan fur. He was the mad Pet Hunter. God, he did
not want to think about that. His head jerked. He thought about
Jane about Karla about Bentley about fat Jessica. He heard a
voice in his mind call Help! Whose voice? Help! He unzipped
Karla's jumpsuit and she smiled at him. Bentley came to him in
her see-through robe. Help! A male voice. Help! And then he
did not think at all. He felt the coolness of the wall against his
buttocks. Coolness becoming warmth. His buttocks slapped the
wall again again again again until the slapping stopped. He felt
warm and his mind was quiet for a moment and his breathing
deep. His head was steady. After a moment, he let the rag he
held in his hand tumble to the floor and he pulled up his pants
and secured them. He heard the voice in his mind again. Help!
It was Brandon's voice. He knew where it was coming from. He
simply knew it. Unbland. He was afraid.

Upstairs, Karla was saying, "I hate to play devil's advocate,
but don't nightmares serve a . . . uh . . . necessary function?"

The others in the room focused on her.

"I know it's trite but without a little bit of fear and negativity
how would we be able to measure the good in life . . . I mean, if
you think good actually does exist," she continued. "Isn't evil
just part of the . . . uh . . . fulcrum that helps lift life up out of
non-existence, up out of death? Isn't evil a . . . well . . . isn't it
necessary? A necessary evil? And when you get right down to it,
doesn't it make some sort of sense that the Nightmare Realm
would begin to overlap with our present reality? It's not as if life
isn't a nightmare already. Things aren't bland-on-bland out there."

She gestured to signify the world outside Bentley's mansion. "They're so fucking unbland it's unbelievable. Now, one nightmare is supplanting another—or fusing with it. It's nightmare-squared!"

Ashley had come into the room. She had been listening by the door to the kitchen hallway.

She said, "Karla, you sound exactly like me."

Karla looked at her friend and smiled, replied, "I always sounded something like you. You've been a big influence on me."

Ashley said, "Next you'll be saying that these nightmare deaths are just some sweaty Darwinian mechanism, some kind of occult natural selection that's paring down surplus human beings in service of humankind's broader goals of survival of the fittest."

"You know," Karla said, "I was just about to say that. On the verge! There must be something to this telepathy thing that everyone is saying is going around."

Dominic started to say something. He was interrupted. Jerry was screaming from the basement. Everyone froze. Then Jane screamed. Jessica covered her face with her hands. Bentley began to shake. This was too much.

Another incident.

Dominic got up and dashed to the basement. Ashley followed. So did Eric. They found Jerry by the coffin. He had opened the coffin. There was a figure wrapped in duct tape inside it. A lot of duct tape had been used. It was a duct tape mummy. Except for one hand which poked from the duct tape. Except for the eyes and nose. The terrified eyes. Brandon's eyes. Brandon shook violently—he vibrated—in the coffin. Jerry stood off to one side. He was slightly bent over. He held his arms, his hands in front of his face. His hands and arms were rigid. A continuous scream emerged from his opened mouth, his jerking head.

"So that's where Brandon went," Eric said to Dominic. He spoke loudly so that Dominic could hear above Jerry's scream.

"You help your friend, I'll take care of Brandon." Eric looked down at the quivering mummy. By his feet in the coffin he saw three empty cardboard spools which had held the duct tape. He took them out of the coffin and showed them to Ashley. She smirked. It was an intense scene. She was trying to take it in stride. She lit a cigarette. The smoke felt good in her lungs. She held it there for a long time, then exhaled. She had an intuition that things were about to take a turn for the worse. Dominic ushered Jerry away from the workshop. He took him over near the oil burner and tried to calm him down. After a moment Jerry grew more quiet. Eric began to pull at the duct tape. Unwinding Brandon. First, he lifted Brandon's feet in the air so he could unwind the tape from his legs. It was going to take a long time— Ashley could see that. Now Bentley was there. Jessica and Jane were there too, hovering behind the others. Bentley looked down at Brandon's face, his eyes. They looked back at her pleadingly. She threw her arms around him. Eric stopped what he was doing for a second. Bentley gathered the upper half of Brandon to her chest. To Ashley it looked like she was holding a large sack, a cocoon. It looked weird. This was weird.

"Brandon," Bentley cried. "Oh, Brandon."

She and Eric lifted him out of the coffin and put him on the floor.

"Wow. It's going to take while to unwrap him," Karla observed. She had just arrived, taken in the scene. She looked around, found a pair of scissors on the workbench, said, "Here, use these."

Eric took them, clicked the blades together a few times. He began cutting the cocoon of duct tape away. Jane was weeping now. She was repeating the phrase "I'm tired of this stuff" over and over. Jessica had walked away. She watched what was happening from near the shelves that ran along the south wall of the basement. Karla looked on with interest. Ashley did too. Jerry began screaming and flailing again. He was trying to wrestle free of Dominic. Bentley knelt on the concrete floor, stroking Brandon's duct tape encased head, his chest, murmuring reassuring words. Eric cut lengthwise along the top of Brandon's quivering body. When he got to the neck, he and Bentley peeled the shell of tape off to either side. Brandon was naked. The smell of feces and urine filled the room. Ashley turned her face as her stomach flipped.

"Get a robe from my room," Bentley cried, looking around. Her eyes seized on Jessica. "You. Fat girl. You go!"

Jessica looked hurt, betrayed. She cried out, "No way! I'm not fucking going. I'm not going anywhere." She sat on her haunches and gave Bentley the finger. Eric cut the tape from Brandon's mouth. He was burbling nonsense. Brandon began to pull at the tape which enwrapped the rest of his head.

"Atrophy, man!" Eric shouted, pushing Brandon's hands away. "Do you want these scissors to cut off your nose?"

Bentley looked at him.

"By mistake I mean," Eric said. "He's hyperkinetic."

"Calm down, Brandon," Bentley said. She stroked his body as one strokes a nervous animal. Eric cut the tape in a line from the tip of Brandon's nose to the crown of his head, then he peeled the tape away. Ashley could see that pieces of Brandon's hair were being pulled out as the tape was pulled away. That must have hurt, but Brandon did not seem to notice. He was beyond that. When Eric was done, Bentley folded the young man in her arms. Brandon was silent for a second and then he was convulsed by sobs—huge, sporadic, sickly inbreaths.

Jerry was calmer now. He and Dominic walked back to the woodshop.

"Come on, Eric," Bentley said. "Help me get him upstairs."

"He's covered in shit, Doc," Eric said.

She made a sound of disgust.

"Hello, someone, anyone! I really need a blanket or a towel here," Bentley said.

"Here's something," Karla said, striding away from the woodshop. She grabbed a sheet of canvas which covered pieces of old furniture and pulled it off. A cloud of dust rose into the air from the canvas. She sneezed, brought it to Bentley. They laid the canvas out beside Brandon, then—Eric taking his feet, Bentley his shoulders—they lifted him onto the sheet. They wrapped him in the canvas, the shroud. Calmer now, Jerry looked into the coffin.

"What's this?" he said.

No one noticed that he had said anything.

"What's this?" Jerry repeated more loudly.

"What's what, sweaty?" Eric asked.

"This," Jerry said. "These scratches in the lid."

Dominic stepped next to the coffin, bent down, examined the lid.

"Oh, no," he said.

"What?" asked Bentley.

Dominic said, "Brandon scratched Ashley's name in the lid." He reached into the coffin, took out a nail, held it up. "He must have used this."

Standing in the basement shadows, only her face touched by the light which shone on the casket, the woodshop, Jane looked intently at Dominic, then looked away. She began to twitch. She put her hands to her throat, to her stomach. Her tongue moved uncomfortably in her mouth. She lost it, keeled over.

"No!" Ashley cried. "Let me see that." She stepped to the coffin, looked at the lid. She turned away, shaking her head. "You've got to believe me . . . it wasn't me," she said.

"Shut up!" Bentley barked. Then she asked Brandon, "Brandon, did Ashley do this to you?"

Brandon gurgled and moaned.

"I think . . . I think that was a 'yes'," Jerry ventured.

* * *

"Ooof."

Morris felt the impact of the helmet to his midsection. The

little bastard had leapt at the last moment. Now another one was running toward him. A boy wearing a football helmet. The helmet was too big for him; it rattled on his head.

Morris shifted his hips so that the boy's head missed his scrotum.

"Ugh."

Morris looked up. Another child was waiting at the head of the line of children, waiting another turn to run and butt him. "Go," one of them urged. The child came at him. It had gone on like this now, off and on, for two days or so—one vile child following another following another.

"Ouch."

They were eerily quiet. Another one came now. He did not hate them. No. He did not hate them. It was an ordeal. He recognized that. He looked at it as some sort of test, something with almost religious or spiritual implications. At first, the impact of the little heads on his body had been merely annoying. No one blow hurt that much. But as blow supplemented blow, his body had begun to feel the cumulative force of the hurtling bodies. He imagined that his thighs, his midsection must be black and blue.

"Ooof."

It was slow torture.

In the beginning he had growled at the children like an animal. He had spat at them, drooled, barked, howled, bared teeth. After a while, he had stopped doing that. It was as if the children—the trial by child—was knocking the feral out of him.

The ordeal had not been without interruption. Sometimes the children sat down or lay down panting, exhausted. Sometimes they slept. Sometimes they left for hours. Sometimes they ate, eating pastries and canned goods they had shoplifted or small animals—two rats and a cat—they had caught in the clever traps they set in and around the old warehouse. At times the co-leaders, the little girl with the stained face or the taller, older boy, stood off to one side watching. Their eyes were blank, uncommit-

ted. It was these blank stares which unsettled him most deeply;
the stares were wearing him down.

"Ouch."

Bound behind the column, his hands worked to free themselves. The children had done a good job tying him up.

*　　*　　*

"You've got to believe me," Ashley pleaded, looking first at
Bentley, then at the others in the basement. Bentley stood a foot
from her. She was staring hard at Ashley. Emanations of anger
were almost visible around the psychologist's body, her head: an
aura, a halo of negative, retributive emotions. Ashley could see
Bentley's body twitch, her hands ball into fists. A door on the
other side of the basement—a door to one of the locked rooms
which ran along the north wall—creaked open. Everyone looked.
Alvin, the retro-hippie who had died at Final Rapture Cemetery,
emerged from the blackness of the smaller room into the half-
light of the basement. His features were indistinct, shadowy, but
he appeared damp, besmirched with graveyard dirt. He pointed
at Ashley. Ashley gasped, put her hands to her open mouth.
Disbelief. The others watched in silence. Except Brandon and
Jane. Balled on the floor now, she began to retch. Another door
opened. Irma Gamerman emerged. She was shadowy too. More
than shadowy—wraithlike. Ghostly. A ghost daubed with
sewerflow, with feces. The gnomelike artist looked sad, grim.
Ashley wept. She felt tears cross her cheeks. Hot tears on shamed
flesh. Irma pointed at Ashley. And then the third door along that
wall opened. No one was there. Just the utter blackness of the
tiny storage room.

"Bruno," Ashley wailed. "It must be Bruno."

A figure appeared in the darkness. Briefly. No one could
make out who it was. It was just one darkness moving within
another. The door slowly closed. It creaked as it closed. It shut
with a tiny oompf. At the same time the figures of Alvin and Irma

melted from view and the doors from which they had emerged closed also.

"I know it was Bruno," Ashley said to Bentley. Her voice was pleading. Bentley slapped her hard across the face.

"Oww! Jesus, why'd you do that?"

Bentley slapped her again. She attacked Ashley furiously, hitting her with her fists in her face, her chest, driving her backwards. Dominic, Eric, and Jerry grabbed the doctor, held her back. She kicked. Jerry held her from behind with his arms around her. He could feel the softness of her breasts. Ashley slumped to the floor, weeping. Devastated. Karla came to her, knelt beside her.

This made Bentley more angry.

"Get the hell away from her, Karla!" she screamed. Her voice sounded insane. It contained all the rage, the helplessness, the anger of the past weeks. Bentley threw off the three men who held her. "Take this bitch and tie her up. Put her in my meditation room and watch her. Guard her." She spoke to them in a voice of shrill command.

Dominic and Jerry moved towards Ashley. Dominic and Jerry lifted Ashley by her armpits. She acquiesced. She was limp between them. They began to lead her away.

"What are you going to do . . . with her?" Karla asked the doctor.

"We're going to have an exorcism," Bentley replied. "Tonight."

*   *   *

At last.

The little girl rushed him now. The angel. Beatrice. The co-leader. She wore a construction helmet. She was taking little steps, running as fast as she could. At the last moment she jumped, pointing the top of her head right at his groin. It was at this moment that Morris swung with his freed hand and grabbed her from the air. His large hand was around her neck. He shook her in the air.

All the children in the room went still. They could see that all of Beatrice's face was becoming red. The lavender swath of color on her face became darker. Her eyes bulged. She kicked, flailed arms, tried to bite, to yell, but his grip enveloped her throat.

"Listen to me very closely, children," Morris said. "One of you will untie me or I will kill the girl." He swung her in the air, a rag doll, in emphasis.

Some of the children started to cry. Others looked to the lean, wiry boy. The leader. The boy fixed Morris with hard eyes. They stared at each other. The boy shifted his gaze to Beatrice whose eyes were rolling up into her head. Strange sounds came from her throat. Her arms and legs flailed weakly.

"It's only a game, mister," the boy said. "Don'cha want us to have any fun. We're homeless children."

"Fuck you," Morris responded. "I'll kill her."

The boy considered a moment longer. Then he said, "Danny, you go untie the man."

*   *   *

Strom Varnish bent over his workdesk. He was working on something new—a baby rattle which would emit a poison which would kill the adults in the area, but not the baby. Damn difficult. A discriminating death device. Special order. He was listening to a wild bit of music on the record player: *The Lamentation of Dr. Faustus*, the last work by the ill-fated, early 20th Century composer Adrian Leverkühn. Leverkühn had gone mad composing this piece, this symphonic cantata, Varnish mused. Maybe that's what it takes—madness—to have great thoughts, great ideas.

"Ahem."

Someone was making a sound.

Varnish looked up. His eyes focused slowly. He said, "Hello Rex. What brings you down to the basement? Slumming?"

"No," Rex Quick responded. "Ahh, I won't be seeing much more of you, Strom. I just came by to say goodbye."

"Come again?"

"They've fired me, the bastards. It's because of the goddamn chair policy!"

*　　*　　*

Police Commissioner Raymond Trump and Lieutenant Francis Finnerty stood before the mayor's desk. Mayor Edgar Paninni poured himself a tall glass of water from a glass pitcher. The pitcher was beaded with moisture. So was the glass. It was too hot in the office. The heating system in City Hall was malfunctioning. There was either too much heat or none at all. Paninni drank. On his jacket he wore a pin with Tater's picture on it. He bent his head back to drain the entire glass of water.

"Ahhh," he exclaimed, putting the glass down on the table. "Nothing like a glass of water. Do you gentlemen drink a lot of water?"

The two police officials shifted uncomfortably.

"Probably not," the mayor continued answering his own question. "So, tell me, please, this Morris . . . this Morris Tantone . . . where is he? Is he in custody yet?"

Trump looked at Finnerty; Finnerty looked at Trump.

"I don't hear an answer, gentlemen."

Paninni poured himself another glass of water.

Trump spoke, "Not yet, sir. But we are doing everything we can. As you know, we've mobilized the entire city government work force. We're chasing every lead."

"We're closing in, sir," Finnerty added.

The mayor nodded. He considered. He said, "You are worthless, fucking assholes. In twenty days you've done nothing. This fucking Pet Hunter—the killer of my Sophie's Tater—is still on the loose, still killing pets."

"Actually, sir, there hasn't been a confirmed pet killing or abduction since Tater's . . . uh . . . murder." Trump said. "We feel our all out push has got the Pet Hunter against the ropes."

"Since Tater's murder?" Paninni repeated. "That's eight days ago."

"Yes, sir. Eight days."

"Except for Costello," Finnerty said. He was trying to add levity to the situation, trying to refocus the mayor's mind.

The mayor seemed to take the bait.

"Costello lost a pet?"

"I didn't know that, Francis," Trump said, agitation flickering for a moment across his otherwise impassive features.

"I hate Costello. Did you know that, Finnerty?" Paninni asked.

"Yes," Finnerty smiled.

"What did he lose? A cat? A dog?" the mayor asked.

"A dog, sir."

"And what was his dog's name?"

"Kitten," Finnerty replied.

"Vixen?"

"Kitten."

The mayor's voice escalated in intensity and volume as he responded, "What kind of status report do you think this is, Finnerty? I ask you to catch one man, one large and easily-recognizable man, a man who is very tall and is bald and is often seen in skin tight shorts with a leash and a dog collar around his neck, and you tell me someone I hate, a piece of human shit who is now a lowly traffic cop because I hate him so much, has lost his dog and his fucking dog's name is Chicken."

"Kitten, sir," Finnerty said.

"Kitten," Paninni screamed. He was up from his chair now, walking around his office, screaming and gesticulating. He turned to look at the two police officials. He stopped. Finnerty and Trump saw the mayor's face, as red as tomato sauce, turn white. Sheet white. The mayor gasped, backed slowly around his desk to his chair, sat. With trembling hands he poured himself another glass of water. He spilled water all over the desk as he poured. He took a long slow drink.

"You may go," he said.

"Sir?"

"Get out," Paninni said softly.

Exchanging glances, Trump and Finnerty left the office.

Paninni was glad they were gone. When he had looked at them in the midst of his tirade, he had seen that the two officers were not men anymore. They were huge, clothed, talking Dachshunds standing upright in front of his desk.

The enhanced Nightmare Therapy drug, Nightmare Plus as Eric liked to call it, was beginning to permeate the city's water supply.

*   *   *

It was between 9:30 and 10 p.m. when Morris entered the club in the warehouse district. The club was loud and dark. Just what he needed. His pockets were full of the money he had taken from the children's piggy bank. $325 in bills and coins. The club was called Little Dutch Boy. He had never been there before. That was good. Maybe no one would know him. He looked different anyway. He had a new growth of hair now and a beard. He was wearing an old T shirt and some soiled slacks the children had brought him after his arrival at the warehouse. His thighs and lower torso hurt him. He sat down at the bar, ordered a drink. The bartender brought the drink and some stale chips. He ate them greedily.

On the stage at the end of the long, thin, low club, a band was setting up. Dozens of young people were milling around. He saw that many of them were wearing fur coats and strange fur hats—raccoon hats with tails.

Uh-oh, someone was taking a place next to him at the bar. Just what he did not need. Company. Conversation.

"Hey, blandboy, here for the Petscapade?"

He ignored the voice.

"Ugly, I'm talking to you. What's your mindset? Rule of engagement—I talk, you respond, huh?"

He turned, looked at this unwanted conversationalist, drained his drink. She was petite, plain. She wore a fur coat and a raccoon hat. Her fingers were covered with rings. She had a dog collar around her throat.

"Excuse me?"

"Here for the Petscapade?"

"What's that," he smiled.

"My, what big teeth you have," the woman replied. She reached out, tried to touch his teeth with a finger. He drew back.

"Oh," she pouted, "are we shy?"

"Yes."

"Napping. I like shy."

He turned away. Maybe she was done. The bartender brought him another vodka and water. He drained it. Bitterness and cold mixing in his mouth, his throat; a pleasant fire being stoked in his stomach. She was not done.

"So," she said, "I take it from your question that you have been out of circulation for a while. The Petscapade is devoted to the Human Pet, a.k.a. the Pet Hunter. You know who he is, don't you? No? He's the guy who is slaying all these pets. He's a napping counter-cultural hero! A deprogrammer with a vengeance! A virus for pets!" She took a vial from her purse, removed the top, held it to her nose, sniffed. "Here, have some of this."

She extended the vial towards him. The bartender brought him another drink.

"What is it?"

"Henry James."

"Henry James?"

"Just snort some. It's petalicious."

He snorted some of the powder, gave the vial back. The room began to glisten with a tranquil interplay of light and shadow.

He drew back, said, "So you . . . you celebrate this pet slayer?"

"Bland on bland, we do. We even have an anthem. A song. *Pet Hunter.* It's a napping song composed by Bruno Passive before he was . . . uh pacified. That's a joke, a witticism. He committed suicide."

"An anthem?"

"Are you just going to repeat what I say to you?"

"Huh?"

"Repeat?"

The band on the stage began to play. The music was soft and out of tune.

He drank his drink. He was feeling lightheaded. The chips were gone. He listened to the song.

Whatcha going to do when you're feeling low?
Going to a pet show.

"That's nice," he smiled.

"Yes, it is. Would you like to dance?" she had moved very close to him. She was whispering in his ear. He liked the feel of her wet, soft breath on his ear. He turned and looked at her. Her eyes glimmered. Her lips glimmered. Behind her, in front of the stage, figures moved slowly, with serenity almost, jostling each other without rancor or animosity.

"One more drink first."

They had one more drink.

She removed her fur coat.

She was not wearing anything but a short, leather mini-skirt. Her breasts were small, non-descript. She turned. Her back was covered in fur. Instead of flesh, she had a black pelt.

"Wow," he exclaimed. "Your back!"

"Yes. Doberman fur," she smiled, looking back at him over her hairy shoulder. "Fur sure. Get it?"

"What?"

"I had Doberman fur grafted onto my back. A fur graft," she smiled. "Dr Reginald Kidd did it. It's the next wave. Absolutely. You can pet it if you like."

He reached out tentatively, felt it, stroked it. It felt like fur.

"Isn't it lifelike?" she said. "Do you think I'm a dog or what?"

"Huh?"

"It's a little joke. But actually, I'm going to have my whole body done, except my head. It's expensive. He charges by the square inch."

Morris was dumbfounded. He like the way the fur felt, warm and smooth. He kept stroking her back.

"Can we dance now, master?" she laughed.

"Yes."

"Well then, bow-wow!"

They danced among the other dancers. The room was dark and pulsated with soft music. Morris was quite high. The rolls of bills, the accumulations of coins swung in his pants pockets. Maybe money was falling out of his pockets, but he could not have cared less. He felt he might fall over at any moment but, still, he felt there was a sort of buoyant fluidity to his moves. The dancers would bark and make other animal noises as they danced. It was the new style. Abruptly his partner stopped.

She stood on tiptoes, pulled his ear down to her mouth. She said, "I know who you are. You're him—Morris Tantone."

"No, I am not. Who?"

"Yes you are! Yes you are. This is so bland. I'm dancing with the Human Pet." She stepped away from him and yelled, "Hey everyone! Hey!"

Everyone stopped dancing. The band stopped playing. The club was silent. Morris saw that all the eyes in the club were on him and the topless woman with dog fur on her back. He looked above the heads. There was a mural of the little Dutch boy with his finger in a dike painted on the wall.

His companion pointed at him, yelled, "This is him. This is Morris fucking Tantone! The Human Pet! The Pet Hunter!"

"No, you're wrong," he said, speaking to her, to everyone, shaking his head.

But she was right. The others could see she was right. They surged at him, chanting "Bow-wow, bow-wow!"

Morris turned and ran. She leapt on his back. He shook her off. A young man tried to bite his leg. He kicked him. Passing the bar, he grabbed the woman's fur coat and raccoon hat. He would need it. It was cold outside. He was amazed he could run so fast.

Some of the club's patrons chased him for a couple of blocks.

Chapter 25

When Bad Things Happen to Good People

The exorcism began at midnight in Dr Bentley's expansive third floor meditation room. The furniture had been pushed to the walls. Dozens of candles lit the room and Ashley, her body bound with rope, lay in the center of the chamber. Holding hands, sitting on meditation pillows, the group formed a semi-circle around her. Jerry, Dominic, Jessica, Jane, Brandon, Bentley, Eric, and Karla. Brandon had not recovered fully from his ordeal. He looked shaken. Ashley had given up struggling. She looked through an oily cloud of incense at a ceiling which danced with the light of candles. Everyone was very quiet. Ready. Eric had made coffee for everyone before they came up for the ceremony. Strong and black. Saying his stomach was upset, he had not had any himself.

Now in their third night of sleeplessness, the group was exhausted beyond exhaustion. Only Bentley's amphetamines and coffee kept them awake. The common mindset of the group was one of punchy, wired blankness. Thoughts and emotions flitted through each individual's subconscious like fish in a tank—darting, confined, observable but lacking the energy to break through the glass wall into full consciousness, into the dryness of rational consideration.

Meanwhile, outside the mansion, the city was going crazy as

the result of Taylor having spiked the water supply with Nightmare Plus. Those inside the mansion could hear the sounds of distant screams, sirens, gun fire. Had they looked out the windows of the mansion, they would have seen the glow of flames from many points in the city as well as terrified citizens running or driving along nearby streets. But they did not care to look. Their business was before them.

"First, a cleansing prayer," Bentley said. Her voice was calm, low, solemn. She wore a black robe embroidered with arcane symbols. She led the group in the prayer, the cleansing prayer, with which they opened their nightly sessions. As she spoke, she dipped her hands into a bowl beside her and flicked droplets of water onto the participants, onto Ashley, onto herself. Jerry felt the water on his face and arms. It seemed to burn then dissipate in coolness.

Closing her eyes, Bentley began to speak in some strange, foreign language. A language guttural and blunt.

"Here we go!" Jerry whispered to Dominic.

Jane moaned.

Jessica felt a ball, a balloon, of fear form in her stomach and rise into her throat.

"What language is that?" Karla whispered to Eric.

"Pig Latin," he replied, smirking.

Bentley rose. The bowl of water, of cleansing water, was in one arm. She circled Ashley's body, speaking now in the voice of command, issuing short, decisive bursts of words in the old, obscure tongue. Her hand dipped into the water, ladled liquid onto Ashley, tossed liquid over the group and around the room. Candles sizzled as droplets touched them. The room grew darker, more smoke-filled.

Jane moaned in horror.

Ashley was rising off the floor. She hovered a foot off the floor. A greenish light emanated from her body—a green, palpitating aura which interacted with, illuminated the whirling clouds of incense. When water touched her body, it turned to steam. A wind rushed through the room. The candles were blown out. The only light now came from Ashley. The room, the house, began to shake. It was hard for those seated on the floor not to fall over. A low sound, a humming, a rumbling beginning almost under the auditory range of the participants, filled the room like the sounding of dozens of low-tuned gongs or bells. From the corners of their eyes, the members of the group saw, or thought they saw, little figures dashing at the edges of the room.

The gremlins, the fecal elves, were back.

They made chattering noises.

Then the shaking, the sounds stopped. The little creatures did not exist. The candles relit. The room was silent. Completely silent. Ashley floated.

Dominic closed his eyes. Opened them. He was in a different place.

*　　*　　*

Ashley is a woman on an operating table held down by leather straps. Bentley is wearing a lab coat. She holds a scalpel which drips blood. The others in the room, the group, stand around the operating table. They wear lab coats too, lab coats spattered in blood. "It is interesting to see how much pain the patient can endure," Jessica says. "A very interesting experiment." Her accent is foreign. He looks at himself. He is wearing a military uniform and then he knows where he is and what he is doing.

God, how evil he is. How vile. He can not stand it anymore. He can not stand it! How can he live knowing what dark secrets his soul holds? He notices he is leaving the room. He hears a voice calling after him. Jessica's. She is a participant too, a participant in the obscene experimentation. She too is a war criminal. Damn! He never even suspected that. Well, all of us are, he says to himself. That's why we must be punished. Punished now. He sees himself going down the hall, going down the stairs of a building in the death camp. The medical research center. He wonders:

is he in a dream now? A nightmare? He can not tell anymore. It does not matter. His life is a death camp. He has a room in the research center. A living chamber at the bottom of the stairs. He goes to it now. He has a suitcase there. He opens it. He seems to remember he has another life. Isn't he Dominic Fanelli, living in the early 21st Century United States, working in an advertising firm? No, that is the dream. The illusion. That is the elaborate escape mechanism his mind has created to remove him from his reality.

His only life has been here in the camp.

He knows what he must do. It's so obvious. So obvious. He reaches into his suitcase, feels under the clothes neatly folded there. There it is! At the bottom of the suitcase is his revolver. He has never told anyone about it. It is his safety valve. He is sick of knowing who he is. He walks across the room to a mirror on the wall next to the door to the hallway and the stairs. In the mirror he sees himself. He is wearing a green and gray uniform. A high peaked military hat. Skulls are embroidered into the collar of his jacket. Twin insignia. Reflected in the mirror he sees the gun going up to the side of his head. He sees his finger tensing on the trigger.

* * *

Though Morris was having difficulty walking, he knew where he wanted to go. There seemed to be some sort of disconnect between his mind and his body. His mind seemed articulate, glib, reasonable. Weaving a pattern down the dark, lonely streets, his feet took him first left, then right. The ordeal with the children, the flight from the bar, the lack of nourishment, the drinks and James had wasted him. Finally, he reached the wall of the Talcott Arboretum. How was he going to get over that, he wondered. Then with an effort that surprised him he managed to pull himself to the top of the wall. He lay there, panting, sweating. His mind swirled. He started to fall asleep. He fell. The ground woke him. He struggled up, stumbled into a wooded grove. Branches scraped his face and hands. He walked into a number of trees. He reached a little clearing. A path maybe. It was a path. He moved along it. His inebriation gave him a strange momentum. After he had covered 400 yards the momentum dissipated. He lay down on his back. He would sleep. He saw the moon in the sky. Nearing full. The moon began to whirl in the sky. He turned over onto his stomach. Better not to look. He still had his raccoon hat in his hand. That surprised him too. He laid it on top of his head.

*   *   *

Jessica called after Dominic as he rose, departed. She felt the impulse to follow but she could not. Something kept her there. And then her attention was riveted by Ashley. Ashley's skin was gone. Jessica could see her organs. She could see the beating of her heart, the action of her lungs, the glistening of her musculature. Grotesque. But fascinating—the way arteries and veins encased her muscles, throbbing with life. Hovering suspended in the air, the skinless body altered again. It changed into a figure made of red liquid— blood—which, against the laws of physics, held Ashley's form. Jessica and the other participants could see a beating where Ashley's heart would have been, the rising and falling of her belly and chest, the action of her lungs. Then, Jessica was conscious of a hideous smell. No! Was it happening again? It was. Ashley was turning into a figure of putrid waste. Jessica pressed her hand over her nose but she could not avoid the overpowering odor. She heard Jerry scream. She heard a blast outside the room. What was it?

"This isn't working, Doctor!" Jerry yelled. "This isn't working!"

"Silence," Bentley commanded. "We must not let our concentration be broken."

Now Ashley exploded. Jessica felt her body spattered with

gobs of hot waste. It was everywhere, covering the room, the walls, Bentley, the participants, and where Ashley had been there was nothing, less than nothing. A darkness, a vacancy, occupied the space of her body. Jerry was on his feet; he was trying to shake the shit off.

"I'm covered in shit. I'm covered in shit. I'm covered in shit!" he yelled.

Jessica could not help thinking how redundant he was being.

"Sit down, Jerry," Bentley commanded.

"Fuck you, Doctor Twat," Jerry yelled, his face twisting in anger.

He exited the room.

*   *   *

Jerry is in the bathroom. His mind races. He just wants to be clean. He throws off his clothes. Throws them in a pile on the floor. He will never wear them again. He will shower and leave this house and never look back. He sees himself in the mirror. Oh, no. Huge, bulky roll-sized pimples are growing on his body. They rise, red hillocks, on his pasty flesh. His head twitches. He takes a hillock on his chest between his hands and pushes. He wants to break the thing, to pop it. His forearms shake with the strain. His face forms a grimace of effort. To no avail. Damn it! He opens the medicine cabinet. There! He takes out a pair of gleaming scissors. He stabs the pimple in his chest. He feels it give. An eruption of pus issues forth with a palpable release, spattering the wall, the mirror. Jerry begins to stab at all the pimples on his body—on his arms, his legs, his back, his torso, his neck.

"Ow! Ow! Ow! Argh!"

His body is covered with blood and pus. He looks again into the mirror to see himself. He looks like he is covered with strawberry cheese cake. Oh god! He can not believe what he sees. His entire head has become one huge pimple. One huge twitching pimple. His mouth and nose are gone. Of his features, only his eyes are visible in the taut, stretched, pink-white flesh. His eyes are wide with fright. His hair tops the head of the pimple. He screams. He stabs the scissors into the top of his skull. He stabs again. Again. Again. Then he throws the scissors aside, throwing them with such vehemence that they lodge in the wooden door of the bathroom. He takes his head, his skull, between his hands and pushes. He feels the insides of his head begin to give way. He sees gray pus emerge from the top of his head. But it is not pus. It is his brain. This does not deter him. With all his strength he pushes. He see his brain rise slowly from the top of his head— gray coils streaked with blood. Then with an audible pop his brain slides from his skull. His brain hits the mirror and tumbles into the sink. He looks for a second at his brain in the basin. Then he collapses onto the floor. For a moment he is conscious that he is dying. Then he is no longer conscious.

*　　*　　*

Bentley, covered in filth, was speaking English now.

"In the name of good, of gods and goddesses who protect the human realm, in the name of Nature, of all that is good, all that is clean, I compel you to disperse your power, disperse your evil and return to the other side of sleep," she intoned. "You have no business here. I compel you. Return."

Karla said something to Eric. He got up and left the room. Now there were only Jessica, Jane, Karla, Brandon, and Bentley.

Jessica could see that Bentley was fighting with all her heart. She stood upright and alone next to the vacancy which had been Ashley. She spoke clearly and loudly. Her gestures were stately, priestly in the now otherwise silent room.

Bentley continued to intone, yet the vacancy which had been Ashley expanded. Jessica moved back. So did Eric and Karla. Jane crawled to a side of the room. She hid under a display case which held various gem-encrusted magical daggers. Brandon did not move. He sat behind Bentley. Ashley's absence grew—an expanding airborne intimation of nothingness. Vile nothingness. The nothingness swelled right up to Bentley's body, her gesturing arms.

"Back. Back to your Realm, I command you!" Bentley cried. She spoke again in the long-forgotten tongue, issuing a stream of crisp, multisyllabic words. The cloud of nothing receded. It receded slowly, coming together in one small ball, one dark node of anti-matter perhaps, Jessica thought, and then it was gone.

It was gone.

"Yes," Jane shouted from her hiding place. "Yes!"

Brandon, partially re-energized, stood.

Bentley slumped into his arms. She was sobbing, exhausted with her efforts, covered in filth and sweat. Jessica and Karla were on their feet too.

"Napping, Doc, you did it! You did it," Karla said. "That was some show!"

Karla and Jessica moved close to Bentley. Jessica took her hand.

Bentley smiled weakly.

"Yes, I did."

Abruptly, the expression on her face changed from exhausted satisfaction to excruciating pain.

"No," she screamed. "No, it's in my head. It's in my . . ."

Her head began to bob and shake on her neck. It vibrated. It oscillated at an increasing frequency until it became only a blur. It exploded. Hot blood, brains, bone, eyes, lips, hair covered the room, the participants, especially Brandon.

"Ick!" Karla cried.

Brandon screamed. Bentley's head was gone. From her neck gushed a geyser of blood. A shower of blood rained down on everything. Then the geyser stopped. Bentley had bled out.

"Look, oh look!" Jane cried from her spot beneath the display case. Karla and Jessica turned.

Ashley had reappeared behind them. She was lying unconscious on the floor. The ropes which had bound her lay loosely
under her.

"Ashley," Karla cried. She knelt beside her. "She's still
alive."

*   *   *

He was depressed. Depressed and almost blind. He had lost
his goddamn glasses down a storm drain as he had dropped over
the wall into the Arboretum. Now he moved slowly, blindly towards his destination. He walked by feel and by memory. He
had to get there. To his cave. To his lair. He needed to be in his
seat of power. He was so down.

It was late. The night was chilly and quiet except for the
noise the wind made gusting forcefully through the trees and the
sounds of his tentative steps through a carpet of leaves. Looking
up at the sky he made out the blurred shape of the moon. Ahead
of him now he saw the shape of the hill which covered his cave.

He was almost home.

Strange that he should choose that word. But more than any-
place it was his home. What? He tripped, sprawled face first onto
the path. Smells of moist leaves and dirt and chilly air filled his
nostrils. The wind was knocked out of him. He heard a grunt.
Not his own. He turned, felt with his hands. He had tripped over
a mound. A big, furry mound.

The mound rose and fell slightly, slowly. It breathed.

"Hmmm, a mammal of some sort," he said. "But what kind?"

He felt some more.

It must be a dog of considerable size, he said to himself. Or a
pony!

"In either case what a spectacular find," he exclaimed out
loud.

His mind grew quiet. He pondered his good luck. To find
such a magnificent animal just when he was at his lowest point

emotionally—it had to be fate working on his behalf. This was almost as good as the time a plump German Shepherd had walked into his lair. What a delicious Shepherd's Pie that had been! Ahhh. He smacked his lips. He felt aroused. He felt a snowflake touch his face. Out of nowhere it was beginning to snow heavily. Funny, he had thought the sky was clear. No time to lose then.

Huffing, puffing, he pulled the unconscious creature into his cave. First he lit a candle or two, then he set about building a fire. As he worked he sang a little song that arose almost spontaneously sometimes when he was involved in his nighttime activities:

Airedales and Cocker Spaniels, Bassett Hounds and Pulis,
Bloodhounds and Borzois, Huskies and Border Collies,
Newfoundlands, Akitas, Greyhounds and Pugs:
These are a few of my favorite dogs.

When the Chow Chows, when the Shih Tzus,
When I'm feeling sad,
Then I remember my favorite pets
And then I don't feel so bad.

The melody was based on a song from some movie he had seen as a child. He could not remember which.

Imprisoned in his pen, his legs bound, Kitten opened his exhausted eyes at the sound of his captor's arrival. He hated this strange man, but, though he had been able to work the muzzle the man had put on him off his head, he was too exhausted now or too terrified to bark or growl or bare his teeth. He lay there watching.

*   *   *

Ashley opened her eyes.

She saw Karla's face.

"Where am I, ugly?" she gasped.

"Ashley! Thank god you're alright," Karla said. She stroked Ashley's brow.

Ashley looked around. By the light of the few candles which remained lit, she saw that Bentley's meditation room was covered in shit and blood. She saw Brandon kneeling, holding Bentley's headless torso. She saw Jessica, wide-eyed, recoiling. She saw Jane trying to hide.

"I guess the exorcism didn't go all that well?" Ashley asked.

"Chip Suey," Karla responded. "Double-o-nined to the nth power."

"Karla, do you feel it?" Jessica interrupted. Her arms hugged her chest. She shivered. Her teeth chattered.

"Feel what?" Karla asked.

"It's worse now. Worse than it was. The place feels evil. This house is evil!"

Karla and Ashley surveyed the room.

The masks on the walls, the demonic statues exuded menace. The triptych of the blasphemous Passion caught Ashley's eye. How horrible. How maleficent. Yes, there was an evil presence in the room. An almost greasily palpable dread permeated the air.

Bang!

Jessica, Karla, Ashley started, turned their attentions toward the sound.

"Oww," Jane whined, standing, rubbing her head. She had hit her head on the display case as she was getting up from her hiding place. Then she whispered, "I think we should go. I think this house has become part of . . . part of . . . the Nightmare Realm. I feel like we've become part of some group dream. A group psychosis. We've got to get out of here and get help."

"Look . . . look," Karla moaned. She pointed. Everyone followed her finger.

Above the display cases under which Jane had just been

crouching, a thick greenish aura of oily light pulsated, quivered, expanded, grew, receded, grew again. At the fringe of the light was an area, a margin, of dark vacancy, of absence.

Jane dashed towards the door, stopped at the threshold. She hesitated there, turned.

"Come on," she begged. "Let's go now. Please!"

"She's right," Ashley agreed, struggling to her feet. "Time to get hyperactive."

"But where will we go?" Jessica moaned.

"I know," Karla said. "The Arboretum. There's a ladder against the wall in the backyard."

"How do you know that?" asked Ashley.

"I saw it there earlier, silly."

The glow from the cases throbbed, bathed the four women and Brandon in a surge of light, a surge of vacancy. It made them feel, before it receded, like they had ceased to exist: a momentary, chilly nothingness.

"Use you later," Jessica cried. "See you at the Arboretum."

She ran to the threshold, pushed past Jane, ran down the hallway. Jane ran too. Ashley looked at Karla; Karla at Ashley.

Ashley spoke to Brandon. She said, "Time to go, Brandon."

He did not respond.

She yelled at him.

"Brandon!"

"What is it?" he said.

"It's time to go."

"No, I'll stay."

Ashley moved towards him, but Karla tugged her away.

The two friends hurried from the room.

When the two of them reached the backyard, Jessica was already half way up the ladder. Jane was right behind her.

"Wait," Ashley said.

"Wait? For what? For the house to do some more sweaty shit? I'm into being, not nothingness."

"You sound like Jean-Paul Sartre," Ashley said.

"I do not," Karla countered. "Just look."

The entire inside of the mansion now throbbed with the green light.

"I've got to go back in," Ashley said. "I've got to make a phone call."

"A phone call? Have you been completely deprogrammed? The place is hyper-k!" ·

"Sorry, Karla. See you on the other side."

"What? The other side of what?"

"The wall."

"I'll wait. Don't be long."

Ashley ran back into the kitchen. The light throbbed around her. She forgot who, where she was. The light receded. She picked up the phone and dialed. She remembered the number this time. She spoke hastily into the phone. She ran.

Karla asked her who she had called.

"Psychic hotline," replied Ashley.

The entire house—walls, window, roof—glowed.

They ran, climbed, jumped.

*   *   *

Costello arrived later than usual. He was drunk. What he saw as he drove up to the house made him slam on his brakes. The house was glowing with a sick green light. I should radio this in, he thought. Then he remembered he did not have a radio anymore. "I am a traffic cop," he muttered. He got out of the car, stumbled towards the house. He stopped, pondered. Traffic cops do not go into buildings that are completely aglow with otherworldly light, do they, Thomas? he asked himself. No, they do not. He heard a scream coming from behind the house. Giving the glowing house wide berth, he ran to the backyard. He saw a dog there, a German Shepherd. The dog glowed too. Then the dog disappeared, becoming before its disappearance the black shape of a dog. He saw a ladder against the wall to the Arboretum, heard another scream. Beyond the wall. He started to run towards the wall. He stopped. He vomited. He was too drunk to climb the ladder, run through the Arboretum. He wobbled back to his car. He drove to the nearest gate. It was locked. He thought about crashing his economy model sedan through the wrought iron. Thought better of it. He got out of the car. Unholstering his revolver, aiming, he shot at the lock. He missed. He shot again and again. The lock exploded. He looked at his gun, smiled, pushed open the gate, drove in. Flakes of snow appeared in his headlights.

*   *   *

Karla and Ashley hurried through the Arboretum. The trees, the cold ground exuded menace. Looking at the trees waving in the wind, Ashley thought they looked different—as if they were no longer trees, but shapes and lines of nothingness. It was as if the night were a dark curtain held against a darker void from which shapes of trees had been cut or ripped, leaving upright absences, waving shapes filled with nothing. Then, out of nowhere it began to snow heavily. The wind abated. Ashley looked up at the sky. The moon, five-sixths full, was surrounded by a mantle of gray-white. A snow moon. She felt her spirits rise, then fall.

"Snow! Isn't this nappingly lifelike," Karla said.

Ashley looked at her warily. Karla looked like a child walking through the snow. Her cheeks were pink, her eyes sparkling.

"Does this snow remind you of something, Ashley?" Karla continued.

"Like what?"

"Like some bland expanse to the north, for example? Some place called Canada?"

Ashley said, "It's you, isn't it, Karla?"

"It's me?"

"You're the link to the Nightmare Realm?"

Karla eyed her mischievously.

"You guessed it!"

"You bitch!" Ashley cried. She started to run away. She wanted to run into the waving non-trees, to become nothing herself. She made the motions of a runner. She ran nowhere.

"Ashley," Karla giggled, "you can't go anywhere. You've got to come with me."

Ashley saw that it was so. Her will was no longer her own. The voice, the intruder voice, which had appeared in her mind in recent weeks, now became the predominant voice in her mind, her will. It was Karla's voice. It had been so obvious all along. Why hadn't she known it? They walked together. Ashley felt flakes of snow on her face. Touching, then melting.

She asked where they were going.

"A rendezvous with . . . uh . . . destiny," Karla laughed. "Your destiny."

"What happened to the shit, Karla?" Ashley asked. "Why isn't it snowing shit. You seem so fond of it?"

"Don't try to hurt my feelings, ugly," Karla responded. "I just got tired of it. It was so icky."

"You're vermin, Karla," Ashley said. She felt anger stirring inside her. Betrayal. But her emotions were distant voices. They were pointless.

"Why don't you hush now?" Karla said.

Ashley became silent. Her words would not move from her mind to her voice.

They walked through trees down a hill. They walked towards a part of the Arboretum which glowed with the sick greenish light. The light hovered like a fog over a clearing. Snowflakes filled the green air. Eric was standing there. Smiling. Leering.

He and Karla embraced, kissed.

"I see you brought, Ashley," Eric said. "Hello, Ashley."

She did not respond.

"Ashley isn't talking," Karla smiled.

"Unbland," Eric said.

Ashley recoiled. Across the meadow she saw a figure standing in front of a tree. It was Sebastian.

"Hello, Ashley," Sebastian called. "How are you?"

Ashley said nothing.

"You'll have to excuse Ashley, Sebastian," Karla called. "She's not herself."

"I hope you'll appreciate the sacrifices I've made to bring Sebastian here, Ashley," Eric said. "The viral rabbit hopped out on a debt he owed me a while ago. I've only let him live so we could have some fun with him and you."

"I guess Sebastian's a welsh rabbit, then?" said Karla.

"Huh?" Eric asked.

Even under the near total domination of Karla's telepathic force, Ashley winced at her tormentor's pitiful pun.

"But will she be able to do it?" Sebastian called back, his voice stamped with its usual odd formality. "Yes, will she be able to end what she started so many years ago. I've been waiting a long time."

"Of course she will, you hyperkinetic fuck," Karla smiled. "I wouldn't miss this for the world. It represents such a . . . uh . . . perfect resolution to your situation." Then she turned to her now robotic companion.

"Here you go," Ashley," Karla said, picking something up from the ground, shaking off thin, dry flakes of snow. The snow looked green in the green light. It was a bow and several arrows. "Time for some . . . uh . . . regression therapy."

A flood of lifelong fears and negative emotions—self-hatred, anger, betrayal—welled up in Ashley and then, overloaded, her mind went cold, static. Her will was no longer her own in any way. She took the bow and arrows.

"There's your target," Eric smiled. "Let's see if your aim has improved since you were a little girl?"

"Eric," Karla said, "get out of here."

He looked startled.

"What? Why?"

"This is between me and Ashley."

He sounded like a little boy as he said, "But I want to see this, Karla."

Then his face was changed by fear.

Ashley could see Karla had changed. She had become old, wrinkled, plump, white-haired, Asian. She looked like Tang's mother. Eric recoiled, whined.

"Please. Please. Please don't do that! I hate it when you do that, Karla."

"Get out of here, now," Karla, no longer Karla, commanded. Tang ran off into the woods.

The old woman changed back into a smiling Karla.

"I'm like a mother to him," she said.

* * *

His pants were around his ankles. He was aroused. He thought he saw the dog eyeing him. Of course, he could not be sure. He was nearly blind. He could only make out larger shapes, but he hopped over to the pen anyway, whacked the dog on the head.

"What were you looking at?" the man asked.

Kitten cowered.

The man hopped to the mound of fur which rose, a breathing heap, from the floor of the cave.

"Ohhh," the Pet Hunter, the real Pet Hunter, moaned, mounting the heap, beginning to move back and forth.

The mound groaned.

"Ohhh," moaned the Pet Hunter.

In his laboratory, Strom Varnish was working late, working on his adult assassination baby rattle. It was almost ready. He held it in his hands. Must not shake it. It held a specially developed neuro-toxin designed to work only on fully matured human brains. Project code name: Spare the Child.

One of the three television monitors clicked on.

"Oh-ho," Varnish exclaimed. The image was fuzzy, distorted

by static. Varnish carefully set the rattle down on a soft rubber tray, turned in his swivel chair, rolled to his stereo, turned it off. Mahler's unfinished symphony ended without finishing. Varnish heard static intermixed with faint sounds from a speaker connected to the TV display. He rolled across the room to the Canine Surveillance Unit control console. His whispy Afro waved back and forth as he rolled. He stood and fiddled with one of the sets of rabbit ear antennae.

"Come on, Satan. Come on, boy!"

The image cleared. So did the audio transmission. Varnish could see one dark shape moving back and forth on top of another dark shape. Some kind of light—a fire maybe—illuminated a semi-sphere of white which moved back and forth rhythmically.

"Uh-uh-uh, you're the sweetest pet in the world" were the sounds that came over the speaker. A man singing.

"What the hell?" Varnish wondered.

Then, to the left of the screen, another block of light appeared. An oval. A face? Varnish heard "Hey, you god damn mutt, I told you not to watch!"

"I know that voice," Varnish mused. "Jesus."

He flicked a switch on the control panel, picked up the microphone.

He said, "Rex. Rex Quick? What the hell are you doing?"

The Pet Hunter stopped in mid-thrust. He looked at the dog. No! It could not be.

"Quick, what are you doing?"

Quick jumped up. Varnish could see his naked legs on the screen. He saw them hopping. The screen became darker, the image unreadable. He heard unrecognizable sounds. Tearing perhaps. Rubbing? Cutting?

"Quick?"

The screen went black.

Then less black.

It was hard to tell but Varnish thought he saw the image of

rapid movement—at close to ground level—through trees. The dog was free! That must be it. He was running through a forest.

"Halt, Satan. Sit," Varnish commanded. The movement on the screen—fast, reckless, forward movement—continued. Varnish tried the nobs and buttons on the control console. They did not arrest the progress of the dog.

*   *   *

Ashley pulled back the arrow, aimed, let it fly. It hit Sebastian in the knee. He writhed. Blood spurted onto the snow.

"Napping shot, ugly," Karla chirped. "A little higher next time."

Mesmerized, Ashley complied. In her mind she saw herself as a little girl shooting arrows at a little boy.

"Shoot me again," Sebastian pleaded. "Ashley, kill me."

Ashley heard Sebastian speak, but it was the voice of the boy Sebastian she heard.

"No," Ashley muttered. But she did not, could not, stop.

This time she hit an arm.

Karla, apparently in a philosophical mood, began to speak.

She said, "You're probably wondering what's going on? Huh, Ash? It all started, of course, with these Nightmare Therapy sessions. One day, I found I was having other people's nightmares—the nightmares of the members of our little class. It was scary at first. I mean, it was really sweaty but then I . . . uh . . . I got used to it. I liked it. And my powers grew. I discovered I could make nightmares happen to other people whenever I wanted. I could make our classmates experience their nightmares when they were awake. Neat, huh? And I also found I could enter people's minds telepathically and just atrophy there or speak to people if I wanted to. I spent a lot of time in your mind, Ashley. It was bland. For me at least. You heard me, didn't you? I know you did.

"But wait, there's more. As my telepathic powers grew I found that controlling what people think and do is pretty easy. Inducing group psychosis is . . . uh . . . child's play for me. I can make things—actual bad things—happen just by using my will. Just ask Dr Bentley! Am I special, or what?"

As Karla spoke, Ashley fired arrow after arrow at Sebastian. He was full of arrows now. Blood poured from him. His head lolled to one side. He was dead. His face radiated contentment.

"Nice work, Ash," Karla said. "Isn't it satisfying to complete something you began long ago? A real feeling of closure, I'll bet. I'm glad I could help."

A car slid into the snowy clearing, stopped. A man jumped out, aimed a gun at Karla and Ashley, moved towards them.

"Hands up," Thomas Costello shouted.

"Unbland," Karla said.

Ashley dropped her bow, moaned, wept.

"Hands up," Costello commanded, pointing his revolver at Karla. "What the hell is going on here?"

Karla concentrated on the newcomer, tried to look into his mind, to see his worst fear.

She saw nothing.

"You're an alcoholic, aren't you?" she asked Costello.

"Jesus, that's personal, isn't it?" Costello replied.

He recognized Karla, though her horns had grown. Then when Ashley turned towards him, he recognized her too. She looked terrible. Tears streaked her face. Her lips quivered.

Karla said, "It's just that alcohol fucks up my abilities to get into someone's mind, as my friend here found out. Bet you could use a hefty drink now, Ashley?"

Costello said, "If you don't put your hands in the fucking air, I'll blow your head off."

"No you won't," someone behind Costello said.

"Eric! Back just in time," Karla smirked.

Having emerged surreptitiously from his hiding place in the woods, Eric held a revolver to the back of Costello's head. The policeman felt the barrel against his skull. He dropped his weapon into the snow. He raised his hands.

"What the fuck am I doing here?" he said aloud.

Karla moved close to him, looked into his face, scrunched up her nose. The cop smelled like vomit on a barroom floor.

"Dying," she answered him.

Then Karla told Eric to take Sebastian down from the tree to which he was now held by arrows and to tie Costello to the trunk with the rope that he had brought along earlier just in case Sebastian had changed his mind. Eric did as he was told, keeping his attention and gun on the police officer as he worked. Ashley stood unmoving, her mind filled only by terror and complete passivity. She watched as Eric bound the policeman, as he finished his last knot, as he tried the ropes, found them secure. She watched as Eric finished pulling the arrows all the way out of Sebastian's corpse and brought them back to the two women.

"Ready," he said, "for round two, if that's what you're thinking?"

"You're reading my mind, ugly," Karla replied, stroking his cheek. Then she turned. "What the hell is that?"

Eric turned too. Costello shifted his attention, looking in the direction his captors looked.

They heard a metallic voice approaching them at a rapid pace. They heard something crashing through brush. They heard these words repeated over and over again:

"Return this dog to Crowe Poussin Enterprises immediately. There will be a substantial reward."

A dog ran into the clearing. It's mouth was open. The words were coming from its mouth. Eric lifted his gun.

"Kitten, no!" Costello shouted.

Eric fired, hitting the dog again and again. The dog leapt, tore off Eric's arm at the shoulder. Varnish had equipped the dog with a hydraulic jaw. Eric's arm, still holding the gun, fell to the snow. The dog, carried by the momentum of its leap, arced to the ground. Wires were interwoven with the blood and brains which poured from Kitten's bullet-shattered skull. Blood spilled from several bullet holes in the dog's body. Once more the voice spoke from the dog's mouth:

"There will be a substantial . . ."

Then, with finality, the dog's jaws closed and the voice stopped. Eric looked pleadingly at Karla. Blood was spurting from his shoulder socket.

"Karla, do something."

"Not my department," she said, spreading her arms.

Eric fell down. Blood poured from him. The blood saturated the accumulated snow. The blood looked gray in the green light of the clearing. Eric died.

"So many interruptions," Karla said. She handed the arrows to Ashley. "Look who you're shooting at now."

"No," Ashley mumbled, moaned.

It was not Costello she saw tied to the tree. It was Bruno. She heard Bruno's voice, not Costello's, imploring her not to shoot.

"Do you have something to say, Ashley? Would you like to talk this over?"

Ashley nodded.

"Napping. I always liked our conversations. Didn't you, ugly?"

"Karla, why are you doing this?" Ashley said. For the moment, she could speak.

"Why? Why? I think you'll be very proud of me, Ashley. I'm involved in a very . . . uh . . . philosophical exercise," Karla said. "Did you know there are those who view life as a dream? You know, mystical types? Eastern meditative types. They're the ones who say that we've got to wake up from the dream of our existence to . . . uh . . . appreciate reality. Well, what better way to wake up from a dream than with a nightmare? You're waking up now, aren't you, Ashley? How do you like our new reality? Ha-ha! I woke up to it long ago."

"That's bullshit, Karla."

"If it's worth anything, I think so too," Costello called from his tree.

"Shut up, imbecile," Karla called to him, "or Annie Oakley here begins to use you for target practice."

"Annie used a gun actually," Costello observed. "But don't worry, I'll just listen from now on. Just try to forget I'm here."

"Where was I?" Karla asked herself, then remembered, answered, "oh yes, 'bullshit'. Well, maybe it is, but so what? It was you, Ashley, with your philosophy about how worthless human life is that gave me the . . . go-ahead, the green light, to take this thing to the nappingmost, the blandest limit. Don't you remember? We're all cancer and there are so many trillions of us that our lives—our deaths—don't mean shit. Get lifelike, Ashley! If we don't matter, what's so bad about controlling a few minds and causing a little mayhem just for fun?"

Ashley replied, "Karla, we were only making conversation; that was just idle speculation. I didn't mean for you to . . . uh . . . actualize all that crap. I didn't believe it myself . . . well, most of it. Lesson number one in my philosophy is: don't believe your own bullshit. Didn't I tell you that?"

"No, you didn't. I'm shocked."

"And, Karla, isn't jealousy the real reason you're doing all this? You're jealous of me and Bruno. Admit it."

"Oh, Ashley," Karla sighed. "I was jealous, yes. But I didn't hate you. I hated myself. I wanted to be just like you, to emulate you. That's the reason I started spending so much time in your mind, at least initially. I wanted to figure you out so I could be like you. And I will be, after you're gone. That isn't the point though. I'm so far beyond petty human jealousy and envy now it's ridiculous. Hey, ugly, I'm the Nightmare Realm. I'm Evil Incarnate."

"You're fucked, you silly bitch," Ashley said.

Karla looked hurt.

"Try to explain yourself and see what happens," she said. She shrugged. Then she turned towards Costello, called, "Ready by the tree?"

"Actually, I'd like minute or two here," the policeman replied. He was quite sober now.

Ashley felt Karla re-enter her mind. She fought it, was overwhelmed by the stronger, the elemental, mental presence. She looked towards the tree. Her lovely Bruno back from the dead only to be killed again.

By her.

"No, Ashley, please," she heard Bruno plead.

She fitted an arrow in the bow, drew it back, aimed. She fought the telepathic command to loose the arrow. The bow and arrow quivered in her shaking hands.

Something rushed by her ear. She heard a sickening thud. Karla cried out. The presence in her mind evaporated.

She shot the arrow into the air.

The clearing became bright green and hot. The snow on the ground and falling through the air turned to shit, then blood.

Karla looked at her. A spear was implanted in her chest.

"Ashley," she gasped. Then Karla's eyes rolled up into her head.

Immediately the snow, the shit, the blood disappeared. Standard night returned.

Two men emerged from the woods.

Costello recognized them.

"Morris Tantone and Rex Quick," Costello cried. "Your timing is exquisite."

Tantone walked over to Karla's prostrate form, looked down at it. He was shaken. Quick stood unmoving by the edge of the clearing.

"What happened?" Quick asked. "I can't see."

"Dad," Ashley exclaimed, running towards him, "what are you doing here? Am I ever glad to see you!" She hugged him.

"Ashley! Is that you? You're glad to see me? That's a change."

"Of course I am, dad. Can't you see what's been happening here?"

"No, I can't. I just said that I can't see. My glasses are lost."

Costello hailed them from the tree.

"How about a hand here?" he yelled.

Ashley walked her father to Costello. Tantone met them at the tree, began to untie the bound man.

Ashley said, "Dad, this is Detective Thomas Costello."

"Actually, it's Patrolman Costello now," Costello said. "They made me a traffic cop."

Quick cleared his throat.

"A police officer. Then I've got to turn myself in," he said.

"For what?" Costello asked.

"This is painful," Quick replied, "but I promised Morris I'd make a clean breast of things—a total confession. It's the least I can do after he caught me humping him. That was my wake-up call."

"Dad, you were humping this guy?" Ashley gasped. Tantone looked down at the ground. He was still wearing the fur coat and the raccoon hat.

"Yes," Quick responded. "But that's not the worst of it. The worst of it is . . . well . . . uh . . . that I am the so-called Pet Hunter. I've been terrorizing the pets of the city."

"Jesus!" Costello exclaimed.

"That means you killed Charlie. Our Charlie," Ashley said.

Quick looked in the direction of his daughter. He could make out the general outline of her form.

"Yes."

"Why?"

"I don't know, Ashley. For these past few months I've been living in a kind of nightmare. I haven't been able to control my dark desires. I've been inhuman."

A flood of emotions would have coursed through Ashley at any other time, but now they did not. She was too emotionally spent. She hugged her father again, said, "We've all been living in a nightmare, I think."

"That's true enough," said Tantone. "I've been in one for years, living as a domesticated man, as the Human Pet. Now, I'm ready to give that up. I'm ready to live as a man, although I want to dedicate myself to the well-being of animals."

"Unbelievable!" Costello said. "It looks like the two of you have had quite a revelatory evening."

"Yes, Officer, we have," Quick assented, "after we moved beyond the initial peculiarities of our meeting. I've sworn to stop hunting pets—and eating them and having carnal relations with them—and Morris has resolved to stop being one. Now, I put myself in your custody."

"For what?" Costello asked.

"I'm the most wanted criminal in the city."

"A week or two ago when I was leading that investigation, I would have been happy to arrest you, Rex, but now that I'm a traffic cop I think we'll let it go with a verbal warning. How about that?"

"A warning? Are you sure?"

"Yes. Go and kill pets no more."

"How about me?" Tantone said.

"Morris, just stop at red lights and keep within the speed limit and you'll be okay."

"Well then," Quick said, "maybe Morris will lead me home. I think I have some explaining to do to your mother, Ashley."

"I'd be happy to," Morris said.

"I love you, dad," Ashley said. Quick looked at her in surprise. She seemed to mean it.

"Just one more thing," Morris said. "What about the woman I speared here. Wasn't that a crime or something?"

Costello replied, "Seeing as she was about to use some sort of weird telepathic power to get Ashley to kill me, I think we can overlook it, Morris. But, one question, why did you two have a spear?"

"Rex took it from his cave as a sort of cane since he can't see," Morris said. "When I saw Ashley here—though of course I didn't know who you were at that time—when I saw you about to shoot the detective I threw the spear."

"How did you know to throw at Karla," Ashley asked, "and not me?"

"I didn't," Morris said. "I missed."

Ashley watched Morris and her father depart. When she turned, she saw Costello kneeling over the dead dog. He was weeping. She went to him, put her hand on his shoulder.

"This was my dog," he whispered. "Kitten."

Ashley looked at the wires and other electronic gadgetry spilling from the dog's head. She remembered too that the dog had been Irma's, but she did not say anything about that.

"Do you think we should bury him?" she asked.

"Not now," he said. "We should go. The police should be here soon."

"But you are the police?"

"Do you know how much paperwork it will take to clean up this mess?" Costello asked. As he spoke, he stroked the dog's flank sadly. "A dead guy over by the tree. Cause of death: multiple arrow wounds. An armed guy there—a one armed guy. Cause of death: arm bitten off. A dead, horned woman. Cause of death: speared. Not to mention all the dog blood and scattered electrical components."

"Dog blood?"

"Yeah, I'm taking the dog." He lifted Kitten's body up, folding it in his arms. He carried it to his car and put it in the backseat. "I'll bury him later. Somewhere nice."

He closed the backdoor of the car. The sound of the closing door seemed loud in the relative quiet of the nearly vacant park, though from off in the distance the sounds of alarms and sirens persisted, punctuated by an occasional explosion. Night was ending. A night sky which had been brightened by the flames of burning city blocks was growing lighter still with the approach of dawn.

"Well, Ashley, care to join me for a drink?" Costello asked. "I think we've earned it?"

"Bland," Ashley replied.

"Hop in then."

Ashley hesitated, eyeing the car. She reached out, opened the passenger side door.

Five women arrived on bicycles. They jumped off and ran towards Ashley.

"Oh shit," Costello muttered to himself, standing next to his vehicle. "Not this again."

"Esmeralda!" one of the black-clad, gun toting women yelled. "We got here as soon as we could, but you wouldn't believe what we went through. The city's gone crazy. People are overloaded. They're fucking out of their minds."

"Yeah, not to mention the disappearing snow, shit, and blood storm here at the Arboretum. That slowed us down," snarled another of the new arrivals. Costello recognized her by the hatchet she carried. Lizzie Borden. Borden recognized him too. She said, "Where's this viral cop trying to take you. You want me to scalp him before we decommission another one of his fucking vehicles?"

"Esmeralda?" Costello blurted. "Is Ashley Quick Esmeralda?"

"Who's asking, shitheel?" Lizzie fired back, punctuating her question with a swing of her hatchet through the air.

"It's bland, sisters," Ashley said. They stopped, looked at her. "This guy just helped save my life."

"He did?" another of the Women Against Cars asked. "Well then, maybe we should give him a free pass for tonight?"

"More than that," Ashley smiled. "I'm going to go have a drink with him. In his car."

By now, the five had taken in the scene: the carnage, the blood, the strange weaponry. This made them more accepting than they might have been otherwise.

"Bland," another said. "We'd better get hyperactive too before more cars show."

"Yeah, cars with sirens," Borden sneered. She looked back at Costello. He smiled at her, waved meekly, got into the car.

Ashley got into the car too, rolled down a window, smiled at her fellow anti-car terrorists.

"Don't make a habit of this riding in cars shit," one of them said, not unkindly.

"I won't. Use you later."

Costello turned the car on, backed up slowly in a semi-circle, then began to drive up the path on which he had entered the clearing. He heard a mild thumping on the trunk of his car. He looked in his rearview mirror. Lizzie was tapping his car with her hatchet.

She smiled at him—only half-menacingly—when he turned to look at her. Then she gave the car one more good-natured whack and waved.

He pulled onto the road which would lead them out of the park.

"Ashley," he said, "ever since that first night we met, the night you carjacked and destroyed my car, I've wanted to see you again. I've been looking all over for you."

"One night you almost got me."

"That's right. The night of Irma's murder," Costello nodded. "You must have dropped your jumpsuit and red wig somewhere, huh?"

"Had you fooled, didn't I?"

"Yes. But what I was saying was—I think I'm in love with you."

He was looking at her intently.

She looked back at him, said, "Jesus, Costello, don't go all sweaty on me now." She smiled as she said it.

"Right," he responded. He moved his eyes back to the road. They were approaching the gate. "Where do you want to go?"

"Anywhere," Ashley replied, "as long as it's outside the city."

Printed in the United States
22771LVS00001B/343-354

9 781401 039844